# DEVIL'S PARODY

## BY TOM RIEBER

## A NICK THOMAS NOVEL

©2011 by Tom Rieber
Published by Nick Thomas Mysteries
Cover Design: Mark Tuttle, Tuttle Designs
Format & Packaging: Sylvia Graham
Editing: Tiffany Graham

Printed in the United States of America
ISBN: 978-0-9847500-0-9

This book is a work of fiction. All characters in this book have no existence outside the imagination of the author and have no relation whatsoever to anyone bearing the same name or names except where permission has been granted.

### Dedication

*This book and all subsequent works are*
*dedicated to my dear mother, Marie,*
*who passed on to a better place on February 6th, 2011.*
*Without her love, belief and encouragement,*
*when mine had left me,*
*none of this would have been possible.*
*Smile down, Mom,*
*the world is a better place because of you.*
*Of course, I thank my beautiful wife, Kibbi,*
*who never gives up on me and*
*supports my work with complete faith and love.*

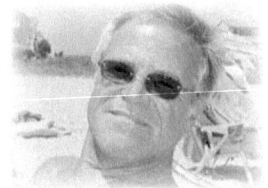

# DEVIL'S PARODY

# PROLOGUE

## COLD RIVER, VERMONT

Time stood still in the stark white chamber. It could've been midnight or morning for all they knew. There was no way of telling in the windowless room. There were no clocks, and no sound except the roaring in their ears—white noise. It was as if they were in a vacuum—suspended by deadly anticipation, afraid to breathe, afraid to move. All eyes in the room were on one man, because it was his play—if he dared.

He looked around at the four others seated at the big, round oak table. As if he were seeking their approval, he gave each a slow and deliberate look. He was deciding if he dared to cross the line between sanity and a world they knew little about. Small beads of sweat formed on his forehead while his prominent Adam's apple bobbed up and down. His tongue darted, snake-like, over his dry lips. His bloodshot eyes searched again and caught each of the others for a brief second. At that precise moment, they all knew what he was going to do. Chance Hartigan was probably going to kill himself. He was going to pull the trigger of that big, ugly .357 Magnum and pray the odds fell in his favor. If the hammer fell upon an empty cylinder, he would walk away with the five million dollars. If his seemingly uncanny good luck ran out, he would be leaving in a body bag, and all the others could do was to sit and watch. He could hear the strained breathing of those around him as they watched him stare once again at the large black handgun that the host had placed precisely in the center of the table. They had all witnessed their host, Sebastian Black, insert one bullet into the chamber, spin the cylinder and then snap the chamber closed. None of them had ever been at a place where the stakes were this high. This was the ultimate game of Russian Roulette. It had all built up to this.

They watched Chance with a mix of fear and macabre fascination as Black, the man they all had come to fear so much, stood by the door with his usual expression of haughty amusement. His arms were crossed and his thick eyebrows were raised in expectation as he watched the game unfold. He loved the game—it was what he lived for and he honestly didn't care which way the pendulum swung—win or lose, it didn't matter. It was all about the game.

They had been told that the prize was in the five gleaming aluminum cases, which were filled with stacks of banded money. The stainless steel cart on which they sat loomed large, very much a presence next to the wall. There was little else in the room with the exception of the monolith—the solid round oak table with the high-backed chairs where the players sat. It was five of them against Black. The way it had been since the game began. They never had a prayer, because their host held all the cards.

All eyes moved back to the gun as Chance reached for it. They could see the rapid rise and fall of his chest, and how his hand trembled as his fingers curled tightly around its polished wooden grip. He looked closely at the weapon in his hand, turning it over, inspecting each minute detail and then unexpectedly, he turned slowly and raised it to bear upon their tormentor, their master of ceremony, Sebastian Black. Black didn't move a muscle as he stood there with his raven-like eyes locked on Chance's—not on the gun. He knew Hartigan wouldn't pull the trigger—it wasn't in the rules.

Everyone knew it was too late for words. The cards had been dealt; the stakes were set and the consequences known. Chance had waited for this moment all his miserable life—it was all or nothing, the ultimate high, the game of games. It was the dream, or more appropriately, the sealed fate of the consummate gambler. The woman next to him sucked in a short breath. Chance looked over at her again as if to ask her blessing and she just shook her head as he turned the gun slowly away from Sebastian and pointed it toward himself. The end of the barrel loomed like a big black hole, an abyss with the power of death waiting patiently to be called upon with a mere squeeze of the finger. The woman, whom he had slept with, cried out for him to stop, pleading, but she seemed like she was far away in some long, dark tunnel and he paid her no mind. He brought the gun up to the side of his head, pressed it hard into the skin on his temple, and held it there for what seemed like an eternity. His hand began to shake, and sweat ran down his forehead as he held his breath—one long, sweet breath that he knew could be his last. Then he yelled, wide-eyed, piercing the heavy air with a scream that came from the depths of hell as he closed his eyes and tightened his finger on the trigger. They all watched in paralyzing horror as the hammer fell with precision upon the waiting cylinder.

# CHAPTER 1

## NORTH TRURO, CAPE COD

When Chris first mentioned the fact that her Uncle Skyler was missing, I honestly didn't pay a whole lot of attention. Uncle Skyler was an enigma. He was the family's black sheep, a toothache from hell, but Chris loved him to death. She was all he had, and Chris had promised on her mother's deathbed that she'd look after him no matter what. Skyler was a creature that only another drunk could understand and appreciate. He'd venture off into thin air with the swagger and ease of a cat and then show up broke and battered weeks later with his tail between his legs and a story that would make Hemmingway proud. In the meantime, Chris would be frantic; the police would smile and assure her they were doing all they could, while dear old Uncle Skyler was shacked up with some exotic dancer in a drunken blackout. Skyler liked to gamble, and at one fuzzy point in his checkered past he had the money to do it. You see, Uncle Skyler had been rich for a brief period of time. He'd invented a hand-held laser device that could measure distances accurately for the construction and home building industry and had made a fortune overnight, which was not a good thing for an alcoholic and a gambler. To make a very long, ugly, story short; he lost it as quickly as he'd made it—actually quicker. He'd found the ponies, three-card Monty, basketball, baseball, football, and then the crowning blow came when the Indians in Connecticut started building casinos. I think the Pequot Indians named a wing after him, or at least they ought to. Skyler found ways to lose money that nobody had ever heard of. He was a gambler through and through, and gamblers usually met with some pathetic fate. Just like alcoholics, if they don't surrender to it—unfortunately, he was blessed with both afflictions. Skyler was prone to bizarre behavior, and that's why I didn't pay much attention when Chris said he was missing. In retrospect, I was wrong this time.

It was a breezy April afternoon and I was up on my deck looking out over my kingdom, which was Cape Cod Bay at Provincetown Harbor. I was slouched contentedly in my Adirondack chair, bare feet up on the railing, with a hot mug of coffee and some drafts of the new book I was working on. I'd stopped red-penning for a moment, and watched some fool try to navigate a small sailboat through the swirling wind and choppy water in the bay with very little success. Not that I could've done any better—a sailor I'm not.

April is the start of nice spring weather and my deck up on the roof was where I went for solitude and serenity. I'm Nick Thomas. I'm forty-ish, which I'm told is the new 25. I am a moderately successful mystery writer who lives in a cottage on the beach. I drive a temperamental old MG, have and adore a vintage Harley Police Special, and have a very diverse love of music. My blue jeans seem to be shrinking and my hair is getting gray around the temples, but I'm happy with life. I'm also a recovering alcoholic. I tell you that up front, because it's a fact I'm proud of. The key word here is recovering. That means I don't drink anymore, I go to meetings in smoky church basements, and I try to live a better life. It's not the scarlet letter or something you whisper to your kids after I've left the room. It's a disease, it's life and it was hell, but I've fought my way back and I'm able to walk with my head up again. It's been eight hard, self-discovering years, but I've done it sober. However, it seems that every time I try to settle back and enjoy the life I've worked so hard for, or attempt to write that serious Pulitzer Prize winning novel that is rolling around inside my head, something happens. Most people call it bad luck; some call it fate, and the adjusted few call it life. I've come to believe that there is a reason for all that happens, and that there is a master plan that we may never be privy to and don't really need to understand. However, I really hate it when life rears its ugly head and messes with my happy little world. There are days that I think I'd love to write the script for my own life. At least I think I would, but God doesn't allow us that luxury. Someone told me once that life is what happens while we're busy making other plans. Isn't that the truth?

Chris, my ladylove, called me earlier in the day and said that she still hadn't heard from Skyler, and that she wanted me to drive down to Boston with her to look for him if he didn't turn up by morning. Skyler loved the city: bright lights, cheap booze, stripper bars and derelicts. He was at home there and it was usually where he headed after he got his monthly check, which was a miracle in itself. I don't know how, but when he did have money he managed to put some away in an annuity that gave him a modest monthly income now that he was "retired". However, after he got his check in the mail—watch out! It was like watching a dog chase a rabbit. Then a week later he'd be at Chris's asking for a loan till his next check.

In spite of my better instincts, I told her I'd help her find Skyler once again, and that I'd pick her up the following morning in the MG. We would check his room in Hyannis first, but I seriously doubted we would find him there. He rented a small room in a house off the main drag in Hyannis for three hundred a month. His landlady, Abby Pierce, would feel sorry for him and feed him when she could pin him down. They fought like they were married which was why I thought there was some type of love-hate relationship between them. She'd scold him on the evils of drinking and gambling and he'd give her this million-dollar smile that could melt stone. He told me that he gave her flowers once but she threw them out the window at him. Mrs. Pierce later informed me that he did indeed give her flowers once but that it was two-o'clock in the morning; he was drunk, and that the flowers came from her carefully manicured garden. I always secretly hoped they would pair up. Abby Pierce would be good for Skyler.

I knew Skyler wouldn't be in Hyannis. Chris had already talked with Abby and even she sounded worried. He never had the resources to stay gone long. It was the call of the wild that lured him and I was sure that's where he'd be found if he wanted to be found. The thing I didn't like was the growing feeling of apprehension in the air, hanging like a dark cloud.

It was supposed to be a nice day and with any luck

we could put the top down and enjoy the ride. Spring on the Cape is incredible: the sun is always brighter, the wind always a bit sweeter and the sky definitely a lot bluer. Besides, Chris and I have fun together no matter what we do and can make an adventure out of anything. So I said, what the hell, packed a small bag and made reservations at a bed and breakfast that I knew in Cambridge. I figured we could have a nice, romantic dinner in some out of the way nook downtown and then locate Skyler. It sounds easy, doesn't it?

# CHAPTER 2

The instructions he'd received were precise. Skyler was sent a bus ticket from Hyannis to Boston by a special messenger and was told to be in front of the terminal at 1 PM on Saturday. The typed instructions told him that there would be a limousine waiting and he was not to mention this to a soul or else the deal was off. Not wanting to jeopardize his chances for the five million that he'd waited for all his life, he'd done as he was told. When he got off the bus in Boston's Port Authority, he pulled his bag out to the sidewalk to find a sea of taxicabs and limos waiting. Skyler stood and shielded his eyes from the sun and scanned the line of cars. About half a block down, he saw a tall, dark-skinned man in a dark suit standing next to a gleaming ebony Lincoln Stretch. The man looked directly at Skyler and motioned him toward the waiting car. Skyler almost tripped over himself as he pulled his tattered bag toward the Lincoln.

"Hey, I'm Skyler Todd," he said panting. "You must be my ride."

The chauffeur ignored the outstretched hand, looked at Skyler and then down at what appeared to be a photo in his hand. He seemed satisfied that Skyler was indeed who he said he was and without saying a word he popped the trunk and tossed in Skyler's bag. He closed the trunk and opened the rear door of the limo for Skyler. There was no change of expression and no words spoken or encouraged, so Skyler climbed in and the door slammed shut behind him.

"What an asshole," Skyler murmured, as he surveyed the plush interior of the limo in which he was the only passenger. "But ... I could get used to this," he said smiling.

The long ride in the fancy Lincoln Limo was one of intense expectation for Skyler. He'd read the ad a thousand times, but wished he'd remembered to bring it along. Abby would probably snoop in his room, find it and think he was foolish. Skyler knew better. He knew this was his chance. He knew that the Good Lord sent him that ad and he was doing his duty to follow the directions sent to him divinely by way of the *Boston Globe*.

The Lincoln had a mini bar that Skyler happily discovered early in the ride, but desperately tried to ignore. Clear heads prevail, he chanted to himself. This firm resolve lasted until the Limo cleared Boston proper and swept onto the highway north without incident. Skyler figured this to be another sign from above and promptly broke the seal on the new bottle of *Jack Daniels* he'd discovered. It was the only bottle in the mini bar. How did they know, he wondered, dropping several ice cubes into a heavy crystal tumbler and drowning them with a hefty splash of *Jack*. Might as well sit back and enjoy the ride, he mused, turning on the rear stereo. To his immediate delight, Frank Sinatra, his all-time favorite, began to sing to him.

Skyler pressed back into the leather and knew his life had just changed.

Skyler closed his eyes and imagined that this was all his; the limo, the mini bar loaded with *Jack* and Frankie telling him life was good. He could not have written the script any better. Skyler laughed and saluted the dark glass that separated him from the silent driver. "Fuck you, buddy. You'll see. Maybe I'll hire a female limo driver with nice tits who will talk to me. Who needs you, Peckerwood?" he laughed aloud. "Hell, maybe she don't even need to talk at that." He laughed some more at that thought and helped himself to just a tad more whiskey.

The miles passed, Frank sang and the bottle of Jack evaporated. By the time he saw the green sign that said *Welcome to Vermont,* Skyler was already shit faced and had to pee. He was clearly on familiar ground.

# CHAPTER 3

I woke to a brilliant morning sun that washed over the wooden floor of the loft and onto my bed. I could see the water from three sides of my bedroom and hear the gentle cadence of the morning tide as I shook the sleep from my eyes and the cobwebs from my brain. It was a bit chilly in the loft but under my comforter, it felt good. I rose up on one elbow and smiled at God. It was going to be a beautiful day for our ride. I always marveled at my fortune. I had so many things in my life to be grateful for. I made a living doing what I loved, I had a great woman in my life and I lived where most people would love to live.

I'd bought this old cottage a few years back from a friend, and with a lot of sweat, hammered and nailed her into my home. The moment I had laid eyes on her I knew I had found my heaven. The weather-beaten cottage was nestled comfortably amongst the dunes on a small bluff that looked out over the bay. The road wound through a series of small dunes littered with scrub pines and sparse brush and ended abruptly in a sandy cul-de-sac where my driveway began. There was a wooden sign nailed to the telephone pole at the beginning of the road that read DEAD END, and somebody scrawled in magic marker underneath it the words *No Trespassing!* Actually, it might've been me who wrote that. There were two other cottages tucked off on each side that belonged to my neighbors, Rudy Kemp, a retired professor of English and a privately frustrated novelist who had yet to darken a publisher's door, and Ms. Regina Lambert, who was an obscure screen figure from the sixties. She'd boasted about a role in a *James Bond* film once after having had a few drinks. They both lead private lives, but we all seemed to get along when we bump into each other.

I showered and brought the paper and my coffee up onto the deck. When the weather cooperates, this is how I like to start my day. I stood at the rail and stretched— head back, eyes closed and breathed in the salty morning air. The bay had a nice even ripple with a whitecap popping up here and there, but it was not as choppy as the day before. Shading my eyes from the morning sun, I looked to my right, toward Provincetown. The town sparkled like the water and I could hear the sounds of the day coming alive. I watched a young couple, bundled in sweats, walking on the beach in front of my cottage as their dog chased some elusive seagulls a little farther down. Spring on Cape Cod had a life of its own, as does everything, but most people don't take the time to notice. They just do what they have to do—no more, no less. Imagine doing that your whole life, just trying to get by and never stopping to watch a great sunset or sit on the beach before a storm and feel the wrath of Mother Nature. I take the time for sunsets now because I know that the one unknown thing God gives us all is time. Some have more than others do and that's what makes life interesting, because we never know how much. I have learned to be grateful and to use my time for things that really matter.

I hated to leave this place, but duty called. In this case, it was Chris and frankly, any reason to be with her was a bonus in my eyes. I spent the next half-hour buttoning up the cottage and loading the MG. I put the top down, snapped the tonneau cover in place and checked the oil and water for the trip into Boston. I learned a long time ago that with this car it paid to take the extra few minutes and check everything. The MG is a temperamental breed of cat. When she felt loved she roared and purred like the fine British sports car she was designed to be, but when she felt neglected—look out!

The MGB was built in 1966 in a small factory outside of London. She was outfitted with a strong 1800cc motor, dual side-draft carburetors and a four-speed synchromesh transmission with overdrive. Her interior was black, with rolled and pleated leather, a polished walnut dash, wood-spoke steering wheel and chrome Smith gages. The only thing I had to change was the sound system. I take my music seriously so I splurged and had a kick-ass CD sound system installed complete with a power amplifier in the trunk. The only thing critical I felt they missed was a cup holder for my coffee. I remedied that challenge by installing my own. One must have his priorities.

I loved to hear her throaty roar on a nice, cool spring day. I popped in an old *Doors* CD and listened to the haunting voice of Jim Morrison as I embarked on my own mission of doom much like Martin Sheen heading up river in *Apocalypse Now*. I stopped and grabbed a coffee for the ride then hit the road. Route 6, which is the main thoroughfare on Cape Cod, was quiet and the

MG hummed as I put her through the gears heading toward Falmouth to pick up Chris. I knew the futility of this whole exercise before I even started but one does many things in the name of love and I knew that I was a lot better off giving in and going with Chris to look for Skyler. I'll say one thing, it was always an adventure when Skyler was involved—and I didn't want Chris wandering around the places he roamed in Boston by herself. Chris wasn't a lightweight by any means and wouldn't think twice about hunting Skyler down in the bowels of Boston's embarrassment and drag him home by his ear, but she liked to have me along for moral support.

Chris is a special lady that I met a couple of years back at an AA meeting down in Falmouth. She's my love and my best friend, and more importantly, the one who tries to understand me when all others have failed. She is a vibrant, intelligent, beauty of thirty-something, with a quick sensual smile, rich short brown hair, and soft brown eyes. I always tell her that it was her long, beautiful tanned legs that got my attention, but it's her smile that keeps it. She suspects that it's the opposite.

Chris is also my informal therapist. She sees things in a way that eludes most people and rejoices in the good in almost everything. I call her Sunshine because she is. She was the one who helped me slow down and take in life before I had a mass coronary and she's also the one who kept telling me I could write. I never believed for a microsecond that I could sell something that I wrote. It was a dream and one that I had put where I thought all impossible dreams went but Chris wouldn't hear of it. She pushed me into finishing my first book, which is a kind definition at best, and helped me go out and find an agent. I know that God was watching, because things don't usually happen the way they did. I found an agent—a feisty woman who took a liking to me and kicked my ass daily until my pile of papers read like a book. And guess what? It sold. Yes it did, and so did the last three. So I do owe Chris. If it wasn't for her I would probably still be working at doing something I hated for too little pay and not enough self-respect.

It was about nine-thirty when I pulled up to Chris's condo, located on the marina in Falmouth. She loved the atmosphere and the hubbub it offered. It drove me nuts. I felt too confined in the condo and there was too much noise in the marina. I enjoy the solitude of my place, which is one reason why we still maintain separate residences. She does spend a lot of time at my house and I cherish every minute, but we both agree that if it ain't broke we ain't gonna fix it—for now.

She must've heard me pull in because she bounded out the door with a bag slung over her shoulder, looking as beautiful as ever. She had a way of arriving. There was a surge of energy, and sometimes I would swear there were trumpets, and then Chris was there, breathless and smiling, with her tousled brown hair poking out from beneath a white sailor's cap with her eyes aglow. My heart skipped a beat as usual. I thanked God every time I could for putting this woman in my life.

She slid into the passenger's seat of the MG and gave me a warm kiss. "Hi baby. I missed you."

"I know."

"Aren't we cocky this morning," she teased and gave my shoulder a punch as I backed out of the parking lot.

I smiled and reached over for her hand, "I miss you the minute you are gone and every second until we are together again. How's that?"

"You're laying it on a bit thick today, Mr. Thomas. You trying to get lucky?"

"It's possible."

"It's inevitable," she said in a mock-husky voice, batting her lovely eyelashes. "But you'll have to wait until tonight." She reached over and ran her slender fingers lovingly through my hair as I roared out of the marina lot.

My thoughts traveled back to the business at hand. "Anything new on Skyler? What exactly did Abby Pierce say?" I asked as I gunned the MG up the ramp and onto Route 28 heading toward Hyannis. A school bus with a load of screaming kids came up next to us and they all were waving and cheering like we were celebrities or something. Chris laughed as she waved back and even I managed a little wave before I downshifted and nailed the accelerator to put some distance between us. While I happily watched the bus fall back in my rear view mirror, I could've sworn some kid gave me the finger out of one of the windows. I made a note to make sure my vasectomy was holding.

"Mrs. Pierce said he came down and paid her the rent two weeks early and said that he'd be gone for a few days. That was a week ago and you know as well as I do that Uncle Skyler has never paid rent early in his life—even when he had money. Poor Mrs. Pierce almost had a stroke."

I had this picture of Skyler leering at Abby Pierce trying to look down her dress when he paid her. "Think Skyler's ringing her bell?" I asked with a laugh. I always liked to concentrate on the important issues. "He's a horny old dog, especially after a few pops."

Chris shot me a look. "That's the most disgusting

thing I think I've ever heard you say. That's like trying to imagine your parents having sex. And no, I don't think they're intimate. I prefer the word intimate, by the way, instead of 'ringing her bell.' Mrs. Pierce is a nice old woman and I happen to know that she thinks Uncle Skyler is a pervert."

"He is. But you think I'm a pervert too, and you still love me don't you?"

"Yes, but it took some getting used to. Abby Pierce has been a widow for a long time and the last thing she needs is Uncle Skyler with all his problems."

"Where do you think he went?" I asked.

"He must've hooked up with Rose for a wild weekend and decided to stay in Boston. I hope that's all there is to this. I would like a simple solution and then as a reward, a romantic weekend," she said, trying to convince herself not to make more of this than it was.

I liked the romantic weekend part but somehow I was less than optimistic about a quick and simple resolution. Skyler could screw up a wet dream. There might be something to him hooking up with Rose. She was Skyler's soul mate—his partner for his train ride to hell and back. Rose was an over-the-hill exotic dancer who worked as a barmaid in one of the finer establishments Skyler had discovered on one of his research weekends a few years back. Rose was a looker in a trashy sort of way. Pushing fifty, she still had curves in all the right places, long, wild raven hair, polished toenails, and legs that are illegal in most states. You know, the kind of woman men fantasized about but never let on to their wives. Actually, Rose had a heart of gold and her only mistake was hooking up with Skyler and I'm sure that most of the time she rues that fateful day when she surrendered to his dazzling smile. Each time Skyler roared into town he would deposit his bag at her apartment, to which he had a key, and head directly for trouble. In Skyler's case, trouble was spelled many ways. He was the biggest shit magnet I ever saw. If there was a scam or somebody looking for a sucker, they didn't have to look too hard. Once while he was drunk, he told me that he worked hard to get the reputation he had. I didn't feel the need to argue.

I looked over at Chris and saw she was lost in thought. She had taken off the white captain's hat so the cool wind was blowing her short chestnut hair back revealing her fine features. She had a small delicate nose and nice defined cheekbones with a smattering of light freckles. She sat with her hands folded in her lap and her eyes closed as we rode in silence for a few minutes.

"You okay?" I asked, as I reached over and closed my hand around hers.

"I was just thinking. You know, why do some people do what they do even when they know it'll never get any better?"

"You really have to ask that question?"

"No … no, I guess not." She paused then said, "I know what you're saying Nick. You and I, of all people, should understand because we're alcoholics and went through that insanity time and time again. It was terrible and maybe I do understand." Her voice had gotten softer and now she was quiet. I looked over and saw she had closed her eyes tight as a single tear traveled slowly down her cheek.

I let her be for a while as I drove and went back to my bottom. Every alcoholic has one, and some are worse than others, but they all seem the worst to those living them. I remember my last few years with the bottle as a living hell. I always started with all the right intentions. I would just have one. You know, that famous "one beer." Well, in my case one was way too many and a thousand wasn't enough and it was the same—day after miserable day. I'd wake up in my car, or the bushes, or somewhere strange and all I would remember was that first drink. The rest was black. My world crumbled around me along with anything that meant anything to me: jobs, my marriage, relatives, and friends. But most of all I couldn't look at myself in the eye anymore. I couldn't bear to look at that man in the mirror as he looked back at me in disgust. He knew what was wrong. He saw what I couldn't. He knew I was methodically killing us both. And I didn't care, or didn't think I did. But I took to shaving in the shower to avoid the confrontation. I did that for the last I-don't-know-how-many-years. I would tell myself it was to save time. But I knew the truth. I was scared of those bloodshot eyes that would look back at me and cause me to scream inside. I would cringe at what I had become. Knowing the truth, I would say to the man in the mirror that today would be different. I'd tell him that I wouldn't stop for that *one* today. I wanted a better life, I did, but I didn't know how to shed the old one. Four o'clock would roll around and I would hear the bottles clinking, smell the smoke in the stale air, hear the mixed laughter of men and women having an after work cocktail. I would hear the music from the jukebox and the smell of excitement and know that I had to be there too. What I didn't know was that there was a big difference between those laughing people and me. They went home after a few drinks to their families, their wives, husbands and children. They didn't wake up on the cold tile floor of their bathrooms in their own vomit, night after night. They could remember what they did and with whom they did it to. I never did. That was how I ended up. That was my bottom and one I never wanted to forget.

Then one day it all changed for me. Don't ask me why, because I don't know. But my life changed in one fell swoop that I still believe came from the hand of God. It was one night like a thousand others where I started with the *one* after work and ended remembering very little past eight o'clock. When I awoke I was in a very uncomfortable cell in a very unfriendly police station. Not to say I was a stranger to these finer bed and breakfasts, but this morning was different. A cop who looked like he was seven feet tall came in, shook me awake and handed me a cup of coffee. I remembered that conversation as if it were yesterday. I was hung over. I was sick and I was scared. I knew my job was gone if the sun was up and I was in jail instead of at my desk. He asked me if I needed help. I remember looking at him and crying. "Yes," I answered him, I needed help but I didn't have a clue how to get it. He said he'd show me, and he did. He put me in touch with a friend who just happened to be in Alcoholics Anonymous and I must've been ready because I heard what the man said. And for the first time in my life I felt that there was some hope for me. Years later, I know that cop was an angel and that he saved my life.

So, I could relate to Skyler and I knew Chris could also. I looked over at her and saw the soft rise and fall of her chest as she had her head back on the leather headrest. She was fast asleep. The sun was just climbing into its midday cradle of warmth as it cast a golden glow on her face and the wind played with her soft brown hair. The smooth hum of the MG and the kiss of nature had put her to sleep. She looked peaceful and I let her sleep. I had a feeling we'd need all the rest we could steal.

# CHAPTER 4

Skyler wasn't sure how long he had been in the dark. He knew he hadn't seen the sun since he'd arrived at the house. He remembered the long black Lincoln going through a gate that was overgrown with ivy. The driver stopped and spoke into a phone that was mounted on a stone post. After a long moment, the heavy, iron gate swung open to a winding gravel drive that had neatly manicured pines on either side. A few hundred yards later, the road opened up onto the most magnificent setting he had ever seen. The house itself was a gothic style stone castle, a towering entrance with massive wood doors and long two-story wings on either side of the main turret stood sentinel. Everything was stone, wrought iron and granite and the grounds were flawless. It was cold looking—almost too perfect, he had thought.

Then Skyler remembered the dogs. They had come out of nowhere when the car had stopped near the front entrance. Three huge Rottweilers watched him when he opened the door of the Lincoln. The dogs were still as statues ten feet away. The alpha among them, a huge sage-looking beast, stood slightly ahead as the others flanked each of his sides. They just watched him, heads cocked, not moving.

Skyler got out of the car a little unsteadily and the trunk popped open so he could get his bag. He'd only brought one. He only had one. He remembered standing there with his bag in hand as the Lincoln drove off and disappeared behind the mansion. Skyler looked around. The dogs were still there, moving closer, circling and herding him toward the steps. He turned and hurriedly climbed the long steps up to a wide stone porch that wrapped the front of the house.

The dogs stood guard on the lawn, eyes intent. Stopping to catch his breath, Skyler looked around him and marveled at the opulence of the castle. The wide porch had archways covered with thick ivy going in both directions and stone benches by the main entrance. There was a granite waterfall next to the steps that cascaded into a small pond with lily pads and flowers. The massive door opened before he could use the brass knocker and Skyler stepped into the darkened foyer. The inside was just as eerie as the outside. The house looked like a castle from the movies, Skyler remembered thinking.

His eyes took a moment to adjust from the sunlight as a low cultured voice said, "Skyler Todd, I presume. Welcome to my home. I am your host, Sebastian Black."

# CHAPTER 5

Hyannis was busy. Hyannis was always busy, even when the tourists went home, and it was probably the main reason Skyler lived there. He never wanted to be far from the action. He loved Cape Cod and said he could never leave it for long. Boston was his office as he put it and Hyannis was his home.

We found Abby Pierce's neat little house where Skyler lived on the second floor, tucked behind a t-shirt shop and small restaurant. She was out of the house before I shut off the engine and was making mewling noises at Chris as she hurried toward us.

"I'm so worried," she sobbed. "He's never been gone this long."

Chris took her in her arms and held the slight woman tight to her chest.

"It's okay Abby. We'll find him. I'm sure he's alright."

I went around the car, joined the group hug for a brief moment, and then steered us toward the little yellow Cape with window boxes, bright flowers and red trim.

"Relax Abby," I said, smiling. "We'll find him. I

guarantee he'll be back here falling down the stairs and peeing in your flower beds before you know it."

"You're not funny, Nick," Chris said over her shoulder. "Uncle Skyler has a lot of good traits."

"Such as?" The question went unanswered as Chris and Abby Pierce went arm-in-arm into the house ahead of me. Some people don't appreciate a sense of humor. I find that a lot. Couldn't be just mine though, could it?

"I'll put some coffee on and I think I've got some cinnamon rolls I can heat up right quickly," Abby said, with a new purpose now. Most women her age equate everything with food. Food and coffee always made everything better, and mind you, I believe it does also.

Over coffee and rolls we managed to find out that Skyler had indeed paid his rent two weeks ago—early. That should've started ringing the alarm bells right off the bat. Skyler had never paid anything on time in his life—especially the rent. Abby told us he was acting strange a few days before he left. She said he was singing and whistling around the house and making references that his ship had finally come in.

"He told me he was going to take me to the Caribbean and ply me with those drinks with little umbrellas in them," she remembered, her eyes sad. "Then he said he was going to marry me right there on the beach. I called him a silly old fool. I said first of all, I'd never marry a sort like him and that he couldn't afford to take me to a movie, never mind the Caribbean. Nonsense, I said, pure nonsense. He laughed at me and said, 'We'll see about that, Abby old girl. Yes indeed. We'll see about that when I get back.' I asked him where he thought he was going, and he just smiled at me and said his ship had docked and he was going to meet her. That's all he would say. I saw him the morning he left. He had on his only suit. You know that old blue thing with the pinstripes?" She looked down at her coffee with moist eyes and said softly, "Still, he looked handsome in that old suit with his white shirt and that red tie he was so proud of."

She looked at us as she dabbed a small tear that was sliding down her cheek. "He did look handsome, though. I wish he wasn't such a maverick. He's really a good man, you know."

Chris and I both nodded as convincingly as we could. You could tell she was fond of old Skyler. It just wasn't in his blood to be tending flowerbeds in Hyannis when the music was calling him in Beantown.

Chris put her hand on Abby's arm and asked, "Is there anything you can tell us? Did he mention anything about where he was going? Was he headed to Boston?"

Mrs. Pierce frowned as she thought back. "No. Nothing stands out. Oh, wait ... maybe ..."

She straightened up as if she seemed to remember something important. "He did say he would be riding in style. Something about a limousine and that he was being picked up in town. I never paid him any attention. I just thought he was talking foolishness like he always did. Who in their right mind would send a limousine for Skyler and where in God's name would they be taking him?"

That one had me stumped. "The casinos have limos that pick up wealthy customers and drive them down to Connecticut, but I can't imagine them picking up Skyler. You gotta have money first." I looked at Chris who looked as puzzled as I was.

"Is there anything else, Abby? Anything?" I asked her.

"There was one other thing," she said rising from the table. She went over to an old wooden hutch that dominated the small kitchen and rifled through a stack of papers. "It was right here," she mumbled to herself. "I know it was. I found it when I went upstairs to close his windows. The damn fool left all the windows open and we were expecting a storm. You know how it rains a lot here in springtime. He left the windows open so I went up to close them. I wasn't snooping mind you." She shot us a stern look over her shoulder.

We both said, "No. No, of course not!" as quickly as we could. Abby nodded and went back to the pile of papers on the hutch.

"Here it is!" she announced. "I knew it was here. I wasn't snooping. It was just there on his kitchen table and I saw it when I reached over to fasten the window." She looked to us once again for validation, which we readily proffered.

Of course she was snooping. There was no doubt in my mind. But I also knew it was a labor of concern if not love. She cared for Skyler, she was worried and it showed.

She found what she was looking for and came back over to the table with a folded section of the *Boston Globe*. It was part of the classified section and when she set it down in front of us I saw an ad circled with black marker. Chris and I moved closer, so we could both read the ad together.

---

*$$$$$$$$$   GAMBLERS   $$$$$$$$$*
*I PROMISE TO GIVE FIVE MILLION DOLLARS*
*TO ONE PERSON.*

*Is that you? Are you interested in the ultimate game of chance? We are looking for a select group of people to participate in an experiment in human nature. Must be of legal age, single, divorced or widowed.*

**Investment:** *1 week of your time with all expenses paid.*

**Return:** *Minimum payment of $50,000. Cash*

**Maximum:** *$5,000,000 cash to the winner. No strings, no hoax.*

*Please respond with a detailed letter as to why you should be chosen.*

**Ask yourself one question:** *What would you do for five million dollars?*

*Serious Inquiries only. Respond to:*
*P.O. Box 251, Cold River, VT 05461*

---

The ad was dated February 27th and I swear I could still see Skyler's drool on the page. Of course he responded to this ad. It was written for him. Hell, I'd respond to this ad for fifty grand and a chance for a cool five mil. I looked up at Chris and our eyes met. She looked worried.

"Nick, this is too good to be true. Somehow, Skyler got suckered into something and now he's missing. You know what they say about when something seems too good to be true."

"Yeah, yeah, then it usually is. Come on, Chris. Maybe Skyler hit the big one and is off on the tear of his life. Why is it always bad?" But I knew the answer to that one as it came out of my mouth. Because it was Skyler, that's why! The best thing that could've happened to him would be that he was turned down from this offer and he was drunk somewhere in Boston with Rose. But the limo thing and his seemingly euphoric mood prior to his disappearance were saying otherwise. Giving Skyler fifty thousand dollars was like giving a five-year-old a can of black spray paint in a white living room.

I looked at Abby and her eyes searched mine for answers. "Okay, we'll look into it," I said quickly. What else could I say, not that I had any choice.

"Can we see his room, Abby? Maybe there's something else up there that can tell us something." I was almost afraid of what we might find, but we had to look.

"Of course," she replied. "Let me get the keys."

The three of us poked around in Skyler's efficiency apartment for the better part of an hour, finding nothing but evidence of the sad life of a gambler. The furniture: the bed, a tattered dresser, a threadbare recliner with a broken foot rest, and a Formica kitchen table with two ripped chairs, that Abby got for him at a yard sale. The top dresser drawer held his life's treasures: a yellowing baseball signed by Ted Williams, a box of old coins, a few crumpled foreign bills, packs of matches from the casino in Connecticut, a few service medals from the Navy, lottery slips, cufflinks, a tie clasp, a broken watch, and a bundle of old photos secured by a rubber band. On top of the dresser was a photo of Chris and her mother, when Chris was about ten-years-old. She'd never been up in Skyler's room and didn't remember the picture. We were all sad. The mood was infectious. This was all he had aside from the modest income from his trust and a small Social Security check.

Chris sat on the bed and I could see she was about to cry. I sat next to her and put my hand in hers.

"We'll find him Chris. We will."

She put her head on my shoulder and said nothing. I don't know why but I had a feeling of dread also. I didn't feel like there was a happy ending in this. Abby Pierce excused herself to fix us some lunch before we hit the road and Chris and I just sat there on the bed with her head on my shoulder.

After a sumptuous lunch of thick ham and Swiss sandwiches on homemade bread, corn chowder and an apple crumb pie, we said our good-byes to Abby with promises to let her know what we found out. The day was young, bright, and a bit breezy as we climbed back into the MG and set out for Boston. The little guy that sits on my shoulder was screaming in my ear to turn around and head home, and as usual, I didn't listen.

# CHAPTER 6

The first night was quiet. Skyler was served dinner in his room, and told to relax, as the other guests got settled and that all would be explained in the morning. The woman who showed him to his room and brought him his food was cold and brisk and offered him no further information. The food was excellent and to his delight, Skyler found a small refrigerator that held a bottle of expensive chilled vodka and some beer. By nine he was passed out on the bed with his clothes still on and the near empty vodka bottle cradled in the crook of his arm.

Skyler awoke the morning in pain—his mouth dry, head throbbing, and his stomach on fire. He remembered finding the vodka and that was it. Must've been spiked, he remembered thinking. He looked around his room. It was richly furnished as one would expect a castle to be; heavy drapes, bulky solid dressers and four poster bed with expensive sheets and a thick luxurious bedspread that faced the ever-crackling gas log fire.

"I could get used to this," Skyler said aloud, rolling his neck to get the kinks out. Snap crackle pop. His mouth tasted like he ate a beach towel—a sandy one at that and his temples throbbed. Shit, I can't keep doing this. I'm getting too old, he thought, knowing that he would continue to drink as he had daily for many years to come.

There was a sharp rap on the heavy oak door and in walked the man Skyler had met upon his arrival, Sebastian Black. He was a small fierce looking man with black slicked back hair, raven eyes that looked like two coals burned into a thin white face, and a pencil-thin moustache above a small tight mouth. He was impeccably dressed in a dove gray suit with a black turtleneck and highly glossed black loafers. The only misnomer, thought Skyler as he looked over the man as he emerged from his fog, was the large diamond earring in Black's left ear. He couldn't remember if that meant the guy was gay or not. He sure looked like it, Skyler mused.

"Good morning, Mr. Todd," said Black crisply, taking in the surroundings. His eyes rested on the vodka bottle lying on the tousled bed. "I trust you had a good rest?"

Skyler stammered a bit, "I ... I slept good sir. Now what is this all about? What happens next? You promised me fifty thousand dollars." He ran a shaky hand through his thin rumpled hair. He looked like he'd slept in a ditch and knew he didn't smell too good either.

Black held up a manicured finger and looked at Skyler in obvious distaste. "Mr. Todd, a word of advice. If you want to walk out of here with the prize you will have to have your wits about you. I strongly suggest you stay away from the booze. There's soda, juices and anything else you might want. Just let one of my staff know what it is you desire and we would be happy to provide."

His eyes rested on Skyler. "Breakfast will be served in the main dining room at 8:30 sharp and please don't be late. We have things to go over. Your questions will be answered then."

He turned to leave. "You have twenty minutes, Mr. Todd, and remember, everything here is a game of chance. Nothing is as it appears ... nothing," Black said and walked out into the hall. He turned to Skyler and added, "You will find new clothes in the closet—your size, of course, so please dress appropriately."

Skyler stood there by the door not sure what to say, so he just closed the door and headed in the direction of the shower.

"That guy gives me the creeps," he said to his rumpled reflection in the bathroom mirror.

# CHAPTER 7

Boston, Beantown, home of the Red Sox, city of Tea Party fame and signers of the Declaration of Independence, was a place of incredible history and cultural diversity. On one hand, you had the hallowed halls of learning at Harvard and Boston College, on the other the sub-cultural allure of the combat zone, where titty bars, hookers and drug deals flourished. This was where the inner-city culture of perversion attracted people from all walks of life; college kids, executives, blue collars, gays, straights, derelicts and dangerous people with varying degrees of pursuit abounded. This was, of course, where I thought we'd find Skyler. He loved it here. He loved the lights, the action, the booze, and the women who danced naked on the bars mere inches from the melting ice cubes in his whiskey. This was Skyler's home and where we would find his friend Rose. I knew where she worked. It was a fine establishment called *High Heels* located smack dab in the middle of hell.

I deposited Chris at the B&B in Cambridge and told her that I'd be back in a few hours and that I'd call the minute I found anything. She wasn't thrilled with the fact that I was going down there on my own, but she did have the common sense to know that a white, seemingly normal couple would stick out like Jessie Jackson at the Vatican on Sunday morning. She told me she would browse some old bookstores and do some shopping but would be close and have her cell phone if I needed her. Cell phones have changed the world the same magnitude as the automobile. I've yet to determine if it is a good influence or a bad one. It seemed to me that the world had functioned pre-cell phone just fine, however, I am as guilty as the next and feel naked without mine.

*High Heels* is one of those social enigmas that are an embarrassment for most, and the things that dreams are made of to some. My opinion fell somewhere in-between. I found a spot for the MG a block away in front of a store that boasted the lowest prices in town for car stereos and beepers. I glanced lovingly at the Sony in my dash and prayed that it would still be there on my return. Needless to say, I put the top up and locked the sports car even though I knew how foolish that exercise was. It was in God's hands. Still, I cringed as I walked away from the car while looking back at her. I loved my car.

I crossed the street and walked briskly in the direction of the bar. One doesn't linger in these neighborhoods. I felt good though, dressed as I usually do with jeans, my well-worn black cowboy boots, black tee shirt and a brown corduroy sport coat. You can get away with this outfit almost anywhere. You can mingle with the snots at a party and they think its casual-cool but you are not so pretentious roaming the lesser restrained bowels of humanity as I was now. A lot of cops dress the way I do—less formal, more relaxed. I took a deep breath as I approached the brightly adorned neon entrance to *High Heels*. There were two black kids leaning on the graffiti wall next to the entrance eyeballing me closely as I walked up.

"What's up?" I asked as I smiled and reached for the door. Never show fear, even when you're scared shitless.

The older of the two, who had a red knit hat pulled tight to his head, moved in front of the door blocking my way. He smiled back at me with a gleaming gold tooth, "Goin' on, man? You lookin fo' sumptin over here? Never seen you befoe. Maybe you a cop, huh?"

I smiled and said, "I'm not the heat, man, and I'm not buying dope or pussy. I'm looking for Rose. She's a good friend. That cool?"

Gold tooth seemed to digest that a moment and then looked at his buddy and back at me. "Know Rosie you say?"

I nodded, "We go back, man."

"That's cool. She inside. Tell Tiny inside Jo Jo sent you in." He offered his hand, thumb up and I shook it. I thought for a second and turned back to him. I had to ask just one little favor now that we were blood.

"Jo Jo, I'm Nick and would I be insulting you and your associate's integrity if I offered twenty bucks as an insurance policy on my little green MG over there?" I pointed down the block and across the street where my car sat conspicuously alone.

"She pretty, man. What year?"

"66. I got a lot of love on those wheels man. I know you can hear that."

Jo Jo laughed and patted me on the back. "Keep the twenty man. The car's cool. Rose is my friend too."

I shook his hand again and his friend's, who hadn't spoken a word during the exchange, before I pushed my way into another world.

It was like passing through the gates of hell, out of a world of bright sunshine to darkness permeated by a throbbing disco beat, clinking bottles and thick cigarette smoke. I paused in the foyer to let my eyes adjust and I became aware of a very large, bald black man in a threadbare white tank top that stretched across an impressive expanse of chest and shoulders. He was perched on a wooden barstool just inside the door. I'd say he went about 280. He didn't offer the same warm smile like the guys outside.

"Fifteen dollar cover, cracker," he growled at me. I wanted to explain that I wasn't your run of the mill pervert but I saved my breath.

I tried my smile. That always worked. "Jo Jo sent me in. I'm looking for Rose. I'm a friend."

He eyed me like I was an insect, but I held my ground.

"Still need the fifteen bucks, Holmes. I don't give a fuck if you Wild Bill looking fo' Monica."

I decided this guy wasn't worth arguing with and besides, I'd just saved twenty outside. I peeled off a twenty and told him to have a beer on me and I walked past him through a beaded curtain into the world of sin. The music was loud, the smoke thick and the two girls on stage were into something that I'll leave to your imagination. Let me say that it sort of got my blood pumping and I was trying hard not to watch—honest. I sidled up to the large horseshoe shaped bar and gave a wave to the barmaid. She was a looker in her early thirties, long blonde hair, a lot of leg, plenty of cleavage, and painted toenails in very high-heeled sandals—the kind with the sexy ankle straps. She flashed me a smile and walked my way slowly so I could get the full effect.

"What can I get for you, handsome?" she said with a low sexy voice. My thoughts went quickly to Chris in her sailor hat waiting for me at the B&B. I felt I needed that affirmation.

"Hi, beautiful," I smiled and flirted just a little. "I'm looking for Rose. I'm a friend."

Her smile faded a bit and she leaned on the bar in front of me showing me two creamy mounds with nipples hard as pebbles through her tiny tube top. "I'm Amy and I can be very friendly, too! Not many guys like you come in here. Mostly we get perverts pulling their puds in the dark over by the stage. Besides, I'm a lot younger than Rosie."

I smiled and swallowed my tongue. "I … I can see that Amy, but I'm here on business." I held out my hand and shook hers. "I'm Nick Thomas, could you please tell Rosie that I'm here and that it's important."

She pulled back from the bar and looked at me skeptically. "You a cop?"

"No, actually I'm a writer, and I'm looking for her friend, Skyler."

She laughed a low husky laugh. "A writer, huh? That's a good one. Skyler owe you money?" she asked. "He owes everybody money, even me." She leaned a little closer and I could smell a soft powdery perfume. She had perfect white teeth and the greenest eyes I ever saw. I shuddered a bit when she ran a perfectly manicured French nail over my forearm. The roaring I heard in my ears felt like I was on the beach.

I recovered and remembered what we were talking about. "No. He doesn't owe me money but he seems to be missing and some people are worried. Have you seen him in here lately?"

I watched her tongue circle her wet lips. Her eyes never left mine for a second and I was very aware of her breasts just inches south of my nose. Man, this lady put off some heat.

Then thank God the spell was broken. "Leave that poor boy alone, Amy, he's spoken for," came a loud happy voice from behind me. I was relieved to turn around and see Rose standing there in electric- blue sequined hot pants, matching bikini top, black fishnets, and very hot looking heels. We embraced. Rose was all nice smells and warm skin with a wild mane of sexy black hair that hung to her waist and a body to kill for at fifty-something. I pulled back and kissed her on the cheek. I knew I couldn't stay here long or I'd be in serious trouble. This was not the type of place a recovering alcoholic needed to be and certainly not a place a man in a committed relationship belonged—too many hormones in the air.

"Good to see you, Nick. What brings you down here?" her eyes searched mine looking for a clue. *"Heels* ain't your regular type of haunt. You'd never stay sober in here, that's for sure, and Amy over there would have you for breakfast." A worried look crossed her face. "It's Skyler isn't it? Something's happened to him, hasn't it, Nick?"

"I don't know Rose. I honestly don't know. I was hoping he'd be here with you. He's missing and we're worried. When did you see him last?" I was beginning to get that feeling of doom. "I figured if he called anybody it would be you."

"That's a good one, Nicky." She tossed her hair back in a stripper's gesture. "I haven't seen him in weeks. The only time I see Skyler is when he's on the way down. I love him to death but I've long since given up any notions of having a normal relationship with him. Come on, let's sit. I need a drink now, a nice stiff one and you can give me the gory details." She took me by the arm over to a quiet corner of the bar and asked Amy for a club soda with lime for me and a double Jose' Cuervo on ice for her. Amy was still glowering at me when she brought us our drinks. She looked me in the eye with defiance and informed me that she got off at eight if I was man enough, and then she strutted away. I watched out of pure respect.

Rose laughed. "You still got the charm, Nicky Baby. You got her bumping into things."

I can't say I wasn't flattered. Amy was made for wild weekends and the things dreams were made of.

Rose laughed in Amy's direction and said, "Remind me to tell you something before you leave, lover. But now let's talk about Skyler."

Rose asked me a lot of questions that I didn't have the answers for. I showed her the classified ad from the newspaper that I had borrowed from Abby. Rose kept shaking her head as she read it. She told me she hadn't heard from Skyler in a couple of weeks. He had called her and told her much the same as he told Abby; that his ship had come in and that when it docks he was going to whisk her away from all of this. The crew on his ship was growing. I wondered how Rose and Abby would hit it off.

"You believe him?" I asked her, stirring my club soda.

"Come on, Nick. You know Skyler as well as I do. He's as full of shit as a Christmas turkey, but loveable as hell. I figured he had another sure-fire scheme to beat the track or something. You know. He was always talking some shit about getting rich quick."

"I know that and so does Chris. We were just hoping he'd be down here with you."

"Speaking of Chris, where is that lovely creature? You lucked out there, my friend."

"I know. Shopping. She didn't feel like she'd fit in down here."

A hurt look crossed her face for a second and then she took a long swallow from her tequila. Rose was a beautiful woman in her own right, just a few too many years in the wrong place and a few too many promises from the wrong men. A different life, a different set of cards and Rose could've been a star or something. She had a way about her—a charisma.

"You're right, Nick. She doesn't. Hell Nick, I wish I didn't," she said, swirling the ice cubes in her glass with a long slender finger. "Think he's dead?"

"Rose, I honestly don't know. I don't know if he even answered that ad."

She took another long pull at the tequila, finished it, and slapped the glass on the table. "Ahhhh, that's good. Listen honey, if Skyler didn't answer that ad then I'm the Easter bunny. They wrote that ad for his sorry ass."

We both laughed. I told Rose that I'd call her the minute I found out anything and vice versa. When I got up to leave, Amy appeared in front of us and asked if we wanted *anything* else and she did stress the word *anything*. I smiled, took her hand in both of mine and told her that another day, another set of circumstances, and she'd be in trouble big time. And that I thought she was a gorgeous creature. That seemed to pacify her. She pouted her full lips and strutted away to a group of suits loudly drinking martinis at the other end of the bar.

Rose walked me to the door where Tiny loomed, still

eyeballing me with a scowl on his huge face. I'd bet the farm that he loved raw meat.

"Bye, bye." I waved at him and blew him a kiss. He gave me the finger and said something politically incorrect about white people and their mothers.

I thought of something and turned back to Rose before I pushed open the door.

"Rose what were you going to tell me before? Remember you said you wanted me to remind you to tell me something before I left?"

A smile played across her lips and she looked at Tiny. "Tiny, Amy got the hots for my friend Nick here. What do you think?"

For the first time I saw a small smile cross his massive face and then a short, loud bark that was probably a laugh erupted from him. "Tha'd be real funny, Rosie. I'd pay me some big money to see that." He looked at me between a few more of those barks and said, "Hell cracker, Amy probably got a bigger dick than you." They both broke out laughing, as I turned beet-red and hastened my retreat out into the world I knew.

# CHAPTER 8

Chris was back at the room when I got there. She was waiting for me, curled up on the window seat in the growing shadows of late afternoon, looking comfortable and warm in gray sweats and turtleneck. She had her knees tucked up under her chin and her fingers were laced together around them. She watched me throw my coat on the bed, waiting patiently to hear about what I'd found.

"Hi Baby," I said softly, kissing her tousled head. "You okay?"

She knew what I was going to say by the look on my face. "She hasn't seen him, has she?" she asked me in a small voice, almost trance-like, still looking out at the city from her perch.

"No, she hasn't. The last time Rosie heard from him was about three weeks ago. She remembers him babbling on about how his ship had come in and told her not to worry about a thing. Sound like Skyler to you?"

Chris ran a hand through her short chestnut hair. "Of course it does, Nick. Did you tell her what we think might've happened? Did you tell her about the ad we found in that paper?"

"Yes, I told her and she thinks the same thing we do," I said slowly. "She's worried about him, too."

"What are we going to do, Nick? How can we find out where Skyler went? I don't have a good feeling about this and I don't think this is like the other times. I don't think he is going to pop up again hung over and broke this time. I'd almost welcome that at this point."

Her eyes were moist and a tear traced its way down her cheek. She made no move to wipe it away. "I know something bad has happened and that this is not going to have a happy ending."

I sat down next to her on the window seat, put my arm around her, and tried my best to sound optimistic. "Come on, let's go have some dinner. I always think more productively on a full tummy and I happen to know where we can get the best baked stuffed lobsters and clam chowder on the East Coast. We can walk and soak up some of Boston's ambiance. Maybe we could stop and get a cappuccino and listen to some jazz.

Maybe," I kissed her ear and said in my terrible French accent, "we could discover a little romance later—perhaps you'd be interested in having a mysterious interlude with a tall dark stranger named Nick." I kissed her ear again and I felt her shudder. "You know what the French say about all work and no play?"

She pushed me away in mock anger, "You're not French, Nick Thomas, and neither am I. I'm glad to see all this hasn't affected your appetites. By the way what *exactly* did you find at *High Heels?* You certainly were gone long enough. See anything you liked?" Her green eyes flashed with just the right amount of jealously. "Is that why you're so amorous? A little fantasy got stirred up perhaps?"

This was potentially dangerous ground and I knew I would never tell her about Amy. She'd never let me forget that one.

I smiled my tender, sincere Nick smile. "I work hard on maintaining my priorities. Food and sex happen to be high on that list," I said sliding my arms around her. "I have all I need right here, so why look elsewhere? Besides you are not ready for what I came across there." I thought back on my encounter with Amy at the bar.

I snuggled into Chris and smelled talc and fresh cotton. I kissed her exposed neck and she began making soft cat-like noises and shuddered into me closer. I kept kissing down toward her shoulder, slow and wet, devouring her inch by inch.

"Hey, Nick Thomas," she purred in my ear with hot breath. "That's not fair. I think we need to go cuddle a while. It would make both of us feel a whole lot better." She swung around on the window seat and wrapped her legs around me, rubbing the backs of my legs with her feet. We kissed slow and deep for a long time. It was like our souls were renewing.

I've always said Chris would make a great therapist.

The afternoon sun was gone. The lampposts cast a glow on the darkening street, where happy sounds of dinner and play replaced the urgent din of the day. We laid there on the huge New England featherbed, entwined, content, spent and in love, lingering and listening to the sounds of the city coming alive. Everything had a life and Boston had its own distinct pulse.

Chris loved the same things I did and appreciated the

re-born commitment to the life of a recovering alcoholic. We had both learned to pause for that moment and to take it all in. But we were both troubled by the feeling of impending disaster.

# CHAPTER 9

I didn't believe there was anything else we could do in Boston. The trail didn't lead there. We had to find out more about that ad and I had a feeling that's where we would find Skyler. You know that old saying that if something seemed too good to be true then it usually was. That's what came to mind when I thought about that ad—too good to be true.

The next morning we woke early and decided to head back to the Cape. We agreed to stop back in Hyannis on the way through to see if there was anything we missed at Abby Smith's. Downstairs at the B&B, over corn muffins, bacon, eggs and hot coffee, we both looked one more time at the folded newspaper that Abby found in Skyler's room.

"It's a P.O. box, Nick. I'll bet we can't even get a phone number."

"There's a way, honey, and we'll find it. It looks like a trip to Cold River, Vermont, wherever that may be. We'll find him, Chris, I promise you." I hoped I sounded more convincing than I felt.

Her soft brown eyes searched mine and she reached over the table and put her slender hand on my cheek.

"I love you, Nick Thomas. Thank you for doing this."

I took her hand and brought it to my lips. "You're everything that is good in my life sweetheart and this is where I belong. I know Skyler is important to you. We'll do this together no matter what we find. Okay?"

"Okay," she said in a small voice.

✠

It was another glorious spring day so the top on the MG went down and we loaded the car for our ride back to the Cape. Chris loved the wind and the feeling of freedom as much as I did so there was no argument. We both, however, were quiet with our thoughts.

We didn't find anything new in Hyannis except an increasingly concerned Abby Pierce. She apparently searched his room police style when we left and came up zero. Our only link to Skyler was that folded up section of newspaper with the five million-dollar promise.

As I drove the remaining few miles to Falmouth, the fragments of a plan began to form in my mind. We decided to stop by Chris's place to gather some essentials and she agreed to come back to the beach house with me. She didn't want to be alone and she was not about to let me wander off on my own to find Skyler.

✠

That night I grilled some steaks and baked potatoes on the deck. Chris set the table with a red checked tablecloth, candles and some fresh cut flowers she'd picked up in town, adding a feminine touch that I usually go without. We ate in thoughtful silence as the red sun disappeared over Provincetown Harbor. After a pound of New York strip we sat in some Adirondack chairs with our coffee and watched the passenger ship, *The Cape Cod Princess,* steam slowly across the bay, headed to Boston, along with a few straggling trawlers coming in for the day. It was a sight I never tired of. There's wasn't much more I could ask for in a perfect world—a beautiful woman at my side, good food, and a view to die for. The sky was a beautiful vivid mix of pastels: oranges, yellows, reds and blues that cast a warm glow over our little world.

"What now, Nick?" Chris asked, her hands clasped around her coffee mug.

"There's only one answer, Chris. We have to retrace Skyler's steps and I think the only way we can do that is to track down that ad. I have a friend at *The Globe*. I'll call him in the morning. Maybe he can find out for us who put the ad in and where in Cold River, Vermont this originated from. There must be some kind of record."

"Then what, Nick?" She asked me.

I took her hand in both of mine and raised it to my lips, kissing it gently. "Then, my dear, I will go to Cold River, Vermont. I've never been to Vermont."

"*We'll* go to Cold River, Vermont, was what you meant to say," she said firmly squeezing my hand. "We are going. No argument, Nick. We're in this together."

I knew from the beginning that the battle had been lost, but I had to put up a token effort for the men in this world. I held up both hands in resignation. "Okay, okay *we* are going. Think there is such a place? I've never heard of it. Sounds like something out of the old movies."

"It must be a real place, Darling. You know that as long as we're together, we'll figure it out."

"We usually do," I answered.

The sky was darkening, and we could see the lights of Provincetown twinkling off in the distance. Chris stood and pulled me up to her. My arms slid around her and our mouths found each other's hungrily in a long deep kiss.

"Make love to me, Nick," she said in a husky voice as she turned and led me by the hand into the cottage. I fought valiantly but lost.

The salt air and the fresh wind that comes off the bay had this therapeutic quality and things usually felt better in the morning. We slept to an uncharacteristic 10 a.m. and just laid there spooning, with my arms around her and our bodies meshed together.

My oldest and dearest friend, Nick Jr., woke us up.

Over coffee and bagels, I made the call to my friend, Charlie, at *The Globe* and he said he would get back to me by the end of the day. Chris had my old atlas opened to Vermont and happily informed me that Cold River actually did exist, at least in 1956 when this particular atlas was printed it did. I think I found that precious book at a yard sale a few years back for a dollar and I loved it. It was an oversized maroon-colored hardcover edition with yellowed pages and extremely small print. I told her that we could look on the Internet and she told me that would take all the adventure out of it.

"There it is," she announced tapping the page with a perfect pink nail. "It looks like it's about fifty miles northeast of Burlington. Hey, I hear Burlington is a jumping place—big college town."

"Cold River," I said, "hmmm, let me see." I hunted around for my glasses so I could see. We squinted together at the small dot in the middle of nowhere just south of the Canadian border. The town itself looked small and wasn't represented in bold letters so the population was less than five thousand back in 1956. I doubted if there was much more now but I would check on the Internet for my own piece of mind.

"Long way from here, sweetie. You sure you want to go?"

"Don't be an ass, Nick. Of course I'm going. We're in this together, right? I have plenty of vacation time on the books. I just have to call the Institute."

I nodded with my mouth full of bagel knowing, there was no arguing with her on this and besides I wanted her company and Skyler was, after all, *her* uncle.

Chris looked at me and asked, "So when are we leaving?"

# CHAPTER 10

Charlie from *The Globe* called back about three in the afternoon with some news about the ad. He told us that the ad had come in prepaid, and that the contact information just listed the same P.O. Box that was mentioned in the ad. He said that was not unusual, and since the ad met all their legal criteria, no questions were asked. He did tell me that this was not the first time the ad had been run. According to accounting, the same ad had been run once about six months ago. It had the same wording, same box number, and was prepaid then as well. Charlie said he was sorry he couldn't be of more help, made noises of getting together someday soon and hung up. He was a friend from another lifetime. Charlie and I worked *The Globe* together many years and many changes ago. He had marriage problems, and I was a drunk, so we helped each other as best we could at the time. Now we lived in different worlds.

I told Chris what he'd found out. Next we thought we should try the local police up there to see if they knew of anything going on that could have involved Skyler. But I also didn't expect the Vermont police to be overly zealous over a missing drunk. I called information and was given the phone number of the Cold River Police Department. I dialed it right away while Chris sat at the counter with her coffee and watched me with a little smile on her lips. She knew I was in for the count.

A plainly annoyed voice finally answered after four rings.

"Hello." It sounded like I woke someone up. I checked my watch, and it said it was 3:30 in the afternoon.

"Is this the Cold River Police?" I asked. "I'm looking for the Cold River Police Department."

The man growled at me over the phone, "This is the police, is there a problem?"

"Is it possible to speak with the Chief or Sheriff, whoever is in charge there? We believe we have a missing person and he might be up there."

"Hold on," Mr. Personality barked and I was put on hold. A long moment later, I heard a click. He was all warmth, so much for the northern hospitality that I've heard so much about.

A clipped voice answered, "I'm Sherman Cobb. I'm the Sheriff here. Is there some sort of problem?"

"No sheriff, I don't think so. Well maybe there is. Actually, I'm looking for a friend of mine, and we think he may be in Cold River. We're worried about him." I realized that I probably sounded like an idiot.

"Nobody lost up here far as I know," he said. "Who's your friend? And why do you think he's here in Cold River? Wait a minute. First of all, who are you? And where are you calling from?"

I told him who I was and why we thought Skyler was in Vermont. After a few minutes of skeptical dialogue, he agreed to listen to the classified ad. I offered to fax him a copy but he told me to "just read him the ad or hang up and quit bothering him." I read the classified ad to him and the answer was a long moment of silence.

"Sheriff? Sheriff Cobb, you there?"

"Yeah, I'm here. Keep your pants on. I never heard of such a thing. Don't you city folks come messing up my nice quiet town. I don't know anything about any classified ad and sure as hell don't know anything about fifty thousand bucks. I've never heard or seen anyone by the name of Skyler. I think I'd remember that one. So, go away. Do you get my message Mr. Thomas?"

An odd feeling traveled up my spine. Was he threatening me?

"Sheriff, believe me the last thing we want to do is to cause trouble. We just want to find our friend. Is there anybody up there who might know about such an ad? Is there someone else we could talk to?"

"Nope. I know anything that is worth knowing in this county, and believe you me, there are no long black limousines bringing people up here to gamble. You think this is Connecticut? Seems to me, somebody's playing a joke on you. So why don't you go and have yourself a nice day, Mr. Thomas. If I hear of anything that might help you, I'll be sure and give you a call immediately. Just give me your number."

I gave him our number, knowing full well he never wrote it down then thanked him for all of his valuable time. I think he might've sensed some sarcasm on my part but chose to let it go by slamming the phone down in my ear.

I told Chris that I had the feeling he was trying to get rid of me and after a very short discussion we decided to drive on up to Cold River and poke around a bit. Chris was excited. She was acting like this was some *Nancy Drew* mystery, and we were going to save her missing uncle from a dreadful fate. I didn't want to verbalize the fact that Skyler could be already dead and that we might be walking into a hornet's nest. I just prayed that we could pull this off and there would be a happy ending somewhere in all this.

I had the feeling that Sheriff Cobb was not telling me the truth, and it'd be prudent for us to steer clear of him, which might prove a tad difficult in his small town.

That night Chris and I got ready for the trip, armed with some education on Cold River that we'd gleaned from the Internet. I was right on a few counts. The population was only 4207 people, there were some farms, and virtually no industrial or commercial properties, but there were three golf courses, all private, and a number of extremely wealthy people who resided there. There was even a private airstrip of some sort that was used exclusively by the residents of this elite community. It seemed that Cold River was not the backwater hick town I'd initially thought it was. The median income was well over the norm for Vermont, the schools in town were privately funded and the police department had eight members besides my new friend Sheriff Cobb. There were already some things that did not seem to fit.

We did find that Cold River boasted several fine bed and breakfasts, most included a complimentary river ride for those who wanted a romantic get-away so we chose one that spoke of character and booked a room online for the following night. We'd be tourists: lovers looking for a quiet weekend in Vermont. We felt that the discreet approach would be the best, seeing that I didn't think I'd made a new friend in Sheriff Cobb, and that I'd probably end up in his jail if I didn't watch my step.

Chris set things up with her boss at Woods Hole, made a call to a girlfriend to look in on, Bob, our shared custody kitty, and then checked back with Abby Smith who still hadn't heard anything new. I noted that I didn't have to call anybody, being my own boss and all ...

The following morning was another masterpiece of nature with bright sunshine and a warm spring breeze blowing off the bay. We had our coffee up on the deck and mapped out our route. First, we had to stop in Falmouth to gather some of Chris's things, kiss Kitty goodbye and to check in at the Institute. At The Woods Hole Oceanographic Institute, she was known as Dr. Christine Todd, one of the chief oceanographers in the Institute's deep-water research program. I'm proud of the fact that my girlfriend is one of the leading ocean research scientists in the country if not the world, and that she loves me—imagine that. Chris spent her working time either in a lab or aboard the *Cousteau,* their new 30 million-dollar toy that did everything but fly and bake bread—actually it can do those things, too.

After Falmouth, it was straight to Vermont. The trip looked to be about five hours and I figured that if all went well we'd be checking in sometime in late afternoon. That would give us a little time to cruise around Cold River and get the proper ambiance of the town, or lack thereof, before it got dark. We had no idea what we were about to do, but it seemed like the logical place to start. No cop in the world would take an active interest in what we were selling until we had some proof that something had actually happened to Skyler. We were still not convinced that he was there, but it was all we had. Our cover story was a simple one if anyone cared to ask. We were getting away for a romantic vacation with no specific destination or timetable, and that's how we'd ended up in Cold River.

The ride off the Cape was fun. The MG was running like a puppy on the beach with eager power and a happy heart. I loved driving with the top down on a day that's alive and bright and the water blue. It was a bonus that my love, Chris, was but inches from my side with somewhere new as our destination. It made it an adventure. I just prayed that we'd be returning in the same frame of mind. A nagging dread made that notion seem remote.

Off Route 91 in New Hampshire, we stopped for lunch. I pulled off the highway and about a mile on the right was exactly what I was looking for. There was a real honest-to-goodness hot dog stand named *Frankie's* next to a small river with picnic tables in a shaded area near the water. It was an oasis in the dessert—a Norman Rockwell piece of Americana. I just knew they had all sorts of fried, greasy health food waiting for us. Chris groaned knowing there would be no Caesar salad to be had.

"Nick you're going to kill us with this stuff," she said. "I'm serious. I want you around for a while."

I smiled, "Sweetheart, as we're posing as a couple on a romantic get-away, we have to play the part." I pulled the MG off the road and parked under a huge maple, and we just sat for a second. I put my arm around Chris, and she rested her head on my shoulder. We heard the water from the small river gurgling over some rocks; it had a calming effect on both of us.

"Hungry?" I asked her, breaking the spell.

"Starved, but I'm afraid of what we'll find over there."

I rubbed my hands together. "I'm thinking clam roll with fries, something cold and maybe, just maybe, I'll buy you an ice cream for the road. What do you think about that?"

"I can hardly wait," said Chris as she wrinkled up her nose. "Maybe they'll have a pita or something."

"I'll bet."

We got out of the MG, stretched, and walked across the dirt parking lot toward the stand. It was about thirty feet long with a shaky wooden overhang supported by a couple of weathered 4x4's decorated with bags of potato chips, pork rinds and cookies. I didn't dare look at Chris. Oddly enough, we were the only customers, so we marched bravely up to the window.

A fat woman wearing a filthy flowered apron, gnawing on a toothpick was cleaning the grill with what looked like an old ice scraper. I tried my best to shield Chris so she wouldn't run back to the car screaming.

"Be right with you folks," she said, the toothpick bobbing as she spoke.

"Take your time. We'll just look over the menu," I said. "See anything you like, Honey?"

Chris just glared at me not even looking at the greasy blackboard that was propped up on the counter telling of *Frankie's* rural culinary wonders. "Nick, next time I pick the restaurant. Okay? I can't do this. I just can't. You have to promise me."

"Okay, I promise, as soon as we get back to the Cape." I nodded and proceeded to increase my cholesterol considerably. Actually, it wasn't all that bad. Chris managed to get the woman, whose name was Jessie, not

Frankie, to open a can of tuna so she had tuna on whole wheat with a pickle. I'm ashamed of what I had so I'll leave that to the imagination. We ate on a picnic table down by the river and enjoyed the day.

We finished lunch and then spread the map out on the hood of the MG to get our bearings. It looked like Cold River was about two hours north. We'd hit town in late afternoon, which was perfect. It would give us plenty of daylight to get settled into the hotel and see a bit of the town before dark. I couldn't imagine that Cold River had a thriving nightlife. I just hoped there was a decent restaurant in the vicinity. You have to maintain a set of priorities in life. Chris mentioned that an AA meeting wouldn't hurt either one of us and I agreed. I didn't like going too long without one. It was our medicine for a healthy life.

# CHAPTER 11

The rest of the drive was uneventful but therapeutic. The Vermont roads were winding and treed and the MG loved it. We had the top down and a nice jazz CD in the changer as I became part of my car and the road. Chris had her head back, eyes closed, and the hint of a satisfied smile as she raised her face to the afternoon sun. She looked beautiful, and I felt very lucky as the soft wind played with her hair. We passed old farms with white wooden fences; some had cows, horses, dogs and chickens. Some were beautiful with magnificent red barns that had ominous pentagrams painted on their lofts and some were in disrepair with old trucks, cars, and bicycles left to rust in their yards. We passed through several sparkling towns that still had the ambiance of the small country stores and shops with front porches set with benches and rockers where one could pass the time. Their main streets were lined with tidy New England houses with picket fences, nice lawns, and colorful tin roofs—some red, some green. There were the crisp white churches with tall crosses, manicured town greens, and tree-laden lanes with small shops and stately colonial houses.

"This is nice," Chris said. "I can't remember the last time I was at a place like this and now that I'm here I can't believe we don't do it more." She put her hand on mine, resting on the shifter. Her hand was warm and I felt loved.

"I know. We should start a thing," I said. "A tradition. Let's try to come up each spring for a weekend. Let's pick a different place each year."

"Yeah, we always say stuff like that and never do it," she said.

"How come people do that? We should keep a book—a journal of ideas like that. Write them down so we don't forget."

"We'd forget to read the book," Chris said with a laugh, and I agreed.

"Let's not forget why we are coming up here in the first place," she said in a somber voice. "I'm worried, Nick. This hasn't happened before. It's just not like Skyler. First of all, he never leaves the Cape except to ferry over to Boston to see Rose—he never has. Second of all, even though this is a wonderful day and the weather is awesome, I still have this feeling of dread. You know, Nick, like something bad has happened or is about to happen."

"I know, me too. I feel it, but I am trying to make this as light as possible while we can. You know? It might get rough later." I reached over, picked up her hand and brought it to my lips, kissing her fingers. "I love you, Chris and I feel what you feel."

She squeezed my hand. "I love you, too, my hero, My Don Quixote."

"I was never anybody's hero before. Is the pay any good?"

Chris leaned over and kissed my neck as I drove and said in my ear, "The pay, comes a bit later and it *will* be good. You can bet on that."

I stepped on the gas harder and drove on with a renewed sense of urgency.

Miles later, I said, "Hey look." I pointed to the green Vermont road sign up on our right. It said *Cold River, VT. Population: 4207. 5 miles*

"It looks like we've found the jewel of the north. Hey, how do they know the population is 4207? What if someone died this morning or a woman gave birth to twins yesterday? That would make it 4208."

Chris turned and gave me that 'you don't know shit' look and said quite seriously, "They have a little man who comes out and changes that sign every day. You just never see him do it. I heard he does it at midnight."

"I thought it was something like that." I looked over at her and gave her my best, confused look. "You're goofing on me now, huh?" I said.

"No, you think?" We both laughed as I down shifted the MG into a nice curve and gunned the sports car through it. She roared like the happy thoroughbred she was as I came out of the corner and slammed it into 4th, giving the car gas as we shot into a nice tree-lined straight away that looked like it stretched for miles.

"Nick, slow down. You act like a kid sometimes," Chris said. "You're going to get a ticket. Mark my words."

"I am a kid. Don't worry, I don't get tickets. I never get tickets," I answered her with a smug smile.

Chris smiled back at me, patting my hand on the shifter and said, "So you think that cop you just blew by was sleeping in those pine trees?"

I looked up. "Huh? What cop?" I asked a moment too late. Looking up in my rear view mirror, I saw him pull out of a dirt driveway that ran between a stand of pines with dust and gravel flying and blue strobes flashing about fifty yards behind me.

"Son of a bitch," I said. "Why didn't you say something? You saw him, didn't you?"

"Well," Chris said in a calm voice. "I saw him as we flew by him, Mr. Never-Gets-A-Ticket. Let's see you charm your way out of this one." She laughed as I downshifted and pulled the MG off the road with the cruiser pulling up right behind me, strobes flashing.

"Damn," I said, pounding the wooden steering wheel.

"Ten bucks I don't get a ticket," I said to Chris with resolve as I leaned over and kissed her. The cop might think we were on our honeymoon and give us a break.

She gave me an impish smile and said, "You're on, Cowboy, but you don't have a chance."

I watched the cop step out of his cruiser and head in my direction from my side mirror. He was right out of central casting, young and lean with a pressed khaki uniform and sunglasses. He was hatless and had handsome chiseled features complete with the dimple in his chin and a full head of black curly hair.

Chris turned a bit in her seat, enough to watch him approach our car, and said under her breath just loud enough for me to hear, "Oh my."

I slapped her hand and said to her out of the side of my mouth, "Maybe you should talk to him then. And stop batting your eyes. It's not polite."

"You folks in a hurry?" the cop asked as he walked

up to my side of the car. He had his hand on his gun, which looked like a .357 Colt Python. His voice was firm but not rough and he had a friendly face. His name was Adams according to his nametag and his star told me he was a Deputy Sheriff.

"I'm sorry, Deputy Adams. I got carried away. It's a nice day with no traffic and the car seemed to have a mind of its own," I said.

"Then I hope it has a job of its own to pay for the ticket. I have you doing 65 in a 30 with that fancy little machine there. We don't like speeders here. Can I see your paperwork—license, registration and insurance card, please?" He was all business. Chris giggled at the line about the car having a job. I'd set some time aside to laugh later.

"Sure Deputy," I said handing him what he asked for. "But could I talk to you a little before you write all that down?"

He ignored me and walked back to his car with my papers.

"Boy you really charmed the hell out of him," Chris said. "I'm impressed."

"You can bat your eyes now. Maybe that will help."

"I thought he was nice. You were the one speeding, you know," Chris said.

I saw Deputy Adams get out of his cruiser and head back to us in the nick of time—I was ready to strangle Chris.

"Mr. Thomas would you please get out of the car and put your hands on the fender?" he asked.

"You're kidding, right?" I asked, hoping he was.

He just stared at me unsmiling. I got out of the car, knowing not to mess around with cops. I even complied without a wisecrack. He patted me down and asked me to turn around.

"Deputy did I do something wrong besides going a tad too fast?" I asked.

"The Sheriff wants me to bring you in. Said he thought you might turn up."

I looked at Chris who shrugged her shoulders but had a concerned look on her face. This was not turning out as we had planned. How would the Sheriff of Cold River, Vermont know that I would show up? I had just called him yesterday, and I hadn't said anything about coming up there.

"Okay Deputy Adams, but may I ask why? We're just here looking for Chris's Uncle Skyler. "I nodded toward Chris. She flashed him a smile and gave him a cute little wave, and he smiled back.

This was too much. I continued, trying to keep my temper under control, "I called Sheriff Cobb yesterday and asked if he had seen or heard of him. That's all. Do you know something that we don't?"

"Afraid I don't, Mr. Thomas, but the Sheriff will tell you all you need to know. All he said was to bring you in. You ride with me, and your friend can follow us. It's only a few miles."

"Am I under arrest?" I asked. "I didn't do anything wrong."

"Besides speeding," he corrected me.

"Besides speeding," I confirmed. "You going to give me a ticket?"

"Haven't decided yet," he answered with a chuckle. "Now get in my car and we'll find out what this is all about."

Chris climbed over the shifter and got behind the

wheel of the MG and I got into the front seat of the cruiser with Deputy Adams. At least he didn't cuff me. That was a good sign.

# CHAPTER 12

Deputy Adams and I had a nice chat on the way into Cold River. He told me that he'd been with the Sheriff's Department for about four years and prior to that he'd been an Army Ranger. He looked the type: young, strong, serious but polite. He asked me about myself so I gave him the brief history minus the gory details of my alcoholism, and told him that I was a mystery writer. He liked that and seemed to loosen up a bit after he decided that I wasn't a mass murderer or real threat to society. Chris followed closely in the MG and I listened subconsciously to her shifting the gears and to make sure she was using the clutch and shifting at the right times.

"Tell me again why you folks are here," he asked me. "Maybe I can help."

I proceeded to tell him about Skyler and the ad that we'd found in his room pointing us to Cold River. His face got grim. I saw his hands grip the wheel harder as he drove, and he stopped being conversational.

"Did I say something wrong?" I asked.

"No."

"Does this ring any bells with you?" I asked, trying

to get him to open back up. I definitely hit a nerve somewhere.

"I don't know what you're talking about and let's leave the rest of your questions for Sheriff Cobb," he said.

Our nice little conversation was over. I looked out the window of his spotless navy blue cruiser as we entered the small borough of Cold River. It was a Currier & Ives postcard of New England. The houses that lined Main Street were large, expensive and well maintained, with washed cars parked in the driveways, the yards raked and shrubs pruned. Many properties were bordered by low stonewalls or white rail fences while some had pillars at their entrances with stone lions or engraved medallions on them.

The town center was a poster child for what every small town in New England should be. The small shops and stores all had common, classy facades with green awnings and benches lined the cobblestone sidewalks. We passed a coffee shop and bakery that had tables with umbrellas outside, a bookstore, and a magnificent white colonial inn across from the town green that looked like it stepped out of the 19th century with a wide wrap-around veranda and huge white columns. I recognized its name as the place where we had booked our room, the Cold River Inn. It looked warm and inviting, as did the rest of the town. So why was I getting the chills? I doubted there would be any AA meetings here but one never knows. I'd certainly check. It's an easy way to make friends in a strange place and I had the feeling we would need a few friends before this was over.

Deputy Adams pulled his cruiser into the parking lot of the Cold River Town Hall and Police Station. It was an immaculate two-story brick and clapboard structure with a lot of activity going on around it. The front parking lot was full and people were coming and going with briefcases and folios. There was a either a Lexus or Land Rover in most slots with a Jaguar and Mercedes salted in here and there—most were the four-wheel-drive SUV types. I don't know why I'd expected pickups and Oldsmobiles. The entrance to the Police Department was around the side and Deputy Adams slid his car in next to several other official looking vehicles.

"Okay, Mr. Thomas, we're here," he said and shut off the car. "Sheriff's waiting."

"Deputy, please, can we take a second here?" I asked. "I don't know what I said to upset you, and I'm sorry if I did, but listen to me. We're not here for trouble. We're just looking for a loved one who we think could be in trouble, and we need some help."

He turned in his seat to face me and seemed to ponder my words. He had a strong face—someone I would like in a different setting. He took a deep breath and said, "Mr. Thomas, let me give you some advice, Okay? Go in there and don't be a wise-ass with the Sheriff. He can be a real prick. Tell him what you told me. He's going to tell you that he'll do everything he can to look into this matter, and he's also going to tell you to stay the hell out of his way while he does. Don't let his size fool you. Where are you and your lady friend staying?"

"We're staying at the Inn we passed. It looks nice."

"It is. Go ahead and check in, see the town, but keep a low profile. Don't go asking a lot of questions. I'll be in touch with you." He held up a finger of caution and said, "We never had this conversation, understand?"

I nodded and wondered what he meant by that. I filed that little talk away to review later.

Chris roared in and parked a few spaces down from us. He looked over at me as if to say something else but changed his mind when he saw Chris park the MG. "Let's go, we'll talk later," he said. "And remember what I said."

"Gotcha, low profile," I said as I got out of his car and waited for Chris.

Chris walked up and linked her arm into mine and the three of us entered the station. Adams motioned for us to sit in a waiting area saying he'd be right back and for us not to go anywhere. Normally, I would've made a joke about climbing out the window and escaping, but somehow I didn't think he'd laugh.

Chris was brushing the tangles out of her hair from the ride with the top down as we sat. She looked at me and reached for my hand. "What's going on, Nick? What's up with the police escort into town? Do they think we did something wrong? I don't get this."

"Honestly I don't know. He was fine until I told him about Skyler, and then he got all quiet and weird. Something's not right here, Chris, and I'm getting the creeps. He also said not to piss off the Sheriff. This Sheriff sounds like a real jerk to me and we haven't even had the pleasure of meeting him yet."

"You're about to get that pleasure, Mr. Thomas," said Deputy Adams walking into the waiting room. "Sheriff Cobb will see you now."

I felt like I was in some B movie where the giant ants from Mars were invading the town and nobody would believe us because they were all pod people too. We stood and followed him through a polished wooden door into a huge mahogany and leather office with walls full of plaques and pictures. Sheriff Cobb was not at all what I'd expected. I had stereotyped a big-bellied, beer-drinking farmer in a cowboy hat. The man seated behind the desk was a far cry from that caricature. He was a neat little man with silver hair and moustache, horn-rimmed glasses and he sported a gold Rolex on his wrist. He was wearing a dark blue tailored suit, white shirt and a blue striped tie. Clipped onto his jacket was his gleaming gold star that said he was the Sheriff. He did not speak or rise to greet us, but instead, motioned to a couple of chairs in front of his massive oak desk.

"That will be all, Deputy." His voice was clipped and dry like a stack of leaves. He didn't sound like the same man I had talked to yesterday. Gone was the country bumpkin I'd thought of as Sheriff Andy. He eyed both of us for what seemed like a full minute before he spoke again.

The voice was educated and used to being in charge. "I guess I wasn't explicit enough when we spoke yesterday, Mr. Thomas. I'm fairly sure I told you to stay home and that we'd look into your inquiry." His sharp gray eyes bored into mine and he raised his eyebrows expecting an answer. He waited as I formed my words.

"We didn't mean to be a bother, Sheriff Cobb. We are just concerned about ..."

"Your Uncle Skyler," he interrupted. "I pay attention, and I've put an APB out on him. I also took the liberty of doing a little background check and found some interesting facts out about your Uncle Skyler. Whose uncle is he?" he asked looking from me to Chris.

"He's my mother's only brother," said Chris. "And I made a promise to look after him when my mother died."

"From what I see here, that's not an easy task," said Sheriff Cobb picking up a file from his desk and pulling some papers from inside. "Seems like your Uncle Skyler has a history of, shall we say, sordid behavior."

Chris looked at Cobb and said almost in tears, "Yes he does, Sheriff, but he's a wonderful man who is alone in this world with the exception of us. We're worried to death that something bad could've happened to him. He's never been gone this long. It's not in his character."

"Character is not the word I'd use in describing your uncle, young lady," he said taking off his horn-rimmed glasses and placing them neatly on top of the file. "I told you that I'd look into it, and I will. What I will not tolerate here are a couple of amateur detectives running around my town causing a stir. We have a wealthy community that doesn't even like the hint of trouble and they pay me to keep it that way. I can't tell you to leave, because other than speeding you haven't done anything wrong. And if you behave, I might even let the speeding ticket slide. But I will tell you to walk softly while you're here. Deputy Adams tells me you have a room at the Inn. Enjoy the town for a couple of days, there are some good places to eat and some nice stores. Spend some money, go on the river ride, then go back home to Cape Cod. If your uncle is or was here, I'll find out and let you know."

He paused for effect and continued, "the flip side of that whole, sweet scenario is that if you so much as spit on my sidewalk you will both be guests in my jail. Trust me when I say this," he leaned forward and spoke through clenched teeth, "that is not a pleasant option. So in plain English, don't fuck around in my town. Do we understand each other?"

Chris and I both nodded in unison and I replied, "Yes sir. Message received loud and clear. We free to leave?"

"As birds," he said. "Now goodbye, Mr. Thomas, Miss Todd, and don't feel like you have to stop in and say farewell when you leave. The mere act will be testimony enough."

Chris and I got up and couldn't get out of his office fast enough.

"What an asshole," I said as we cleared the door.

"But a well-dressed asshole," Chris said.

# CHAPTER 13

We walked outside to find that Deputy Adams was nowhere in sight. His car was gone. We leaned against the MG and looked around at the quaint town. It was a sunny afternoon and there was a slight breeze on this perfect New England day. I wondered if it was always like this, where the town never changes. I told Chris what Deputy Adams told me in the car about talking to us later.

"What do you suppose that means?" she asked. "Think he knows something?"

"Of course he does, and I think he might help us. But I'm not too sure about the little Napoleon sheriff in there. I got a feeling he's not going to look too hard, do you?"

"No, I don't think we'll get much help there except to pack. Ever seen the Stepford Wives?" Chris asked. "This is the town. It has to be."

"It does have a surreal quality about it now that you mention it. Actually, I've had the chills since we rolled into town."

"Me too, but we've come this far. We have to try, Nick. I know Skyler was here. I just feel it. Know what I mean?"

"I do. I think so, too. Hey, let's go over and check into the Inn. Remember you promised me a little special attention," I said. "You know what I always say."

"What do you always say, Nick?" she asked. "I'm afraid to ask."

"An opportunity lost is one you can never get back."

She smiled and put her arms around my neck as we leaned against the MG. "I might've known it had to do with either food or sex, but I think we need to reflect on those thoughts," she said as she kissed me. "We're not over there yet?"

We hopped into the MG like a couple of kids and drove around the town green to the Inn.

The Cold River Inn was stunning. Its driveway wound through a stand of large oaks and past a huge expanse of lawn around to the front of the hotel where we parked. We unloaded our things and climbed the stairs, finding ourselves on a long wide porch framed with rich splashes of flowers and there was a row of inviting rocking chairs on each side of the massive double front doors. It was a page from the past. The foyer was all polished mahogany, thick carpeting and tapestries. There was even a bellboy. His name was Billy and he was sixty if he was a day, but he grabbed our bags and told us to "follow him." I felt as if I was in a movie.

Billy led us upstairs to a pleasant room that had a great view of the town green. He opened the windows, and the white linen curtains billowed in with the breeze.

I handed him a five-dollar bill that disappeared with lightning speed into his pocket.

"Thank you, Sir. If you need anything else …"

He looked like a friendly sort, so I took a chance, decided to ask him a few questions, and showed him the photo of Skyler that Chris had brought.

"Billy, have you seen this man anywhere? He was came up here a few days ago," I said.

He didn't even look at the photo. His manner got brisk all of a sudden. "Nope, never seen 'em. I don't remember faces much anymore."

"You didn't even look at his picture," said Chris. "Please take a look. He might've stayed here, or you might have seen him in town."

He glanced quickly at the dog-eared photo that I held out to him and said, "Nope, I told you. Never seen him. I gotta go now. I don't want to get into trouble."

"You won't get into trouble. We're just trying to find this guy. He's our uncle."

"I gotta go now. You folks have a nice evening. Dinner's at six-thirty. Try the pot roast." He opened the door and made a hasty retreat into the plush hallway, closing the door behind him.

After he left, Chris said, "That was strange. You get the feeling the whole town is in on this or are we getting paranoid in our old age?"

"Good Ol' Billy didn't want to talk to us. That's for sure." I said. "We have to come up with a strategy that won't ruffle any feathers and we have to be careful who we talk to."

"Remember what Deputy what's-his-name said. Low profile."

"Adams, Deputy Adams. I'm tired," I said. "This whole thing has got me confused. And I have the feeling that Sheriff Cobb is going to keep a real close eye on us."

"I'm tired, too." Chris flopped onto the large

featherbed, kicked off her sandals and patted the bed next to her. "We need to recharge," she said with a sly wink. "Come hither, my big strong man."

"Ah," I said. "Duty calls."

The afternoon had turned to evening when we finally woke from our "nap." We heard soft music and the clanking of dishes from below through the open window. The smells of food brought me back to life, so I hopped out of bed and patted Chris's magnificent posterior.

"Sweetheart," I said. "Do you smell that? I think I've died and gone to heaven. Let's get up and eat. I'm starving."

"I swear, Nick Thomas, food is more important to you than sex," Chris said, still half asleep.

"No, my love, they are both equally important. One precludes the other at certain times."

"Then get back over here and wake me properly."

What could I do? I was trapped.

We finally got dressed for dinner and went downstairs. The dining room was as splendid and rustic as the rest of the Inn and it was packed—a good indicator that the food was good. A pretty, young hostess sat us at a cozy table near a huge stone fireplace, chit-chatted with us for a moment about how we would love Cold River, and then told us that our waiter would be right with us.

Chris said. "I had the strangest dream. Someone was standing over me with this sick smile, and I couldn't move. He didn't touch me, he just was watching. And I smelled cigarettes. Something is off here, Nick. I don't have dreams like that at home."

"It's the kind of stuff that scares me. I guess the

question is, why is it weird or is it our perception that's off? I mean we're used to the Cape where everything is out on the table. This is a different world. It's like we stepped back in time."

"Speaking of weird, look who's coming this way," Chris said, taking a sip of her lemon water.

I turned to see our new friend, Sheriff Cobb, threading his way toward our table, stopping here and there to shake a hand and exchange some pleasantries. He reminded me of a politician working a room before election—all smiles and totally full of shit. He had on a fresh gray suit with his precious Sheriff star clipped to his breast pocket, and he had the same cold, pasted on smile. He saw me notice him, patted the man he was talking to on the back and walked toward our table.

"Evening Mr. Thomas, Dr. Todd," he said. "What do you think of our little Inn here?"

"It's just fine Sheriff. You have a lovely town," Chris said. "I never told you I was a Ph.D."

"I like to know who's in my town."

"And what other profound nuggets did you uncover?" I asked, annoyed. "Our records are clean. Hell, Sheriff, Chris here could run the good ship *Lollypop* and my worst offense is bad writing."

"Actually, Mr. Thomas, I picked up one of your paperbacks this afternoon and started thumbing through it. Not my normal reading, but it looked interesting. I might even give it a read."

"I'm honored. I'll sign it for you if you like."

Cobb acted like he didn't hear that. He had his hand on the back of one of the vacant chairs at our table and looked around the crowded dining room with a sense of pride. "This is my pearl, my kingdom, and it's my duty to keep it just the way it is," he said slowly, looking at me. "That's why I get concerned when there's any hint of trouble. I will look into the whereabouts of your Uncle Skyler, Dr. Todd, and I will do it as fast as possible so we can all get on with our boring routines and can get you fine folks back to Cape Cod where you belong. My point is that I'll do the looking, not you. Are we clear?"

"You made your point this afternoon, Sheriff," I said. "We're just going to take a couple of days and enjoy your lovely countryside. If that's okay with you?"

"Ahh, then you asking Billy the bellhop if he'd ever seen or heard of your uncle Skyler was just idle curiosity then," he said, and his smile faded and his eyes turned to flint. He waged a manicured finger at me and said in a low growl, "Don't fuck with me Mr. Thomas, or you will find yourself neck deep in a basket of rattlers. I'm the law here, and I do the investigating. Do I make myself clear?"

"As a bell," I said, and nodded that I understood. He looked at Chris, and she did the same. I had the feeling that if this were the old days we'd be run out of town by a bunch of screaming farmers on horses and wagons, waving burning torches and jabbing pitchforks.

His smile and good manners returned. "Good then. We finally understand each other. Be sure and have the pot roast. It's excellent, and please do enjoy your stay." He left our table, skirted the room bestowing a few more handshakes and nods and then left the dining room. More than a few of the diners had taken in the exchange and continued to stare at us.

Chris said, "Nick, this place gives me the creeps. That guy has eyes and ears everywhere. We have to be more careful who we talk to."

"Why should we have to be careful? See if that over aged bellhop gets another tip from me," I said. "Anyway let's eat. We've got to eat, right?"

"Right, then I'd like to take a little walk and see the town before it gets too late."

"You're on."

The meal was great and both of us ate more than we should have. I had the Yankee pot roast with broiled potatoes, gravy and baby carrots, and Chris had the grilled salmon with asparagus. I have this way of justifying things, for example, I figured this to be a working vacation/research/find Skyler type excursion and that as payback I could have the carrot cake for dessert and not feel guilty. Chris usually ignores my rationalizations and me. Therein lays the guilt.

We still had our share of curiosity-minded people who stole stares at us as we left. Not one person said hello or smiled back at us. No one would even make eye contact, and the dining room became very quiet as we made our way to the door. No dishes rattled, or silverware hit the plates, no one coughed, laughed, or even argued. The silence was heavy as we left the restaurant and exited through the lobby and walked out onto the porch.

"That was creepy," Chris said.

"Not one of them would look at us, did you notice that?" I said, looking back over my shoulder.

"Let's walk, Nick. I want to get away from this place."

I offered her my arm as we stood on the wide veranda. It was a nice spring evening, so we decided to stroll along the streets of Cold River. Small landscaping lanterns lit the hotel's long driveway, and spotlights cast warm shadows in the garden areas beyond the stand of maples.

We walked hand in hand and I felt so very much in love. I looked at Chris, so beautiful, so young and vibrant, and who just happened to love and believe in me. I thanked God for those moments of appreciation, when time slowed a bit and you realized what was really important. Staying sober helped me do that even though there were times my ego erupted and tried to take over. That night I felt humble and happy, but also very nervous. Something was going on here and the key to it was the ad. Whatever it was, it was bigger than Skyler. The problem was that we still didn't know who placed the ad. That would be the next step, and it was becoming increasingly apparent that we had to be careful in going about it.

We hit the bottom of the hotel's long drive that emptied onto a deserted main street. Most of the small shops were closed. The coffee shop, the bakery, the bookstore, the stationary, and the hardware stores were all dark and deserted. We walked hand-in-hand—relaxed and full. I stopped and pulled Chris to me and kissed her soft lips—we closed our eyes together, holding the moment.

"I love you, Nick," she said. "I love all that you are, my handsome writer-person. You *are* my hero, you know."

I smiled and held her back so I could see her eyes and said, "And I love you, and I am so proud of you, who you are, and how completely you love me. I never thought I'd ever have what we have—the friendship, the laughing at the same stuff, liking the same people, crying over commercials and even going ga ga over the same books."

Her eyes smiled into mine as we stood there on the

deserted sidewalk of Cold River, Vermont. The moment could've lasted an eternity. It said all that needed to be said about life. I felt that at that precise moment in time I had everything I'd ever need.

# CHAPTER 14

That happy moment was short lived as a loud blip from a siren made us jump. We turned and saw a Cold River Sheriff's Dept. cruiser pulling up to the curb.

"What now? They going to arrest us for making out in the street?" I asked Chris.

"Let's keep cool, Nick," said Chris. "Let's not give them a reason."

We walked to the cruiser, and the window buzzed down, so I leaned in.

"Get in the back, both of you and be quick about it." It was Deputy Adams.

I pulled open the door, and Chris and I got in. I was pulling the door closed as the cruiser pulled away from the curb.

"Deputy, what the hell is going on?" I asked him.

"Hang on a few and trust me. Let's go somewhere and talk."

I looked at Chris who shrugged her shoulders.

"Seems like we're in your hands, Deputy," I said.

"Call me Ted. Ted Adams. He drove us out of the main area of town and then followed a small road out to a bluff that overlooked the river. It was a fast moving river that looked rough and wild with rocks and white-tipped rapids that reflected off his headlights. He parked in the dirt lot and shut his car off.

"Okay Ted, we're just simple people. Can you please tell us what the hell we've stepped into?" I asked him.

Deputy Adams turned in his seat and faced us. His face shone in the meager light of the darkened car. He had a handsome, clean-shaven face, the type people liked and trusted.

"Do you have the ad with you?" he asked.

"It's right here." I reached into my back pocket and pulled out my wallet. "I put it here so I wouldn't lose it." I thumbed through the bills and papers in my wallet and was stunned when I could not find the article.

"I know it was here. We just looked at it this afternoon. I put it right back."

Chris said, "I remember, Nick. I saw you do it."

I continued to search but had to accept the conclusion that it was not there.

"Has anyone had the opportunity to look through your wallet?" Deputy Adams asked.

"No. I never had it out of my sight. The only time I had my pants off was this afternoon." I glanced sideways at Chris, and she nodded. "I doubt if anyone could've of slipped into our room when we were napping. Could they?"

"It's possible and probable," said Adams. "Can you reconstruct the ad?"

I looked at Chris with the creepy revelation that someone was in our room as we slept from our lovemaking. I remembered Chris's dream, or was it a dream? Had she felt that sick presence in our room—leering down at her? I flushed from the anger growing inside me. I looked over at her and knew she was reading my mind. I reached over and gripped her hand.

"Oh my god, Nick, what did Uncle Skyler get himself mixed up in? This is freaking crazy. Now people are breaking into our room when we are sleeping and who knows what else," Chris said in a trembling voice.

Ted Adams turned around to face us. "Listen, I'll help you and I think I can help you. But right now you got to tell me what you know. Now what about this ad? Can you tell me what it said?"

I took a deep breath. I was still pissed about the stranger in our room and that fucker of a sheriff, but knew I couldn't do this alone. "I suppose I could. I remember the P.O. Box number and it offered a lot of money to gamblers if they wanted to participate in some sort of experiment or study. The prize was five million dollars in cash going to the winner. Hell, what kind of seasoned gambler wouldn't take that chance?"

"Write it down for me," he said, handing me a small notebook and a pen.

I did the best I could from memory and with Chris's help we sketched out the ad and then handed it back to him.

"Deputy what is your interest in all of this? You seem to be the only one who believes us," I said.

He stared out toward the river and seemed to be thinking and weighing what to say. "I think I know who's behind the ad. We have a history … of sorts."

Chris tapped his shoulder, "What kind of history? Do the police know about him?"

"It goes deeper than knowing, Dr. Todd." He turned to fully face us. His expression was grim. "My mother worked for his family. She was their housekeeper for many years. Now the grandson of the original owner of the estate lives there in seclusion. His name's Sebastian Black and he's rich and powerful. My mother would never speak much of him, just that he was a sadistic, evil child. The funny thing is that the Sheriff's not at all interested in looking into Mr. Black, and he makes it clear that we should follow the same philosophy if we want to continue to enjoy our present employment status."

"What …" I started to ask when Deputy Adams jerked his head around and looked beyond us toward the road. A pair of headlights bounced off the main road and a car turned into the parking lot by the river.

"Get down and stay there," he hissed. "Someone's coming. Don't make a sound."

Chris and I slid to the floor of the cruiser in a tangle of arms and legs. We heard a car coming toward us. Gravel crunched as it pulled up alongside and then stopped. The window of the Deputy's cruiser buzzed down.

"Evening Sheriff."

"Deputy. What are you doing out here this time of night? I thought you were in some kind of trouble."

"No trouble, Sheriff. I just scared off a few kids making out is all. I was just getting ready to head back into town and call it a night. My shift ends in twenty."

"Could you stop by my office for a minute? There's something I want to talk to you about."

"Tonight?"

"Tonight."

"I'll be there in ten minutes, Sheriff. Anything wrong?"

"I'm not sure, Deputy. There's something I want you

to look into for me." The Sheriff put his car in reverse and spun gravel as he left the lot.

My heart was pounding and my mouth was dry. Chris had my hand in a death grip.

"That guy is everywhere," she whispered as we started to untangle. "He gives me the creeps."

"Stay down," Adams said over his shoulder. "I don't trust that bastard. Wouldn't be out of character for him to wait down the road and watch me pass. He pops up in the most unexpected places. He's got eyes in the back of his head, I swear. I'll drop you folks on one of the side streets near the Inn. We need to talk further."

"Name the place and we'll be there."

"Tomorrow's my day off and I go up to Burlington to see my mother. She's in a rest home there. We can meet in a place I know for lunch. It's called *Anchovies,* near the University on Park. Ask a student if you can't find it. It'll take you about an hour to get there from here."

"We'll find it. What time?" I asked.

"Be there by one."

# CHAPTER 15

We opened the door to our room, and Chris screamed. The room had been tossed. All of our things had been pulled out of the drawers and suitcases, the mattress was flipped over and the pillows were sliced open, leaving piles of clothes and feathers everywhere.

"That does it, Nick, let's get out of here right now! We can call the State Police from the road."

"Whoever did this wants to scare us off. They got what they wanted this afternoon. What did they expect to find here?" I asked as I looked around the trashed room. "Maybe they weren't looking for anything. Maybe they were telling us that our blissful stay in Cold River should come to an end."

"Nick I know that creepy shit sheriff is behind this. I'm scared, damn it, and I'm scared to death that Skyler is dead. I just know it, Nick."

I held her trembling body next to mine, stroking her hair as I looked over the mess that was once our cozy room. I got madder by the minute.

"I don't know what's going on, Chris, but I sure as hell am going to find out." I stalked over and picked up the phone.

The next couple of hours were a large pain in the ass. The Sheriff and two of his deputies arrived quickly and made the motions of being concerned.

"Seems like someone doesn't like you, Mr. Thomas," the sheriff said.

"You mean besides you?" I asked, my tone harsh. Chris came over and linked her arm in mine to calm me down, which didn't work. "You know Cobb, all we have gotten from your nice little town is a load of shit from a bunch of snotty people. What happened to your famous New England hospitality?"

The sheriff held out both hands. "Now hold on Thomas, I know you're upset and can't say as I blame you. But—"

I cut him off. "No buts, Sheriff. I'm pissed. Someone came in here this afternoon while we were taking a nap and stole something very valuable and now this. So, no, I am not going to hold on."

His eyebrows rose. "What's this about this afternoon? You didn't tell me anything about that." His beady eyes searched my face.

"We can't be sure but Chris said she felt someone's presence here and now something is missing."

The Sheriff took a deep breath and looked at me and then back to Chris. "What was taken? And why wasn't I told?"

I answered for her, "We weren't sure until just a little while ago when I discovered it missing." I didn't want to tell him what it was but he wasn't going to let it go.

"Mr. Thomas, again, what was taken?" This time his voice was rising. "Don't you think I would be the one to call?"

I sighed, "The ad, Sheriff. The ad from *The Globe* I showed you about "Gamblers Wanted." The one that led us here. It was in my wallet and now it's gone.

He nodded and looked around the room at the mess. "Anything else taken that you know of?" he asked.

"I ... I don't think so." I turned to Chris. "See anything else missing, Honey?"

"I don't know, Nick. We didn't bring much. But what else could they take? My panties?" She asked with her voice trembling. She was unnerved and I didn't blame her. "Nick, I want to go home. Let's just call the State Police and go home. This is a bad place." She looked directly at Sheriff Cobb when she said that.

"Now hold on Miss Todd, let's not get crazy here. The last thing we need is a bunch of State cops trampling through my town. Let me—"

I broke in. "Then *do* something Sheriff. I want someone to go out and check this Black character out and I want it now!" I realized my mistake as soon as I said it.

He looked at me sharply. "Black? Where'd you hear that name? I never said anything about Black or anyone else for that matter. You had an ad with a P.O. Box number and that's all. I said I would run it down. I also said that you were *not* to be poking around in this. If there was a crime committed, and I stress the word *if,* I will find out who did this. Until then you get in your pretty little sports car and go home."

I covered the best I could and looked back at him evenly. "Sheriff, we're not as stupid as you think. I have sources too, and like you, I do not like to be fucked with. And someone is fucking with us right now. I don't scare easily. I want to stay right here until I am satisfied that

Skyler Todd is not in this town. I happen to know a bit about the law and I happen to know a lot of people period, including your fine state governor. I've met her several times and she loves my books."

I made that up and wasn't sure he believed it or not. "We have not committed a crime and certainly do not intend to, but we want to know what happened to Skyler. Now if that means we call in the State Police and the media, then that's what we'll do.

Cobb studied me for several long seconds, his cold eyes unwavering. "Mr. Thomas, and Dr. Todd, it appears we have gotten off to a rocky start. Why don't we begin anew as they say. I will do all I can to track down your Uncle Skyler immediately if it means getting rid of both of you sooner." There was no humor in his thin smile. "Give me a couple of days. I assure you we will turn over every rock. If nothing turns up, then by all means call whomever you like. Does that sound fair?"

Chris and I both nodded.

He held up a finger and said, "But that means you will let me do my job, Okay? And that also means that you will stay clear of the investigation. Are we all on the same page here?"

We nodded again.

"Good," he said finally. "I'm sure the Inn will find you ... ahh ... alternative accommodations for this evening." He looked at the night manager who had accompanied him up to the room and was standing in the hall behind the deputies. He was small man with a bowtie and a red vest.

Cobb added, "Maybe even a nicer room."

"I shall see to it immediately, Sheriff," the manager said quickly.

With that, Cobb motioned to the two deputies and headed toward the stairs. He stopped suddenly and the deputies stumbled into each other trying not to bump into him. It was almost comical.

"Mr. Thomas, I will call you. Do not continue to be a pain in my ass or you will find yourself sleeping in my house." He looked around. "Less ambiance … if you get my drift." He turned again and left without hearing my answer which wasn't even close to "Goodnight."

In minutes, a bellboy had our stuff loaded onto a cart and asked us to follow them to our new room. The night manager apologized all the way down the hall. He was an annoying little man named Chester.

It seemed we rated an upgrade as we entered what must've been their Presidential Suite. We walked into a beautifully furnished sitting room with a large screen TV mounted over a stunning stone fireplace. Chester picked up a remote and clicked toward the gas logs that lit immediately.

"Lovely," Chris said. "Now this is more like it."

"Our best, Madam," said the manager. "The bedroom suite is this way, if you would follow me please."

We followed him into a spacious high-ceilinged room with white wainscoting, red walls and a king sized four-poster bed that faced yet another fireplace that was already lit and warming the room. The furniture was heavy and rich and the high windows looked out onto a magnificent view of the mountains all lit by the moon.

"I hope this will do and please forgive the inconvenience. We are all shocked and beside ourselves that something like this could happen here," Chester said heading for the door.

"I have one question," I asked him, pointing at the

door. "If I lock this deadbolt from inside can anyone come in?"

"No sir, I can assure you it is secure."

"That's what we thought before," I said, opening the door for him. "But thank you for the room. We'll say goodnight now."

"Goodnight, sir," Chester said stiffly and scurried out.

"The little turd," I muttered. "He was probably the one who tossed our room."

"The governor, Mr. Thomas? I didn't know you knew the governor." Chris asked playfully punching me in the arm after the door closed.

"I wasn't even sure if it was woman. Good guess," I laughed.

"Lucky one," said Chris shaking her head. "You get away with so much B.S., Mr. Thomas."

"He bought into it, and often you do, too. You can't resist my charms," I said with a big grin.

"This is more like it," Chris said, ignoring my comment and taking in the spacious suite. "It's been a long night. What do you say we try that fancy bed, Mr. Thomas," she said leading me by the hand into the bedroom, kicking off her pumps as we went. "We need to renew our attitudes and you need to rub my feet."

"Be a shame to waste their hospitality," I said, already at rigid attention.

# CHAPTER 16

I opened my eyes to the sun streaming in the high windows of our new suite. I patted the bed next to me to find Chris was not there and I immediately panicked for a second.

"Chris? Chris?" I called out. The bedroom door opened and she walked in with a newspaper and cup of coffee. It was dreamlike. She had on a Red Sox t-shirt, a smile and nothing else. I reached for the coffee.

"You are so predictable," She laughed.

"One must have coffee before anything else. It's a law somewhere, I'm sure."

Chris sat cross-legged next to me on the bed and opened the paper as I gratefully sipped my coffee, propped up on one elbow. I began rubbing her toes, to which she gave a slight moan and said, "Nick, stop that. I ordered us breakfast. It should be here in about ten minutes."

"We need to get an early start to Burlington, remember? Deputy Adams?"

"Oh, yeah." I'd completely forgotten after last night's fiasco. "We need to meet him at someplace near the University, Pepperoni's or something like that." I was still in a fog.

*"Anchovies,"* Chris laughed and began running her bare toes under the covers to explore. "I bet if we hurry we can beat room service. Do you think we have time for a little you know what?" She had my attention literally in her hand so I surrendered gallantly. The things we men do in the name of love.

A little while later, after our morning revival and the hearty breakfast that Chris had ordered, we were bumping into each other in the bathroom as we rushed to get cleaned up and dressed. Not long after, we were out in the MG with fresh coffees and warm raspberry scones, compliments of the Inn.

"Know where you're going cowboy?" Chris batted her big brown eyes.

"I'm actually part Indian," I said, putting on my sunglasses. "The Fucawi Tribe, ever hear of them?"

"Nick you're full of shit. You are not an Indian."

"Ah, the lady has not heard of the Fucawi. They were a great tribe of proud men who never asked directions and when lost, they would ask each other "Where the fuck are we? The Fucawi!""

She laughed and punched me in the arm. "That is so you. Bet you were chief," she said. "You are indeed crazy."

"I know, but we have fun. Look, I got me a map from our buddy at the desk. I know it kills him to be nice to me." I put my arm around her and kissed her ear good morning. "What was that for?" she asked.

"Cause, I love you."

"And as well you should," she said with a mock pout. "We better kick up some dust, Mr. Nick Thomas, or we'll miss our chance to talk to that deputy. I have a feeling he's important."

"So do I, my dear. Something definitely stinks up here and it all starts with that creepy Sherriff. We've got to find this Black character. I'm sure he's the one behind this."

"That's where I think the deputy will come in handy. He seems to know something about what we are looking for. He might also have an agenda. You hear him mention about his mother?" she asked me.

I nodded and pulled out onto Main Street and roared south.

According to Chester at the Inn, the University at Burlington is about one hour drive southwest if we don't know where we're going. "Forty-five for us locals," he had said, indicating that they are smarter than we are. I won't even go there.

Forty-eight minutes later I slid the MG in front of a neat, ivy-covered brick building that housed *Anchovies*. The town had that charged, college town feel—bookstores, clothes shops, bars, trendy restaurants and young good-looking people everywhere. I got a wink from one of the co-eds walking by, all blonde and tanned and about twenty and, of course, I didn't notice the strappy high-heeled sandals she was wearing. "Nice car, mister," she flashed a coy but knowing smile and kept walking. I was tongue tied and looked over at Chris who had her hands on her hips and an amused look on her face. "Don't even dream, Nick Thomas. You have jackets older than her. Hell, you probably got jackets older than me."

"Trust me, honey, I'm yours heart and soul."

"I know." She smiled, and linked her arm in mine as we climbed the four short steps to *Anchovies*. I took a mental inventory of my jackets as we entered the restaurant. Maybe I should buy a couple of new ones.

# CHAPTER 17

Skyler tried to shower away the cobwebs, mindful of the time. He didn't dare be late to breakfast. He guessed that he would be meeting the others that were summoned there by Black. Now there was one strange freaking character, thought Skyler as he toweled off in a hurry. The ornate bathroom was nothing Skyler was used to. He felt like an intruder, but who cares? For a minimum of fifty large ones he would do just about anything.

He dressed quickly in a beautifully cut blue suit that just happened to be his size. He chose a crisp white shirt from several hanging in the armoire and a nice blue and white striped tie that screamed *power*. He looked at himself and felt proud. At seventy-one, he still cut a distinguished figure; silver-gray hair, trim with crystal blue eyes, and a friendly smile that usually charmed the pants off the most unsuspecting of women. Even though the way he lived had dulled the shine a bit. He wondered if he could keep the suit—after all, he had come all the way up here.

Skyler took a deep breath and tried to calm his stomach. It was doing flip-flops as he reached for the brass-handled door to the dining room. "I can do this," he said aloud with meek confidence. The room was huge and splendorous with high ceilings and a bank of windows that looked out over spectacular grounds. There was a heavy oak table with high-backed chairs. The walls of white wainscoting met gracefully with a red velvet paper adorned with art that was exactly as one would imagine in a castle. One massive portrait dominated the room. It was of a florid, angry looking man who had bushy eyebrows, and was wearing a tuxedo.

Sebastian Black stood at the end of the long table glancing at the clock with apparent irritation. It was 8:35. The other guests, two men and three women, were already seated.

"Glad you decided to join us Mr. Todd. Please be seated. I will warn you that the next time one of you are late it will cost you five thousand dollars. Actually, it will cost each of you five thousand dollars. That might put the test to some of your defective characteristics and help you encourage your fellows to be prompt." Sebastian Black waved Skyler to a seat. Angry glances from the other five bore into Skyler as he took his seat.

"I'll be brief to start. We will have breakfast to get to know one another, and then we'll begin. I'll start here on my left and each of you will introduce yourselves briefly, and tell why you think you should win the prize ... five million dollars in tax free cash."

Six people sat around the big table in a heavy uncomfortable silence. Skyler wanted coffee and decided that he would establish himself as a maverick to this arrogant little prick right away.

"So, can we eat in the meantime?" Skyler asked, trying to talk with some authority.

"By all means, Mr. Todd, eat … eat." Black said looking to his left. "Now let's start with you Mr. Hartigan."

A tall military looking man with cropped dark hair stood. He was broad shouldered and there was an amused look in his eyes that said, "I'm not scared of shit." "My name is Chance Hartigan. I'm from New York, retired military and I like to gamble. I have seen things in my life that put things into perspective. I have nothing to lose."

He looked deliberately at each one of the other five seated around the table. "Let's get something straight right from the beginning. I'm not here to be your friend. I could give a fuck less about anyone of you. And I intend to walk out of here with the prize." Hartigan sat back down apparently finished.

Black winced a bit but seemed unruffled. "Okay," he said crisply. "Miranda?" He motioned to the striking woman next to Hartigan. She was maybe fifty but had an air of confidence. She was dressed in elegant black with pearls, complete with black sheer hose and sleek black pumps. Skyler couldn't help but notice. Woof! He sucked in his gut and ran his hand carefully through his hair.

She didn't make an effort to rise as she took a slow deliberate sip of her coffee and then placed the cup with care back on the saucer, making sure it was exactly in the center. "First, Mr. Hartigan, I find your language offensive and I'd appreciate a little courtesy." She looked directly at him and smiled. She had ash blonde hair that fell gracefully to her shoulders, long elegant nails, and a slim Cartier watch. She was thin, classy and very self-assured. Hartigan nodded quietly at her and it seemed an understanding was established.

She remained seated. "As our kind host said, my name is Miranda. Miranda Bell. I've been widow now for about five years. I live in New York and I can afford to wager as I see fit." She looked at each of the men at the table and said, "I'm not here to find a boyfriend or to get a little on the side—I have two very accommodating pool boys for that." There was a slight gasp when she said this. She seemed to enjoy the impact and smiled indulgently. "Why am I going to win the prize? That's easy. I'm convinced that I've already won." She picked up a spoon to stir her coffee apparently finished.

Skyler watched everyone with interest. This was his competition and so far no one looked to be a pushover. He was next, but Black ignored him and looked to the other side of the table at a burly, older man dressed casually in a golf shirt that stretched over a barreled chest and the beginnings of a paunch. He looked like a Mafia bodyguard—about fifty-five or so, with thick hairy arms.

"My name is Anthony. Anthony Frascarelli. My friends call me Tony."

Skyler snorted and almost choked on his coffee. "Sorry," he said sheepishly. "Went down the wrong pipe." Of course his name was Tony, thought Skyler amused by his prophetic powers.

Frascarelli waited until Skyler was done, then continued.

"As I said my name is Anthony Frascarelli. I'm from New York. Brooklyn. I ah, I sorta worked in the business and now I'm here to win this five million bucks. The ad said how far would you go? Well there ain't nothing I ain't done and I still sleep like a fucking baby. So don't go getting in my way." He looked right at Miranda who chose not to respond. He sat back down and mumbled, "Nice to meet yous all."

Black cleared his throat before speaking. "As you can see we're all from different backgrounds. I have tried to gather a cross section of society. Now we have Ms. Winfield." He motioned to an older woman, with white hair trimmed in a stylish shag, wearing expensive jewelry and a coy smile. She pushed back her chair and stood. "My Name is Lydia Winfield. I am seventy-two years young, rich and alone in the world and now I spend most of my time gambling and having fun." She winked at Skyler and continued, "I live in Greenwich, Connecticut and live my life to its fullest because one never knows when the big curtain will fall." Her eyes twinkled and she spoke with intelligence.

Skyler appraised her in a new light. She was in great shape for her age. Maybe …

Lydia Winfield continued. "Why do I think I'll win? Well, I really have nothing to lose now, do I? And I, just like all of you, want to go out with a bang—have the big score and then leave it to a charity or maybe to my cat. That's what I'd do," she finished with a matter-of-fact smile and sat back down, patting Skyler discreetly on the thigh, lingering there for a brief second.

His breath caught in his throat and he coughed. There were a few snickers around the table before Black cleared his throat with an air of impatience.

"Miss Lee?" he asked, motioning to a young vivacious girl.

"Hey y'all, I'm Donna Lee." She popped up out of her chair with a big smile on her face.

"I'm a North Carolina girl. I'm thirty-one, single, and, my dear old daddy died with me being the only relative alive and all. … Well, I gots me some money to play with. And you see, most men I gamble with are way too busy trying to figure out how to get my pants off and never see me coming."

She was a firecracker all right, thought Skyler, with short brown hair and a quick smile that would melt mortal men.

She concluded in an exaggerated southern drawl, "I like to win, y'all. And I usually do." And with that she winked, gave us all a wide innocent smile and plopped back into her chair.

Black smiled at Donna Lee and said, "Your energy is refreshing, my dear. I look forward to the competition. Now that leaves us Mr. Todd, your turn sir."

Skyler had the last of his English muffin in his mouth and tried to swallow it quickly, coughing. He felt Lydia's foot lightly rubbing against his leg under the table. He cleared his throat, took a loud sip of coffee, and stood, leaning against the table for support. It seemed as if the vodka from last night was crawling through his skin. He tugged his tie straight and smoothed his coat. He remembered how handsome he looked in the mirror upstairs. That seemed to help him straighten up.

"Hi everybody, I'm Skyler Todd from Cape Cod, Massachusetts. I'm retired, sort of, and I have made my living most of my life trying to beat the games of chance. And I am also single," he said pointedly looking at Miranda Bell who completely ignored him. "I like to live it up, guess I have all my sorry life, but am too damn old to change now. So this is my retirement. My big score and I plan to go home with it."

Black cut off further talk by putting both hands up

in front of him. "Okay, now that we know a little about each other we will move on."

Skyler, not done, sat down reluctantly. *This guy is an asshole, he thought to himself. But remember all that money.* The thought cheered him immediately.

"We don't know much about you, Mr. Black," said Donna Lee. "I like to know who I do business with, if you know what I mean. You living here in this big ol' castle out in the middle of nowhere. Hell, you could kill us and no one would know."

"I assure you Miss Lee that nothing like that will happen. I inherited this castle from my Grandfather Rudolph, who, by the way, is the one looking down on us as we speak ," he said, pointing to the angry looking man in the huge dark portrait. "My family has always had an interest in human nature as far back as I can trace."

The room was silent as Black paused to look at his grandfather for a long moment before continuing. "I have done research on the gambler's mind for many years. This experiment goes to the basics, my friends. It goes to the very heart and soul of people just like you. The one and only question is, what would you," he paused for effect and then continued in a much softer voice, "do for five million dollars? Everyone has a price … everyone! Now," he clapped his hands together, "some quick housekeeping before we begin."

The tall man, who had picked him up at the terminal, appeared beside him. He was dressed now in black military garb having exchanged the black suit and tie. The man was in good shape with a seriously stern face, quick eyes and cropped steel colored hair.

"This is Dieter. He's in charge of security. We keep large sums of cash here and we like to discourage unwanted visitors. You all met the security force when you got here—the three Rottweilers led by my lion of a dog, Zeus. You don't want to meet Zeus without one of us around. He likes to eat things that move."

Skyler was hung over but instantly got a chill when he looked up and found Dieter smiling at him. It was a "Don't-mess-with-me-or-else" look.

"Dieter runs the outside of the estate and he is my driver. He's been with our family for many years. He also has several well-trained men to assist in the security detail. You will have no need to interact with these men and I highly suggest that you don't. Dieter's wife Helene, who is serving your food, runs the house. Any household needs should be directed to her. The girl you will see is their daughter, Kristen, and she is most definitely off limits for any stray ... um, thoughts, if you get my meaning, because that would just annoy Dieter to a bad end I'm afraid. So, ladies and gentlemen, for your own safety please do not try and leave the castle for the duration of the experiment. Once our business is concluded then you will all be free to leave. Some richer than the others I would think."

Skyler raised his hand and asked, "Mr. Black, are we prisoners here?"

Black smiled thinly, "Mr. Todd, you came to me, did you not? I'll keep my end of the bargain as long as you keep yours and do what you're told. You are free to go right now—no money of course—but you are free to leave." Black looked around the room with a questioning look and said, "Anyone else? Speak up now or forever hold your peace." There were no takers. Everyone was looking at their hands and fidgeting in their chairs. Black continued, raising a finger, "I will make this a bit more interesting and add this one thing to the dynamic. If any of you decide to try and leave without my permission or urging from this moment on—none of you will get a penny. All bets are off and you will all be sent home." The room was heavy in silence and then the room erupted.

Tony was the first heard over the other's protests. "Now wait a fuckin' minute Dracula. I came here to gamble not baby sit. I want my money. Are you going back on your word?"

Black unruffled, put his hands up. "No. You will get your money, Mr. Frascarelli, once the contract is fulfilled. You agreed to a week. If you all play ball, do what is asked of you, and participate in the spirit of the game, then you can come out of here with a lot more than fifty thousand dollars. I've just added an extra incentive for all of you to help spur each other along. The final caveat, is that if you are assessed a fine, it will come off the total prize. For example, if Mr. Todd here decides to be late for a gathering again, his fine will be deducted from everyone's money. I'm sure we'll see less tardiness now." Black chuckled and all eyes went to Skyler who felt very small in his chair. He smiled feebly and nodded his understanding.

Black went on, "Be mindful and be on time. These things are essential if this experiment is going to work. Are we clear?" Black scanned the six faces seated before him and then nodded to Dieter, who then left the room. "Good, now we can begin."

Skyler was less than reassured. He locked eyes with Miranda Bell and she nodded slightly as if to say "Let it go for now but we'll talk later." Of course, he just knew she wanted him, too. Skyler sat back and accepted his situation as a good thing. He was in a magnificent castle, with a beautiful woman to charm, plus there was a whole lot of money here, he just knew it. The prospect of sweet Miranda Bell with her black pumps and stockings ... he forced himself back to reality.

What the hell had he gotten himself into? Locked away in a remote castle with fierce, blood-thirsty dogs and a madman in charge? Skyler didn't have to look. He knew the shit fairy was hovering close.

"We will now move to the game room," said Black amiably. "Let the games begin." There was a hint of a cold smile on his paper-thin lips.

# CHAPTER 18

Chris and I pushed the heavy wooden door of *Anchovies* open. We were greeted by a wave of wonderful smells, the pleasant sounds of clattering plates, rattling silverware and laughter.

Chris cocked her head, straining to hear above the mild din, and held up her finger, "Listen Nick, I think they're playing our music, suh!" She added the last in her sexy southern drawl. "This sweet little ol' girl from North Carolina knows her Allman Brothers when she hears it."

I heard *Ramblin Man* floating through the air and smiled. "You heard correct, my dear, this place is cool," I said, taking it all in.

The place was small and busy. It had quaint tables with red-checkered tablecloths and a Chianti bottle with a single red rose centered at each table. The staff consisted of young college kids having fun and flirting with each other as they bustled about. I spotted a nervous Ted Adams along the side in one of the booths. He motioned us over and we threaded our way through the busy restaurant. He kept glancing around, looking past us as if he thought someone might have followed us.

We got to the booth and I offered my hand, "Hey Ted. You got to relax man. You look frazzled."

He had on a red flannel shirt, jeans and a John Deere hat. He looked like in the majority of people from Vermont or Fargo. Probably on purpose, I decided. Maybe it was his version of being undercover.

"You never know who's watching, Thomas. You have no idea who you are fighting and what the stakes are." We sat across from him and a waitress appeared and took our order for coffee. She nodded and dropped three art-deco menus on the table, which we busied ourselves with to offset the awkward silence. The waitress came back fairly soon and took our order.

Although Chris did her best to shame me, I homed in on a piece of pepperoni and anchovy pizza. She ordered a small Caesar salad and Adams had a cheeseburger.

"First thing I'll say to you both," Ted said looking very serious, "is that you have to be extremely careful of what you do and who you talk to from now on. Sherriff Cobb is very annoyed with the both of you and make no mistake, he has eyes everywhere."

I looked at Adams. "Cobb is an asshole. You're all nuts up here, you know that?" It just slipped out but there it was. Now, I was annoyed. "Ted, let me tell you something, okay? We're not some stupid city slickers up here on a lark. We're here because Chris's Uncle Skyler is missing and we believe him to be in Cold River and nobody seems to give two shits about that. That damn sheriff is more worried about his image than anything else. I really have a mind to call in the state police or even the freaking governor (that had worked before). Believe me, Deputy, if anything else, I know how to make noise."

He looked me dead in the eye and said evenly, "You

can't make a lot of noise buried in the woods, my friend."
*That got my attention.*

He continued, "What I'm saying is that we have to be careful. I'll help you find your uncle, but trust me, if he's out at Black's estate it will be extremely dangerous."

"Sounds to me like there's a book here," I said. "This whole thing is bizarre enough to rate a novel. Now, tell me why did we drive forty miles today, Ted?"

"Well, Mr. Thomas as I said, I have a bit of history with man Sebastian Black. He owns a very secure estate outside of town and it has been rumored that some very strange things happen up there. He seems to be legally untouchable, at least on a local level, and I'm fairly certain that Sherriff Cobb is on his payroll."

"What makes you say that, Deputy? I don't like Cobb, and I'd love to see his ass in hot water, but that's a strong accusation."

Adams stopped talking as the waitress came and delivered our food.

"Let's eat. Then we can talk." He began to attack the most delicious looking cheeseburger I ever saw. I watched as catsup oozed down the sesame bun and mixed with the tasty looking grease. The fries were in a basket the size of Red Riding Hood's and we all started digging our paws in the second they were set on the table. There was just the right amount of salt and they were handmade and hot. I started to get aroused ... not really, but it was so good. My pizza turned out to be a great choice as well. It was well laden with cheese and generous slices of pepperoni. Heaven would have food like this, served by naked ...

Ted shattered my fantasy. "Let me start at the beginning and tell you what I know, and maybe we can help each other figure this out. First, I'm not the backwater deputy sheriff that you may have me characterized as. I'm a decorated Desert Storm veteran. I'm going to UVM full time to study law. I want to go to the next level—FBI or Homeland."

"Lofty aspirations," I said, with sarcasm in my voice. "Glad you have eyes beyond the trees as they say." The pizza was wonderful and I immediately regretted not ordering two pieces. I'd never get that past Chris now.

"Shut up, Nick," Chris smiled through clenched teeth. "Go ahead Ted, we're listening." I'm pretty sure it was her heel that was pinning my foot to the floor with a good deal of pain. See if she gets her feet rubbed tonight.

"Anyhow," he continued, "I can't very well take an oath in good faith with so much corruption around me. I can't prove anything, but it seems funny that Sherriff Cobb gets a brand new Mercedes Benz every two years—brand spanking new!" He pounded the table and coffee cups, saucers and spoons rattled. "He doesn't make that much as Sherriff, I looked it up. Fifty-three thousand dollars, plus benefits. Ever see his house?" he asked us in an incredulous voice. "It's a freaking mansion. And his wife is some under thirty hottie from Romania or Russia. And she's quite the little shopper, I'm told. You can't tell me this is all happening on fifty-something thousand dollars a year. I think not."

Several people were staring at us from the nearby tables. He was getting worked up. "It's just not fair to honest people like me."

"Ted, you gotta calm down." I said into the tense moment of silence. "What about calling in the State Police? Cobb got real nervous when we threw that out at him last night."

"You ... you saw him when last night?" Adams asked quickly. Apparently, he didn't know that we were terrorized last night.

"Ted couldn't know what happened to us last night." said Chris, elbowing me. "Tell him Nick."

"What happened, Thomas?" insisted Adams.

"When we were out with you someone broke into our room and trashed it. Trying to send us a message I guess. Everything we owned was spread out all over the place, pillows slashed, drawers dumped. The only thing missing was the newspaper ad and we think that was taken from my wallet while we napped in the afternoon. We called Five-O and our friend the sheriff showed up."

Adams looked at us both as if not comprehending.

"Cops, Teddy. We called and your fearless leader came to our rescue." Chris added, wrapping herself around my arm as we sat.

"Anyhow," I broke in, "let's get back to the reason we're here. Ted, we have a missing loved one and we are fairly certain he might be holed up in that estate by this guy Black. That's all we know. Your turn my friend. Help us out."

Ted Adams spent the next hour painting a bizarre picture of the Black Mansion and the secrets it reportedly held. People had been reported missing but never found. Sebastian Black was an extreme recluse. He did not go shopping, dine out, or have any direct connection with the public. He donated scads of money to the town so they tended to look the other way at his eccentricities. Adams told us how his mother was employed by Black as a nanny and housekeeper and that it did not end well. I assumed it had to do with sex. It always does. That's the guy in me. Adams wouldn't elaborate and I didn't push. But he did say that his mother was never quite the same. She was withdrawn and humorless and she absolutely refused to talk with her son about it. The odd thing, he told us, was that she had a lot of money in her bank account. Money that she'd refused to touch.

"Okay Ted, we know that Black's a weird character, but what the hell is he doing up there? You saw the ad."

Chris was looking out the window lost in thought. I knew she was thinking about Skyler and the danger he could be in.

"I think he lures unsuspecting souls up there who cannot resist the temptation of easy money and then has some type of game or something. I don't know. I couldn't track down anyone who has been there, and when I asked Cobb about it awhile back I was told that if I wanted to make law enforcement a career that I should forget that Sebastian Black existed. Ever since then, Cobb has watched me like a freaking hawk. I was thinking of hiring a private detective to see what he could find on Black. It's a mission with me now. I want to take him down. I don't know what he did, but he made my mother unhappy and because of him she stayed that way."

Chris came back. "You know Ted, we're a great team, quite resourceful and we don't cost a dime."

"You're also quite visible to Sherriff Cobb. He'd love to throw your asses in jail."

"Yeah," I answered, "but he's afraid of what I can do publicly. I can make a lot of noise."

"Remember what I said about the woods, Mr. Thomas. This isn't a joke or a lark. I know you have a vested interest in this with your Uncle Skyler missing and all, but you got to be smart or you both will end up missing. I have a plan and I have someone on the inside. But that's all I can say right now."

Chris gripped my arm and I let this sink in. My swagger was waning. *There were a lot of woods around Cold River.*

"Tell us what to do, Ted."

# CHAPTER 19

We got back to the Inn a little after four and found a nice little surprise waiting for us in our new home. On the polished table, in the foyer entrance, was a silver bucket with ice and a beautiful bottle of Dom Perignion. Two chilled glasses were stuck in the ice next to it.

"Apparently they don't know we don't indulge. Nice thought, though," I said fingering the ice cold neck of the bottle wondering what it would taste like after all these years.

Chris stared at the bucket with the two glasses chilling next to the bottle of Dom. "Nick, I just don't get a good feeling here. We're here in this Currier & Ives town with that creepy Sherriff and this Black character with a castle. Sounds like a bad movie."

"Yeah, and we're in it," I said, still eyeing the bottle of Dom. "Want to have something cold? Maybe some O.J.? I saw some in the fridge. It would be a shame to waste these nice chilled glasses."

Chris saw me looking at the bottle. "I think we need to find a meeting, Nick. That's what I think."

"You're right as usual," I said opening the small fridge

and grabbing the juice. We both knew the consequences if we popped that Dom. Alcoholism waits forever with the patience of death and the seductiveness of a woman to those who have dared to defect. That was not an option for either of us.

I poured the O.J. into the two chilled glasses and handed one to Chris.

"Okay sexy, let's review. What exactly do we have here? First, Skyler is missing, which in itself is not entirely unusual. But the trail leads here and here we find Creepy Town, USA, a bad impression of a tough guy sheriff and some sort of weirdo in a castle. To top it off, we are being threatened by forces unknown and a quasi-hero rides to the forefront offering to help save the day. Have I got it right so far?" I asked as I sat down next to Chris on the plush couch as she stared, lost in thought.

"I think we need to take a ride and find this so called castle," she said.

"Agreed, how about first thing in the morning?"

Chris nodded and we toasted our glasses to a plan and drank.

"What say a little nap before dinner?" I asked, setting down my empty glass.

"Nap?" she asked setting down her glass and reaching for me. "I think we could be a bit more creative than that, Mr. Thomas."

"Semantics, my dear," I said pushing her gently back on the couch, my lips finding hers.

We made sweet love right there on the couch with euphoric abandon and drifted off in each other's arms, spent and very content as the afternoon sun started to fade into evening.

I had no idea how long it had been when I came out of the heavy fog. Jesus, I thought, I felt like I had the worst hangover of my life. My temples throbbed, and it was like my skull was in a vice. My mouth felt like I'd swallowed a beach towel, sand and all. I was afraid to open my eyes and my thoughts tried to go back in time. Did we drink the Dom? No, we drank the orange juice. I slowly and painfully opened my eyes to see the sunlight streaming into the living room. I was still on the couch, naked and alone. Chris? I looked around the room. No Chris. I still couldn't move. Everything hurt … screamed. She must've got up in the night and went to bed. We missed dinner and slept right on through. Why did I feel like this?

"Chris?" I called out feebly. Christ that hurt. I tried to prop myself up on an elbow, head throbbing with the effort. "Chris?" No answer. I managed to get up on shaky legs. The room spun. Something was wrong. I was not supposed to feel like this. I didn't drink anymore, damn it!

I went to the bedroom door expecting to find Chris cuddled up with a pillow. Instead I found the room empty. The bed had not been slept in. I felt the bile rise up in my throat and ran to the bathroom, fell to my knees and got violently sick for what seemed like forever. Finally able to stand again, I washed my face and looked at myself in the mirror. I looked like hell. My eyes were bloodshot and my skin a deathly pale. I hadn't felt this bad in many years.

"Chris? Where are you?" I cried out again. The room was silent and then my eyes went to the vanity where our toiletries were and at first didn't comprehend what I saw, or rather what I didn't see. Chris's cosmetics were not there. Her makeup case, her perfume, even her hairbrush that we always shared was gone.

I stumbled back into the huge bedroom and didn't see her green and tan Louis Vuitton suitcase. I yanked open the drawers where her clothes had been and saw that they were also missing. I sat on the edge of the bed with my head in my hands not comprehending what I saw. Chris was gone and all her stuff as well. This was not good. This was not Chris. She would never leave without telling me. Did something happen? Did I somehow get drunk and blackout and did we fight or something? No, I assured myself. We made love on the couch and fell asleep in each other's arms. That's all I remembered. I had to find her.

I found my pants and dressed quickly, threw on my corduroy sport coat, and then realized my keys were not in the pockets. I panicked. I raced around the suite turning over cushions and looking under everything. After a furtive ten minute search I came to the conclusion that the keys to the MG were also gone. Could Chris have taken her things and the car and left? Never!

I pulled out my cell phone, checked to see if I still had signal, started to dial the sheriff. I hesitated and decided to wait until I had more facts. Him, I didn't trust in the least. I hit the speed dial for Chris and it rang until her voicemail picked up. "Hey this is Chris …"

I paced the room with the phone to my ear and waited for her message to end.

"Chris? Chris, honey, it's me. Where'd you go? Call me please as soon as you get this. I … I don't know what happened. I hope you're okay. I love you." And then I hung up. Puzzled, confused and fuzzy headed, I couldn't imagine what was going on.

I looked around the suite once more for any clues as to what had happened. My eyes fell on the table in the foyer where the ice bucket that had held the Dom had been. It, too, was gone as were the glasses that we had toasted with orange juice. Had the juice been spiked? I ran over to the small fridge at the mini bar and checked to see if the O.J. was there. What I found to my growing apprehensions was a fresh bottle, unopened, exactly where I had taken the one from yesterday afternoon. This was all too strange. I know I wasn't crazy. Something fishy was going on and now my Chris was missing.

I took one last look and slammed the door shut on the way out. I took the stairs two at a time as the fog started to lift from my brain. I hit the bottom floor running and raced out to the parking lot knowing what I would find. The MG was gone. I wanted to scream. This couldn't be happening. I knew Chris would not leave me here like this.

I turned and ran back into the Inn and to the front desk. The same older man with the caterpillar eyebrows and florid face, who had checked us in, was there reading the morning paper and drinking coffee. He looked up at me as I approached and smiled. "Good morning Mr. Thomas. Can I help you?"

"Where is the woman I checked in with? And where the hell is my car?" I demanded.

I must've scared him because he backed away from the counter and looked frightened.

"Mr. Thomas wha … what are you talking about?" He managed to croak out.

"Chris, my girlfriend, the woman I checked in with, is gone. Have you seen her?"

"No, Mr. Thomas. Not since yesterday when you came back together. Has she gone missing?"

"I don't know. I don't know what's going on here but I intend find out!" My voice rose to a fever pitch. "If for some reason you see her or my car for that matter please let me know or the sheriff. I'm going to see him now. I need to get to the bottom of this. I hate this freakin place!"

"Yes … yes sir, Mr. Thomas," he stammered. "The minute I see anything—"

This he said to my back as I raced out the double doors. I stopped, and turned back just in time to see the desk man pick up the phone and dial. He didn't see me and I thought I could see a small thin smile that play across his lips as the man spoke softly into the phone. I stood there looking through the doors, my anger making the top of my head ready to explode. Then I turned and headed down the wide stairs to the circular drive.

# CHAPTER 20

Sheriff Cobb was sitting behind his desk when I burst into his office. He was wearing his ever present perfect gray suit, crisp white shirt and dove gray tie with his shiny silver star on the breast pocket. His gold rimless glasses perched on the bridge of his nose as he peered at the computer screen. Still, I had the feeling he was expecting me.

"Cobb, what the hell is going on? Where's Chris? Where's my car?"

He put his hands up in a back off gesture. "Whoa there, Thomas. What do you think you're doing bursting into my office?"

The deputy that I blew past in the outer office appeared behind me red faced with his gun drawn.

"Good way to get shot," Cobb continued with a calm voice, nodding toward the deputy.

"Everything okay here, Sheriff?" the deputy asked, looking at him expectantly.

"Wait outside, Harlan. I'll call you if I need you. Do I need him, Thomas?"

I shook my head impatiently. "What happened to Chris? She's gone. She's missing and so is my car. Someone drugged us last night and now she's gone."

"What do you mean someone drugged you? You have proof?"

"Someone sent us a bottle of champagne, but we don't drink, so we drank the orange juice instead and passed out. When I woke up this morning, I was dazed like I'd been drugged and Chris was gone—so is my car."

Cobb smiled at me indulgently over the top of his glasses. His hand formed a tent on his desk. "Let me get this straight, Mr. Thomas, someone sent you a bottle of champagne which you didn't drink. But you did drink orange juice. Then you passed out and now your pretty girlfriend has flown the coop, so to speak, with your little sports car. Am I getting all this right Thomas?"

"No Cobb, you're not," I snapped. "Chris would not just take off. Something has happened to her. All her things are gone. No note, no nothing. It's not something she'd do. She's missing and I know something bad has happened." I collapsed wearily in one of the green leather chairs across from his desk.

Cobb eyed me with a faintly amused look on his face. "Thomas did you at least give the idea some thought? Maybe she was tired of playing detective in one of your dime *Eddie Kane* novels and decided it was time to go home."

"Damn it, Cobb!" I shouted pounding on his desk. "She didn't leave and something is definitely wrong. Now will you help me or do I call the State Police and tell them about your lack of concern?"

Harlan poked his head back in, with hopes of maybe shooting me. Cobb waved him off as his smile faded into a look of cold steel. He rose from behind his desk. There was no humor in his expression.

"Mr. Thomas, you are starting to really piss me off. I

run a nice little town here. No problems. That is, until you showed up with some wild story about a missing uncle."

I started to speak but his quelling look told me to be quiet.

"I humored you, Thomas. I even made some discreet inquiries and found nothing. Do you understand me?"

I nodded numbly. "Sheriff you have to look at this from my side."

"Thomas I don't have to do anything. What I ought to do is to put you in jail until I find out exactly what's going on here. For all I know, you killed your girlfriend and staged this whole thing."

"Now you wait a freaking minute, Cobb," I said jumping out of my chair. "What we have here is two people missing under some very bizarre circumstance in this backwater town, and you won't to do a damn thing about it! It is me that's had it. Screw you, Cobb. I am done playing around." I got up, my eyes still deadlocked with his, and then I stalked out of his office, slamming the door behind me as I left.

I eyed Harlan fingering his holster as I marched through the front office and said, "Don't worry Harlan, you may get your chance yet."

I thought about things as I stood on the sidewalk outside the police station trying to regain my cool. It had become personal, now. They, whoever they were, had Chris. I was sure of it. And now I was on my own.

# CHAPTER 21

The six people were led by Black's man, Dieter, to yet another magnificent room in the castle. Inside, the drapes were dark and closed. Skyler couldn't tell if there were actually windows beneath them or not. Heavy tapestries hung tastefully on the walls and the ceiling was mirrored. The room had an eerie quality. Directly in the middle, on an expansive Oriental rug was a huge round oak table surrounded by six massive and intricately carved high-backed chairs. They were placed neatly around its six-foot diameter. An ornate chandelier hung low, illuminating the table. The rest of the room was bathed discreetly in shrouded sconce style lighting. The only other thing in the chamber was a large stainless steel cart with five aluminum cases lined up on the shelf.

"Please sit," Dieter commanded in a heavy accent. "Mr. Black will join you shortly."

With that, he was gone, leaving the six to settle in at the table. Skyler hurried to sit next to Miranda Bell. He was afraid to sit next to Lydia again. The woman was relentless.

"What do you think he's up to?" he asked her in a whisper, leaning close to her ear. She pulled back, eyeing

Skyler as if he was a cockroach. Miranda took a long breath and leaned away him. "Why don't you shut that fat mouth of yours and we'll all find out. You, Mr. Todd, are destined to screw this up for all of us. And listen to me, you little toad, I will cut your throat as you sleep if that happens. Do I make myself clear?" Only he could hear as she'd hissed at him under her breath. She smiled at Skyler with her lips clamped tight and her eyes flat. His hand went unconsciously to his throat as he truly believed her.

He nodded and sat back quickly to see the other four looking at him.

He put up his hands and said, "This all seems a bit weird, that's all." And before anyone could rebuff him further the heavy door opened and Sebastian Black strode in. He was a small man with a large presence. They all looked at him expectantly.

"Mr. Todd," he started slowly. "All of your questions will be answered in due time. I truly hope for your sake that you will make an attempt to fit in here. As I said, if one of you becomes a problem you will all go home with nothing. Do I make myself clear? This is a case of all or nothing."

All eyes were on Skyler, who composed himself quickly. *How had Black heard him? Do the walls have ears?* He thought. Skyler knew then that he had to be careful. He didn't get to this age by being totally stupid.

"Mr. Black, Sir, I apparently have given you the wrong impression. I will be the model guest and none of you will have anything to worry about from me. I promise." He held up his right hand as if swearing an oath. "I apologize to all of you ... sincerely."

Miranda Bell met his eyes and held his gaze and

Skyler firmly believed that she would do what she had said she would.

Chance Hartigan said, "Todd remember this, if you fuck this up for all of us you are a dead man."

Frascarelli seconded the motion by pointing his finger at Skyler like a gun. Skyler licked his lips, and to his credit, remained quiet.

Lydia spoke up and smiled at Skyler, "I think Mr. Todd has made his amends. I think we should all move forward and let bygones be bygones."

There were a few grumbles and a few nods as everyone looked back to Black.

Sebastian Black studied the group. "Good, I think we all understand each other. Remember; do not try to venture outside this house. I'll not be responsible for what the dogs or the snakes do to you."

You could have heard a pin drop even on the thick carpet.

"Now let us begin." Black clapped his hands together and smiled. "Let's try to lighten things up a bit. This is supposed to be fun. Now, I'm going to give you an opportunity to make some money. The game will begin at a moderate level but I warn you the stakes will grow as the reward does. My purpose is to see just how far any of you will go for the money. What would you do for five million dollars?" He looked at each one of them pointedly and continued, "that is the ultimate question." He turned and motioned to the cart with an exaggerated flourish, the way a game show host would do—arm extended, palm up with a big phony smile. *The survey says …*

Gasps and sighs came from around the table. All eyes were wide as they stared at the cart. Frascarelli rubbed his hands together. Donna Lee giggled. Skyler licked his lips.

"That's right folks. The cash is right over there." Black held up a manicured finger and continued, "Please don't get any ideas about … ah … helping yourself prematurely." He allowed himself a short laugh. "I'm afraid Dieter would enjoy the challenge of hunting you down." He paused, looking from one startled face to another. "There are 127 acres of forest that surround this estate. Forty acres are swamp with some very unsavory creatures, including snakes and bears. Some of which I have imported myself."

There was a quiet murmur around the table. Skyler looked at Miranda Bell who stared straight ahead at the table.

Dieter appeared carrying a large covered silver tray.

"Game time," Sebastian stated in a cheerful voice, rubbing his hands together.

# CHAPTER 22

The whole thing was too bizarre to understand. Chris was gone. My car was gone, and I was alone in this backwater town in the middle of nowhere where the people were none too friendly. It was like they were all in on a big secret that only I didn't know. I crossed the street from Cobb's office and walked slowly back toward the Inn. It was a warm, sunny morning and the day had that glow, but all that was lost on me. I paused on the sidewalk and turned my face skyward, closing my eyes for a second in a silent prayer.

"Please God, have Chris be safe," I said quietly to myself. I opened my eyes, looked around me and squinted up at the clear pastel blue sky with its puffy white clouds drifting lazily overhead like islands in a vast ocean. There was a gentle breeze brushing against my face. It was almost too perfect. It looked and felt like a movie set. The shops that lined the main street were open and tourists walked with bags and small children clutched in their hands. The colorful awnings that adorned the entrances were flanked by potted plants and flowers, tables of books, t-shirts, art and all the typical shit tourists buy when on vacation. It felt like it was all staged for me.

The door to the small coffee shop that Chris and I had passed just yesterday was open and wonderful bakery smells drifted out onto the cobblestone walk. I hadn't eaten since lunch the previous day when we met Deputy Adams and even though my mind was spinning trying to make sense out of what was happening, I was hungry and knew I had to keep a level head. I went in, ordered a large coffee and two warm cinnamon buns to go and then headed back over to the hotel to regroup.

The Cold River Inn sat back majestically through a gauntlet of carefully trimmed pines and boxwood hedges along its gravel drive. There was a large circular pond on the front lawn to the left of the drive that had several fountains of water shooting twenty feet into the air, which kept the water fresh looking and moving. There were even benches around it for the guests. The Inn was an impressive three-story presence in itself with its high roof spires that reached toward the peaks of the Green Mountains off in the distance. Three long banks of large, crisply pained windows with hunter green shutters ran its vast length and a grand entry was flanked by heavy white columns that were set into the wide Victorian porch, which wrapped around the massive old beast. On the sprawling veranda, there were rockers and tables placed in clusters where guests could sit to enjoy their gin and tonics or iced tea and take in the ambiance of Cold River. This morning, there were only a few people sitting about drinking coffee and reading the morning paper. Nobody seemed to pay me any attention. I climbed the stone steps and walked down the wide planking of the porch toward a shady spot near one end with several white rockers. I passed an old couple who smiled automatically at me. I nodded and mumbled a good morning to them with a tight smile, and quickly walked on. The last thing I wanted was conversation about the weather right now. I needed to think.

I sat in one of the rockers and looked out over the expanse of lush gardens that were bordered by tall pines and oaks with the powerful, misted mountain peaks looming in the background. Birds chirped and the small brook that ran near the porch babbled. This could have looked beautiful had I not been so insane with worry over Chris. I expected or rather prayed for her to come up behind me and kiss me on the neck or something. She didn't.

I took off my sport coat, threw it over the rocker next to mine and proceeded to drink my coffee and eat a cinnamon roll. I leaned back in my chair and put my feet up on the rail. I tried to will myself back to normal. I felt some semblance of life returning to my body even though my head still throbbed. I was certain I'd been drugged but couldn't figure out how. We didn't drink the Dom so how did we get drugged? What was I missing? And of course, the big question was what was I going to do now to find Chris?

I thought for a long moment and then made a decision. I knew I wouldn't have a lot of help from the police and I was a sitting duck if someone wanted to make me disappear too. I needed help and I knew there was only one man I could trust with this. I fished my cell phone out of my coat and punched in the number for my one hope. Ray.

Ray was my friend. He's the guy I call when I need help with anything and he's instantly there without asking why. A year back he covered my ass when I was accused of murdering my ex-wife, Carla, and her slimy business partner in an insurance scam that left me framed and wanted by the cops. Ray is an extremely resourceful Jamaican who stood about six-foot-three, all ebony muscle and raw confidence. Ray's massive head was shaved which gave him an even more menacing look. He had a wide intelligent face, sharp, raven eyes, with arms the size of Cleveland. He sported a large, gold hoop earring in his left ear and had a gleaming gold tooth smack dab in the middle of his puss. He liked to smile a lot and said the gold tooth gave him character. No one ever felt the need to argue. Back in the day, as Ray discreetly called it, he was part of a Navy Seal Team unit in Viet Nam that did things most people would never hear about or could imagine. He didn't talk about that much. He didn't need to. Ray had that quiet confidence that comes from having seen it all and was certainly not afraid to see it again if need be—he might even enjoy it a bit.

My cell phone purred as it rang several hundred miles away on the Cape and I felt instant relief when I heard Ray's deep voice.

"Talk to me, Hemmingway," the deep Jamaican accented voice said without ceremony.

"Ray, I need you."

"Where you at, mon?"

I told him and outlined briefly what had happened. He asked me a few pointed questions and told me that he'd be there before breakfast the next morning. He said he needed to gather up a few things and then he hung up. I held my phone against my cheek and breathed a sigh of relief. Ray hadn't even questioned it—he was on his way. How many people have friends like that? I felt relief and thought that maybe this day would get better. Turns out, I was very wrong.

# CHAPTER 23

I sat there a moment, finished my now cold coffee and decided that I needed to do something. This Black character was the key. There wasn't a shred of doubt in my mind that it was all connected—Chris disappearing, Skyler missing and me sitting there with my you-know-what in my hand. I looked over at a small neat man drinking his coffee and reading the morning paper—*The Cold River Gazette*. Good a place as any to get information.

"Excuse me," I asked the man. He ignored me.

"Sir?" I asked again a bit louder.

He looked over at me as if I was panhandling, pointedly folded his newspaper in annoyance and replied, "Yes, what can I do for you?" His tone was nasal and I immediately guessed him to be a lawyer. He was dressed expensively in a perfectly pressed black suit with a grey turtleneck and gleaming black loafers. His dark hair was slicked back neatly with a thin well-trimmed mustache over his pencil thin lips and he had piercing dark eyes. There was no warmth here, I thought.

"Are you from around here?" I asked trying to

be cordial. I even smiled and I don't think I actually said "asshole."

"Yes, I am. What do you want?" he answered curtly. "I'm a busy man."

I eyed him and said a bit sarcastically, "I can see that. I just want to know where the newspaper office is located."

The annoying little man gave an exasperated sigh and nodded to his right over my shoulder. "It's down Main about four blocks. I'm sure even you couldn't miss it. It says 'Newspaper' on the sign—*The Cold River Gazette.* Now may I finish my paper in peace?"

I couldn't help myself and answered, "Sure, thanks for all your warm hospitality. I can see why people flock here." This time I might've actually said "asshole" out loud.

He ignored me and snapped open his paper as I stalked past him.

"Have a nice day, Mr. Thomas," he called after me in a nasally voice, not looking up from his paper.

I was halfway down the stone steps when it hit me. *How did he know my name?* I whirled around to where the man had been seated with my mouth open. He was gone. I looked in both directions on the veranda and there was no sign of him. Where could he have gone so quickly? I bounded back up to the porch and opened the lobby doors. It was deserted except for my friend behind the desk. This time he did not smile at me.

"Did you see a man in a black suit come through here in the last minute?" I asked him from the door, a bit out of breath.

He shook his head as he looked around at the empty front lobby and spread his arms wide to demonstrate. "I'm afraid not, Mr. Thomas. Seems you are having a rough day," he said with a condescending expression. "Nobody's come through here in the last ten minutes."

I didn't say what came to mind and walked back out into the sunlight. "I hate this freaking town," I said loudly to no one in particular and headed down the drive, kicking the loose gravel as I walked.

I found the newspaper office with no trouble. The walk did me good and I had calmed down a bit. The bright shops ended after the third block and the town's industrial area began. It was what you would expect on the outskirts of a small New England town. Old mill-type buildings that were converted to small machine shops, art and dance studios and office space, crowded both sides of the narrowing street. There were a few ramshackle houses with peeling paint and sagging porches and some battered cars and trucks parked on the street. I made a note not to venture down here alone at night.

*The Cold River Gazette* was in a low brick building with a dirt parking lot on the side. Dying flowerbeds filled with cigarette butts and road trash were on either side of the entrance. There was an old Chevy van with a logo in fading paint beside a newer yellow VW bug. The bricks were well worn and there was an aging sign over the front that actually did say "NEWSPAPER." Under it was the scripted logo of *The Cold River Gazette,* noting it was established in 1927. It looked out of character in this Currier & Ives town. It was run down and musty looking, much like the rest of this seemingly forgotten neighborhood.

I stepped through the door that had one of those obnoxious little bells that tinkled when the door opened. I closed my eyes and took a deep breath as I walked inside. It was just as I had imagined; dusty, cluttered and noisy, with the hum of large machinery emanating from the back. The pleasant surprise was the striking young blonde girl who greeted me.

"Good morning, sir. May I help you?" She asked. She was bright and cheery with a smile that could melt a young man's heart. I guessed her to be about twenty-five, tall, slim and tanned. She had on a turquoise halter that exposed a sleek belly and white shorts that barely covered legal areas and she wore flip-flops. Her honey blonde hair was tied back loosely in a ponytail. I must've stood there a bit longer than I should have without a response.

"Sir? Can I help you?" She asked me again, still smiling.

I felt foolish. "Hi ... er ... yes. Sorry. You look like someone I used to know." I countered quickly. God, she was a pretty one. I had a hard time forming words.

She extended a tanned slender hand, which I took immediately. "I'm Sandy Adams, reporter, photographer and anything else that comes along." I noticed there was not a ring to be seen. I am trained to notice these sorts of things.

I smiled. "I'm Nick, Nick Thomas."

"The writer," she pronounced quickly.

"Guilty as charged." I smiled, sucking in my tummy. I might've blushed a bit, but then regained control.

"My brother, Ted, he's the deputy you met. He told me about you." Her eyes darted back over her shoulder to a large door that must have led to the pressroom. "Mr. Moon is the owner and he's in the back running the ad sheets for tomorrow." Her glance was furtive and then she turned back to me. "What can I do for you Mr. Thomas?"

"Nick. Please call me Nick." I put on my charming smile. "Sandy I need some information and I figured this was the best place to start. What do you know about a man named Sebastian Black?"

She flushed a bit, looked at me warily and then back over her shoulder. I got the impression that she was scared of something. "He won't like me talking to you but screw him. Okay. Look Nick …"

She was interrupted by the sudden silence from the back. Whatever machine had been running had stopped and a fat red-faced man in a gray apron over a dirty white shirt came through the wide doors from the back, wiping his hands on a rag. He was short and almost as wide as tall with a small head and no noticeable neck. His face was sweaty and he had bushy white sideburns and small tufts of white hair on each side of his gleaming head. He looked like a big rat that had just finished with a dumpster. His tail was probably under the apron.

"Who's this?" He asked in a low flemmy voice. "I'm Louis B. Moon, the publisher and owner of this paper." He made no attempt to shake hands and I instantly disliked this man.

"My name is Thomas. Nick Thomas and I am …"

"I know who you are. You're that guy who has come into our town and has caused quite a ruckus." His beady little eyes bored into me.

I stepped back and spread my arms wide. "Whoa, Louis, I think you got the wrong idea here. I'm looking for someone that was supposed to be here and nobody's telling me squat. So I figured …"

He cut me off. "Whatever you figured, Mr. Thomas, was wrong. There's nothing I can or will help you with so quit bothering my help." He glanced at Sandy who had retreated behind the grimy counter and busied herself with something on the desk behind it. I looked over at her and she averted her eyes. This was a no win, I decided.

I looked back at Louis B. Moon and shook my head. "Seems to me that everyone here's hiding something. That just makes me all the more curious. Have a nice day, Louis." I turned to leave, sick of this whole mess.

Sandy hurried over and pressed a rolled up newspaper with a thick red elastic band around it into my hand. Here is the paper you paid for, Mr. Thomas."

She winked at me quickly as she passed me the paper. I looked at her for a long second and nodded. "Thank you, Sandy. At least someone's nice in this town." I turned and walked out slamming the door. The little bell fell off the door and hit the dirty floor with a clatter.

I walked out into the sunlight with the rolled up newspaper in my hand thinking about what I was going to do next. Ray was on his way, and that was comforting, to a degree. I knew the first order of business was to find Chris. She would never have gone off and left me. Christ, we never even had an argument. We seldom did.

I was curious about why the perky little Sandy had given me a newspaper I hadn't asked for so I stopped walking long enough to pull off the elastic. A small piece of notepaper fluttered out and fell to the sidewalk. I stooped to pick it up, looking around to see if anyone was watching me. Nothing looked out of place so I looked at the note. I read it several times before it sank in. It said: *Mr. Thomas, please be careful here, you are in great danger.* She had scribbled her number at the bottom and signed it *Your friend.*

Now I was really confused as I stood there. What

did this woman know? I hastily shoved the note in my pocket and stuffed the newspaper in a trash can in front of one of the old houses and walked back to the center of town. I had one more stop to make.

I pushed the door open of a neat two-story building with a blue canopy. It was located right next door to Sherriff Cobb's office and shared a paved parking lot. *Town Offices* was stenciled on the glass door. I scanned the glass-framed directory in the small lobby and found what I wanted. I headed up the stairs to the Tax and Records Department that was located on the second floor. I'd find out where Black actually lived—maybe get a map. I knew these things were supposed to be public knowledge. Hell, I was public.

A brisk woman scowled up from a cluttered desk and asked me in a clearly annoyed voice, "May I help you?"

She had the gravelly voice and lined face of someone who'd had too many cigarettes for too many years.

I leaned on the counter and smiled my best Nick smile, which usually always worked. "Yes Ma'am. I'd like to look up a piece of property and I'm not sure how to go about it."

"What for? Who are you?" She snapped at me.

"I might want to purchase it."

She peered at me for what seemed like a long moment. I smiled again and she seemed to thaw a bit. She pointed a bony finger at a set of double doors with big windows so you could see if someone was coming or going. "Go through there and you'll see the computer on the counter. You can use a computer, I assume."

I nodded.

"Good," she responded. "Just type in the name or address you want and then hit search. It will tell you what volume and page to go to. If you want the plat map you will see where it says *Plat Map* and it will tell you where to find that also."

I just knew there was a warm nurturing woman in there just dying to get out. I nodded, thanked her and went bravely into the vault.

I found what I was looking for in ten minutes. Sebastian Black owned a parcel of 127acres off Cedar Swamp Road in Cold River. The deed had been transferred by probate to him fifteen years ago by someone named Augustus Black. I assumed that was his father or Grandfather. I wrote the information in my pocket pad and looked for the reference to the map, which I found fairly easily. I managed to print it out after feeding it a dollar's worth of change.

The map showed a large irregular track of land with the footprint of a huge structure on the southeastern corner. It also showed a small road that led from Cedar Swamp Road that wound through and crossed what looked like wetlands and dense woods all the way to the structure. There were also several small outbuildings that I assumed were a garage or servant's quarters. This was a castle after all, I mused. I studied my findings for a moment and decided to get out of there before the woman decided to check on me. I folded the map and tucked it into the inside pocket of my sport coat.

As I exited, she looked up again and asked me, "Find what you need Mr …?

"I did and thank you for all your help." I smiled at her again and headed straight for the door and freedom.

"I didn't get your name," she persisted.

"No, you didn't," I answered, as I opened the door and left quickly before she could make a fuss.

That was when my day turned to shit in a hurry. Waiting for me on the steps was Sherriff Cobb wearing a wide smile on his face. His idiot deputy, Harlan, had his hand on his gun nervously. Several passersby stopped and watched as the spectacle unfolded. I saw the lizard lady from the tax office smiling at me from the steps.

"Mr. Thomas," Cobb said with obvious pleasure, "you're under arrest."

# CHAPTER 24

It was dark, cold and damp. There was dripping water somewhere off in the distance but otherwise the silence was heavy. Consciousness came slowly like swimming toward the top of a murky pool—far away, elusive and cold. Chris couldn't breathe and her head was exploding with shards of brilliant light from behind her eyes. Then she was aware how bizarre all this was. Her eyes snapped open to the darkness and she shook her head to clear the dream and the cobwebs. Her mind raced with questions. Where am I? How did I get here? Where ... where was here? Nick? Oh my God! Where was Nick? Am I dead? No ... death was not supposed to hurt like this.

Chris squeezed her eyes shut and then opened them again. Her mouth was dry and her temples pounded. The darkness surrounded her and her eyes fought to adjust. She shivered and wrapped her arms around herself. She was covered with something coarse that smelled old and dirty. She reached up and felt her face gingerly. Her mind was still spinning, not sure what had happened. She took both hands and pulled her hair back, kneading her scalp hard and breathing fast. She laid her head back down. It hurt too much to raise it. She sensed she was naked under the blanket and on a cot of some sort. Her feet were cold and uncovered. The mattress was thin under her and there was no sheet or pillow, just the musty fabric, rough and uncomfortable, with hard springs poking from beneath.

What had happened? They were in the hotel room at the Inn, where they had made love and then fallen asleep. That's all she could remember. She and Nick were lying naked and spent on the sofa in the hotel room, entwined in each other's arms. And now she was here. She was alone in the dark.

As quickly as consciousness came it faded away as she dropped back into deep sleep.

# CHAPTER 25

Skyler had lost all track of time. He didn't know what time of day it was—maybe it was even night. He knew he had been here at Black's castle more than a day but most of that was a blur. It was like a vacuum with the absence of any external stimulus. He hadn't seen the trees or the sky since he had gotten out of that limo before those fucking dogs had herded him into Black's web. Every window in the castle was frosted or covered and they were told never to attempt to go out any of the doors.

He was sitting on the king-sized bed, fully dressed leaning his back against the massive oak headboard with a fresh vodka and ice in his hand. He thumped his head back against the oak several times in absent frustration. Had he gotten in too deep this time? he wondered. Skyler had survived all these years on the edge by paying attention to the little voice in his head and this time the voice was screaming to get the hell out of there.

Black was a shrewd character, thought Skyler. He made the game so we would police each other. If one quit they all would lose and the others had made it perfectly clear that they would kill him if he messed it up for them. What would happen then? He wondered if they would even find his body. Probably not and no one would shed a tear or even look real hard. Well, maybe Chris would. But Skyler knew that Chris would think he went off on a tear and would never think of looking for him here. No, he was truly alone in this and he realized then he had to be smarter and keep a clear head if he was going to survive. He slammed the empty glass onto the nightstand and smiled to himself in grave resolve. "I will come away with the prize," he said aloud. Yes sir, Mr. Black, that five million dollars is mine. You just wait and see. It was then he decided that he would stay away from the drink until the end. Then he would get drunk in style. He would keep his wits and outsmart them all.

Not much had happened yet. Black had them play some cards and some simple games—child's play actually. Skyler was up by four thousand according to the big tally board that hung in the game room. They were all getting impatient and anxious for the real games to begin. Or had they already, Skyler mused. They hadn't moved the cart with the aluminum cases and they all eyed the prize constantly. Dieter would watch them and smile as if to dare them to even touch the cases. Skyler knew Dieter would enjoy hurting them. He had that look, cold and calculating with a hint of sadistic amusement. Hell even his name sounded like a Nazi and that weirdo wife of his who never said a word or even looked at you was scarier still.

Skyler shivered. This place gave him the creeps. Black told them at dinner the real fun would begin in the morning and, while eyeing Skyler, suggested that we all have our wits about us. Why was he always picking on me? Skyler fumed, debating whether to have just one more before going to bed.

Skyler had kept his flimsy resolve, remarkably enough. The next morning he dressed carefully after a long hot shower in a nice dark blue pinstripe suit that he'd found in his closet. It fit him perfectly, along with a starched white shirt and dark blue striped tie. He thought of Miranda Bell as he shaved and combed his steel gray hair. He looked like a million dollars. Skyler smiled to himself as he took one final look in the full-length mirror in the spacious bathroom. He would show them all who was the real winner. He took a deep breath and smiled. "Yes indeed, this day is going to be different," he said aloud, as he shut the door to his room and headed down to breakfast.

He didn't know just how right he was.

# CHAPTER 26

I looked at Cobb incredulously. My mouth was dry, I couldn't believe what was happening.

"I'm what?" I asked in a strained voice. "Are you freaking nuts?"

"You heard me, Mr. Thomas, you're under arrest. Now turn around and put your hands against the building." He helped me turn around to face the rough concrete wall and I felt my feet being kicked out from behind me so I was leaning on my hands. Harlan awkwardly patted me down checking for weapons. I could've had an AK-47 in my back pocket and that idiot wouldn't have found it.

I spun around furiously, almost knocking Harlan down as he was still running his hands down one of my legs.

"Cobb are you fucking nuts? What is going on?" I shouted and then realized that I was looking down the barrel of a very nasty automatic that had materialized in Cobb's hand.

"Don't move," he shouted and then roughly spun me around again and cuffed me with my hands behind my back.

"Wha … what am I under arrest for pray tell me?" I screamed back at him.

Then I felt Cobb's hot breath in my ear. "You killed your girlfriend, Thomas. I know it, you know it, and I … will prove it. So, now just come along with us next door or I'll shoot you right here for resisting arrest and nobody but nobody here will give a shit. We're all sick of you. Do you read me, Thomas? Right now you're being arrested for suspicion of murder and I can probably find more charges to sweeten the pot."

I was numb. Murder? Chris? This was all too much. My head was spinning.

"Wait a minute Cobb! Did you find … did you find Chris?" I was afraid of the answer. I felt sick. Was my Chris dead? I had to know.

"No, smart guy, we didn't find the body yet. But we found your car and we found bloodstains in it. And also we found one of her shoes in the car. It's looking like you two had a nasty row and you lost your temper. We'll find her, Thomas. You can bet your city ass on that."

"Cobb, I had nothing to do with that. You got it wrong," I said seething but controlled—barely. I also knew there was nothing I could do right now to change the situation so I knew I had to go along before I made things worse. I almost laughed at that. How could I possibly make things worse than they already were?

"That's why we got lawyers and courts, Thomas. Now let's go before the whole town turns out. A small crowd had gathered in the parking lot between the buildings and was watching Cobb manhandle me toward the jail next door. He pushed me from behind and I trudged toward my insane destiny.

The accommodations that were afforded me were,

let's say, less than comfortable, even in their neat and clean jail house. The cell was 10 x10 with a steel bunk, a sink and a toilet, both made of cold stainless steel so I wouldn't smash them and cut my wrists with the shards of porcelain. There was a single harsh light behind a mesh cage in the ceiling giving off more light than one would like and there was no window. There was nothing in this concrete tomb but walls and bars. A small camera was mounted by the door that I assumed could see everything inside the small cellblock. A tiny red LCD was on under the wide lens of the camera. There were identical cells on either side of me that were empty. I was the sole guest of honor.

Cobb read me my Miranda rights and Harlan shoved me in the cell after taking my sport coat, my belt and my shoelaces so presumably I wouldn't hang myself.

"I want a phone call and a lawyer right now, Cobb," I managed to say in a level voice. "I know my rights here."

Cobb looked at me coolly and just nodded. "You'll get your call, Thomas." He paused and gave me a thin smile, "When I'm good and ready." With that, he followed Harlan out through the steel door and left me to reflect on my good fortune.

I'm not a violent man. I've evolved via the recovery process. I've learned to forgive, to love my enemy and all that happy shit. But right now I could've strangled Cobb without batting an eye. I sat heavily on the thin mattress that lie atop the steel bunk, and put my head in my hands. This was all too much, I thought. Chris and I came up here to find Skyler. That's all. We figured he was gambling to his heart's content in some private club and we would simply convince him to come home with us. Now two days later, I'm in jail, suspected of doing harm to the woman I love, and it looks like justice will be extremely hard to find up here in Cold River, Vermont.

The thought of Ray heading this way was comforting. He would know what to do. But … hmmm … yes, there would be a big "but." How would Cold River, Vermont react to a 6'2" black Jamaican rolling into town and asking for me? Come to think of it, I hadn't seen a black person the whole time I was here.

Ray is not what one would call inconspicuous. I almost laughed aloud when I pictured his first meeting with Cobb. Ray would smile his gold-toothed smile and intimidate the shit out of Country Boy Roy.

I knew that if we were going to be successful in getting out of this mess we'd have to be careful and go about this very quietly. Exactly how Ray and I would achieve this would be the challenge. My immediate problem was how I was going to get out of this jail so I could find Chris. I knew she was alive—I could feel it. The light of my life couldn't have gone out without me feeling it.

I must've dozed off during the night despite my new gated accommodations. I awoke, craving coffee and food. They hadn't bothered waking me for dinner. I laid there with my head spinning, when loud voices rocked me back to reality. I wasn't sure how much time had passed or what time it was, but I recognized Ray's baritone immediately. He was demanding to see me. Ray! Thank God. I jumped up and smoothed myself out the best I could.

"Ray! Ray! I'm in here," I yelled out.

I could hear voices from the front and they were growing louder. I could hear what Ray was saying now.

"No you listen to me, Mr. Sherriff. Do you see this badge?"

Oh no, I groaned aloud. Ray was using one of his fake ID's.

"I'm with the FBI and Mr. Thomas is helping us with a very important investigation," Ray said forcefully. "Do you understand me, mon?"

"Investigating what?" Cobb shot back, not to be intimidated. "Who the hell do you think you are barging in here and demanding to see one of my prisoners?"

"Let me spell it out for you. You can open that fucking door right now and let Mr. Thomas out of that cell or you will have more federal agents just like me up your ass than you ever dreamed of, and you never know what they might find, Mr. Barney. You all that squeaky clean, mon?"

There was a moment of silence from the front and then the door to the back opened and in stepped the most beautiful sight I have ever seen. There was Ray, my crazy-ass Jamaican friend strutting in with a sharp blue suit, crisp white shirt and a red tie, standard issue FBI sunglasses and a smile that spoke volumes. As the crowning touch, he had an ear bud in his right ear that probably went to his iPod. I had to admit, he looked like a real fed.

"Mr. Thomas, you remember me, no? I'm thinking we need to have us a talk."

I played along and nodded. "You're the agent I spoke with on the phone about Skyler Todd. You're with that task force, right?" What task force, I had no idea.

"That's right," he said smoothly giving me the slightest of winks. How he pulled this one off I'd never know. Ray just had instincts. "Now suppose you tell me what's going down here, mon, and why this Sherriff has you locked up."

"It's bullshit. Mr ... umm Mr. I never did get your last name, Sir." I thought the sir with a touch of fear would work well.

"My name is Montego. Like the bay. Special Agent, Ray Montego." He turned toward Cobb. "I want this man released in my custody right now Sherriff. We're working on a major case and Mr. Thomas is helping us."

Cobb was not totally convinced ... yet. "No way, mon," he said defiantly, making a jab at Ray's accent. "He's my prisoner and I have him booked on suspicion of murder."

"You have a body, Mr. Sherriff?" Ray asked him smoothly. "Why don't you and me go over all this evidence you say you have here on this man." Ray jerked a thumb in my direction. I looked on, keeping my itching mouth shut. This was Ray's show and there was no way I was going to screw it up. I got to admit, the man had balls—big ones. I wondered how he managed to get the garb and the creds, but he always told me not to ask stupid questions and "jus' roll with it." I kept quiet.

"No we don't have a body. We found this guy's car two miles from town this morning with blood on the seat and what we are surmising is his girlfriend's sneaker on the ground next to it. Wise guy here says they were drugged and doesn't remember a thing that happened last night when his car was stolen." Cobb was smug for a second.

Ray shook his head and peered at Cobb as if he were a small child. "You can't hold him without a body and the rest is bullshit, Mr. Cobb. You say Mr. Thomas here woke up in his hotel. How did he manage to get back to town without anybody seeing him. Huh? You unlock that cell now and give him to me. I'll personally guarantee that Mr. Thomas here stays in town where you can find him if you need him. Fair enough, Sherriff Cobb? Meanwhile you might want to take a look at some other suspects."

"Do I have a choice?" Cobb asked in a resigned voice. I couldn't believe it. This was going to work.

"Not really, mon. You don't have a case here and you know it."

"Okay, take this asshole out of here but I want to know where he is at all times. Do we understand each other Agent Montego?" Cobb was still trying to hold some ground.

Agent Montego? I fought to keep a straight face and Ray shot me a glance that said to keep my mouth shut. I did.

"Good, now let's get you out of there, Mr. Thomas," Ray said turning back to me. I was still standing there behind the bars holding on with both hands like they do in the movies. I wished I had one of those tin cups to rake across the bars a few times. That would really piss Cobb off.

Ray looked down at Cobb again who was a good foot shorter than and said, "Later, you and I need to talk, Sherriff. Something here stinks and my office is concerned that there might be some funny business happening here. You know anything about that, Sherriff Cobb? I'm interested in this fellow Sebastian Black."

I wanted to strangle Ray. Enough was enough. Now he was pushing his luck. The color seemed to drain from Cobb's face but he managed to nod and said graciously, "I am at your disposal, Agent Montego. Let me know how I can help."

Ray got me out of there, shoelaces and all within five minutes and as we walked out into the early morning air, I began to breathe again.

"Ray ... I ..."

"Shut up now, mon. Let's get away from here before you say a word."

Outside sat Ray's gleaming Black Hummer that I had bought him after the last time he saved my ass and I had smashed up his Explorer. He gave me the first gold-toothed smile of the day as we climbed up into the SUV.

"Ray, I love you man."

"I know. Just don't get all mushy wid me mon, okay? We'll find Chris. I promise you, my friend."

"Deal," I said with a weak grin as he pulled smoothly away from the curb.

# CHAPTER 27

They all assembled for breakfast in the huge dining room and there was a nervous buzz of conversation. Skyler felt that something was going to happen today. He was disappointed that the seats on either side of Miranda Bell were occupied so he had no choice but to sit next to Lydia Winfield. He made a note to get to breakfast earlier. He knew if Miranda took the time that she would like him. Hell, they always did. Skyler knew his charms were lethal.

"Morning," he said brightly to everyone but his eyes were on Miranda. There were a few grumbled responses. Miranda chose not to reply and went back to her bagel and coffee with renewed interest.

Skyler felt a hand on his and turned to Lydia.

"Good Morning, Mr. Todd," she said. Her hand lingered on his for a long moment. "I trust you had a nice night's rest," she said, smiling coyly. Christ, he thought, the old broad is hitting on me already this morning. He shot a quick glace in Miranda's direction but she was engaged with Hartigan and not paying him any attention.

"Morning Lydia," he said as he sat. "I did sleep well. You?"

"I don't like sleeping alone," she said in a confidential tone that only he could hear. She was looking into his bloodshot eyes and leaning very close. Oh no, he groaned inwardly.

"If you ever want some company ... well, you know. You're a handsome man and we are all alone here."

"Uh ... thanks Lydia ... I, er ...," he stammered, not knowing what to say. He didn't want to make more enemies.

She patted his hand again and said, "You just think about it, next time you are laying there and can't sleep. Maybe I could help." She winked at him. "You would be amazed at what I can do to ... ah relax you."

Skyler almost jumped out of the chair when he felt her fingers rubbing the crotch of his pants. It was just wrong. Lydia smiled again at him and picked up her orange juice.

"I think we're going to have some fun today," she said to no one in particular running the tip of her pink tongue over her bright red lips.

Dieter appeared and they all fell silent.

"Good Morning," he said curtly, his English heavily accented. "Mr. Black will see you in the game room in ten minutes." He looked at Skyler when he spoke. They all nodded and Frascarelli shot him a Heil Hitler salute to which Dieter just smiled thinly. "I am Austrian, Mr. Frascarelli, that is where the similarity stops and remember the American saying. How does it go? Oh yes, 'every dog has his day'." He turned and left the room leaving a heavy silence.

"Fuck him," Frascarelli said. Nobody else responded as they filed out after Dieter.

They all sat in silence and waited. It was ten

uncomfortable minutes before the heavy oak door opened and Sebastian Black strode in with Dieter following discreetly behind.

"Good Morning to all of you," he said, unsmiling. "Today you will find out what the stakes truly are."

Dieter stood at parade rest next to the door. Next to him was a small cart with a covered tray that looked like some sort of serving dish. Skyler eyed him with a mix of contempt and fear. He looked like a quiet killer.

Chance Hartigan spoke up for the group. "Yes Mr. Black it would be nice to know why we are here and how we win the prize." He motioned toward the other cart with the five aluminum cases.

"Mr. Hartigan, your questions will soon be answered. Now let me share with you the rules for our next contest." He had their attention. "Tomorrow there will only be five of you."

There was a collective gasp and then the what-the-hells started.

Black held up his hand and commanded, "Silence, all of you. You agreed to come here for the chance to win the five million dollar prize. You will all have an equal chance at that prize. Someone has to win so five of you have to lose. That process will be one of elimination. If you lose the challenge, you go home with the fifty thousand as promised. However, if you refuse to participate in the challenge you will forfeit your share."

Miranda Bell spoke up. "Mr. Black, am I to understand that you will not honor your promise?"

"No, Ms. Bell, read the agreement you signed. It clearly states that all members must participate in the challenges in order to fulfill your end of the bargain. No one is reneging on anything. Now please let us begin.

You want to leave, let me know now and we'll make the arrangements."

Six sets of wary eyes settled on their host. These were not stupid people. They were all professional gamblers and understood the stakes.

Black turned and motioned to Dieter who carried the covered stainless serving tray that he had taken from the cart then carefully placed it in the center of the table. All eyes were riveted on the gleaming dome as Dieter stepped back with a small smile on the corner of his lips.

Black moved forward, stepped between Miranda Bell and Chance Hartigan and placed his hand on the domed cover. The air was heavy and no one spoke.

"Now," he said slowly as he lifted the cover. "Our game becomes serious." He paused for a moment and looked at each of the six people seated around the table.

On the platter beneath the cover was a heavy meat cleaver; one that a butcher or professional chef would use. They all stared at the cleaver, not comprehending the significance it held and there was a murmur of questions. Black smiled at their confusion. Skyler wondered what this sick bastard was up to and had a sinking feeling in the pit of his stomach.

Black held up his hand for silence once again.

He prolonged the moment, obviously enjoying the speculation in the room.

"The prize, ladies and gentlemen, is twenty-five thousand dollars to each of you who chooses to participate. The cost ... is one of your fingers.

There was a stunned silence in the room.

Miranda Bell was the first to break the silence. "Mr. Black, you certainly don't expect—"

He cut her off. "What I expect, Ms. Bell is for all of

you to honor your commitment. Did any of you expect that it would be easy to collect five million dollars?"

"You're fucking nuts," Frascarelli yelled heatedly as he started to rise. "I'm outta here."

Dieter moved quickly behind him and shoved him roughly back into his chair.

"No, Mr. Frascarelli, I am afraid you will let me finish," Black said evenly.

Frascarelli glowered at Dieter. Dieter smiled and no one else spoke.

"Good," Black said rubbing his hands together. "Now let's see what you are all made of. I will actually raise the stakes a bit and offer an additional ten thousand dollars to the first one who accepts the challenge and completes the task. Who will be first?"

Six sets of eyes looked from one to the other and they were all shocked to hear Lydia Winfield, the little old lady, reply, "Hand me the cleaver, Mr. Black."

Skyler almost swallowed his tongue.

# CHAPTER 28

Ray pulled the Hummer into the same dirt lot by the river where Chris and I had met Deputy Adams two nights ago when he had warned us to be very careful. Now, Chris was gone. I wasn't sure if she was alive and I couldn't live with that. But I didn't feel like she was dead. I'd know it down to my soul so I had to believe that she was alive. That's what kept me going.

Ray reached back and pulled a couple of ice-cold Red Bulls from a small cooler.

"Red Bull?" I asked, taking one.

"Gives me pep, Hemmingway. Don't mess with me. I just got your ass out of jail."

"Don't mean I won't be going back with you right next to me, Tonto," I said as I popped the top and took a long pull of the rocket fuel.

"Well genius, what's the plan?" he asked me with a serious tone. His large ebony face watched me for a long minute.

I was thinking. Writers think. "First we've got to find Chris. At this point, I could care less about Skyler. I want to find Chris and if we happen to find that worthless fool in the process then it'll be a bonus. Chris. I need to find her. That's all I want to do." I felt the tears and rage boiling inside. I felt so damn helpless.

Ray put his huge paw on my shoulder and said with his own emotion, "Nick, we gonna make this right. I promise you. Now, tell me everything from the beginning, mon. Don' leave anything out."

And so I did and for the next twenty minutes, I spun the story from the day we found out that dear Uncle Skyler was in the wind, and quite possibly way in over his rum-soaked head, to Ray finding me in Sheriff Roy Cobb's jail.

"Shoulda left you in jail, mon. You'd be safer. This feels like real trouble. The hairs on the back of my ..."

"You don't have any hair."

He smiled at me, gold tooth gleaming, in his thousand dollar suit and asked, "You know where this Black fellow lives? I think it's time we go say hello."

"I think so," I said and brought out the assessors' map of the Black Estate that I had folded in my sport coat pocket. I was surprised that Cobb had overlooked this and let me keep it. "We need a road map."

"How 'bout a G.P.S.?"

"Ray you're a genius."

"I know. Give me the name of the road, mon."

Thirty minutes and four miles later, we found Cedar Swamp Road. The road was canopied with tall pines and oaks and gave me the feeling that we were driving back in time. This beautiful country lane, lined with lush laurels and majestic trees, threw long shadows in the morning sun and had a very sinister feel to me. I shivered unconsciously and shook my head to clear the feeling.

"This feel creepy to you?" I asked Ray.

"Yeah it does. Hey, look at that," He pointed to a tall black iron fence that appeared on our right. It was overgrown, but imposing nevertheless and stretched far beyond as we drove. There were "KEEP OUT PRIVATE PROPERTY" signs every 200 feet or so. Also, "BEWARE OF DOGS" signs were posted on the fence itself.

He slowed the Hummer and pointed to a barely visible coil of razor wire that ran across the top of the iron spears.

"See the wire on top?"

"Nice and friendly. Looks like this might be the place."

Ray nodded and extended his arm across my face again, "There's the gate coming up now. Cameras too. They tracking us now for sure."

"When I started to turn to get a better look he said tersely, "Don't look at them. We have to act like we're lost or something."

I nodded and made believe that I was looking at the map in my hands as we passed the gate with their probing eyes.

The heavy, iron gate hung between two huge stone pillars, covered with thick ivy. The initials RB were chiseled on the pillars which I figured to be Rudolph Black's, the infamous grandfather. Fierce looking ivory colored lions adorned the top of each pillar. Tucked next to them were motion cameras that recorded each vehicle that passed. I saw a small call box mounted on a post before the gate and I had the urge to make Ray stop so I could call and play stupid, but that's exactly what that would be. We needed to keep a low profile, not attract any attention, and see what was inside those gates. We drove on as the iron fence resumed and stretched on seemingly forever.

"Let's see if we can't find a place to lay low till tonight. Then we go in and see. What you think, Hemmingway?"

I was hungry and then an idea came to me. "You bring any food? Ray, we need to do some shopping. Maybe we can find some treats for the dogs."

He looked at me, nodding. "Help them sleep maybe. Good idea. I brought us some clothes. I can't go marching round the woods in this suit."

"Where'd you get that suit anyway? You don't wear suits. I never saw you in a suit. It's kind of scary."

"My funeral suit, mon, and it be for yours you keep running your mouth."

We both laughed. It felt good but the feeling went away quickly when my thoughts averted back to Chris. Then I felt guilty for laughing.

We backtracked to a small gas station/mini-mart on the outskirts of town. The title mini mart didn't do it justice, but we found most of what we needed there. This was rural Vermont where the coffee was right next to the night crawlers and bug spray. We bought an overpriced thermos of bad coffee, cold drinks, four disgusting microwave burritos and a bag of chips the size of a pillow. Ray found some extra special treats in case we ran into the dogs. I had a feeling he was planning to add a bit of something to them.

"Let's go back and find us a spot to lay low to watch and wait."

"Wait for what?" I asked.

"We wait to see if anybody comes and goes, then we go in late for a look see ourselves."

"You're the boss," I conceded gratefully. I didn't want to think. We attacked the suspicious burritos that actually tasted worse than they looked.

When we got back to Cedar Swamp, Ray circled the entire estate, finding a rear gate on the other side several miles away.

"This looks like the only other way in." he said.

"And out," I added. "It doesn't look like it's used much."

He nodded. "Let's get back over to the front side and wait for dark."

Ray found a small opening in the woods on the opposite side of the road not far from the front entrance to Castle Black and wheeled the Hummer through the tangle of laurels so we were out of sight.

"Good a place as any," he said and got out of the truck.

Ray had come prepared to wage war. SEALS were always prepared, or was that the Boy Scouts? It was reassuring to have him here. He popped the rear hatch of the Hummer, which was packed with what looked like an arsenal, pulled out a large green military duffle bag and threw it on the ground. This kind of stuff was a bit out of my depth, but Ray actually enjoyed it. I think he got bored tending his bar on the Cape and loves a chance to be a SEAL again. I've got to admit, he certainly pulled off the fed act with Sheriff Cobb and I have seen Ray in action, so I'm glad he's my friend.

"Let's change clothes and take turns watching the gate," he said tossing me what looked like a black jump suit. "I think we can see it from the top of the truck. I'm gonna take a quick look around. You jus sit tight and I'll be back. Try to get some rest. You're gonna need it tonight."

"I'm going to sit here and poison myself with this burrito and this foul tasting coffee."

"Good. I'll be back. Save me some coffee."

He changed into his commando gear complete with a nasty looking rifle with a scope and disappeared into the thick forest. I swore I saw a smile on his face.

# CHAPTER 29

The room was totally still as Lydia Winfield, the sweet horny old lady picked up the heavy meat cleaver from the stainless steel platter and smiled.

"Now Mr. Black, let me understand this. If I chop my pinky off, you will give me twenty-five thousand dollars."

"No, Miss Winfield, I said I would give you twenty-five thousand plus an additional ten for being the first. Thirty-five thousand dollars for your little finger is the reward. The question is it worth that to you?" His coal black eyes had no smile.

The others, Skyler included, just watched in shocked amazement. It was surreal.

"Christ Black, you can't be serious. This is downright sick," protested Chance Hartigan. The others nodded in agreement.

Black took a deep breath and said as if he were speaking with a small child, "I'm as serious as the proverbial heart attack, Mr. Hartigan. Have some of you lost your appetite for the challenges?" He said, arching his eyebrows.

"We would certainly like to know what they are, Mr. Black, before we go much further," Miranda's cultured voice countered. "You've never told us any specifics of these challenges. We were told that we'd be participating in an social experiment, as I believe you called it, and the winner would walk away with the five million dollar prize. There was nothing ever said about chopping off limbs."

"The rules have never changed, Ms. Bell, if you or anyone else has changed their mind about participating, please let me know now." He scanned the six confused faces. "The ones remaining will be happy to see the odds turn in their favor."

"You are fucking sick," cried Frascarelli, jumping to his feet and kicking over his chair. "I'm outta here."

Black snapped his head to Frascarelli and hissed, "In or out , Mr. Frascarelli?"

Dieter moved silently behind the dissenter's chair, standing at a discreet distance.

"I came here to gamble not chop shit off. Next you're gonna offer me fifty G's to cut off my pecker. Well, Dracula, that ain't gonna happen. Get me the fuck out of here. Now!"

Black looked at Frascarelli for a long moment and then nodded to Dieter.

"Dieter, take Mr. Frascarelli up to gather his things and make arrangements for his … ah … departure."

Dieter nodded with a tight smile and gestured for Tony Frascarelli to follow.

Frascarelli turned and looked at the remaining five sitting at the table.

"You all can stay here with this nutcase. Me, I'm outta here. You're all gonna regret staying here. Mark my words!"

"Goodbye, Mr. Frascarelli," Black said with finality

and turned back to the group as Dieter escorted the still fuming Frascarelli out.

After a long tense moment, Skyler found his voice. "What the hell just happened here? What happens now Black? This is getting weird." He looked to Miranda Bell for support and she ignored him as usual.

"We go on as planned is what we do. Now we have five." Black turned and gestured toward the cases that held the five million dollars. "The odds have improved. Now let me ask you all this," he paused for effect, "does anyone else want to leave right now?" He asked, slowly looking from one to the other. Chance held Donna Lee's hand. Miranda and Skyler flanked Lydia and looked protective. They all glowered at Black.

"Come now. Speak up or forever hold your peace." He smiled at this and then said, "If any of you have anything to say, get it out now."

The group was strangely silent for a long moment until Skyler spoke up once again, "Mr. Black, are we to assume that these challenges get progressively more dangerous?"

All eyes were on Black.

"Remember one thing, Mr. Todd, you all came to me. Am I correct?" He didn't wait for an answer before adding, "Yes, it was *you* who answered my advertisement. *You* are the *ones* who came to me. I promised that one of you would walk away with the five million dollars and I also promised fifty thousand dollars to all the runners up. If ...," he paused again, "and only if, you complete the challenges I have prepared. Will they get harder you ask? Yes, they will Mr. Todd. Let me ask you this, where else in this world would you have the opportunity to win five million dollars? Tax free, I might add. You couldn't have believed it would be easy to attain now, could you?"

There was some grunting and then sighs of resignation.

The classy Miranda Bell said with her eyes locked with Black's, "Well then Mr. Black, let's cut to the chase, shall we? What's next? Come on, I'm ready for you."

The other four nodded in assent and looked ready to continue.

Black stood back, clapped his hands once and smiled. "Good, now where were we before this unfortunate interruption?"

"I believe I was ready to accept your first challenge," said Lydia Winfield in a firm voice. The cleaver was in her hand and she smiled thinly at Black. They all watched her place a frail white hand on the wooden table in front of her as she took a deep breath and raised the cleaver over her head. Black stood at her side watching, like a raven waiting for something to die.

There was no air in the room. Skyler could hear his own heart beating. He licked his parched lips and watched with horror as the sweet little old lady, who had rubbed his crotch at breakfast, took a deep breath, closed her eyes and swung the heavy cleaver down towards her chalk white finger.

"Stop," Black commanded as his hand shot out with amazing speed and strength to catch the old lady's hand a scant six inches from the table and her finger. She looked at him in terror and confusion as he gripped her wrist and carefully peeled her fingers from the handle, taking the cleaver away from her. Lydia slumped back into her chair, pale as a raw chicken.

There was a stunned silence. Heads turned, mouths opened but words wouldn't come to any of them.

"What ... what just happened? Why did you stop me?" Lydia asked Black, not comprehending what had just happened. "I was going to do it. Why did you stop me, Mr. Black? I don't understand."

Donna Lee let out a howl, "Holy shitttttt!!!!"

Hartigan let out a long breath and Miranda just sat back shaking her head. Skyler was afraid he peed in his pants.

Black held up the cleaver as if it were the prize and bowed to Lydia. "You win the challenge Miss. Winfield. That's what just happened. I wanted to see if you would do it for the right ... how shall I put this? Reward." He stood back and smiled at Lydia Winfield. "You had every intention of completing the challenge. So, in my eyes, you win and the thirty-five thousand is yours."

Skyler ran his hand through his sweat-drenched hair not believing what he had just witnessed. "You are truly a crazy fuck Black, you know that?"

"Ahh, Mr. Todd, everything in life is our perception of things and situations. Remember that. Oh, and for the rest of you, do not assume that I will act the same way in a similar situation. Please remember that. Don't try to call my bluff. That could be very dangerous."

He looked at each of them again, focused deliberately, and then said with a wry smile, "I think that will be all for now. I'm sure you all would like a break, so we will begin anew a bit later. I think you'll all enjoy our next challenge."

He turned and left the room like a wisp of bad air.

# CHAPTER 30

They were all seated in the huge dining hall finishing their dinner. Skyler, ever the optimist, had managed to maneuver a seat next to Miranda Bell. She was dressed in a simple black pantsuit adorned by a single strand of pearls around her graceful neck. Her rich blonde hair was pulled back in a tight chignon looking very elegant and sexy. She was in superb shape, Skyler noted appreciably, and she exuded an air of confidence that drew him like a moth to a flame. He just couldn't help himself with her. He felt like a schoolboy even though he was at least twenty years her senior.

The other three were engaged in an animated conversation about Lydia's close call and good fortune and were not paying much attention to either of them.

"Miranda, do you think we could ever be friends? I mean I've been trying to be nice to you since we got here and you treat me like a cockroach or something. I'm just trying to be friendly, you know."

"You don't give up, do you Mr. Todd?" She said and eyed him coolly. She wiped her mouth with a linen napkin and turned slightly in her seat toward him. "We'll talk soon."

He started to speak and she put a finger to his mouth. "Not now and not here and not for what's in your dirty little mind—both of them," she added with a wan smile.

He looked puzzled then got the thrust of her jab. "Hey wait a minute Miranda ..."

She silenced him again. "Mr. Todd, please just shut up and listen to me for once and get your head out of your pants. You'll listen and do exactly as I say. Understand?"

Skyler looked confused but nodded and mumbled, "Sure ... sure, Miranda, whatever you say."

"Good." Then she continued in a hushed tone, "I'll tell you when and where we can meet. Now finish your dinner and stop acting like an ass." There was something in her voice and eyes that stopped him cold. He looked at her for a long moment, nodded again and then went back to his plate. He smiled to himself, seeing a glimmer of hope. He stole a quick glance down at her crossed long legs, sans stockings, ending at the ever-sexy black peep toe pumps.

Chance Hartigan, who had taken a liking to the young and vibrant Donna Lee, sat with his arm resting on the back of her chair and spoke to all of them. "What you think happened to Frascarelli?"

"What do you mean, Hartigan?" asked Skyler, chewing on a roll. "He left. His choice."

"I mean, do you think Black actually let him go?"

The table got quiet as they all seemed to ponder this.

"What would he do, Chance?" asked Donna Lee in a high voice. "You don't think ..."

Chance exhaled a deep breath. "I'm saying that this guy is off and I got a bad feeling that nobody's going to leave this freaking place. I don't trust him a bit and that goon, Dieter, gives me the creeps. Something's not what it seems here. I just got a feeling, that's all."

"Shhh. He could be listening," warned Miranda Bell softly. "It seems these walls have ears. I think we all have to be very careful in what we say and do until we know exactly what we are up against here."

Lydia Winfield, spoke up, looking over at Hartigan. "I'm not so sure anything is wrong. I mean he didn't actually hurt anybody, or for that matter, he didn't let me hurt myself. And I did win thirty-five thousand dollars."

"Lady, you were lucky, that's all, and for that matter, do you actually have the cash? No!" snapped Hartigan. "He's playing with our heads and I don't think it's gonna end there."

"What do you think, Todd?" asked Hartigan, pushing his plate away untouched. "Think this is legit? Do you actually think one of us is going to waltz out of here with five million bucks?"

Skyler pondered this for a second, finished his coffee, and said, "What I do know is that supposedly there's a lot of money on the table here and I'm not ready to walk away from that chance just yet." He looked to Miranda who just sat there watching the other four quietly. "What do you think, Miranda?"

She was silent for a long moment and then said, "I think we do what the man says and see where it goes."

The door opened behind them.

"Excellent idea, Ms. Bell," a voice boomed behind them as Black, followed by Dieter, entered the room quieting all conversation. Black's raven eyes surveyed the five seated at the table and held up a hand.

"Please, I know this is all a bit mysterious to you, but

I assure you I am being sincere and fair. Mr. Frascarelli, who at his own behest, left the mansion about an hour ago and has been driven to the bus depot in Burlington. Quite unharmed, I might add, and I actually gave him a small consolation gift of ten thousand dollars for his trouble. I do not wish to keep anyone here against their will." He paused and then smiled thinly, "Do any of you wish to leave as well? This is the last time I will ask without penalty. I will give anyone who wants to leave the same ten thousand."

He looked to each of them in question. Hartigan shook his head. Donna Lee smiled and folded her arms. Skyler nodded and Miranda simply met his steely gaze with one of her own.

"Not with five million on that table," said Hartigan. The rest nodded in assent.

"We're in, Mr. Black," said Lydia Winfield. "Now what's next?"

Black smiled and turned to Dieter. "Please escort them back to the game room and I shall be along presently."

Turning back to the five he said, "I've some business to attend to but I'll be joining you shortly. I want you all to ponder one thing. Another one of you possibly will be leaving us tonight."

There was a collective gasp in the room as he continued, "That's right. One of you could go, but here's the thing. You will choose that person's fate amongst yourselves. That should be interesting."

"Hold on Black, what the hell do you mean?" cried Hartigan, rising from his chair. "You said if we met the challenges we would stay? What kind of shit are you pulling here?"

The rest sat with their mouths open, except for the cool Miranda Bell who said,

"It seems like you enjoy changing the rules, Mr. Black."

"No, Ms. Bell, you have that wrong. I don't change the rules, I make them and I'm afraid that you will now abide by them," he snapped curtly and left the room. Dieter stared unflinching at Hartigan who still shook with anger.

"Your move, Mr. Hartigan," Dieter said in his thick accented voice. "In or out, I really don't care which."

Chance swallowed and eyed Dieter back. "Every dog has his day, asshole. Remember that."

They stood sizing each other up for a long moment. Dieter had at least three inches and fifty pounds on the big man and had the look of unwavering confidence of one who truly enjoyed conflict. Hartigan broke the eye contact.

Dieter smiled and said, "I shall look forward to that day, Mr. Hartigan. Just remember that dogs do bite. Now shall we go?" He stepped aside and gestured toward the door.

"Do we have a choice?" asked Skyler, a sick feeling growing in the pit of his stomach.

Dieter smiled thinly again and answered, "No, I'm afraid you do not."

# CHAPTER 31

Ray was gone for what seemed like a long time. He finally slipped back into the small clearing about an hour later where the Hummer and I sat waiting impatiently.

"I was worried," I said stretching as I sat on the hood of the Hummer.

"That's touching, but I had to get the lay of the land."

"See anything that could help us?"

"Two ways in, two ways out. I saw some dirt roads but couldn't see where they led. The one gate on the far side opens onto that back road, but it's locked tight with a chain and there's nowhere to hide. The cameras got it covered real good."

"So, let me guess. The main gate is it."

"Right you are. The perimeter fence is wired and cameras are everywhere. Not to mention that the whole damn place is a swamp. Swamp means critters Hemmingway, and this boy don' like critters."

"See any dogs?"

"Nope, and that is what scares me. I know they're there. Quiet fuckers."

"So what do we do?" I asked Ray as he reached for the thermos of coffee.

He took a gulp, made a face and spit it out. "Man this shit is bad. Look, somebody has to come and go through that gate sooner or later. Let's watch and wait to see what happens. Patience always reveals answers, my friend."

"Can I use that? That was poetry, and don't waste good coffee."

He gave me a love tap that sent me sliding off the hood of the Hummer. "You a funny guy, Hemmingway, use my insight and you pay me a fee." Ray said, hefting his frame easily up onto the high roof of the Hummer. "Now let's set up and watch. Pass me my rifle and be careful, don't shoot anything, especially me."

"What do you want me to do?" I asked as I watched him position himself on his stomach. He lay prone facing the direction of the security gate, squinting into the scope.

"Grab some rest, you're gonna need it. I'll roust you if something happens."

"Yeah, like I'll be able to nap."

"Try. Now shut up so I can tune in here. I can't concentrate with you running your mouth."

We waited through the afternoon as shadows started to creep over the dense forest. I think I actually did get a little sleep as I was out of it when Ray hissed at me, "Hey Nick! Wake your ass up. We got some action."

"Where? What do we do?" I asked as I wiped the fog from my brain and climbed out of the Hummer quickly.

"Car coming. We gotta move fast," Ray said urgently.

We heard the sound of a powerful motor in the distance. Then saw a pair of bright headlights snaking through the trees behind the gate.

Ray slid to the ground, grabbed a backpack from the back and threw me the smaller one. He put his pack on the ground and pulled out a Beretta 9mm, a worn leather shoulder rig, and two spare clips from it and handed them to me.

"Come on, put this on and follow me. Move now! We're going in, so stay with me. Don't say a word and follow my lead."

I knew better than to question Ray so I did as he told me, slinging the pack on one shoulder and hustling behind him. We crossed the dark road about fifty feet up from the gate. Now I could see the headlights on what looked to be a big, dark colored sedan, waiting as the gates slowly swung in.

"Keep close to the fence and let's come up next to the pillars," Ray whispered, catching his breath. "I don't think those cameras will pick us up if we stay back against the fence under them. We'll slip in after he goes out."

We were both pressed against the ivy-covered fence behind the cover of the lion capped pillar as the big car pulled slowly through the gates and its headlights swept the dark road in front of us.

"Keep cool," Ray whispered, "when he gets past us we move. Fast, and then run to the right into those trees. Stop when you have cover."

"Right behind you," I managed reply. My heart was thumping as we watched the car clear the gate, turn right, and then accelerate quickly down the dark country lane.

Ray slapped me on the shoulder and we sprinted

through the opening, hugging the side as much as we could and then disappearing into the woods. The gate swung closed and we rested against a huge oak about fifty yards inside, panting.

"Think the cameras caught us?" I asked between gasps.

"Don't know, but we ain't waiting here to find out. Let's move. Look Nick, I don't know what we're going to find in there. This could get real nasty. Are you sure you're up for it?" He said, adjusting the shoulder holster under my left arm.

"Ray, I am going to find Chris. Without her, nothing really matters. I'm in." I said with finality in my voice and a bravado that I didn't feel. "Let's do this."

We plowed through the dense underbrush parallel to the road in the direction we assumed to be the main house. Every few minutes Ray would stop, hold up his hand and listen. We heard nothing but the soft wind in the trees and a loud chorus of night frogs singing from the marsh. Then we moved on. About fifteen miserable minutes later we saw a glow over the trees about a half a mile to our left.

"That should be the house," Ray said, looking around us in all directions and then he got down on one knee.

I knelt next to him, breathing hard. "Okay, Ray, let's go."

He put a hand on my arm and looked me in the eye. "This is RECON, mon, understand? We are just looking around. Shit, Hemmingway, we don't even know if Chris is here."

"She's here, Ray. I feel it. I know it."

"Well then, my friend, if she be here we'll find her."

"Sounds easy," I answered skeptically.

"Can be. Just follow me and keep your head down."

"It's down, Kemo Sabé."

We found the light and the mansion just where we thought it would be. From a vantage point in a small copse of trees, we hunkered down and took in the sight. It was magnificent. The house or castle as it were, was a gothic stone masterpiece that stretched a hundred feet in both directions from the main turret, and was at least three floors high. The roof was a maze of steep slopes covered in terra cotta with copper rain gutters. There was a large lighted fountain and a pond to the right of the wide entry stairs with soft landscape lighting that accented the shrubbery under the high windows, many of which were lit. There was a large stone structure to the rear with six garage doors, so with my superior deductive intuition, I decided this was a garage with living quarters above. There were lights in several of the windows there as well. If I ever had a pre-conceived picture of an English castle, this far surpassed anything I could have dreamed up.

"Wow," I managed to say.

"Looks like a movie set, mon, scary, but beautiful. No dogs yet. We might be—"

Before the words came out all hell broke loose.

We were blinded by the sudden wave of light that illuminated the entire grounds. Powerful halogen lamps swept the area and then we heard the dreaded urgent barking of excited dogs. They sounded like big dogs, many big dogs, coming from the back of the castle and heading in our direction.

"Oh shit," I cried and looked over at Ray who was already running in a low crouch. "Come on, move it," he hissed at me. "We need to get off the ground, fast!"

I needed no further encouragement as we streaked around to the left and headed straight for the back of the huge stone garage. The dogs were not fooled and seemed to have our scent. The barking got louder as we ran for cover. There was a lot of noise now. I heard the sounds of men running and shouting at the dogs. This was not good.

Ray stopped suddenly, dug into his pack and pulled out a white wrapped package that I recognized as the meat he had bought at the mini-mart. He began dropping pieces behind us as we ran.

"Hope that'll slow them down a bit," he panted. "Put something in there to help them sleep."

A loud crack followed by several more pierced the night and I realized that we were being shot at. "Ray they're shooting at us!" I cried. "What are we going to do?"

"Follow me. We're going for that back gate. Keep running!"

We tore through the underbrush. Brambles scratched my face and arms while limbs whipped me as I chased after Ray. We stumbled out of the dense brush onto a small dirt road that led deeper into the woods.

"This way," he called back. "This gotta lead somewhere."

I heard the dogs yelping and barking about two hundred yards back near the garage. Maybe they thought we went in there for cover. Then more shouts. It sounded as if there were two men shouting back and forth and they were closing the distance. A shot slammed into a tree directly ahead of me and that was all the encouragement I needed. We raced down the dirt road and into the darkness. I had the sinking feeling that we were going to die.

We ran for a few hundred yards and then the road dumped into a clearing where a small ramshackle cabin and a tall water tower sat. Parked next the tower was an old white Jeep Cherokee. The cabin was dark and it looked deserted. Ray headed straight for the Jeep and yanked open the door.

"You ever pray, Hemmingway?" Ray yelled.

"Right now, buddy. Right now. Think this thing runs?" I answered holding my sides trying, to catch my breath.

"We gonna find out quick." He yanked open the door and felt around the steering column for keys, of course there were none, so he yanked down the visor, still no luck.

"Shit," he cursed looking around the littered interior. "They gotta be here." He yanked the floor mat out and fumbled under the seat.

With a yelp of triumph, he cried, "There is a God!" He held up a small ring with the Jeep key on it. "Get in!" He pulled his Glock from his holster and placed it on the seat between his legs.

I pried open the passenger door and leaped in as Ray tried to start the old truck. He turned the key and the motor groaned but didn't catch. It ground and whined but still didn't start. Ray gave the gas pedal a few more ferocious pumps, turned the key again and the old Jeep roared to life.

The rear window exploded as Ray whipped the wheel and gave the old girl some gas. I heard the men shouting and dogs barking. They were sprinting into the clearing. I could see two men in black and a big nasty looking dog racing toward us. Ray spun the Jeep, extended his arm out the window and pumped off three quick rounds in their direction.

"Look out!" I yelled as the Jeep headed straight for a huge oak. Ray yanked the wheel as two more shots exploded and the dash splintered in front of me. Damn, I was hit! A piece of the plastic wood-grain dash was sticking out of my shoulder and blood was beginning to ooze.

"I'm hit, Ray!" I yelled.

Ray didn't answer. I grimaced in pain and horror as he rammed the gearshift and mashed the gas. The Jeep sideswiped the tree crunching my door and shattering out the window. I ducked as shards of glass covered me.

"Get down!" Ray yelled over the din of the chaos. "You okay?"

"I'll live. Piece of dash clipped my shoulder."

Two more shots exploded in the night and the Jeep veered and rocked, almost flipping over.

"They got one of the tires! Damn! Hold on, Hemmingway!"

He gunned the Jeep and headed for the dirt road and straight for the two men.

"Holy shit!" I cried as I saw them jump out of the way and into the brush. The big black dog leapt, snarling viciously at the Jeep as we flew past. We hit the road, the Jeep thumping and veering with one front tire blown out and Ray struggling to keep the bucking vehicle on the road. It was our only chance. More shots pinged against the Jeep as Ray fought to keep it on the small road.

"We need to find the fence!" he yelled over the whine of the motor. The road forked and Ray swung the wheel to the right and gave the truck as much gas as he dared with the flat tire. The men had fallen behind but the dog was right by my door, leaping as if trying to tear the door off with his teeth.

"There," Ray pointed. "Hold on." I followed his arm to an opening in the trees and I saw the heavy iron fence. I knew then what Ray intended to do and I grabbed for my seatbelt.

He yanked the wheel and gave the old Jeep the gas. The impact was bone- jarring as metal hit iron at about thirty miles an hour. I was slammed back against my harness as all went black.

# CHAPTER 32

The voice came from a thousand miles away. I was swimming in a fog. "Nick. Hey Nick, come on man."

"Nick!"

I opened my eyes to see Ray slamming his shoulder against his door to open it. He grunted and with one mighty thrust his door creaked and yawned open. "Damn, I rapped my leg real good." He winced and scrambled out and ran around to my side.

"Ray. Shit, I hurt, man. I think I'm bleeding," I said touching my shoulder. My fingers came away wet with blood.

"Yeah, I know. We got to get out of here and fast. Can you move?"

"I don't know," I managed to say. I was covered in glass and felt the shard from dash still embedded in my right shoulder and there was blood—a lot of blood. The windshield was spider-webbed and sagged a mere foot from my face.

I took hold of the shard of plastic and pulled it out wincing in pain as I did. "Shit, Ray that freaking hurt." The whole world was spinning as I ripped off a piece of my undershirt and packed the wound as best I could. It would probably need stitches but that was the least of my worries.

"Did we get away?" I asked, looking back through the shattered rear window.

"Not yet, man. They're coming fast and we got to get the hell out of here now!" Ray barked. "If you can't move, I'll carry you." He wrenched the passenger door open with a loud groan of mangled steel, reached in and helped me out. "Can you walk?"

I felt my legs and they seemed okay. "Yes, I think so. Where are we going?"

"Follow me. We got to find the Hummer and get the hell out of here."

A blast rocked the Jeep and we heard the men running and that damn dog yelping in pursuit. They were coming fast and they were not very far behind us. What was left of the gate lay on the hood of the Jeep in a tangled mess. We were about twenty yards past the fence as the momentum had carried us across the narrow road into a tangle of brush, the rear end sticking several feet out into the road. Technically, we were off the property but somehow I doubted that would stop our pursuers. Two more shots pinged against the Jeep as Ray headed off at a dead run to his right and I followed on his tail. I stole a quick glance over my shoulder and saw two dark shapes running behind that nasty-assed dog. They were just at the point where the gate had been, and I had the sinking feeling that we were going to die real soon unless our buddy above sent us a miracle. There was shouting and barking, and more shots in our direction. Ray was about twenty feet ahead of me sprinting down the middle of the dark country road.

"Come on, Nick. Move your ass!" he yelled over his shoulder.

"I'm here. Just keep going, man. I'm right behind you," I wheezed. My sides ached and my chest felt like it was about to explode, but I kept the pace as we rounded a bend in the road.

Then my heart stopped. A pair of bright headlights cut through the darkness and a dark sedan screeched to a halt directly in front of us. Its roof exploded in a wash of red, white and blue lights. I knew then that we were totally screwed. It was the cops and we had just trespassed, stolen a vehicle and while fleeing, smashed through a gate, along with a litany of other charges, if they had time to think about it.

A voice boomed from a loudspeaker, "Halt! Police! Hold it right there! Face down on the ground and don't move!"

Ray was bent over, hands on his knees panting directly in front of the cruiser. He raised one hand in surrender, still trying to catch his breath. I stopped beside him and raised my hands.

"Get on the ground, get on the ground now!" the cop roared through the speaker. We did as he asked.

"We were being shot at," I cried, lifting my head and pointing behind me. "They … there was … where the hell did they go? There were two men chasing us with guns and dogs. Man they were after us. Honest. We were being shot at."

"Keep your ass down," the cop commanded as he climbed out of the cruiser. The light bars were still flashing against the black sky blinded me and obscured everything else.

I couldn't hear anything coming from behind us. It

was like the men and dogs had vanished into the night, leaving us alone to explain everything to the police.

I rose my head up again to see a tall figure silhouetted in the high beams of the car walking toward us cautiously. The radio squawking on his shoulder was the only sound I could hear besides Ray's labored breathing beside me.

"Officer, we can explain," I pleaded.

The footsteps came slowly toward me, yet the cop didn't say a word. A feeling of dread came over me as I thought he could be working for Black, too. He stood directly in front of me and shined the brilliant beam of a flashlight in my face. All I could see was his black shiny shoes. Ray remained silent and I figured that was the best tact. I waited as the beam of the flashlight washed over me and then flashed on Ray.

"Thomas, are you just stupid or do you have a death wish" the cop asked.

My heart leapt in my throat as I recognized the voice. Deputy Ted Adams. Thank God.

"Ted!" I cried out and started to get up.

"Stay down," he barked. I dropped back to the pavement.

"Ted … Deputy, please let me explain."

Ray spoke for the first time in a bewildered voice, "You know this guy?"

"We met the other night," I said.

"Get up you two, walk over to the car and put your hands on the roof. Now!" he barked loudly. He wasn't at all friendly now.

"But Ted …"

"Do it and shut your mouth, Thomas. You're in enough trouble."

"Do as he says, Nick. Be nice to the cops, man," Ray breathed.

We did as Adams asked, leaned against the roof of the cruiser and spread our legs as he patted us down. He pulled out Ray's Glock and tucked into his waistband. He found my Beretta in the shoulder rig and pulled it out. Adams reached into the car and cut the strobes off. He moved behind us again and said through clenched teeth, "Now you are both going to get in the back of my car and keep your stupid mouths shut until we get clear of this place. Got it?" he growled and I knew he meant business.

He opened the back door of the cruiser, Ray slid in first and I followed. Deputy Adams slammed the door, got in the front and drove off. The crumbled Jeep sat across the road with its cooling engine ticking and hissing. The men and dogs were nowhere to be seen.

"Ted, what the hell is going on," I asked in a strained voice.

"I should ask you the same Thomas. What in God's name were you doing out there?"

"Ted, Chris is missing and I know that bastard Black has her. I know it."

"You know this how, Thomas?"

I told him how we had been drugged and then about Chris disappearing. He already knew about the MG, the blood and that Cobb had arrested me.

"Is this the FBI agent who came to rescue you?" He jerked a thumb back toward Ray. "I don't suppose you have an I.D.?"

Ray piped up, "Sure do, Deputy. Special Agent Ray Montego."

"And you're full of shit," Adams spat out, looking at

us in the rearview mirror. "Cobb called the field office in Burlington and they never heard of your ass. Do you know what they do to somebody impersonating a federal officer? Kiss your ass goodbye, Special Agent Montego. There's a warrant for both of your arrests. Cobb is spitting bullets and wants to have you both for dinner. He is one pissed dude. You pulled one over on him and he is not happy. He's got cars all over this area looking for you as we speak. When we got the intruder call out here, I knew it was you."

"But Ted …"

"Thomas, shut up. Do that for me." He pulled the cruiser off to the side, parked and clicked off the lights. He turned in his seat and looked at Ray and then me, shaking his head. "That was real stupid, Thomas. I told you Black has Cobb in his pocket, or at least I'm pretty sure he does. Now what do I do with you two bozos?"

"Ted, I know Chris is in there and Skyler, too," I said heatedly.

"Do you have any proof?"

"Well, no, but I just know."

"That'll get us a warrant for sure, Thomas. I'll just ask the judge to issue a warrant to search one of our most prominent citizen's estate for two kidnapped people and the probable cause is what? Your instinct? That'll fly. I'll get laughed off the force before I get the pleasure of watching you two go to jail."

"Ted you know bad stuff is happening in there."

"I suspect it. That is the key in my world, Thomas. I suspect it and until I have some sort of proof, it just remains speculation and I can't do a damn thing about it."

"Okay, so how can we help you?" I asked him.

"Help me?" he asked incredulously. "Help me? How can you help me from a jail cell, genius?"

Ray spoke up, "There might be a way."

Adams and I both stared at a grinning Ray.

# CHAPTER 33

The five remaining gamblers sat nervously at the big oak table in the shrouded room. It felt late but they couldn't tell if it was—no clocks were to be found anywhere in the castle and they all had surrendered their watches on arrival. The room had seemed luxurious and comfortable two days ago now felt thick with tension. The game had changed and they all felt it. A foreboding, sinister air hung in the room.

Dieter had left them and said that Mr. Black would join them shortly. He had made a point of silently goading Hartigan with mocking stares. Hartigan, to his credit, ignored the man.

"I don't like the feel of this," whispered Skyler to Miranda, who had for once sat next to him by choice. "I got a bad feeling and I haven't lived this long by not paying attention to that."

She took a long breath and looked at the other three before answering. "Skyler, you have to keep your cool and remember what I told you." It was the first time she had addressed him by his first name and he felt a surge of hope even in this impossible situation. Skyler looked at her as if seeing something for the first time.

"Miranda, why do I have the feeling you know something the rest of us don't?"

She leaned closer to his ear and whispered, "Just keep your poker face on. You know how to do that, don't you? I will talk with you later tonight after everyone has gone to sleep. Leave your door unlocked."

He looked at her curiously with a small smile on his handsome face.

"Don't even dream. That's not going to happen." She sighed. "Do you men ever think of anything but your penises? No, don't answer that. Just leave the door unlocked and try to stay sober." She looked him in the eye pointedly.

"Okay, Miranda. You got it."

Hartigan looked at them with suspicion. "What are you two whispering about?"

Miranda stared back at him steadily. "That's none of your business, Mr. Hartigan." She looked over at Skyler and almost knocked him out of his chair by the seductive smile she flashed for him and everyone else to see.

There was an uncomfortable silence that was broken as the heavy door opened and Sebastian Black strode in. The ever present Dieter was behind him. They both had troubled expressions on their faces.

Black got right to the point. "Good evening, are we ready to begin?"

"Ready as we'll ever be," Chance Hartigan said. "What you got for us Black?"

Black took a moment and then walked around the huge table slowly, pausing behind each chair before moving to the next.

"We now have five. Five people who all want the

prize." He motioned toward the cart with the cases that held their fate.

"One of those cases is empty." He let that sink in as everyone sat in silence. "Good, now I see that I have your full attention. As I said, one of those cases is empty which is unfortunate for one of you because in a short while I am going to ask you all to stand behind the case of your choice. The choice of selection will be decided among you." He allowed himself a small smile and then continued, "That in itself should be interesting. How will you choose? Will you decide to draw numbers at random? Will you let the ladies choose first? Like I said, I am going to leave that choice totally up to the five of you."

Skyler couldn't wrap his mind around this. "What happens to the one who picks the empty case?"

This time Black gave a wide smile before answering. "Why Mr. Todd, that person will die."

Hartigan leaped to his feet and went after Black. "You mother fucker, you are going to be the one—"

Before he could reach Black there was a loud crisp pop and Hartigan flew backward as Dieter shot him in the center of his chest.

# CHAPTER 34

Time froze in the game hall and then the room exploded as the horror of the moment registered. Donna Lee screamed and ran to Hartigan who was convulsing wildly on the carpet. He had what looked like two probes on long wires extending from his chest leading to the device Dieter was holding. Black moved behind Dieter who was holding a large automatic in his other hand that now pointed in their direction. Hartigan gurgled, his legs still twitching as if he had thousands of ants crawling over him. Donna Lee was sobbing and cradling his head while stroking his sweat drenched hair. Skyler sat with his mouth open, not believing what he had just witnessed.

Black spoke over the din. "Not to worry. He'll be fine. Dieter shot Mr. Hartigan with a Taser gun. He was hit with 1.2 million volts of electricity. It is not lethal, but as you can see, extremely effective," said Black calmly. "Now the other gun in Dieter's hand is not so harmless. So I strongly advise all of you remain seated and I will explain the new rules of our arrangement.

"You son of a bitch," cried Donna Lee, still cradling the convulsing Hartigan, her horrified eyes on Dieter.

"He's dying. I can't believe you shot him you Nazi son-of–a-whore. I'll claw your fucking eyes out if I get the chance."

Black gave her a thin smile. "Now, Miss Lee, you are a wildcat aren't you? Mr. Hartigan will be coherent in a few moments. A bit shaken up, but I assure you he'll be fine. I suggest that you refrain from antagonizing my associate here as I'll not always be around to protect you." He looked pointedly at Dieter who remained stoic.

"Black, you've crossed the line. We want out of here and now," bellowed Skyler. "You are totally insane!"

Miranda put a hand on Skyler's arm and forced him back into his chair. "Not now," she hissed.

He looked at her incredulously. "He's going to kill us all! Can't you see that?"

"No, Mr. Todd, not all of you are destined to die—maybe none of you. That will be up to you."

Black looked to Dieter. "Dieter, would you help Mr. Hartigan back to his quarters so he may recover a bit? Now for the rest of you, I hope this served as a lesson. Do not threaten me. That would be pointless, and I promise you, next time Dieter won't be so compassionate."

They watched Dieter lift Hartigan up as effortlessly as he would a child, throwing him over his shoulder and carrying him from the room. Donna Lee chased after them to the door where Black stepped in front of her.

She looked at him and pleaded, "Can I go with him, please? He needs someone with him."

"No, Miss Lee, you may not. Now, sit back down and I'll try and clarify some things for you."

"What exactly is going on here Black," snapped Miranda, seemingly unfazed by what had happened. "You said that one of us will die. That'll get you the needle and you can bet that if you hurt one of us again your little game will be over."

Black eyed her with obvious contempt. "Ms. Bell, I'm afraid that will not happen. You see, we have found the cell phone and the little Sig Sauer that you smuggled in here and so carefully hid in your room."

"What the hell are you—"

He waived this off as if shooing away a fly. "Please Ms. Bell, give me some credit. Don't mistake me for a fool. Apparently, you are not whom you professed to be and you can bet that we will find out exactly what *your* motive is. Actually, *you* can bet your life on it."

Her grey eyes flashed anger and she snapped, "My motive, you asshole, is to win the money. Nothing else, but now it seems as if your motive is quite different than what we thought."

"So, why did you bring the gun, Ms. Bell? My rules were very clear. No cell phones, no weapons and no contact with the outside. But clearly you chose to ignore them. Maybe you should be the next one to … leave us." His eyes pierced hers and she had no doubt to his meaning.

Miranda took a deep breath and sighed in resignation. "Mr. Black, I never go anywhere without my protection, especially in a situation that I know nothing about. I'm careful and I'm sure that you have checked my background. I am who I say I am—nothing more, nothing less. I'm no threat to you. I promise. I've no problem with you keeping my gun and phone but I would like them back upon leaving."

Black's pretense was gone. "That's *if* you leave here Ms. Bell. And that will be entirely up to you." He held up both his hands and then said in a cold, even voice,

"Now the four of you will sit and you will listen as if your lives depended on it." He smiled an evil smile and continued, "Actually your lives do depend on it."

Skyler felt Miranda grip his hand tightly. The only one who hadn't spoken though the entire episode was Lydia Winfield. The old woman sat there staring at her frail white hands on the table in front of her. She cleared her throat as if summoning courage and asked in a small shaky voice, "Mr. Black, are you going to kill us? Am I going to die here? Are we all going to die? Why, Mr. Black, why are you doing this to us? What have we done to you?" She was losing control. You could see it in the tremble of her lips, the lacing and unlacing of her pale fingers.

He smiled at her and began in a soothing voice, "Ahh, Miss Winfield, I'm afraid that you have missed the point. Maybe you have all missed the point and need to hear this. As you probably have surmised, I am a very wealthy man. I do what I please, go where I choose, and have anything I desire. But what drives me is human nature—actually it fascinates me. Years ago, I delved into the lost souls of people much like you who risk all for something so elusive as money and the status of wealth. I found this to be the driving force of evil in most people. Most average, fundamentally good people will often cross a moral line for the chance to live a life they crave. Is money the magic bullet that will solve their problems? Will they become different people? Will their lives become everything they had dreamed of with wealth? Or will it be the bullet that sends them into the depths of a hell that they never imagined?"

He had their rapt attention and continued as if they

were not even there. His eyes had a faraway look as he continued his soliloquy.

"You are not the first, nor will you be the last. I have spent years compiling the data and results of my social experiments and someday the world will take my work seriously."

"Hitler said the same thing," scoffed Skyler. "He was a sociopath much like you and we all know how he ended up."

Unruffled, Black ignored his comment and continued. "Now what we have here," he turned and gestured toward the cart with the cases of money, "is unimaginable wealth, right here in the same room with you. One of you will walk out of here with five million dollars, and yes, one of you will leave with the money. That, I promise you. Contrary to what you may believe, I intend to honor this promise if you all play by the rules."

Miranda Bell stared at him and said, "You said one of us will leave with the money. What will happen to the rest?"

"That will depend on how resourceful you are."

Skyler couldn't keep quiet any longer. "So this is a fight to the death, Black—you and your Nazi friend there, against us."

Black shrugged, "In a manner of speaking, yes, you all could live or you all could die."

In a trembling voice Lydia asked, "How will that be determined, Mr. Black? I'm an old woman and no match for you and your men. Am I to be the sacrificial lamb?"

"No, Miss Winfield, you have every chance in the world of being the one to win. This will be based on luck, wits, intuition and resourcefulness. I'll make this an even playing field—not one of strength, but one of intelligence and the sheer will to survive."

Skyler caught Miranda's eye and she gave a slight shake of her head. "Just listen," she mouthed.

"Okay Black, seeing that we do not have much choice, what's next?" asked Donna Lee in a belligerent tone. "Bring it on, 'cause we're gonna bury your slick ass together."

Black nodded. "As I said this morning, one of you will be departing tonight. One of those cases holds nothing but a card—the four of clubs. This card is called by many as the Devil's Bedpost and is said to deliver bad fortune to any who have been dealt the card. The one who chooses the case that holds the four of clubs will have a special challenge."

"You mean that person will die," blurted out Donna Lee. "Our life depends on which damn case we pick. Is that right?"

"That, Miss Lee, is yet to be determined. The person who draws the unlucky case will have options and they will have a five-to-one chance of survival."

"I don't believe that for a minute, Black," scoffed Skyler. "There's no way in hell you are going to let any of us out of here alive so we can tell the cops who and what you are."

"Believe what you want, Mr. Todd. The reality is that you're not really sure of where you are. Are you sure my name is Black? Think about your credibility Mr. Todd, given your sordid past. Also, if you are the one to leave us, I'm prepared to double my initial offering of fifty thousand dollars and let you walk away with one hundred thousand dollars in cash for your silence and discretion."

Skyler licked his lips and pondered this. He looked at this man. How could he be trusted? Would anyone see the money? Or would they all end up dead as the mice always do when the cat gets tired of the game? One hundred grand was a lot of cash and really, he didn't owe any of these people anything. He would've liked to get to know Miranda better and he would help her if he could—but, a hundred grand? That was tempting. He glanced sideways at Miranada's long crossed legs, one sleek black pump dangled from her foot. He shrugged to himself, it was a toss-up, he decided.

Black went to a teak sideboard and brought out a felt bag which he carried over and placed it in the center of the table. They heard the rattle of something inside when it clinked on the table.

"I have devised the only fair solution to the case challenge. There are five wooden chips in this bag, each with a number on it from one to five. The cases are numbered the same. Each of you will reach in and choose a chip and that will be your case."

"Will someone draw the five million dollar chip?" asked Donna Lee. "Is the game over then?"

Black smiled at her and said, "No Miss Lee, the other four cases hold nothing more than the chance to move on to the next challenge. They will hold the ten of diamonds—another card of significance."

"Are you telling us there is no money in those cases?" Miranda said in an even voice, her eyes unwavering on Black's.

"Miss Bell, there never was actual cash in any of those cases. But I assure you the cash is at hand and will be given to the victor."

They all let that sink in. They had been duped. But

then they'd all been duped before. And they still always come back for more.

"What about Chance," asked Donna Lee. "He's not here to choose. That's not fair."

"Mr. Hartigan will be left with the remaining chip. That is his penalty for his insurgence. This is all by pure chance so it really does not matter if he's here or not. Now, which of you will draw first?"

# CHAPTER 35

Turning down the squawk of his radio Adams said, "I'm listening, Mr. Montego, Or should I say Special Agent Montego? You got a way to set this right without putting my ass in a sling? We've got about ten minutes before I have to check in with Cobb. You can bet your ass that he knows about the breech on Black's estate back there."

"Check in now," said Ray. "Tell him about the breech and that you found the Jeep full of bullet holes with some blood, but that's all. Report that you followed the trail as much as you could but couldn't find anyone out here in the dark. Put out that you saw a red Explorer ripping out of here and were in pursuit. That should keep them busy for a while."

"He'll send everyone in right away."

"That's cool, we'll be gone. Drop me and Nick around the corner by my truck and we'll disappear. They'll never know we were here," Ray said. "We can get this guy, Adams. Just give us a chance. We can go where you can't."

"You two didn't do so hot this time," Adams shot back. "Why should I trust you?"

I piped up, "Because, Ted, we have more to lose. I want Chris back and I suppose in some warped way I would like Skyler back, too. They're family, Ted. Your hands are tied, but I know you want to do the right thing and nail this dude. He's bad and what's worse is that he thinks he can get away with anything. You want a big case, Ted? This is it. Help us and you get all the credit. We'll just disappear."

Ted Adams pondered this, looking straight out into the dark night. The moon shone in the big sky, casting a blue-black hue across the road. There was a nice cool rustling of the night breeze setting the background for thousands of tree frogs in chorus all around them.

"Ted? Yo Ted?" I asked, tapping his shoulder. "We're your only hope. Let us help you."

"I'm thinking, Thomas."

"Yeah, don't think too long. Look there!" Ray was pointing down the road. The flashing from approaching police cars bounced off the sky about a half a mile away and coming toward us in a hurry.

"Shit, where's your truck?" Adams said quickly.

"Up around that corner where the main road meets this one," Ray exclaimed. "Go now and we can jump out before they get here."

Adams already had the Crown Vic in gear and spitting rocks as he wheeled the big car around and nailed the gas. Two hundred yards up he swung the car right and Ray yelled, "Here. Stop here!"

Adams slammed on the brakes and Ray and I rolled out quickly.

Adams yelled through the window as he was pulling away, "Thomas, meet me at midnight at the same place we met the other night. Got it?"

I shot him the thumbs up and we scrambled into the brush where the Hummer was hidden from sight.

"Get down," whispered Ray urgently as the first of two cruisers wailed by with lights flashing in the same direction as Adams. The second car took the forked road where we had just come from. I had a feeling they would converge somewhere on the other side of the estate.

"Hope Adams can pull this off," I panted and slid down the side of the Hummer. I sat on the ground with my back against one of the mammoth tires, trying to get my breath back. Ray was leaning against the hood with his night vision scope, watching the front gate.

"Damn! Deputy Dawg got my Glock. I need that back, Hemmingway. Nobody takes my piece."

"He's cool, Ray. You'll get it back. Is it legal? "

"Sure it is," said Ray not meeting my eyes.

"Ray?"

"Well, maybe some of the paperwork got lost. Hey listen, the point is if we're gonna get this Black, we're gonna need some supplies. And I needs my Glock—that pisses me off. Forgot to ask Barney Fife there for it back, that's all. I like that gun."

"We'll get it back. Now we should get the hell out of here."

"Not yet. Let's sit a minute. They're going to be chasing after their tails for a while looking for that red Explorer. I think Adams is leading them the other way. But I just want to make sure nobody is coming out of that gate and that there are no more cop cars coming this way. Then we go. Nice and easy, and straight the hell out of this county. It's eight-thirty now so we have three hours to regroup and meet your buddy Adams. We got some thinking to do, Hemmingway."

I nodded and closed my eyes for a long seductive minute. I was exhausted. Today was a hundred days packed into one both physically and emotionally. Where was Chris, I asked God. I knew I wouldn't hear the answer but it gave me hope to feel that someone else was in control and possibly on my side. I prayed that she was safe and alive. I might've even bartered a bit. You know the one: if you help us here I'll never do *that* again—whatever *that* happened to be at the time.

"Nick," Ray whispered. "Let's go. It don't look like anybody's coming right now and I don't want to wait too much longer. The cops will be coming back." We climbed up into the Hummer and Ray started the powerful truck. He kept the lights off and rumbled slowly out of the undergrowth and onto the road.

We both held our collective breath. Ray looked both ways and then nailed it getting as far away from Castle Black as fast as we could.

# CHAPTER 36

With a chuckle Black said, "Let the chips fall where they may." The five seated around the table did not laugh. They stared at the velvet bag that held their fates.

"Who will choose first?" asked Black. "All of you have an equal chance."

"What happens then," Skyler asked. "What happens to the one who gets the case with the four of clubs?"

The silence in the room was thick. All five sets of eyes were on Sebastian Black. He seemed to ponder this, not answering right away.

He shrugged and then he spoke, "I have a special challenge for the one who draws the case with the unlucky card. If he or she accepts the challenge and prevails then they would be allowed to continue and we move on to our next elimination. You see, it was beneficial for all of you that Mr. Frascarelli decided to leave us as your odds have improved."

"Is he alive, Black?" Skyler asked. "Or did you—"

Black stopped him with a raised hand. "Mr. Todd, I can assure you that Mr. Frascarelli was quite content with the terms of his departure and do remember that it was his choice to leave us. Not mine." He took a deep breath. "Now please, let us proceed with the matter at hand. Which of you will choose first?"

Before anyone could answer, Dieter entered the room and whispered something to Sebastian Black. Black's eyebrows rose in what looked to be annoyance. He nodded to Dieter and said, "Very well. Have him join us immediately. We're about to begin."

Black turned back to the group and said, "It appears that Mr. Hartigan very much wishes to be a part of this challenge and will be joining us momentarily. In the meantime, while we await his arrival why don't you discuss how you will draw the chips.

"I think Chance should go first," said Donna Lee. "After all, you almost barbequed his ass. It just seems right, that's all." She looked around at the others and they all seemed to nod in assent. Black grimaced at her vernacular.

"Why not," said Miranda. "It's not like there's a clear advantage one way or another. Hell, I'll go next if no one objects." No one did.

"Then me," Skyler said quickly. "I'll follow Miranda."

She gave him a small smile and said, "As it should be."

They all managed a small laugh at this and the tension seemed to ease a bit.

Lydia Winfield looked at Donna Lee and said, "You go next, my dear, I'll be last. I'm not the least superstitious. What will be, will be."

It was settled.

The heavy door opened and Chance Hartigan walked in ahead of Dieter, looking ashen and subdued.

Donna Lee rushed to him, put an arm around his waist and helped him back to his seat.

"You didn't have to do that, you sadistic son-of-a-bitch," Donna Lee screamed at Black. "That wasn't right. How'd you like someone to hook you up? I'd love to use a cattle prod on you and your buddy over there." She nodded at Dieter.

"Oh but I did have to do it, Miss Lee. This is not a democracy and the sooner you all realize that the easier your time here will be. You all need to know that your lives are literally in my hands. Play by my rules and you'll survive. Break them …" He paused for effect. "Break them and there will be severe consequences."

"You're crazy," whispered Hartigan. "You'll regret this. I promise that."

Black smirked and said, "I sincerely doubt that, Mr. Hartigan. Now please, let's proceed. The prize is still very real and you all need to realize that the only way to leave here with anything is to follow my rules."

"You're going to kill us anyway," Miranda Bell said in an even voice. "No one is walking out of here with anything, are they, Mr. Black?"

"That, Miss Bell, is entirely up to you. Now Mr. Hartigan, you go first."

Hartigan pulled the velvet bag towards him, without ceremony reached in, and came out with a blue poker chip. He palmed the chip, not looking at it for several long seconds and then held it out between thumb and forefinger for all to see. The chip was a nice deep blue with a thin white border circling the outer edge and in the center was a bold number "3."

Black smiled and told Hartigan to go over and stand behind case number three on the long cart. He did so without expression. Then he stood back as Miranda

Bell reached in and pulled out number 5. Skyler was next pulling the number 2, and then Donna Lee drew the number 1.

Skyler leaned over to Donna Lee and asked, "Young lady, would you consider switching with me? My lucky number is one. My birthday is 1111. November 11th, and I've always been extremely lucky with that number."

She eyed him with contempt. "Screw you, pops. You get what you draw."

Skyler sighed and shook his head but said nothing. Then Lydia Winfield drew the last chip.

They stood nervously, and one by one, went to the cart to stand behind their respective cases. Donna Lee, behind case number one, was still glowering at Black. Skyler was resigned behind number two. Chance Hartigan stood with his thick arms crossed behind three. Lydia Winfield, passive and quiet, stood behind number four. And Miranda stood in a defiant posture with her hands planted on the fifth and final case.

Black cleared his throat and spoke, "In case you're wondering, I don't know which case holds the four of clubs. This is all purely by chance. Now, Miss Lee, would you be so kind as to open your case?"

The only sound in the room was that of breathing, heavy in expectation. Donna Lee looked down the line at all of them, smiled, took a deep breath and said, "What the hell, guys, you only live once." She reached down and flipped the two hasps up then raised the lid of the aluminum case. She looked inside, picked up a red backed playing card and held it to her chest.

No one spoke.

"Looks like I live to play another day." She laughed and held out a ten of diamonds. The others exhaled with relief before realizing with dread that the odds of any of them pulling the "4" had just increased.

"Well done, Miss Lee. Now Mr. Todd, let's see how your luck is holding out, shall we?" asked Black with a thin patronizing smile.

"You'd love to see me draw that card, wouldn't you Black," snapped Skyler with more bravado than he felt.

"Ahh, Mr. Todd, you are quite wrong about that. I could care less either way. You see, it is about the game, not you. I don't have any bets on any of you and quite frankly I'm glad you all have some passion. It adds to the excitement. Now please," he gestured to the case in front of Skyler.

Skyler took a deep breath and held it as he flipped up the two metal hasps. He paused for a beat and then slowly raised the lid. The red playing card was lying face down in the center of the black felt lined case. Skyler looked up for divine guidance and then, with a deliberate thumb and forefinger, peeled up the bottom edge of the playing card. His shoulders slumped, his eyes closed and he let out a long sigh, resting his hands on the cart on front of him to steady himself.

"Skyler?" Miranda asked.

"Todd? Todd? You okay?" asked Hartigan, who stood next to him.

Skyler didn't move for a second and then looked up and smiled. "Oh yes, I'm just fine." He held up the card for the others to see. "Just fine." The ten of diamonds flashed in the subdued light.

Then there were three.

Donna Lee looked nervously at Hartigan who was next, and now had a one-in-three chance of drawing the fated four of clubs. Miranda smiled at Skyler who winked at her with a broad grin. Lydia Winfield just stood there with her two frail white hands atop her case.

"Now, Mr. Hartigan, it's your turn," said Black. "One of you three will draw the four. Which one will it be? Anyone want to wager? Say ten thousand?"

No one spoke. No one moved.

Black smiled again and looked over at Dieter. "Oh well, Dieter, I thought they were gamblers. Mr. Hartigan, please open your case."

Chance looked over at Donna Lee and then back at Black.

"What happens if I draw the four?" he asked. "I don't think you ever gave us a clear answer."

Black sighed, "Mr. Hartigan, as I said previously, if you are the one to draw the four, you will have a special challenge. It will not be easy and not one for the faint of heart—but certainly winnable. If you pass the challenge then you will move on with the other four to our next challenge. Oh, I almost forgot—the one who draws the four and accepts the special challenge and succeeds, will receive one hundred thousand dollars in addition to whatever other monies you have won."

There was a collective gasp among the five.

Skyler was the first to react. "Hey wait a minute! What do *we* get? That's not fair, Black."

Black sighed, "Mr. Todd, let me put it to you another way. *You* do not want to be in that position. You, personally, do not have the fortitude for that particular challenge. If I were you, I would accept your good fortune and sit back and see what happens."

Miranda spoke up, "This gets weirder and weirder, Black. I just don't see where this is headed."

"You will, Miss Bell. In good time you will all come

to understand that five million dollars does not come easy." He paused and added, "Did you really think it would?" He looked at each of them, clearly annoyed. "Did any one of you think that you would come in here and walk out with five million dollars for a hand of poker? Or maybe a roll of the dice?" His voice rose, "I'm tired of your bickering—all of you. If any one of you wants to leave right now, just say the word. But … you will leave here with nothing!" He rubbed his temples with two fingers of each hand in frustration and anger. "Now either open the case, Mr. Hartigan, or Dieter will escort you out. Am I clear?"

They stood in shocked silence.

"Mr. Hartigan?"

Chance Hartigan looked down at the case in front of him. "Fuck it," he said, and in one motion flipped up the locks with a *thunk thunk*.

# CHAPTER 37

Dieter found Sebastian Black in his study. He was sitting in a leather-winged chair, reading by a comfortable fire. Black carefully placed a silver bookmark in the book, closed it and then looked up at his old friend.

"Is everyone to bed?" Black asked.

"Yes sir. Everything seems to be quiet upstairs."

"I still want a man in that hall tonight."

"Already done." The big man stood rail straight but his face was relaxed.

Black gestured for Dieter to come in. "Dieter, come sit with me. I want to talk to you. Pour us some of that cognac over there." Black motioned toward the small bar built into the bookshelves.

Dieter nodded and poured the fine brandy into two deep crystal snifters. He crossed the room, handed Black the brandy and took the other leather chair facing the crackling fire. The flickering glow reflected off Black's pale face.

Sebastian Black took a deep breath, held up the glass and swirled the rich brown liquid under his nose while gazing into the fire. It was a special Vielle Reserve XO that he had brought in from France.

"Ahh, one of my true joys in life," Black said wistfully. He took a slow swallow and put down his glass.

"Dieter, I believe we have a problem."

"Yes Sir," affirmed Dieter in his heavy English. "I sense that things are getting out of control. It was bad enough taking the girl, but now it seems as if there are other factors we should consider."

Black looked at his ex-commando friend who had served with his father and had remained loyal to his family. For as long as Black could remember Dieter had always been there.

Black gave Dieter's observation some thought and nodded, "I'm not sure who is who out there. I know the girl, Chris, was looking for her Uncle Skyler and that's why this Thomas character is here nosing around. So I understand Todd, and we'll come back to that. I'm fairly certain Ms. Winfield and Ms. Lee are who they say they are. Mr. Hartigan isn't smart enough to deceive anybody so that leaves the mysterious Miranda Bell. What do you think of her, Dieter?"

Dieter sat back in the heavy leather chair with an ease and confidence of a man who feared no danger. He had thick arms, big hands, and a broad Germanic face. His silver hair was short-cropped, military style and he had piercing intelligent blue eyes.

Dieter snorted, "She doesn't flinch. I don't trust a woman who doesn't flinch, Mr. Black. But ... if you wouldn't mind, I would like to maybe—"

"No, Dieter, not this time," Black snapped. "You can't get distracted. Not now. Understand?"

Dieter met Black's eyes with his own and nodded. "Not a problem, Sir, understood."

"Good," Black said as he finished his brandy and

put the snifter down. "If things go well you can have the girl. Be patient."

Dieter nodded in assent and asked, "Mr. Black? Can I be honest?"

"Yes, Dieter, please speak your mind. That's why I asked you to stay."

"I think the authorities will begin to get curious if any more people disappear and we both know that Sheriff Cobb is a spineless shit. He'd roll on you in a minute. I'm getting the feeling that we are running out of time here. We need a plan, Mr. Black."

"We do indeed," mused Black. "We probably should have left the girl well enough alone, but the temptation … the temptation to see just how far the average man would go to find a loved one intrigues me. It is a game within the game, yes?"

"Yes, but I smell trouble. The hairs on the back of my neck are standing," said Dieter. "And I've learned to pay attention to that."

"Why do you think I do this, Dieter?" asked Black, staring into the fire.

"You like the game, sir. You like to put people in … ah, survival situations to see what they'll do and which ones survive."

"I do indeed, my friend. It is all about the game. And I love the power I have over them." He was clenching his fists unconsciously. "But it's always about the game."

"Yes, sir," answered Dieter. He sat forward in the chair and leaned closer. "Mr. Black, I think the guy tonight was Thomas and he had someone with him. My men didn't get a good look, but they said he was big and moved fast. You know, like a man who knows what he's doing. Marco said he could have even been a black man.

We found a backpack with some curious stuff—rope, tools, a flashlight and two spare 9mm clips. There was even a glasscutter. I'd bet it was Thomas with a friend, looking for his lady friend."

"It very well could've been and probably was. I think we might have to get rid of her. Throw them off our scent. We know someone was smart enough to get in here and drug the dogs. Good thing Zeus would rather eat something that's alive," he smiled. They both laughed at the thought of the massive dog chasing his quarry.

"What do you think we should do?" asked Dieter leaning forward, his large hands resting on his knees.

"Take the girl out to the old airstrip tonight and leave her where she will eventually be found. Cobb will see to it that Thomas is the focus of their efforts and I think we need to speed things up here up a bit—wrap this up as quickly as possible."

Dieter arched an eyebrow. "So who goes next?"

Black smiled. "We'll see. It's still the luck of the draw. Is Mr. Frascarelli properly disposed of?"

Dieter nodded and stared at his employer in the flickering firelight for a long moment before asking, "What is it you would like me to do?"

Black finished his brandy and then told his old friend in detail what it was he wanted.

# CHAPTER 38

Chris screamed when the door crashed open. She recoiled in her bunk and tried to cover herself with the rough woolen blanket. Her eyes blinked and tried to adjust when the light suddenly came on and blinded her. She didn't know how long she had been sleeping. She felt like she had been drugged. Her legs and arms felt heavy and her head throbbed.

A powerfully built man dressed in black filled the doorway. He had short-cropped hair and fierce features. He was probably in his fifties, she guessed, and he spoke with harsh authority.

"Get up now," the man commanded in a heavily accented voice. German or Austrian, she thought. He threw a bundle of clothes at her. "Get dressed. You have two minutes. If you're not ready, you'll go as you are."

"Where? Where am I going?" she asked in a weak voice. "Who are you? Why am I here?"

He didn't answer, just turned and stalked out of the foul smelling little room, slamming the door behind him.

Chris stared at the door for a long second and then down at the clothes the man had thrown at her. They were hers, from her suitcase and she didn't waste time thinking about it. She scrambled up and gratefully began to pull on her jeans. What the hell was going on? She asked herself. Where was she and where was Nick? He would never leave her like this. She had deduced that this had something to do with Skyler's disappearance. No doubt there. Was she inside the place where they had him? That would make sense. And who was this creep?

Her thoughts were shattered by the door crashing in once again and the severe looking man in the black military outfit stood in the doorway once again.

"Let's go. Now!" he barked, "and keep your pretty little mouth shut or I'll gag you." He cupped her chin roughly and brought her face to his. "Are we clear? I would just as soon feed you to the dogs." His accent was heavy and his breath smelled of liquor.

"But maybe ..." he paused and looked at her pointedly. "If we could become friends, you and I, things could get a little better for you." He ran a finger down her cheek and she recoiled with horror. It felt like snakes on her skin.

The man laughed—more of a guttural sneer. "Then we do this the hard way."

Chris wanted to vomit but she nodded quickly. "No ... no, please, I won't be any trouble. I promise. Just don't hurt me ..." No sense in putting him on the defensive, she thought. It might come in handy if he didn't think she was a threat and possibly a bonus for him. Her mind was already spinning a way to escape this bastard, whoever he was. He was already using the wrong brain, and if he tried anything with her, he would lose it. She would hurt this guy if she had the chance.

He grabbed her arm as she bent to tie her sneakers and he pulled her to her feet. He was powerful and lithe. His words were clipped and strong and there was no smile in his cold eyes. She knew she had to be careful and would probably have only one chance to get him. Patience, she thought with resolve.

"Now!"

"Okay, okay. Please just let me tie my shoe." He did and then pulled her hands behind her and secured them with a nylon tie. He turned her around and put a black balaclava over her head before pushing her out of the room down some steep steps and into the cool evening.

"If you make a sound I'll shoot you in the back of the head." She felt the cold hard steel of what she believed was a gun. She had no doubt that he'd kill her.

She nodded and said through the hood, "I won't be a problem. Just don't hurt me, okay?"

He pushed her from behind and Chris stumbled. It was hard to walk with the hood over her head and this monster pushing her forward. He had cinched her hands tightly together behind her and her shoulders hurt like hell. Chris vowed to hurt the man. Oh yes, he was going to pay. He pushed her again and she tripped and almost fell in what sounded like a gravel drive but she kept her footing.

"Move it, and if you make a sound it'll be your last," he hissed and kept shoving. Ten steps later he yanked her to a stop and said, "Stop here." Chris obeyed.

She heard a mechanical pop and a noise she couldn't place and then she realized what it was as she was pushed into a car trunk.

"What are you doing? You asshole! You sadistic son-of-a-bitch. I'll get you!" she shrieked and tried to struggle, kicking out blindly. She blacked out as something hard crashed against her skull.

The man looked around and got into the black Chrysler.

# CHAPTER 38

Ray drove into the darkness with his huge hands gripping the wheel and his strong jaw set in a determined look. Neither of us wanted to talk, so we rode in silence for a few minutes.

"Gotta plan, Hemmingway?" he asked staring into the tree-lined road ahead. Tall pines and dense shrubbery loomed all around and over us as the powerful headlights from the Hummer cut through the blackness to more blackness.

I looked over at him and said, "This is a tough one, my friend. I'm a bit out of my depth here. I'm a damn writer, Ray, not a covert ops guy. And shit, Ray, you've been out of Viet Nam over thirty years."

"Hey, don' be dissing me. I still got the mojo."

"That's good, my friend. I have a feeling we'll need all the damn mojo you can muster."

Ray took a deep breath. I could see his strong ebony face in the dash lights. He had a look I had not witnessed before.

"We'll get her back, Nick, no doubt about that and then we're gonna have us a little *Come to Jesus* with this Black fella. The way I see it is we need to get back inside and the faster the better."

"Right," I nodded, "they know we're here now and that could push them to do something neither of us want to think about."

Ray looked at his watch. "Got an hour before we meet that cop. He better bring my gun. I'm still pissed about that."

"Ray, he could arrest you for that gun."

"Details. Anyway we meet Deputy Dawg there and feel him out. Seems he wants to help us. Why is that, Hemmingway?"

"It's personal with him. I think it has something to do with his mother. She worked for Black and something bad happened. He didn't tell me what, but he definitely doesn't like our Sebastian Black and he's convinced that Sheriff Cobb is on Black's Christmas card list."

"So what's he get out of this," Ray asked, braking hard as he took one of the dark corners a bit too fast. "That make me curious. Something about him bothers me. Can't put my finger on it."

"Hey, Adams is okay. He's just a straight hick cop with his eye on glory. Slow down, big boy. I want to die in bed, with Chris preferably, not on this backwater road with you."

Ray looked over at me and smiled with his gold tooth gleaming in the dash lights. "You hurt my feelings. I thought we had something."

"Come on, Ray, be serious. Let's hear what the Deputy has in mind. I agree though, if we can't get the law to go in, then we do, and fast. Every minute Chris is in there is one minute more than I can stand. God, you know how much I love her, Ray."

"I do and we gonna find her."

All of a sudden, the cab of the Hummer was filled

with bright light. "What the hell?" Ray yelled. "It's a car coming up fast with their high beams on. Shit, hope it's not a cop."

I turned in my seat and saw a large dark sedan closing the gap between us. It was about fifty yards behind us. I kept looking hard into the bright lights trying to see if it was a cop. "Ray I don't know. I don't see a roof rack but it could be an unmarked car. He hasn't turned on any lights yet. Wonder why not if it's us he's after."

"Here he comes," said Ray, "and fast." The big sedan shot forward and was only a few feet from our bumper. Ray was going faster than he should have as the small road twisted and turned into the pitch black night, now this car was on our tail with its high beams on.

"Slow down, Ray. See what he does," I said, looking back into the bright wash of lights.

Ray hit the brakes and we heard the sedan's brakes screeching as the driver locked them up so as not to crash into us from behind. I watched the big car fishtail and then straighten. I didn't see any grill lights. This was no cop, no way. He would've had lights and sirens blazing by now. Ray slowed to about thirty miles an hour with the car still right on our tail. Then it swung out into the other lane and pulled even with us. The windows of the dark sedan were tinted and we couldn't see in but knew he could see us. It stayed with us like that for five long seconds on that dangerous road, and then roared past and back into the lane in front of us.

"What the hell was that?" I gasped. The jerk had scared the hell out of me.

We watched the taillights of the big car disappear as the road curved and then curved again, and then he was gone.

"Ray I just got the worst damn chill."

"Thought it was a cop," Ray said.

"No Ray, something was way wrong about that car. I felt it."

"You psychic now?"

"Never mind, can we find coffee somewhere before we meet Adams? I need something hot. My brain is fried."

We drove out of the maze of country lanes and finally hit a real two lane road with a sign that said Riverville 10 mi. Ahead. We found food, coffee and a place to wait behind a 24-hour gas station. And it was time to pray.

# CHAPTER 39

Ray and I sat there in silence, sipping luke warm coffee, waiting for Adams. Ray had tucked the Hummer into the woods across from the road so we could watch without being seen.

"What now, Hemmingway? Let's sketch this out. Skyler's missing, Chris is missing and now we're wanted by the cops. It sounds to me like we're in deep shit."

"Ray, you have a way with words."

Ray crumpled his coffee cup. "What do you think this cop will do to help us?"

"I don't have a clue. All I know is that he's our only friend right now and that he has some sort of history with Sebastian Black."

"He could arrest us on the spot," Ray observed.

"He could have done that already. I think he needs our help to nail the bastard. He wants Black for his own reasons."

Ray grunted skeptically, "I don't trust cops and he's still got my gun."

"Enough about that damn gun. You'll get it back."

Just then, we saw a pair of headlights headed our

way and watched as a Cold River Sheriff's car pulled into the dirt lot across the road and killed his lights.

"That's our boy," I said, grabbing Ray's arm. "Let's go."

"Hope you know what you are doing," he said looking at me intently.

"Not a clue, Kemo Sabé, but let's do this. Right now we really don't have a choice."

"We could get the fuck outta here," Ray said.

"Not without Chris."

"Riiiiiight," Ray reached up and switched off the interior dome light in the Hummer so it wouldn't go on when we opened the door. "Let's move, Hemmingway, but let's make sure it's our boy before we go running up, okay?"

"You bet," I replied, praying it was Adams instead of one of Cobb's boys lying in wait.

We made our way through the brush and across the narrow road to the idling cruiser. A very nervous Adams was waiting, his eyes darting past us and all around as we climbed in.

"Hurry up. You guys come with me," he said quickly. "Grab your gear and leave that truck in the woods. Should be safe there.

We ran back to the Hummer, grabbed our gear and Ray locked it up. Then we sprinted across the road and hopped into Ted's cruiser.

Ted looked back nervously. "Get down until we get farther out."

"Where we going, Ted?" I asked from the back. The rear of the cruiser was a bit crowded with both Ray's huge frame and mine in the back. I was hoping we didn't have to go too far.

"My house. It's just a few minutes down the road. We can get some coffee and talk this out."

"Any chance of breakfast?" I asked hopefully. Real food was but a distant memory.

Adams nodded. "We'll find something and then we need to figure this out. Cobb wants you two characters bad and will stop at nothing until you both are either in a cell, or on a slab."

This revelation bred silence in the car.

My mind was reeling. This had all started out so simple. Chris and I just wanted to find Skyler. Now we were fugitives from a rogue sheriff *and* insane maniac— and we could wind up dead.

"I don't get this, Ted. This is so out of control. Can't we call the State Police or the FBI or something?"

"And tell them what exactly, Thomas? That there's this big conspiracy? Remember they still think you had something to do with your girlfriend's disappearance. You're a wanted man. We need more evidence to go to anybody." He looked over his shoulder at Ray and added, "And your friend here is wanted for impersonating a federal agent as well as aiding and abetting your sorry ass."

I didn't have a reply that made sense and Ray prudently said nothing.

Adams had slowed the cruiser and pulled off into a tree-lined dirt drive that led back through a small stand of pines that opened into a clearing where a small white ranch style house sat with a large red barn off to one side. An aging Range Rover was parked in front.

"Who's here?" I asked in a tight voice looking toward the Rover.

"No one, that's mine. Now get out of the car and inside. And do it quickly."

I looked over at Ray who had not said a word during the short trip. He turned toward me with a grim look on his face and motioned with a quick nod of his head as he unfolded his big frame from the back of the car. We walked quickly from the car up onto the sturdy porch and into the house after Adams.

"Back there," Adams pointed, locking the door behind us. "We'll go back to the kitchen. Can't see the light from the front."

Minutes later the coffee was brewing and Adams was frying bacon at the stove. Ray and I sat uncomfortably at the small kitchen table. I rubbed my temples in frustration and fatigue. It was nearing dawn and the darkness was fading to gray outside the window. The back of the house faced a dense wall of pines and oaks with underbrush that seemed to go on forever. Nobody spoke for quite a while. I could hear the gurgling of the coffee maker and the sizzling bacon. The smell was wonderful, even in light of our situation. I wanted a cigarette even though I had quit a long time ago. It just seemed like a natural thing to do.

"Okay, Ted. What now? What in God's name are we going to do? I've got to find Chris and all I want to do is to get the hell out of this nightmare of a town and get back to Cape Cod."

Ray who had still not uttered a word put his huge paw on my arm and said quietly, "We'll find Chris, Nick. We just need to get back inside that compound. We need a plan. Any ideas, Deputy?" He peered at Adams standing at the stove, still in his uniform with his gun belt on.

Adams was staring out the window above the sink. The smell of eggs, bacon, toast and coffee filled the small kitchen.

"I'm going to lose my badge over this," Adams said

ruefully. "That's all I know. And I'm here mixed up with the two of you. I'll end up in jail myself."

"Not if we're right and Cobb is in the middle of this with Black," I replied, getting up from the table and filling three heavy mugs with coffee. "If he's dirty, and I have no doubt about that, then you could wind up a hero, Ted. Cobb's a bully and he's up to his ears in something very wrong."

"He's a powerful bully, Thomas, and there are a lot more of them than there are of us," Adams said solemnly, plunking down three platters heaped with eggs, bacon and toast.

"Eat," he gestured with his fork, "then we talk, and I'll tell you the whole damn story about our Mr. Black."

# CHAPTER 40

The bumping and jarring shook Chris from a nightmare. She was alone and captive but she knew someone was coming for her. "Nick. Nick, where are you?" she screamed. Was this a dream or was this real? Where was she? Christ she hurt. She could hear the whirr and whine of the tires on the road and music seemed to bounce and echo all around her. Her head throbbed. Violins and pianos roared in a wild crescendo—manic and building. Was she dead, she wondered, still disoriented and blind. *Classical music*—"This must be hell," she confirmed aloud. Then things started coming back. She remembered being shoved toward the trunk of the car and then everything had gone black. Her eyes fluttered against the darkness and she felt the knot forming on her aching head. She had been hit with a club or his huge powerful fist. She felt panic and then anger. That bastard had hit her on the back of the head, knocking her out.

"Let me out of here, you bastard," she screamed and started kicking against the wall of the trunk. "Let me go!" Her legs thudded against the trunk to no avail. Damn classical crap. She kicked harder and the music got louder. He must've turned it up as the strings and piano echoed loudly in her ears.

"I'll kill you, you son of a bitch." She kicked wildly against the lid as hard as she could until her legs could not kick anymore. She began crying. "God, nooo. No. What is happening to me? Help me God. Please help me." She sobbed, her chest heaving and gasping for breath.

Her arms, bound behind her, screamed in pain.

"Help me." She just lay there, exhausted, spent and scared. I'm going to die, she thought. By now Nick must be dead, too. That's the only way he would not be here with me. Oh my God. What have we gotten into? She sobbed some more and then just lay there trying to block out the insanity of the music, and the noise from the road, and the blackness of the pain. It was stuffy and she felt suffocated. No, she was not going to die here in this trunk. Not like this. Not now.

She knew she had to calm down or she would die. She focused on breathing and trying to think. She tried to stretch out as much as possible to ease her legs and shoulders.

Okay, she told herself, relax … think. There was always a solution if you thought things through with a clear head.

Chris started to breathe slowly to try to slow her heart rate. She closed her eyes and went inside herself. She felt her each breath. She felt her lungs fill and expand and her chest rise and then fall. She exhaled deeply and took in long, slow, deep breaths—in and out. She felt her mind clear.

Okay, she thought. She was in the trunk of a car with that German bastard or whatever he was and he was driving somewhere. She would need all the strength and power she had if she were to have a chance. Would she have a chance, she asked herself. Or would he just open the trunk on a dark road, kill her and then dump her body into the woods for the animals to find? Hell, they were in Vermont. They'd never find her body.

Chris felt around in the dark behind her trying to find something to use as a weapon and something to cut the tie that was biting into her wrists. She strained her arms as hard as she could and felt some give in the tie. He hadn't cinched it down completely and she thought she might actually be able to get her hands free. She grunted in pain and tried again. Pulling her arms apart, she managed to slide one bruised and swollen hand free. First one and then the other.

She rolled and brought both aching arms up in front of her and began massaging her bleeding wrists. She reached up and pulled the heavy balaclava off her head and just lay there panting and sweating.

Chris went back in her mind to what she could remember. The last sane thing she could recall was going back to the Inn with Nick. They had made love right there on the couch and fallen asleep in each other's arms. Then she was in that room, locked away, naked and not knowing how she had gotten there. She thought she had been there for a day, maybe more. There was no reference point—no way to tell. The big man had come, knocked her out and dumped her into the trunk of this car. And now here she was. It made no sense. All they were doing was looking for her Uncle Skyler. Damn him!

She lay quiet and soon realized that the music had stopped. Thank God for small favors. She barely breathed as she listened. The tires hummed and she could hear a voice inside the car talking urgently. But there was only his voice, thick and accented. He must be on a cell phone she thought, but she couldn't make out the words—just his muffled voice and then nothing. She remained still, barely breathing, waiting as the car sped on. She heard the *click, click, click* of the turn signal coming from the back taillights, felt the car as it slowed and tried to calm herself. Was this it?

The car slowed, turned and then stopped—the motor still idling. She heard the driver's door open and then footsteps on gravel. Someone was walking away from the car not back toward her. Chris strained her ringing ears and thought she heard a heavy clanking sound. Yes, he was pulling a chain off something. That was it—a chain. Oh shit, she thought, what next?

She heard footsteps on the gravel again and then the car sagged. The driver's door slammed shut.

He must've opened a gate, Chris thought, but to where?

The car moved forward and then stopped again.

What the hell, she thought. What was he doing? She strained her ears and she heard a clanking as if gates were closing and then the rattle of the chain again. He had locked them in wherever they were.

He got back in the car and began moving again. They bounced over a rough gravel surface for a few painful minutes and then the car rolled to a stop and the man shut the engine off.

This was it, if she could surprise him, she would have a chance. She knew she would have only one chance at her captor. He was big and strong and the only way she could come out on top was by surprise. Her legs ached as she tried to stretch and limber her muscles. She twisted her body so she could have a chance to kick. The years she'd invested in Tae Kwan Do gave her hope. Her heart was thumping in her chest and her mouth was dry. He was coming for her. She fumbled around and found the balaclava, pulled it back over her head and then hid her hands behind her. He wouldn't know she was free until it benefited her.

The driver's door slammed shut and she heard the loud crunch of gravel as the man headed toward the rear of the car. Chris heard the jingling of keys and the sound of the trunk lock being turned. She tensed, closed her eyes, and waited. The lid rose slowly and Chris forced herself to lie limp and appear unconscious. It was hard as all she wanted to do was to get out of there. The trunk light washed over her but she remained still. She could feel her captor watching her. Her breathing was shallow. She stayed still, feigning sleep.

"Hey," the man poked at her. "Hey, wake up woman and get out now!"

He poked at her with his gun and she moaned but she didn't open her eyes.

Just a second more, she thought. Be patient. Wait it out.

"Hey," he poked her in the ribs.

Now! Chris thought, and lashed out with a mean kick to her captor's face. It connected. He grunted in pain and fell backward. Chris struggled to get a foothold and to get out of the trunk. She knew one kick would not stop this monster. She threw her legs over the edge and thrust her body forward and out. She stumbled to her feet in time to see the man getting up only six feet from her. He was grinning an evil wicked grin.

"Now we have some fun, girl. You can't get away

from me." He advanced toward her and she could see a menacing smile on his broad face in the wash of the light.

Chris backed up against the rear of the car. "Come get me, asshole. I'm not going down without a fight."

"Have it your way," he said closing the gap between them. "Then I will have my way—with you."

He lunged toward her and in what seemed like slow motion. Chris turned against the car for leverage and snapped out a vicious kick connecting to the side of the man's knee. She heard a sickening crack and saw the man topple in pain, clutching his knee and shrieking, "I'll kill you, you bitch."

She knew she had hurt him. He clawed for the gun he'd dropped. Chris beat him to it and kicked the weapon away just before he grabbed her ankle and pulled her down with a painful crash. Chris cried out as she toppled over her stronger opponent. She rolled away as his fist crashed against the side of her head. Momentum carried her over one more time and she managed to struggle back to her feet. She felt nauseous and dizzy from the blow, but by rolling away she hadn't gotten the full impact. The German scrambled after her, his knee damaged and his eyes wild with fury and pain. Chris did her best roundhouse kick and sent another blow into the side of his head. He crumpled to the ground, dazed and bleeding.

"Fuck you, too," Chris said, leaning back against the car, breathing hard and trying to counteract the dizziness.

She knew she didn't have long. He was not going to be that easy. She had to get the hell out of there. She scrambled over to where she had kicked the automatic and picked up the handgun. She backed away slowly, her eyes still on the unconscious man. He started to moan. Chris stepped over and kicked him in the head again. He went limp.

At this point she didn't care if she killed him or not. It was him or her and it wasn't her day to die.

Chris peered down and looked at him closely. He was alive but seriously out. She had time now.

# CHAPTER 41

We sat in Ted's kitchen devouring the food and drinking coffee as Ted began to paint the picture of a very deranged Sebastian Black. I mopped up the last of my egg with a wedge of toast, leaving the plate dishwasher clean, waiting for Ted to fill us in.

"It goes back a long way," he began, putting his Red Sox mug down on the Formica table. "It started years ago—before my time. My mother told me the story when I was ten or twelve and made me swear never to tell a soul or her life would be in danger, and probably mine, too."

Ted was staring out the kitchen window as he spoke. The morning light crept across the small kitchen bathing us in a warm glow. He seemed to be far away, but he had our rapt attention. We said nothing to break the spell and waited patiently for him to continue.

"Black's grandfather, Augustus Black, purchased the estate back in the late thirties. He bought the castle from a widow whose husband died before he could complete the project and Augustus literally stole it from the grieving widow. Nobody knows the details. That was sometime in the 1930's, and from what Mother told me there were strange things going on out there from the very beginning. Augustus made his fortune on bootlegging and illegal gambling, and local lore has it that he would bring high rollers in for some very unusual high stakes games. I heard one story about a human hunt."

"What?" I blurted out. "What the hell is a human hunt?"

Ray stared and said nothing, his face impassive.

Ted looked at me. "It's exactly what it sounds like, Thomas. They turn a man out into the woods and they hunt him."

"Christ. I can't believe it," I said shaking my head. "I mean how could he get away with that?"

"He had money, a lot of money and you have to understand that this is the woods. There was no FBI up here in Cold River, Vermont. Hell, I'm not sure there was even a town sheriff at the time. But let me finish the story."

"Go ahead," I said, not believing what I'd heard so far. "This is getting good."

Ted Adams snorted and then continued, "Anyway, several times a year a number of big black cars would come rolling through town toward Black's castle. This is a small town and even smaller back then. One black limo would be noticeable, but five or six would definitely be an event. Anyway, they would head out to Black's for the weekend and there would be guards around that high iron fence to discourage anybody from being too curious. Old Bob Winters who lived the closest to the estate says that when he was a boy he remembers his father saying that while he was out hunting near Black's land one morning he saw a group of men chasing a black man through the woods and shooting at him."

"Didn't he call the police?" I asked. "I know this is the back woods, but come on Ted, a human hunt?"

"Winters didn't have a phone and didn't want any trouble. Besides, who was he going to call? Nearest law was in Burlington, fifty miles away. No. People kept to themselves up here. Still do, and most don't have any faith in the law."

"You're the law, Ted," I observed.

"So is Cobb, and he's the Sheriff, and he works for Black. At least I think he does. It certainly explains a lot of things. He sure didn't buy that Mercedes and keep that pretty little wife happy on sheriff's pay. Hell, his suits cost more than my salary."

"I don't like that little fucker." Ray finally spoke, "he's got rat eyes."

"Yeah ... and he's as dangerous as one too. Remember that," Adams said.

Ray smiled, "I'm dangerous, too."

Ted looked at Ray for a long second and had to laugh, "I bet you are."

Ray smiled. I smiled, and then Ted went on with his story. He told us about Augustus Black's two sons and that one had died as an infant. The other son, Charles, was a mean nasty snake of a kid who got worse as he got older.

"What about his wife?" I asked, "Augustus' wife. You've said nothing about her."

"Never heard much about her. Mom said that she only saw her a few times. From what I've heard she was crazy and that Augustus kept her locked away somewhere in the castle. Mom said she saw the white haired woman in one of the top windows a few times and that it looked like the woman was crying out to her. Mom said she couldn't hear anything and the woman disappeared behind the curtains. Mom said it scared the heck out of her."

"This gets creepier but the minute," I said shaking my head. "Okay, we have a psychopath who organizes hunting parties with real people as the prey and a crazy old woman locked away in this castle. Now what of Charles, the son? He must be Sebastian's father."

Ted shook his head, "Not so fast. Charles went away to college and came home with a beautiful young wife. I'm told Augustus was quite taken with Charles' wife. Her name was Mary. They say that Charles would disappear for weeks to go on drinking and gambling binges in Boston and New York. And that left his pretty little wife all alone with Augustus."

"I see where this is headed," chimed in Ray. "Old Augustus had a hard on for the young wife."

"And I bet you'd be right," Ted said. "All I know is that Charles supposedly came home unexpectedly to find his father dead and his wife brutally beaten by an intruder. They were very curious circumstances indeed. Apparently, a robber broke a window out in the study, entered and then killed Augustus, left Charles' wife for dead and proceeded to rob the safe. Funny thing is, that the safe was opened and empty, but had not been forced. Augustus and Mary were found upstairs in separate rooms, both naked. There were signs of Charles' wife having been dragged from Augustus' suite. Charles had staged the whole thing by the time the authorities arrived and he pleaded ignorance. And the cops couldn't prove that he did it or just didn't look too hard. The

Black's were rich and could buy anybody. The kicker is that I don't think Charles knew at the time Mary was still alive."

"But she lived," Ray stated.

"She lived … barely. She was in a coma. She was badly beaten and had severe head trauma on the head but hung on for over a year. She never regained consciousness."

"But where did Sebastian …" I stammered and then it hit me.

"She was pregnant," Ray and I said in unison.

Ted nodded. "She was carrying Augustus' baby and so little Sebastian was born while Mary was still in a coma. Charles was never sure if the baby was his or Augustus', but dutifully took Sebastian home and raised him. Actually he didn't raise him." He looked at both of us with a painful smile.

"What do you mean?" I asked, confused. "Who did?"

Ray answered for him, "Ted's mother."

Ted rubbed his eyes and nodded, "Yes, my mother. Charles Black hired my mother to raise his, or rather Augustus', bastard son, Sebastian. She hated Charles, but she felt sorry for the infant boy."

"What about the mother, Augustus' wife—the white-haired woman in the window?" I asked.

Ted shrugged, "Don't know. My mother said she never saw or heard from her aside from those few times in the window. There were other servants who had been in the household when she got there. Nothing was ever said about her, and as my mother was only allowed in certain parts of the house to care for the baby, she never saw her. She asked Charles about it once and he told her that she was seeing things and that his mother had been dead for many years and that she was buried in the family plot on the estate."

I shivered, "This is too much and way too creepy. Think your mother could've been mistaken?"

Ted shook his head, "She had the eyes of an eagle, Thomas. She never missed a thing. Believe me, I know. She raised me and my sister and we never got away with shit. If she said she saw an old woman in the window then she saw an old woman in the window. I don't doubt any of that."

"What happened to Charles?" I asked.

"Charles was a roamer and roam he did, but when he came home he was relentless in pursuit of my mother. He was smitten with her. He would bring her expensive gifts and tell her how he could make her life better."

"Where was your father?" I interrupted, "what did he think of all this?"

Ted didn't answer right away. He just stared down at his empty coffee mug and I could see something painful building in his face.

"Ted?" I prodded. "What is it?"

I glanced sideways at Ray who remained silent.

Ted looked up at both of us and said in a choked voice, "He was killed."

"Charles?" Ray asked.

Ted didn't answer. He just kept staring down at his hands locked around the mug—his knuckles white.

The silence in the kitchen was thick and we all sat quietly for what seemed like an eternity. I could hear the ticking of the coffeemaker on the counter. Outside, the birds were welcoming in the day with a chorus of song. The sun had pushed dawn aside for the day and washed over the old Formica table where we sat waiting for Ted to answer.

Finally, he looked at both of us and managed to say with controlled anger, "Nobody could prove anything. He was coming home from work one night and they say he was going too fast and missed a turn just a few miles from here. They say he had been drinking. My father never drank. Never. He didn't have any use for it, but they said there was a bottle in the truck and that he smelled of whisky."

I started to speak and felt Ray's vice-like grip on my arm.

Ted continued, "Back then there were no blood alcohol tests—none of the shit we have today so we couldn't prove that he wasn't drunk. Someone started rumors that he was distraught over money. Hell, everybody had money problems back then. We were poor as fucking dirt, barely surviving. That's why Mom took that job at Black's. But he wouldn't get drunk over that—no damn way."

"Charles wanted him out of the way," Ray said.

"Damn right he did," Ted slammed his fist down on the table. "I know the bastard was behind it. Mom knew it too, but for some reason she stayed at Black's."

I looked at Ted and said, "He was holding something over her head."

"That would be my guess. I've been over it a thousand times and the only thing I can figure is that he either threatened her or threatened to do something to me and my sister if she didn't stay. Something died in her when my dad was killed. She was distant and cold, but she went to work every day telling us that we needed the money and that God would take care of things."

"Jesus Ted, that's quite a story."

"It's not a story, Thomas. It's real," Adams snapped, his eyes blazing. "It's my life!"

"Whoa, Ted, I wasn't implying that it wasn't. Honest. I mean it's … just incredible. We believe you," I stammered as I looked to Ray for support. Ray nodded.

I got up with my coffee mug for a refill. "What happened to Charles? Is he still around?" I asked.

Ted shook his head and met my eyes. "A year to the day after my father was killed they found Charles dead in his bed. The Doc said it looked like a heart attack but he couldn't be sure."

We all sat quietly not saying what we all were thinking. The elephant in the room just sat on our table.

# CHAPTER 43

Skyler sat up as if he had been juiced by an electrical charge as something grabbed him from his dream and snapped him back to consciousness. He had been dead to the world after a huge meal downstairs and downing a number of vodkas when he'd returned to the room. He heard it again. There was a soft knock on his door and then watched as the knob turned and the heavy door swung inward. Miranda Bell stepped into the room.

Skyler blinked, "There is a Santa Claus."

Miranda pressed the door closed and eyed Skyler, "Get out of bed and put some clothes on."

"I thought ..."

"I know what you thought," Miranda snapped and flipped on the light, "and that will never happen. Now get up. We need to talk."

Skyler blinked and saw she was not in the mood for playing and did as she asked. He fumbled for his trousers that were in a heap at the foot of the bed.

"What are you doing here, Miranda?" he asked.

She handed him a Coke from the small fridge. "Here wake up."

He accepted the sweating can with shaking hands

and took a long swallow. She watched his Adam's apple bob up and down as he guzzled the soda.

"Okay, I'm awake. What's this about?" he asked in a voice still thick from sleep and booze.

Miranda looked at him as if deciding what to say. She had on a dark *Nike* running suit. Her hair was pulled back in a ponytail and she was barefoot. She looked absolutely beautiful, Skyler thought. There was still hope, he decided.

Miranda spoke in a low voice, "We're all in trouble, my friend, and we need to get the hell out of here."

"What kind of trouble?" Skyler asked.

"Frascarelli is dead."

Skyler didn't get this right away and shook his fuzzy head. "What did you say?"

"They killed Frascarelli."

"How'd you know that?" asked Skyler, trying to understand.

Miranda came over and stood over Skyler who was still seated on the edge of the bed. "I know. Just accept that. I saw the old woman, the maid or whoever the hell she is, rolling Frascarelli's bag down the hall earlier. Now why would he leave without his bag? Tell me that."

Skyler took another long gulp from the soda can. "Miranda, who the hell are you?" He looked up at her with surprising clarity. "Come on now, be straight with me. I can keep my mouth shut when I have to."

Miranda said nothing.

"Come on, Miranda. You just said we are all in danger and I believe you. This gets scarier by the minute here. I'm sorry I ever answered that damn ad. Now come clean with me. If we're in danger it's my life on the line here, too."

Miranda went to the window and pulled back the heavy drape. The window looked out over the moonlit courtyard. She spoke still looking out, "My name is Miranda Aames and I'm a private investigator."

Skyler's mouth opened but said nothing as he stared at her trim back.

"I was hired to look into the disappearance of a man named Malcolm Burke, a very wealthy eccentric from Manhattan. He disappeared last December and the trail led me here. I answered Mr. Black's ad, myself, and got invited. I can be persuasive if need be. And figured out what he wanted to hear."

Skyler nodded, "I knew it. I thought you were a cop or something."

Miranda nodded, "I worked for the FBI, so I do know what I'm doing. Problem is, they found my gun and cell phone and I am flying solo here."

"No you're not," Skyler bounded from the bed. "I know you think I'm a drunken fool, Miranda, but I might surprise you. I can help and believe it or not, I can stay sober. Just tell me what you need me to do."

They heard the heavy footfalls in the hall heading in their direction. All of a sudden, Miranda reached back, ripped her top over her head revealing a perfect set of breasts and pushed Skyler back onto the bed, sprawling on top of him—her mouth finding his in a passionate kiss. She was all over a very confused and suddenly very aroused Skyler Todd. The door crashed open and one of the guards burst into the room with his gun drawn. A very angry looking Sebastian Back was right behind him.

"What the fu …" cried Miranda as she rolled off Skyler and covered her breasts with the sheet.

"Well, well, what do we have here?" Black smiled.

"It appears we have some forbidden romance brewing." His face hardened and he motioned his man to the bed.

"Show Miss Bell back to her room and make sure she stays there."

The man looked at Miranda expectantly and then back to Black.

"No Marco, not yet. You may have her when the time is right."

"Fuck you, Black and you too, asshole," screamed Miranda, scrambling off the bed and grabbing her top.

Skyler rolled off the bed and stood with Miranda in defiance.

Black looked Skyler over and said, "Do you always sleep with your clothes on, Mr. Todd? I think the two of you bear watching more closely. Marco, please, escort Miss Bell back to her room and make sure she's locked in this time."

"What's going on here, Black?" shouted Skyler. "Are we prisoners now? You can't do this!"

Black smiled and nodded to Marco who grabbed Miranda by the arm and pushed her out of the room, his gun held steady at her head.

"Good night, Mr. Todd. We will deal with this in the morning. In the meantime I suggest you get some sleep. You'll need it."

And with that he turned and strode out, slamming the door behind him, leaving a very scared Skyler Todd alone in the room.

# CHAPTER 44

Chris looked down at the now unconscious Dieter and then around in all directions. The night sounds of the crickets and other dark dwellers had been replaced by an eerie quiet. The pre-dawn light was gray and the early spring air had a chill. She shivered and wrapped her arms around herself as her eyes adjusted. There was a squat brick building with a high tower structure next to it about a hundred yards to her left and she could see the shadows of an old truck, piles of dark shapes on pallets, and the hull of a small airplane without wings resting on one wheel.

Everything she saw seemed to be overgrown and in disrepair. To her right she saw a large empty expanse with more shapes of odd-looking mechanical vehicles parked at careless angles. The whole place had the feel of abandonment. It was an old airstrip of some kind, she thought, maybe an old military installation. But how did the German get the key? *Oh shit, the keys!*

Chris ran back to the prone figure, hesitated, and then crouched down to search his pockets. He wore a black military outfit that had Velcro pockets everywhere but she found what she was looking for on the second try and pulled a heavy key ring from his right pants pocket along with a spare magazine for his pistol, which she pocketed immediately. She bent over looked closely at his bloody face, listened to his breathing and found it ragged and shallow. His hideous face was a mask of blood and she knew she had broken his nose with one of her kicks. Oh well, she thought, he would've done a lot more to her if he'd had the chance.

Chris ran back to the car and slid in behind the wheel placing Dieter's automatic on the seat next to her. The car was a powerful Chrysler 300 sedan, the kind that reminded her of a gangster car—black with black leather interior. She looked around her one last time and then she remembered something. He'd have a cell phone. She could call Nick.

Her heart was beating out of her chest as she jumped out of the car and ran back to Dieter who still hadn't moved. She bent down and fumbled with the flap on his shirt pocket. It wasn't there. Must be in his pants, she thought, on the other side where she hadn't checked. She had to roll the big man over to reach it. She hefted and pulled, grunting with the effort, and reaching over his body, found the pocket where his cell phone was. "Ahh, almost," she grunted. And with one final tug she freed it from his pants pocket.

A vice-like grip snatched her wrist and twisted it. Chris screamed in pain as he rolled in the opposite direction pulling her over his body and slamming her onto the ground. The cell phone clattered away in the semi-darkness.

"You bitch. You thought you had me," he hissed as he turned her wrist harder.

Chris screamed out again in horrible pain. "Nooooo," she wailed. "Let me go you fucking animal. Let me go!"

The big man rolled over on top of her and pinned her beneath his body. His face was seething with anger, only inches from hers. She felt his sour breath and the blood from his shattered nose dripped onto her cheek.

"No, little darling. Now I will show you just how much of an animal I can be. Now I will have you, you little bitch." He had her arms pinned and his legs were wrapped around hers. She couldn't move. In a lightning fast move, he let go of one of her arms and slapped her viciously several times. Her head snapped back and forth with the heavy blows. She felt dizzy and began to lose consciousness.

"Nooo," she screamed and tried to spit in his face. She tasted his blood in her mouth and her stomach heaved in revulsion. She tried to buck him off but he was too heavy. He slapped her again and she went limp under him.

"Good," he muttered and stilled for a moment. Her mouth was slack and her eyes closed. "Now, Dieter will have some fun."

He waited a second more and then slowly rolled off her. She was still, and her breathing was shallow and labored. She appeared unconscious. He fumbled with the zipper on her jeans and ripped it down. Then began pulling them down in frantic tugs.

"Now I will have your sweet little ..."

In a move so fast he didn't comprehend what was happening, Chris shot the edge of her hand into Dieter's throat. He screamed out in pain. She hit him again and he rolled onto his side clutching his throat in agony. She followed his roll and jabbed two fingers into his eyes and he screamed again as she rolled back in the opposite direction and sprang to her feet. She yanked her jeans back up, fastened them and moved back toward him. She knew that to run would be foolish. She had to finish him.

"You cunt. I'll kill you," he gasped. "I'll kill …"

He never finished as she kicked him in the face, feeling the cartilage in his nose crush beneath her foot. She saw more blood gushing from his nose. There was a froth of blood coming from his mouth. She knew that he was hurt bad but he didn't quit. The big German rolled away from her, trying to get to his feet, one hand over his eyes. She glanced around in desperation, and in a moment of clarity, retrieved the cell phone, sprinted back to the car, slammed the door, and hit the door locks. The *thump thump* told her they were locked. She fumbled the keys with shaking hands. They fell from her grasp and jangled to the foot well.

"Shit!" she screamed and looked back to see if he was coming but she didn't see anything. She'd left him lying behind the big car. With both hands, she felt around by her feet and finally found the keys near the gas pedal.

"Come on, come on!" she cried in panic as she found the key with the thick plastic fob and tried to fit it into the ignition. The key slid in and she turned it, starting the powerful motor. "Thank God," she cried. "Now please get me out of here." She grabbed the chrome and leather shifter and was pulling it back when the window exploded sending shards of glass all over her. She looked in horror as she saw his bloody face just inches from hers. He had a huge rock poised in his hand for another blow.

"Shit, no way asshole! You're not gonna get me." In terror and a rush of adrenaline, she yanked the shifter down all the way and nailed the gas. Dieter fell away from the car as it fishtailed and swerved, spraying gravel and rock as it gained traction. Chris spun the wheel and headed for the outline of the fence and the gate a hundred yards ahead. She glanced in the rearview mirror but didn't see him. She pressed the accelerator to the floor as the big sedan roared toward the gate.

The big Chrysler crashed through the gate ripping it from its hinge posts, the heavy chain still holding it together in the middle. The gate came down and smashed onto the car as she sped through. The two-piece gate hit the hood and windshield then went over the top as the car lurched through the opening.

Chris had no idea where she was or which direction to head but just went with the momentum. She veered the car to the left and the tires spun trying to gain traction in the gravel of the entrance. She yanked the wheel harder and nailed the gas as the car gained purchase when it hit the blacktop. Then she slowed and straightened the wheel with shaking hands while she tried to get her breathing under control. She'd done it. She had gotten away from that madman, she thought as the headlights cut into the mist ahead and the nightmare faded into the distance.

# CHAPTER 45

I looked at Ray and then back at Ted. We'd decided the only way to find Chris and nail Black was to get back into the estate. Ted admitted that he couldn't and wouldn't trust anyone else in the sheriff's office and he didn't feel they had enough to go to the FBI.

Ted brought out a surveyor's map and a packet of aerial photos and spread them out on the table.

I looked at him in amazement. "Ted where in God's name did you get these?"

"Question is why," added Ray.

Ted shrugged and gave them a small smile. "This day was bound to come and I wanted to be the one to put the cuffs on that psycho and ... my good friend Sheriff Cobb. Let's say this one's for my mom and dad."

We all smiled and Ray said, "Then let's go get this fucker."

The survey map showed the perimeter of the large tract, the roads that bordered it on two sides, and the ominous bog that covered a big part of the woods surrounding the main house. The aerial photos were more help.

"How recent are these, Ted?" I asked.

"I had a friend do them last year as a favor. We were in Storm together and he did some fly overs for me and took some nice pictures."

I looked at Ted incredulously. "You mean you've been planning this for over a year?"

"Much, much longer than that, my friend. I just didn't have the means. I was alone on this remember? We won't have any backup out there." He held up a finger, "But Thomas, if we find something in there, we're calling in the State Police. We are not commandos."

Ray snickered, "Shiiiit. Lot of good they'll do. Don't like cops."

Ted eyed us and said, "No heroics you guys. We're not the Hardy Boys."

"Okay. Okay Ted. Let's get down to it," I said looking back down at the photos and map. Ray went to the counter and poured some more coffee then sat back down muttering something about his opinion of cops.

"Here," I pointed at one of the aerials and drew a line with my finger. "This is the road Ray and I were on. There's the small maintenance cabin where we borrowed that Jeep. See that water tower? And here is where we crashed through that rear gate."

"We can't go in that way," Ray said. "And we can't go in through the front like we did. They'll be onto us now."

Ted nodded and said looking down at the map on the table, "One way would be through those woods. I know it pretty well, my Dad used to take me hunting there. It's nasty terrain, though, lots of brambles and heavy bog."

"What about snakes?" Ray asked. "Somebody said something about snakes. I don't like snakes, mon. Hey that reminds me. Where's my gun? I want my damn Glock back. It has sentimental value."

Ted looked at him. "Is it legal?"

"Sure," Ray said, not looking at him.

Ted shook his head. "I don't want to know." He got up and went down the short hall. A minute later he came back with Ray's Glock, my Baretta and the spare magazines. He handed them to the big Jamaican.

"Please don't make a mess with these. I don't want to end up having to arrest you."

"Scouts Honor," Ray said, smiling now. He planted a kiss on the butt, checked the magazine, slammed it home, racked the slide chambering a round and tucked it into his waistband. "I feel much better now."

I shook my head and said, "Now that we've had this Hallmark moment can we can get back to business here?" I asked. "We know where we have to go. We know why we have to go and that only leaves the *how.*"

Ted smiled and said, "Now that's where I come in. I think I have an idea. We're going to drive right through the main gate."

We stared at the young deputy.

"We're going to what?" I asked not quite believing what I'd heard.

Ted smiled at us. "It is so simple and so obvious that it could work. I've been thinking about it. The woods are dangerous, and more than likely have video and audio surveillance. I doubt Black would leave a lot to chance even though chance is his game."

"So we walk right in and say hello?" I asked. "Come on, Ted, what you been smoking?"

"And he didn't share with us," Ray said with a straight face. "Not polite not to share."

Ted paused a long moment and looked at us. "Think about it guys. Who would be allowed access? The cops, right?"

Ray shrugged and I nodded for him to continue.

"They had a break in last night and it would be my official duty as a deputy to investigate. Right?"

We nodded again.

"Okay so I take my cruiser out there, they let me in and I'm able to investigate the situation."

"What about Cobb?" I asked, "He'll wonder why you have this interest all of a sudden."

"I'll tell him that I saw something last night by the back gate and wanted to check it out. Hell Thomas, the Jeep was wrecked out there and the gate was smashed. It's my job to be curious and unless Cobb gives me a direct order to stay away, it's up to me to investigate."

Ray looked at him and said," Okay, where does that leave us? I want to get in there."

"You and your buddy here," he jerked a thumb toward me, "will ride in the trunk of my cruiser. Hopefully I'll be able to ride out to the rear gate without too much trouble. When I think it is safe I will pop the trunk and you two roll out and hide until dark."

"Ted, what about those damn dogs," I asked. "They are none too friendly."

Ray nodded emphatically. "Fuckers mean. I'll shoot them if they come near me."

"We can deal with them," Ted said, massaging his temples, suddenly weary. "Damn what time is it anyway?"

With that we all glanced at the kitchen clock. It was a little past eight and we'd been there in Ted's kitchen for many hours now.

"What time you got to go in," I asked.

"My shift starts at nine. First I want to make sure you both knew what you could be in for."

Ray smiled indulgently at Ted. "Teddy, no offense, but I been involved with shit you wouldn't know existed and believe me, I can take care of myself."

Ted looked at me. "What about Mr. Thomas here?"

"Don't worry about me, Ted. I've been around this guy long enough to know how to keep my head down and I know how to take care of myself."

Ray nodded and gave me a shot in the arm. "Hemmingway here can be a badass when he wants. Him and his girlfriend into all this karate shit and they both know their way around a gun."

I nodded at Ted. "Chris and I both shoot at the range and I have a Concealed Weapon Permit."

"Maybe in Massachusetts," Ted said, "but not here, and that last thing I want is you two cowboys shooting up the place. More than likely somebody innocent will get hurt."

"Ted, innocent people are already hurt," I said looking down into my cold coffee. I was thinking about Chris and praying she was still alive. "All I want from you guys is five minutes alone with this Black. Five minutes."

"No way, Thomas, this guy is going in alive and he will answer for all his crimes," said Ted raising his voice.

"I'm not planning to kill him, Ted. I just want to scare him a bit. Ray understands, don't you, Ray?"

Ray nodded.

Ted Adams stared at both of us. "No, Nick, you are not going to touch Mr. Black or I will arrest you. Are we clear?"

I smiled and nodded. "Sure Ted, not a hair. Crystal clear. Now when do we go?"

# CHAPTER 46

Sebastian Black had not slept well. He'd had this foreboding feeling that everything was beginning to unravel. He picked up the phone by his bed and punched in the speed dial for Dieter's cell. He should have been back long ago and Black wanted to make sure the girl was disposed of. One less detail to worry about, he thought.

The phone buzzed seven times before going to voicemail.

"Hello, leave a message." The pre-programmed tinny voice said.

"Dieter, call me at once. We have much to do today." Black slammed down the receiver. Dieter always answered his phone. Annoyed, Black picked the phone back up and called Marco who answered at once.

"Yes?" the accented voice of the Mexican said in a groggy voice.

"Marco, have you seen Dieter this morning?"

"No sir. I'm headed to breakfast now," Marco replied. "He should be down there drinking coffee with his wife. You want I should have him call you?"

"Yes, damnit, tell him to call me immediately. I'll be down shortly." He slammed the phone down.

Minutes later, Black strode into the large kitchen to find Marco sitting with Dieter's daughter, Kristen, eating breakfast. Dieter's wife, Helene, was preparing the big morning meal for the guests at the stainless steel stove.

"Good morning," Black said in a clipped tone, looking all around the kitchen. "Helene, where is Dieter? Has he been here?"

Marco scrambled up, dabbing at his mouth with a napkin. He glanced over at Helene, who looked worried, and then back to Black.

"He didn't get back yet, Mr. Black."

Black stared at him with his hands on his hips, "What? What are you saying, Marco? He left to take care of a small errand for me last night and should have been back well before now."

Marco held up his hands, "I don't know, Mr. Black. All I know is the car's not here. I checked the garage after I talked with you."

Helene broke in, kneading a dishtowel in her trembling hands, "I have not seen my husband, Herr Black, and I'm worried. It is not like him to not come home at night. Where did you send him?"

Ignoring her, he faced Marco. "He went to the old airstrip. Find him," Black hissed between clenched teeth, "Now!" He turned to leave and then looked back at Marco.

"I want the guests in the game room with the doors locked. You can serve them breakfast in there and keep them there until you hear from me. Put Sanchez in there with them and tell him if anyone gives him any trouble to shoot them. He would enjoy that. And you find Dieter. Am I understood?"

"Yes, sir," a stunned Marco replied as Black strode

out of the kitchen. Helene sat and put an arm around her daughter.

Five of them sat at the big round table not saying much. Skyler tried to engage Miranda in conversation but she ignored him and concentrated on her coffee. Confused, he went back to his breakfast and waited for her to break the silence. The others ate in uneasy silence. Finally, Chance Hartigan had had enough.

"What's happening? Why are we in here?" Hartigan asked of Sanchez who was seated off to the side by himself drinking a cup of coffee and reading a newspaper, watching them. Sanchez was a big guy, dark hair, dark eyes, and he had ex-Ranger written all over him, down to his Blackhawk jumpsuit adorned with a big ugly automatic prominently displayed in a holster on his hip. Sanchez looked up at them, but said nothing. He shook his paper in annoyance and went back to his reading.

"Come on, Paco, where's Black," asked Skyler in a raised voice. "We're getting tired of all this hocus pocus around here. You Sabé English?"

Sanchez looked up, smiled and still said nothing, but slid off the stool he'd brought in. He carefully folded his newspaper and placed in on top of the stool. Then he walked over to where Skyler sat with the others.

Skyler shrunk back in his chair as Sanchez, well over six foot, loomed over him and leaned close to Skyler's trembling face. He had a dead smile and flat black eyes.

"The name ain't Paco, asshole," he said in a soft voice and backhanded Skyler across the face. Skyler flew sideways knocking into Lydia Winfield sending both of them tumbling to the floor in a shower of plates, cups, food and silverware. Food splattered the wall, the carpet and their faces.

Chance Hartigan leaped to his feet "Hey, leave him alone."

The muzzle of Sanchez's automatic appeared six inches from his face.

"Or what? Come on. Please. How does Clint Eastwood say it? Make my fucking day."

No one moved. Sanchez and Hartigan stayed frozen, daring the other for more than a thousand heartbeats.

Then Sanchez smiled at all of them, the gun not wavering. Skyler scrambled to help the shaken Lydia to her feet. Miranda Bell put her arm in front of Donna Lee and pushed her back into her seat.

Sanchez backed away, the gun still trained on Hartigan who was the biggest threat, and said in a calm voice, "I'm going to say this one time and one time only. My orders are to shoot any of you who becomes a problem." He paused for effect.

"You what?" screamed Donna Lee, straining against Miranda's arm. "You fuck. You're going to shoot us?"

"Only if I have to, pretty lady. I would much prefer to have you in one piece," he said with a chilled smile and a wink.

Hartigan moved forward slightly and Sanchez looked quickly back at him. He thumbed the hammer back on his pistol.

"You want to be the brave one, no? Maybe I shoot you now to show I'm serious. You want to be the first to die, Gringo?" Sanchez pushed the muzzle of his pistol under Chance's chin.

"No, Chance," cried Donna Lee, looking at Hartigan. "Do as he says."

Sanchez smiled and nodded, "Smart lady. Now all of you sit the fuck down and shut up. The next one gets up will die. Sabé?" He pushed Hartigan toward his chair with the gun and snarled at him, "You will be the first one, tough guy. That, you can count on."

Skyler and Lydia managed to get back in their chairs. Skyler used a linen napkin to dab at a bit of blood by his mouth. Miranda stared at the big Mexican with open hostility in her eyes but she was composed. Hartigan reluctantly found his seat while Donna Lee sat rigid, breathing hard and seething with anger.

Sanchez, gun in hand, stood looking at them with a dark scowl on his face. The spark had gone out of Lydia Winfield, the terror of the fall and the threat against their lives was too much for her. She sat quietly and appeared scared, staring down at her trembling bone white hands. Donna Lee had her arms through Chance's and was trying to calm him as he glowered at Sanchez—breathing heavily. Skyler just sat and stared ahead—his lip swollen and bruised.

Miranda Bell spoke up, "Mr. Sanchez, why don't we all calm down."

He shot her a look, "No, you calm the fuck down, lady. Now all of you listen to me very carefully. You will all sit at that table and keep your mouths shut." He held up the automatic as if admiring it, then looked back at them with a smile and said, "The next one who opens their mouth will get a bullet in the back of the head. Sabé?"

He looked at Skyler, who was still staring straight into nothing, and then said with a sneer, "I'll give you Paco, asshole. Just give me a reason."

No one said anything.

# CHAPTER 47

Chris pulled the Chrysler off the road and onto a small dirt track that led into the tree-lined forest. It was time to gather her thoughts. She closed her eyes for a second and awoke three hours later with a start as the warm morning sun bathed her tired face through the dirt-streaked windshield. Running a hand through her tousled hair, she tried to recount the previous night's events. What the hell was going on, her mind screamed at her.

She was cold and shivering and realized that she was covered in shattered glass from the broken window. It crunched beneath her as she wriggled around and opened the heavy door. Hundreds of small diamonds of window glass poured out onto the grass as she got out of the car to stretch and brush herself off.

God, she hurt. Every bone and muscle in her body was sore as she took a quick inventory. Nothing broken, but her clothes were mud-stained and torn from the battle with the big German. She felt her pockets and found the cell phone she had fought him for. The gun she had taken from him was on the passenger seat.

Without thinking, she powered the phone on. There were seven new messages. She knew she wouldn't be able to retrieve them without a password so she went to the text messaging in-box. There were three from the same number:

*Is the deed done? B.*

*Where are you? B.*

*Call me immediately!!!!! B.*

Chris didn't think the German would be calling anybody anytime soon. She punched in Nick's cell number and groaned when it went right into his voice mail.

"Shit!"

She snapped the phone shut then opened it again and redialed Nick. Same result; *"Hi this is Nick. I am not able to answer now but please leave me a message and I will get back to you as soon as humanly possible. Thanks for the call and have a great day."*

Chris clutched the tiny cell phone in frustration. "Nick? Nick, where the hell are you? I'm okay, but not sure where I am. Call me at this number … please hurry Nick. I'm scared."

She leaned against the fender of the Chrysler and tried to think. What would Nick do? He could be in jail for all she knew or worse. She shook her head, *no, I'm not going to think like that.* She thought a moment trying to figure out what Nick would do in the same situation. Then she punched in a series of numbers.

The cell buzzed three times before Ray's wife Jazz picked up.

"Montego Rays," answered a thick Jamaican voice, clearly irritated. "We not open for breakfast. Call back later."

"Jazz? Jazz, it's me, Chris!" she managed to get out in a flood of relief. It was so good to hear a familiar voice.

"Chris? That you, honey? Where you at honey? Everybody be looking for you."

Chris could hear the crash of pots and pans, harried voices and running water in the background. She could see Jazz standing there, all 300 pounds of her in one of her signature electric Mumus, ready to pounce on the kitchen help.

"I don't know where I am, Jazz. I got away."

"Away from who, Darlin'? Who be messing wid you? Hey! Watch what you doing!" she screamed again at someone. "Damn kids. Sorry Honey, the kitchen boys won't live the day. Who be looking for you, girl?"

"I don't know Jazz, we came up here looking for my Uncle Skyler and …"

Jazz spat, "That worthless—"

"I know, I know, Jazz, but we're here somewhere in Vermont and I don't know where Nick is."

"He be with Ray now, Darlin'. Mr. Nick called yesterday and Ray jumped in his big-assed truck and flew up there all commando like, wherever the hell there is."

Something crashed in the background that sounded like glass and Jazz screamed again, "That gonna come out of your pay you stupid skinny ass. You wait till I'm done here. I'm gonna barbeque you and have you fo' lunch." A second passed, Chris could hear commotion on the other end of the line and then Jazz came back.

"Damn help. Okay Honey, now tell Jazz what you need."

Chris bit her lip and said, "Jazz, just give me Ray's cell number."

# CHAPTER 48

We gathered around the trunk of the Crown Victoria as Ted shuffled some gear around to make room for us. He had road flares, a green ammo can, a first aid kit, two pump shotguns and what looked to be a bio-hazard suit.

"How we gonna fit in there," Ray asked with a raised eyebrow. "I don't wan' to be smellin' Hemmingway's ass there, mon."

"You're no sea of fragrance, yourself," I said.

"You'll make do," Ted said to both of us. "You want to get into the compound, and this is your only way. Just keep quiet and be ready for anything." He handed Ray two plastic looking objects that looked like small hand grenades. Ray smiled and nodded, putting them in his pockets.

"Know how these work?" Ted asked.

"Flash bangs, mon. I used to use these on my kids," Ray replied with a straight face.

Ted couldn't be sure Ray was kidding so he added, "Pull the pin, and toss. Cover your ears and shield your eyes."

We nodded.

"They make a hellava lot of noise and whoever has their eyes open will wish they hadn't. Lot of blinding light and noise, but no real explosive power."

Ray nodded happily and looked at me. "We good to go, right Hemmingway?"

He loved this shit, I thought and said, "Riiight. Remember one thing, Ray—actually a bunch of things— they have dogs, cameras, men with guns, and who knows what else in there. Piece of cake, the way I see it."

They both eyed me, two ex-commando types and me; the writer, lover, philosopher, and all that crap. But Ray also knew that I could take care of myself when it counted. Hell, I had been in the Navy, what I could remember of it.

"That's *your* lady in there, Hemmingway," said Ray, giving me a shove, "and *my* good friend, so get your ass in the trunk. Maybe we save her and leave you there."

"Funny man. Maybe when this is done we have the immigration man check your visa."

Ray chuckled, "Call him, mon. He's my cousin. Oh, and I gots me a cousin over at the I.R.S. too, my man. Maybe I tells him to look real close at some writer guy I know who don' pay any taxes."

I put both hands up, "Whoa, we're all brothers here. No need to get nasty."

That broke then tension and we all had a small laugh.

Ted looked me and Ray up and down. "You guys ready?"

"Ready as we'll ever be, Teddy. Just get us inside," I said.

Ray patted his Glock lovingly and nodded, "Let's go, Deputy Dawg. Jus' give us the word when we need to roll out and disappear."

Thirty minutes later, the dark blue Crown Victoria slowed as it approached the front gate to the Black Estate. Ted rode with the window down and left arm resting on the window frame. He thumped hard twice on the outside of his door with his hand. That was the signal. They were there.

"Be ready for anything, Hemmingway," Ray whispered. He was curled up poised toward the trunk latch. I was spooned behind him. It could have been a tender moment had it not been Ray.

"I'm following you, big guy."

He pushed back against me, "Give me some room here and don't you be liking this shit. I'll hurt you."

"No worry, you're way too hairy, mon."

Ray mumbled some expletives I couldn't quite make out and then he whispered with some urgency, "Now be quiet, we need to know what's going on out there."

"Cool."

Ted yelled his identification into the box mounted on the gate pillar. I strained my ears and heard the squawking of the box but couldn't make out the voice. The car was idling. Ray was quiet. Then I heard Ted say something and slap the outside door with his hand three times. There was the whirr of a motor and clanking of metal as the iron gate opened. The car moved forward, tires crunching on hard packed gravel. *We were in.*

The plan was for Ted to drive up to the main house, get out and politely ask Black permission to look around where the intruder had been last night. They would wait silently in the trunk and pray those dogs were not around. Ray had dumped a full tin of black pepper all over the back of the car and along the outside rim of the trunk.

All he said to Ted and me was, "I hate those fucking dogs, mon. They don' like pepper."

I was glad he didn't put the pepper inside the trunk or we'd both be sneezing.

If all went well with Black they would proceed toward the back gate, passing by the watershed and tower. That's where they had hoped to roll out. There was a ninety-degree bend in the road as it entered into the dense forest and the cabin was right there off to the right. It could be a great place to roll out of the trunk unseen and plan from there. We knew we had to be concerned about cameras and sensors but Ray said he had that covered with some hand-held gadget he had in his backpack. It made me wonder how connected Ray was and that maybe he was a real bona-fide spook. I was real glad he was my friend.

The car stopped and I heard Ted open the driver's door. The car dipped a fraction and then rebounded as he got out. I crossed my fingers and prayed. We were in the mouth of the dragon.

I heard the door of the house open and a clipped voice, dry as leaves, said, "Good morning Deputy. What may I do for you? I'm Sebastian Black."

My heart pounded and my mouth went dry. I knew that voice. It was the rude son-of-a bitch I had met on the porch at the Inn yesterday morning—all that seemed like weeks ago now.

Ted was in the moment and all charm when he called back up to Black. "Good morning, sir. I'm here to look over the scene of the break-in last night if I may."

There was a long silence. What was wrong? I wondered and nudged Ray. He elbowed me hard in the gut and I decided to stay quiet.

Black finally said, "Deputy Adams, may I ask who sent you out here? I spoke with Sheriff Cobb this morning and he said *he* would come out himself sometime this morning. I'm a bit confused by your presence."

"Yes sir, Mr. Black. I understand. I live just up the road and wanted to make sure you were safe. I'm on the way into town and to the office. It was my own initiative, sir. I was out here last night after it happened and thought I could see more this morning."

"Well Deputy …"

"Adams. Sheriff's Deputy Ted Adams, sir. At your service."

Goddamn Teddy. I almost laughed aloud. He was hinting that he would like to work for Black and that he wanted to make sure he paid personal attention to this matter. He was trying to reel the bastard in.

I could see Ted standing there with his hat in hand and an "Aw Shucks" look on his countrified face.

There was a long pause as I imagined Black staring down at Ted from the porch trying to determine if the man before him was telling the truth.

"Very well, Deputy Adams, I'll have my man, Marco, accompany you to the rear of the estate. You can see where they appropriated one of my maintenance Jeeps and proceeded to crash though the rear gate. The Jeep is still across the road."

"That won't be necessary, Mr. Black. I can get to the crime scene myself."

"Nonetheless, Deputy Adams, I insist. There are …" he paused, "dangers here that most are unaware of."

"What dangers, Mr. Black? I'm not sure I understand." Ted's voice took on an edge. He was the cop again.

"We have dogs, of course, and there are many types of snakes. Most of this land is swamp."

Ted took some control back. "Mr. Black, I'll only be here a half an hour or so and then I'll be out of your hair. Would you mind putting the dogs away? I know these woods and all about the critters. I was born here. Just put up the dogs for half an hour."

There was silence and another long pause. "Agreed," said Black.

A big door creaked and I heard some muffled voices; they were too far away to hear what they were saying. But the tone was short clipped and irritated. Ray was barely breathing next to me but I could hear my own heart thumping in my ears.

Then Black spoke, "I will have Mr. Sanchez join you at the rear gate. Marco is tending to other matters, I'm told. Stay straight on this gravel road and you will run right into the gate. I warn you Deputy Adams, stay in your car and don't venture out until my man gets there."

"Understood, sir. I'm glad to be of service."

All right, Teddy, I thought. Enough is enough. If he made his ass kissing too obvious, Black would get suspicious.

Ted had the good sense to get back in the cruiser and start the engine before he made a fool of himself.

I breathed a sigh of relief and said to the back of Ray's neck, "Looks like he pulled it off."

"We ain't home yet. Now shut the fuck up," Ray hissed.

I did.

The Crown Vic crunched along the gravel utility road and after a long minute Ted yelled back to us, "Get ready. We're getting close."

Ray thumped the trunk twice to signal that we understood.

"Ten seconds," Ted shouted and popped the trunk latch from inside. Ray held it down in place until the *go* was given.

I could feel Ray tense as I gathered my senses. This would be a fast and furious couple of minutes while we found cover and prayed we didn't get spotted.

"Now!" shouted Ted.

Ray pushed open the trunk and rolled out onto the dirt road with a grunt. I followed not quite as gracefully and ended up with my foot caught on the lip of the trunk for a second and was dragged a few feet by the moving car and then fell in a heap. Ray was already on his feet. God, he pissed me off sometimes. My leg screamed in pain and I quickly prayed I hadn't done any serious damage. Not now.

I rolled over and got to my knees then felt myself being lifted up. Ray, looking around in all directions hauled me up with one hand and barked, "Move it, Hemmingway. Follow me and keep your head down."

"Got your pack?" he asked as he ran ahead of me.

"Yeah," I managed to say while trying to keep up with him.

Ray darted into the woods to the right of the clearing and stopped behind a large thicket of laurels. "Stay here," Ray said and disappeared into the brush.

I knelt there not knowing what to do. The leg that got caught on the trunk throbbed but I could move it and at this point the adrenaline was winning the battle over any pain I might have felt. We were in, so now what? Chris was my priority. Nothing else mattered. Once she was safe then we would deal with any legal bullshit that arose. I just didn't care and besides, Ted was on our side. Of course, Ted could be occupying the cell next door to Ray and me.

I heard a rustle and Ray was back. He crouched down next to me and said in a low voice, "Now listen to me, Hemmingway, we gonna make a break for that cabin. I didn't see any cameras or sensors. I'm thinking they are to keep people out not for people already inside, but stay low and stay behind me. There is a back door that leads to a storeroom that's unlocked. Let's get inside and wait for Teddy to make some noise."

I nodded, "Lead on, Tonto."

He shot me a glare and kept moving. He hates it when I call him that.

We stayed low and circled the small clearing. Ray stopped several times and motioned for silence. Satisfied, he moved on with me right on his heels. We came around the back of the small clapboard cabin and I saw a small four-by- six porch with a couple Heineken bottles on the rail and hundreds of cigarette butts growing out of an old stone urn by the steps. Must be the break area for the health club, I thought.

Ray took the steps in one bound and pushed the door open enough to slip in and I followed. We were in a storeroom off a short back hall. Huge coils of wire, mops, tools, brooms, paint cans, and cases of light bulbs were stacked on metal shelves lining one wall. On the other side sat an old, white refrigerator that hummed in defiance of its age. Maybe it was the source of the mysterious green bottles on the porch.

There was a small dirty window that faced the clearing and the porch. Ray motioned for me to stand to the side and stay put while he moved forward to check the rest of the cabin, his Glock poised as he crept down the hall. I saw him stop at the corner, look one way and then the other and then back at me.

"We good. Nobody home," he said sliding his Glock back into his holster. "Stay away from any windows, mon."

I nodded and opened the refrigerator and smiled. "There is a God."

I handed Ray an ice cold bottle of beer and cracked a can of Canada Dry for myself.

He eyed the soda can carefully. "Scared me, mon. Thought you was going for the beer. Have to hurt you." He twisted off the cap and drained the bottle in one long glug. "Ahhhh. I needed that."

I watched his Adams apple bob as the cold beer washed down his throat. I could taste it myself. It would be ice cold and foamy and good. And I would want twenty or thirty more, so I happily gulped my ginger ale. It did suck being an alcoholic. There was never that excuse of a special occasion, or "I deserved that one." No, that was a poison I'd have to live without and the key word there is "live." I knew that if I took a drink after all these years it would be all over and so did my good friend Ray. He'd kill me before the booze would with Chris right behind him.

Thinking of her immediately brought back my anxiety. "What now?" I asked.

"We wait. Teddy gonna make some noise and we wait for everybody to head back there and that's when we go back to the house."

"How many you think there are?" I asked.

"Hard to say, mon. I'm thinking three or four and

remember he got those fucking dogs. I'll shoot them before I let one get his teeth into my ass."

I smiled at the image of Ray running for his life with a big dog nipping at his ass.

"What so funny, Hemmingway? I hope one of those dogs takes a liking to your ass. We see how funny that be." He tilted the bottle and drained the last bit of delicious-looking foam from it. He eyed me from behind the tilted bottle and smacked his lips.

"You suck, you know that?" I said.

He wiped his mouth with his sleeve. "Yup, but you love me."

It was then we both heard a low beep. We froze, listened, and there it was again. An almost inaudible beep was coming from the pocket of my jumpsuit. My phone, *holy shit!* I dropped the empty soda can and grabbed for my phone. I opened it, almost dropping it in my excitement. I flipped open the Motorola and it said that I had two new messages.

"Ray … I got some messages. I thought the battery was dead long time ago." I pushed the key for voicemail and it asked me for my security code.

My heart sank when Sheriff Cobb's voice came through the speaker, "Thomas, you are in a world of shit. I strongly suggest you and your fake FBI friend turn yourselves in immediately." His tone softened, "I know this is way out of control and that this is not all your fault. I just don't want you getting hurt out there, understand? Now, come on in and we can talk about it. I'll be waiting." Then he clicked off.

"Fuck him," Ray muttered. "Who the next one from?"

"Give me a second." I hit the cue for the next message

and almost dropped the phone when I heard Chris's voice.

"Nick? Nick, where are you? I got out. I don't know where I am. Oh God, Nick I hope you're okay …"

"Chris," I screamed into the phone forgetting for a second that this was a voicemail. Ray moved next to me and was listening as we heard Chris say she was okay but that she was not sure where she was. Then the signal began to fade as the little power I had died.

"Damn it, Ray," I cried in frustration. "Chris …"

"Chris is alive, my man. That's what we focus on. Wish your phone didn't die."

I looked down at the dead phone in despair. "Ray, give me your cell. Come on!"

He pulled his phone from a pocket and checked the screen. "I got no signal out here, mon."

I grabbed the phone out of his hand and started to punch numbers and then realized that I couldn't retrieve the number she'd called me from anyway—my phone was dead.

# CHAPTER 49

Chris leaned against the car and squinted into the midday sun. She looked at her bloody, dirty hands and shook her head. So much had happened in the past 48 hours. Here she was with a stolen car, a stolen firearm and a wild story of being kidnapped by some big German whom she assaulted and quite possibly killed. They had come up here to Bumfuck, Vermont to look for Skyler and then all hell had broken loose. She had no idea where Nick was, or, for that matter, where she was. And really, she did not know for a fact that Uncle Skyler was even here or had been.

I could go to the police, she thought, kicking at a bottle cap in the dirt. But wouldn't they think she was nuts? Or worse, they could be in on this. Great, who else? The FBI? Jazz had said Nick was with Ray and that was somewhat comforting, but she hadn't been able to reach either one of them.

She leaned back and closed her eyes. The sun felt good on her face. God, she would kill for a bath and a cup of coffee. Then her heart stopped as she heard tires crunching on the dirt behind her. She whirled in panic to see the nose of a silver and blue Vermont State Police car, with its tall antennas, pulling down the dirt lane behind the Chrysler and blocking it in. Her eyes darted around her and she realized that there was nowhere to go. It was truth time.

"Stay where you are," the deep voice boomed from the speaker as the car ground to a stop six feet from where she was standing. One big man in sunglasses filled the windshield behind the wheel. There didn't appear to be anyone else in the car.

Chris raised her hands and dipped her head in resignation, afraid to hope. Stick a fork in me, if he's in cahoots with her abductors I'm done, she thought. If not, thank you God.

"Please turn around and put both your hands on the roof of the car."

Chris turned and did as he asked. She heard the door of the patrol car open. "Are you alone, young lady?" he asked. She nodded.

"Are you hurt?" the trooper asked coming up behind her.

"I ... I'm not sure," she said slowly, still leaning forward against the car. "I was kidnapped and attacked. I just managed to get away."

"You can turn around now, young lady. Everything's going to be okay. I'm a cop." His voice was firm but not threatening.

She looked at him. He was a big sucker, probably six-three or four, with blond hair and dark aviator glasses. He had a nice face, she thought. He didn't look like a prick, but looked concerned. If not for the situation, she would have thought him handsome. His uniform was all spit and polish and the patch on his arm told her that he was a Vermont State Trooper, an expert marksman, and that his name was Roberts.

The air seemed to leave her as she slumped down the fender of the car and sat with her back against the front tire. "God, am I glad to see you," she managed to whisper. "It's been a long night."

She was more than ready to let someone else take care of this mess.

# CHAPTER 50

They sat, not looking at one another, not uttering a sound—afraid of what was to come next. Sanchez had retreated back to his perch on the stool at the bar. It wasn't really a bar, just a slab of marble protruding from the wall where he'd placed his coffee cup.

The man's cell phone buzzed. He answered it immediately, "Sanchez."

He listened for a minute and then replied, "Yes, sir. I'll tell them and then I'll go out to the rear gate." He listened for several more seconds and then snapped the phone shut. He slid off the stool and approached the table where the five sat.

"Mr. Black wanted me to tell you that he was sorry for any inconvenience and that he will join you shortly."

Hartigan hadn't calmed down. He pushed back his chair and stood to face Sanchez who had his gun out, poised by his side.

He smiled at Hartigan, "Please Senor', it would make my day."

Hartigan stood with his hands defiantly on his hips.

"You don't scare me. What the fuck's going on here? Are we prisoners? I demand to know."

Sanchez leveled the big handgun right at Hartigan's head. His eyes were coal black and unblinking.

He looked at Hartigan with an amused expression and said, "You demand? Gringo, really? You fucking demand?" Sanchez walked closer so the barrel of the ugly automatic was a mere six inches from Hartigan's face. "You demand? Let me tell you something, my friend, you are only alive right now because Mr. Black wants you alive for reasons of his own."

His voice went up a pitch, "Me? I'd love to put a bullet between your eyes, Mr. Smart Guy. Or maybe cut your throat with my K-Bar." He tapped the knife sheath on his belt. "I may still do it when Mr. Black is done with you."

Chance Hartigan stood there eye-to-eye with Sanchez and didn't even blink. He said with surprising calm, "When that time comes, Mr. Sanchez, I would hope you give me the benefit of a fair fight."

"Guy's got some balls," Skyler muttered to no one in particular. Miranda kicked him under the table.

Sanchez smiled. "We'll see, Mr. Smart Guy, we'll see, when the time comes …"

He turned and looked at the rest of them. "Now, Mr. Black says for you to stay put for a few minutes and that he'll be down shortly. Try to behave yourselves." He chuckled to himself and left—the heavy oak door closed and they all heard the distinct click of the lock.

Hartigan put his hands on the table and said quietly, "We have to get out of here and fast. They're all crazy."

"Exactly how, Chance," asked Donna Lee. "We're locked in this tomb that has no windows. There is only one big-assed door and it's locked. What's the plan?"

A voice came from behind them. "Plan? Plan for

what, may I ask?" Sebastian Black appeared out of nowhere. They hadn't heard him come into the room.

Skyler, mouth open, managed to stammer, "How ... how did you do that?"

"I didn't see you come through the door," Donna Lee gasped.

Hartigan, back in his chair, leaned back and crossed his arms as he eyed Black, "He didn't. Did you, Mr. Black?"

Black just smiled. "That is immaterial. I'm here and we need to move our game along."

"You've got to be kidding," yelled Hartigan. "After all that's happened here you still want to play games? I don't believe you. You got some nerve."

"What exactly has happened here, Mr. Hartigan? I'm confused." He held up his hand to quell any response. "Please give me a minute to explain things and then you can decide if your perceptions are correct or not. What do you all say to that?"

There was a murmur from the group and then Miranda spoke up, "Mr. Black we are dying to know what you're up to here. Oops, maybe a bad choice of words. Anyhow, we have been asking and no one has been telling. Now, we feel like we're prisoners."

Black's face was an impassive mask but everyone could see he was losing patience. He chose his words carefully, "All of you came to me. All of you signed a contract when you arrived agreeing to participate in a social experiment to which you would be paid a minimum of fifty thousand dollars. Now," he paused, "think about this. Everything you have done and been exposed to is part of this experiment. You are not prisoners, Miss Bell, as you so vehemently think. You are free to go. No money, but you are free to go. That was and is still the agreement."

"Just like Frascarelli," Skyler asked. "We know something happened to him."

"You do, Mr. Todd? And how exactly do you have that knowledge?"

"Someone saw the maid wheeling his bag out yesterday. Why wouldn't he have taken it with him when he left?"

Black looked at Skyler with a bemused look on his face, "His bag? Mr. Frascarelli chose to have us ship it UPS for him. He had a satchel with him that he was more concerned with and we offered to ship his bag to him at no cost. He accepted. That is what you saw. Now, when you get home any of you are free to call him to assure yourself of his safety. Now," he clapped his hands, "let us get to the real matter at hand."

Hartigan stopped him again, "What about that commando goon, Sanchez? He said you were going to kill us all. Hell, he said he wanted to kill me."

Black laughed. "Mr. Sanchez still thinks he's in a war somewhere. My apologies. He's a good man and loyal, but I'm afraid a bit overzealous. He will not hurt any of you. I promise you that. Now please, let's move along to the next challenge. Actually, first we have the special challenge for Mr. Hartigan." Black looked at him and said, "remember that I told you this would be the toughest and that you can opt out. But then you are out. No money. You will leave with nothing."

"Yeah, I heard you before. Bring it on," said Hartigan.

Black was quiet for a long moment, looking them over one by one, and then finally he said, "Good. Now that we understand each other, we can begin." He pulled a large revolver from his jacket pocket. The five stared at him with open mouths. He held up his hand for silence. He took a few steps toward the table, leaned over between Lydia and Miranda, and quite deliberately placed the handgun in the center. No one said a word as he stepped back.

As if addressing a classroom he continued, "That is a Smith & Wesson .357 Magnum revolver. It is reputed to be one of the most powerful handguns made to date." They all just stared at him. He reached into his other pocket and came out with his fist closed and then opened his hand slowly to reveal one large brass bullet in his palm.

"And this, my friends, is a .357 158 grain XTP hollow point round." The room was quiet.

Black bounced the round in his hand and looked at Hartigan. "Now Mr. Hartigan, you are asking yourself 'what does this have to do with me?' My answer to you is 'everything.'"

They waited for Black to drop the bomb.

Black smiled at the group and walked back over to the table. He carefully placed the round upright in front of Chance Hartigan.

"Mr. Hartigan, in front of you is your chance to remain in the game for the five million dollars. You were the one to draw the four of clubs, now this is your chance to remain in the game," he paused. "Or not."

Hartigan looked horrified at his host. "What the hell are you talking about, Black? You want me to shoot somebody? You're insane, you know that?"

"That's debatable, Mr. Hartigan, but the fact remains. No, I don't want you to shoot anybody. I want you to pick up the pistol, load in the round, spin the chamber, put it to your head, and pull the trigger. Then we'll see just how much of a gambler you really are."

"You gotta be kidding," shouted Skyler. "That's total insanity."

"You can't do that," cried Donna Lee, grabbing Hartigan's arm. "Chance, you're not going to touch that gun. I won't let you."

Hartigan shook his head as if trying to clear his thoughts. "You mean Russian Roulette, Black? You want me to play Russian Roulette?"

Black just stood there looking at Hartigan—an amused expression on his face.

"Let me get this straight. If I don't blow my brains out all over everybody here then you will give me a hundred grand and let me stay in the game?"

"That's about it, Mr. Hartigan. So ... are you in or out?"

"If he doesn't do it, I will." They all turned to Miss Lydia Winfield.

"What? What are you saying, Lydia? This man's crazy," said Skyler. "You can't do that!"

Lydia smiled and patted Skyler's hand. "Yes, I can, sweetie. I can do anything I want. I'm not afraid to die and that's what this is all about. Am I right, Mr. Black?"

Black smiled at Lydia and said, "Yes, Miss Winfield, you are exactly right. Would you risk death for all that money? That's what it all boils down to. We first have to see what Mr. Hartigan decides to do."

Hartigan stared at the bullet in front of him and then reached out and picked it up.

# CHAPTER 51

I was standing to the side of a small window in the storage room, peering out. "Shit, I can't believe I missed her call.

"Calm down, mon, it means she's alive. Now we go find her if she's here."

"What is Teddy doing out there?" I asked in frustration. "We need to move."

"Right now, mon, we don't need to do anything but wait. We don't want to go running into a hornet's nest. Let Ted do his thing. You just be ready to move when I say." He looked at me. "You good?"

"Good."

Ray moved to the hall and crept down its length. "Stay here. I'm going to check the front. You watch the back." I nodded and went over to the window. The woods beyond the small clearing where the cabin sat were thick with tangles of brush and tall pines and oaks that gave it a dark, ominous look. I decided that I would not want to try and go through those woods.

My mind went to Chris and I felt an immediate stab in my gut. All I saw was the image of her next to me in the MG, laughing and in love on our trip up here, her short hair blowing in the breeze, the light freckles across her pert little nose and the contented comfort of her hand in mine as we laughed at the absurdity of our mission to save Skyler. We both knew Skyler was beyond saving, but he'd been harmless enough in the past. I was afraid that had all changed.

It had started out as an adventure of sorts. The writer in me being drawn to things like this. But this was much more than any of us had bargained for. Chris was missing now, we weren't sure if Skyler was even here in Cold River, but everything kept pointing to this Black character. It felt right and if there wasn't anything to hide, why all the resistance to us looking for him? It all pointed right here.

Ray came back down the hall and said, "All clear, mon. Now we wait. It shouldn't be long now."

As if on cue a loud explosion rocked the windows of the cabin, followed by another, and yet another rumbling boom.

"Teddy likes those flashbangs, too, mon," Ray smiled and tapped me on the shoulder, "Showtime. Follow me and keep your head down."

"You bet, Kemo Sabé."

Ray looked back at me and said, "I find out what that means and I don't like it, they be calling you Hop-a-long. Now, come on."

"Wrong show," I chuckled and ducked his backhand just in time.

We ran out the back door and, staying close to the cabin, sprinting to the south corner. Ray put his hand up and stopped. We heard the roar of an ATV coming fast from the direction of the house and then the barking of the dogs in pursuit.

"Damn Ray, thought we had the dog thing under control."

"Too late now, mon. As soon as they pass by, we go. I want to check the garage first. The upstairs might be a good place to hold a prisoner where nobody be looking."

I put my hands on my knees, panting, my sides aching. "Right behind you."

The ATV grew louder as it approached and screamed by. It was driven by a tall man in black with a rifle slung across his back. Three snarling dogs were right behind him at a dead run. Ray swept me back with his arm. "Stay back. Don't want those dogs getting sight or wind of us now. Wait. Now, when I tell you, get behind me and don't stop until we reach that garage, and stay to the side of the road."

"I'm with you."

Ray waited a beat and then said, "Now!"

We sprinted around the cabin and headed for the gravel road. Ray slowed the pace when we came to the road, looked both ways, and then continued to his left toward the house and garage. My heart was beating out of my chest as I tried valiantly to keep up with him. We rounded a bend and there was the garage about fifty yards ahead. It was a huge two-story stone and wood structure that was larger than most houses. There were six massive double doors with an entry door on each end—the bay door, closest to us, stood open. Must be where Black's man had gotten the ATV, I thought. On the side of the building, we saw a steep stairway leading to a landing on the second floor.

"Which way?" I asked between gasps.

Ray looked up and then back to the front of the garage. "Up," he said, "but I don't want to be caught on those stairs. Let's see what's inside. There must be a way up in there.

Hugging close to the building, we made our way to the open doors and slipped inside the dark bay. There were two more Honda ATV's. Ray straddled one then unscrewed the gas cap and shook the bike. He was rewarded by a sloshing sound. "Sucker's full. Nice of them. We probably gonna need these. Ever ride one, Hemmingway?"

I shook my head. "But, I learn fast."

"Hope so. Let's keep moving."

Ray swung off the ATV and walked quickly to the back of the bay where there was a sturdy looking door. He tried the knob and it opened.

"This way," he said as he disappeared through the opening. There was a long hallway that ran the length of the structure with doors that presumably led to each bay with several doors on the opposite side.

Ray pulled on one that was locked. "Bet one of these leads upstairs."

I nodded and pointed, "How about that one?" There was a heavy oak door that was larger than the others. It had a small intercom box mounted on the wall next to it.

"Right." Ray jogged over to it and tried the knob to no avail. It was locked. He looked around for something to pry open the door. The hall was immaculate, no hope there, and then he brightened.

"Hemmingway, get back to where those ATVs were. I saw some tools on the bench. Get me something to pry this lock. I could shoot it out but I don't want to make any noise or waste the ammo. See if there's a crowbar or a big screwdriver. And bring a hammer if they got one."

I was already on my way back to the bay. I found

a workbench on the back wall that had tools in outlined places on the wall. After a few moments, I saw a black crowbar propped up in the corner next to a sledgehammer. I grabbed them both and was back to Ray in under a minute.

He grabbed the crowbar and growled, "What took you so long?" Then immediately went to work on the doorjamb.

I might've said something about his mother's lineage.

Ray managed to get the tip of the crowbar between the door and the jamb and ripped it open with one loud splintering crack.

"Too bad, "he said, yanking open the door. "Was a nice door."

The stairwell behind the door was flooded with a shaft of sunlight from a window at the top landing. Ray drew his Glock and crept up the stairs with me close behind. He stopped halfway to listen, nodded, and then motioned for me to move up. It appeared to be empty so far. No one came charging onto the landing with a gun, no alarm bells were going off—only the ones in my head, along with the hairs standing on the back of my neck. What would we find up here, if anything? Chris? Was she still alive?

Ray hit the landing, flattened against the wall and held up his hand for me to stop. He peered around the corner. Satisfied that we were alone, he nodded.

"Clear," he whispered. "Let's go."

We went in and saw a large open living area with two well-worn couches, a big TV, a small kitchen and several cots against one wall. Everything was neat and tidy and the place was empty. No dishes in the sink, the beds were made, and the ashtrays on the wooden coffee table were clean. Ray went to one of the large windows and looked out, scanning the parking lot from side to side.

"We still good."

"Ray," I said in a quivering voice. I was pointing to a door to the left that had a hasp and padlock hanging open on it.

"Stay here," he commanded and walked quickly over and opened the door. Of course, I was right behind him.

"Chris?" I called out, pushing past him. "Chris?"

"Room's empty," he said, switching on the light from the outside wall.

The room was a small, bare windowless cube that was empty with the exception of a metal cot with a jumble of old blankets and a small dirty pillow on it. We both stared for a second and then I rushed over to the cot, pulling the blankets back in a fury. I picked up the stained pillow and put it to my face.

"She was here, Ray. I can smell her. I know she was here and not too long ago."

Ray nodded. "Look around. See if she left anything—a message or something."

We looked around for several minutes to no avail, but I knew Chris had been here. I felt her presence, her smell. It's just something you know about the person you love. I sat heavily on the bunk that groaned under my weight. I put my head in my hands.

"Ray, what have we gotten into here? I feel so helpless."

He came over and put his huge paw on my shoulder. "Come on, Nick, we gotta keep moving. She's not here, so the house is next.

# CHAPTER 52

All eyes were on Chance Hartigan as he held the long brass bullet between thumb and forefinger, staring at it. He was making the most insane decision of his life. He looked from the bullet to Black, who just stood there stoically—no expression on his face, no flicker of emotion in his eyes.

Donna Lee broke the spell. "Chance there's no way in hell you're gonna do that. He's crazy, man." She held out her hand and pleaded, "Please, Chance, give that to me. Come on, we don't need the money that bad."

Chance looked at her and snapped, "It's not about the money, Donna Lee. It's never been about the money for me." He looked back at Black. "No, I just want to beat this bastard at his own game."

"Nooo, Chance, it's not worth it," Donna Lee persisted, but the fight in her was gone. She could see that Chance had made up his mind. She slumped back in her chair with a pout and a piercing stare at Black.

Chance looked around at the others seated around the big table, giving each a slow and deliberate stare. It was as if he was seeking their approval before deciding to cross the line between sanity and a world they knew little about.

Chance reached out, picked up the gun and expertly flipped the cylinder open, spinning it several times. He dropped the shell into the chamber and snapped it shut.

No one said a word.

Hartigan spun the cylinder again.

He looked up and said to Black, "This is what this whole thing is about, isn't it, Black? How fucking primal are we? Huh?" He looked at Skyler, "Would you do it, Todd? No, you wouldn't in a million years. What about you, Miranda? Come on, tell me." His voice rose and he turned back to Black. "What about you, Black?"

Chance shook his head to his own question, "No, you wouldn't know the fear of not having money. You never spent a day in your miserable, pampered life, hungry or needing a job."

Black stood there with his arms crossed and said nothing.

Hartigan looked closely at the weapon in his hand, turning it over, inspecting each minute detail. And then he slowly turned and pointed it at their tormentor, their master of ceremony, Sebastian Black. Black didn't move a muscle as he stood with his raven-like eyes locked on Chance's—not on the gun. He knew Hartigan wouldn't pull the trigger—it was against the rules.

"Kill me, Hartigan, and you lose. You'll die and there will be no money," Black said still holding Hartigan's penetrating stare.

"Fuck it," Hartigan said. Small beads of sweat formed on his forehead while his prominent Adam's apple bobbed up and down. His tongue darted snake-like over dry lips as his bloodshot eyes searched again and caught each of the others for a brief second. At that precise moment, they all knew he was going to do it.

Hartigan brought the gun up to the side of his head, pressed it hard into the skin on his temple, and held it for what seemed like an eternity. His hand began to shake, and sweat ran down his forehead as he held his breath—one long, sweet breath that he knew could be his last. Then he yelled out, piercing the heavy air with a scream that came from the depths of hell. He closed his eyes, tightened his finger on the trigger, and they all watched in paralyzing horror as the hammer fell precisely on the waiting cylinder.

Everything moved in slow motion. Donna Lee screamed and grabbed for Hartigan who sat there holding the smoking .357. The deafening explosion filled the heavy chamber and the air was filled with screams of chaos and horror. Hartigan was still for one long second and then he slumped over onto the shocked Donna Lee—very dead.

Donna Lee screamed and fell backward, pushing herself away from the bloody mess as he slid sideways and landed on top of her. The side of his head was blown completely away where the powerful .357 slug exited. She kept screaming as she saw she was covered with blood and brain matter. She tried to push Hartigan's heavy mass off her.

Miranda had pulled Skyler off his chair and down with her. Lydia Winfield had passed out and was lying face down on the table with her mouth gaping open.

The room was thick with the smell of cordite. Miranda scrambled up, looked over the table and scanned the room. Black was gone. Where did he go? She wondered. Miranda wished she had her gun as she turned, checked the room the way she had been trained to. Black had disappeared.

Miranda looked down and grabbed Skyler's arm. "Listen to me very carefully and don't say a word." Her voice had taken on a controlled command.

He nodded with numb understanding.

"We need to get out of here before that maniac kills us all. Do you understand me?" She took him by his shoulders and looked into his bloodshot eyes," I need you to focus and I need you to help me. Understand?"

He nodded and straightened with resolve. He said in a level voice, looking at her, "Miranda, you can count on me. I was not always a drunk. I can do what needs to be done. What do you want me to do?"

She pointed, "Check that door and see if we can break it down. Donna Lee, get up and tend to Lydia. Do it now!"

"I can't," Donna Lee wailed scrambling to her feet. "Chance, Chance what have you done?" She was staring down at his bloody head, hyperventilating and sobbing uncontrollably. "Noooo, Chance, no."

Miranda stomped over to her, and slapped Donna Lee hard across the face. "Donna Lee, listen to me. You have to help me if any of us are going to get out of here alive." Miranda shook the panic-stricken girl again, "Come on, Donna Lee, I need your help!"

Donna Lee looked at her and finally nodded through the snot and tears. Miranda reached over and brushed the girl's hair back from her face.

"Skyler, get over here and wet one of these," she commanded, throwing him one of the table napkins. "Come on man, move it!"

Skyler moved to her side immediately and dabbed

one of Black's fine linen napkins in a tumbler of ice water. Miranda grabbed it and began cleaning the blood and tissue from the girl's face and hair.

She glanced back at Skyler. "Drag Hartigan over there." She pointed to a spot against the wall a few feet away. "And put something over him. Nothing we can do for him now, the damn fool. Skyler, pull him by his feet." Skyler had never touched a dead body before and thought he might get sick but did as asked.

He bent down, took hold of Hartigan's feet and began to tug the man's body across the blood-stained oriental carpet. Hartigan was a big man and Skyler strained and puffed but finally moved the body out of the way.

"Donna Lee, tend to Lydia. Splash some water on her face. Try to rouse her. Damn I hope she didn't have a heart attack. Get her some water." Miranda Bell was in her element and fully in command. Skyler was relieved that someone else was in charge. Donna Lee appeared to be still in shock.

The girl started to babble, "I ... I can't." Miranda turned the girl by her shoulders and hissed through clenched teeth, "Donna Lee if you want to get out of here with your pretty little ass intact, you'll do as I say. Now tend to Ms. Winfield!" She pushed the girl toward the old woman slumped on the table. Donna Lee hesitated but then straightened and looked back at Miranda and Skyler.

Brushing her hair back with a trembling hand she spoke with resolve, "I'm okay. I'm a tough North Carolina girl, remember?" She moved in the direction of Lydia Winfield and said as if building confidence, "I'll take care of her."

Miranda nodded at her and then turned to Skyler. "We have to get out of here. I wish I knew how Black disappeared so fast. You take that side. Look behind the drapes. If you see anything that looks like it could be a door let me know." She began inspecting the room that was shrouded in heavy drapes and tapestries. "There has to be some sort of panel. We know he didn't come in through the door.

She came to the marble shelf where Sanchez had left his coffee cup on, stood back and looked at the wall. This was it. She gripped the face of the marble shelf and pulled. It didn't budge—solid as a rock. The wall behind it had an ornate wooden frame that looked like there should have been artwork inside and it seemed to serve no purpose. *This* had to be it, she thought. This was just about where they saw Black when he had appeared and this niche would've been close enough for him to have darted into when the gun went off.

"Skyler, over here," she grunted as she pulled hard against it. It didn't budge.

Skyler hustled over, out of breath, and asked her, "What've you got?"

Miranda tugged at the shelf mantle again and then banged her fist down on it. "Damn, I thought this was it. Maybe there's a secret catch or something."

Skyler stood back and looked over the small recess behind the shelf, leaned forward and pushed on one end of the marble. There was a loud click as a man-sized opening in the wall swung outward.

"Come on, let's go," she yelled, and gave Skyler a tight smile. "Nice work."

Before Skyler could bask in his glory, Donna Lee called over, "Excuse me … hey, guys?"

"Donna Lee, for Christ's sake, get Lydia up and let's get out of this room." Miranda snapped. "Carry her if you have to."

I think Lydia … I mean … she ain't breathing. Oh shit, she's turnin' blue and she's cold. Oh shit," she wailed, "I think she's dead, too."

Miranda raced over and felt the side of Lydia's neck. "She's dead all right. Okay it's just the three of us. Let's move!" She grabbed Donna Lee's arm roughly and tugged her toward the secret door.

"Come on, you guys," yelled Skyler, as he held the door wide for the two women. "Let's go!"

Now there were three.

# CHAPTER 53

Ray jogged ahead of me toward the massive stone castle, alert and competent. We could still hear the dogs barking at the rear gate where Ted seemed to have done his job. Pure adrenaline pumped through me and gave me the strength to keep moving.

A muffled boom came from inside the house and we both dropped to the ground within fifty yards of the mansion.

Ray raised his hand for me to stay put. I nodded as he rose and ran low toward the back of the castle. There was a stone arched portico that covered the rear entrance where green benches and wide stone urns brimming with flowers flanked the walkway. The sun was throwing long shadows from the huge pines and I watched Ray slip from one dark spot to the next, flattening against the wall next to the portico. He looked both ways and then into the recess where the door was. Satisfied that we were alone he signaled for me to join him.

Panting, I crouched next to Ray at the wall. He peered again into the dark alcove for a long second and then back to me, nodding. "We good, so far."

"What now?" I whispered. "Was that a gunshot we heard?"

Ray nodded, "Big gun. Let's go in."

He snaked around the corner with me on his heels. Under the large portico was a thick wooden door with heavy strap hinges and a small window head high. There was a buzzer that had a placard under it stating that all deliveries were to be brought through this entrance by appointment only. Like someone was going to drive a Little Debbie's truck through the gate. Ray pushed the heavy iron door lever down and it opened, to our mutual delight.

"There is a God," I exhaled.

"Yeah and he black."

"Riiiiight!"

Ray pushed the door open several inches and waited a beat—nothing, so he opened the door wide enough so we could slip in and closed the door behind us without making a sound. We stood in a cavernous hallway of cobblestone and dim lighting that seemed to be the main entrance to the castle's kitchen. There were two large walk-in coolers on our right and racks and racks of dry stores on the other side. Wonderful smells of bread baking filled the air. My stomach rumbled on command.

Ray put a finger to his lips and motioned for us to move behind the food racks. He knelt down, checked his Glock and readied the two flash bang canisters from Ted. I got the hint and pulled out the compact 9mm Beretta he'd given back to me.

We were ready.

Ray leaned toward me and whispered, "Could be some kitchen help in here. Let's try to take them quiet and put them in the cooler."

I nodded and he pointed for me to go around to the far side of the food racks. He went around the other way.

I heard a muffled sound and a squeal when I rounded the corner and saw Ray holding his huge black hand over a plump middle-aged woman's mouth. Her eyes were wide and her body began to sag. Ray pulled her up and hissed in her ear, "Listen, honey, I'm not going to hurt you. Do you understand me?"

The woman's grey head bobbed in earnest with her eyes the size of saucers.

"Now," he continued, "is there anyone else in here right now? Be honest with me. I would hate to slice your throat open."

The woman looked like a wet dog the way she was shaking her head.

"Okay, okay," Ray tried to sound soothing. But I guessed the fact that he was a 6'3", bald black man dressed in commando gear and holding a gun worked against him.

Ray pulled the frightened woman over and dropped her in a chair, his hand still clamped firmly over her mouth. She had paled considerably and I was afraid she was going to have a heart attack and die right then and there.

Ray leaned down and put his broad face in hers and said in a quiet but menacing voice, "Now I'd like to take my hand away from your mouth. I know you're scared but if you scream or do anything stupid others will die. And it'll be your fault." Ray could be real convincing when he wanted to be.

She nodded with vigor and tears streamed down her cheeks. Ray removed his hand but stayed within inches of her.

"Please," she whimpered with a thick accented voice, German was my best guess. "Don't hurt us, please. We are only the help."

I picked up on this and walked over to her. "We? Who else is here? You just said there was no one else here."

The woman said nothing, holding Ray's intent gaze for several seconds, but then her eyes darted toward a small hallway on the rear wall of the kitchen.

Ray nodded to me to check. "Careful Hemmingway. Could be armed."

I raised my Beretta and crept in the direction she inadvertently gave us.

"Nooo," she wailed, "my daughter. Don't hurt her, please I beg you."

I was already at the hallway and saw that it led to another pantry. I raised the Beretta and stepped cautiously inside. Crouched in a corner was a beautiful young girl in her teens with long blonde hair and fine patrician features. Her pale blue eyes flicked to mine and I smiled reassuringly at her.

"No one is going to hurt you. I promise," I said in a soothing voice. "We're here looking for someone, we're the good guys, I swear."

She said nothing, just turned her gaze to the floor.

I knelt down in front of her. "Please, we need your help."

"I don't know what goes on here," she spat. "Leave us alone."

"I'm looking for a girl ... my girl."

"I don't know nothing about a girl. Did you hurt my mother?"

"No, your mother's fine. We just need information."

"Are you the police?" she asked me in a trembling voice.

I chose to stretch the truth a tad. "We're working with the police and are looking for some people who we think are here against their will." I pulled a picture of Chris from my wallet and handed it to the girl. She glanced at it and shook her head.

"No. No girl like that here."

I searched her face. "Are you sure? We know she was here over the garage in a cell."

Her eyes widened. "I don't know anything about a girl or a cell. We are not allowed to go to the garage. It is forbidden."

I tended to believe her. The fact she was stunningly beautiful lent a certain credibility to her words—always the sucker.

Ray appeared behind me leading the older woman who broke down into sobs when she saw her daughter. The old woman fell to the floor and hugged her daughter babbling in German.

Ray looked me and asked, "Anything from her?"

"No, except they are not allowed to go near the garage. She didn't recognize Chris and I believe her."

Ray arched his brow, "Okay." He looked down at the two women and said in a low growl, "Where's Black?"

"We don't know," the old woman said. "He was here before breakfast and then left. He was looking for my husband and he was very angry about something."

"Who is your husband?" Ray pushed in closer. "How many men are here?"

The old woman shook her head, "I'll tell you nothing. How do I know you are who you say you are?"

Ray thumbed back the hammer on his Glock with

a loud click, but she held his gaze, unflinching. She was no longer scared but indignant.

"Go ahead, I'm not afraid. I will not betray my husband."

Ray bent down to her and hissed, "Listen lady, we are not here to hurt anyone. We need to find two people and then I don't care what you do. But make no mistake if you don't start talking things could get very bad around here real soon."

The girl broke in, "I'll tell you what you want to know. Just leave my mother alone."

"Kristen," the old woman cried, "Don't tell …"

The girl pushed away from her mother and said, "Black is usually upstairs in the big game room. That's what he calls it. It is there he has his guests.

"Guests?" Ray and I said in unison.

"Yes, his games, or whatever he calls them. People come and people go and all sorts of strange things happen here. He scares us to death. I see many things,"

"Are there guests here now?" I asked. "How many?"

The girl looked away for a second as if thinking and then said, "Five, I think. There were six but one man is gone."

"Is there a white-haired older man? Sort of handsome? Name's Skyler."

She nodded, "Yes, a man who always smiles at me as if I don't have clothes on. I remember that strange name."

"That would be Skyler," I said looking at Ray. He nodded.

"Kristen," I said, "Where are they right now?"

"I … I'm not sure. We were told by Mr. Black to stay down here and not to come upstairs to do our work today. He's looking for my father."

Ray took over, "And now who be your father?"

"His name is Dieter. He has worked for Mr. Black's family a long time."

"Is he here now?" I asked.

The old woman grabbed her daughter's arm and hissed to her, "That's enough, you have said enough!"

The girl pulled free again and cried, "No Momma, no more! We've lived here with this monster long enough. We are nothing but prisoners here and I am sick of it!"

She looked at Ray and said in an even voice, "I help you, you get me and my mother out of here—somewhere safe. That's the deal."

"Kristen," her mother carried. "What are you saying? You cannot leave your father!"

Kristen snorted, "I can and I will. Momma you can stay here for the rest of your miserable life being a servant to that bastard and a slave to Father, but not me!"

She turned back to us with her hands on her hips and her blue eyes ablaze. "Do we have a deal or not?"

"Kristen," I said, "If what we think is going on here, that will not be a problem. I think you'll *all* be going someplace else."

"My father went somewhere with the car and that pig Sanchez raced off on that motor thing."

"That's all?" I asked. "Nobody else?"

"That's all," she said and pointed toward a narrow stairway cut into the stone toward the rear of the kitchen. "And that is where the monster is. First floor. The door opens to a big hall. Game room to the right with a big door and his study where he hides is past that to the left."

I looked at Ray and said, "What do we do with them?"

He thought for a second and then said to the women, "Ladies, for our own protection, I am going to lock you in here until the shouting is over."

Kristen's eyes flashed, "The hell you will. I helped you. You will not …"

We didn't hear her finish because Ray swung the heavy pantry door closed behind us and all we could hear was the young girl pounding on the door screaming in German.

"Hemmingway, get me one of those chairs over there," he said as he leaned on the door keeping it shut. "That's one pissed off fraulein. That how you say it?"

I nodded and dragged back a heavy wooden chair from the table, which he promptly wedged under the doorknob. "There, that should hold them. Nobody gonna hear them banging down here."

"Where to now?" I asked him, "Up?"

"Up," he said, already disappearing up the narrow opening. "Keep your eyes open and watch that gun. I don't want you shooting me in the ass."

I almost laughed in spite of the situation.

We crept up the narrow stairway that wound around inside a turret. There was a muted light at the first floor landing and we saw that the stairway continued up into darkness.

"Hey, this is kinda cool," I observed. "This must be his escape route."

"He ain't escaping nowhere," Ray said as we stood before the door on the main floor. "Now be quiet and let's see who's home."

He turned the knob, glanced back at me and pushed it open an inch, leaning his head against the door so he could see through the opening. All seemed quiet—no movement, no sounds. He opened the door farther and poked his head around the corner, looking both ways.

"Clear. Let's move. Remember where this door is, Hemmingway. We may need to scram in a big hurry."

I nodded and followed him into the hall—both weapons were at the ready as we crept along the wide hallway. The entire castle was silent. Twenty feet ahead, we saw the large oak door Kristen had said was the game room. Ray motioned for me to position myself on the wall on the other side as he reached over and tried the iron lever. It didn't budge. He leaned over, inspecting the lock, took a deep breath and delivered a vicious kick just below the lock. We head a cracking sound but the door held solidly. He kicked again and the jamb began to split.

"One more," he huffed. He centered himself and spun thrusting a side kick that shattered the jamb and door. The door blew open crashing into the wall behind it. Ray flattened back against the wall and waited— nothing. He signaled for me to follow left as he breeched right. We both swept the empty room with our guns drawn and found it empty—almost.

The large ornate room was in shambles. Overturned, dishes, chairs and glass lay scattered and broken on the expensive oriental carpet.

At a large table in the center of the room, an old white haired woman was slumped forward with her head resting on the table, frail arms dangling stiffly at her side. Her mouth was open slightly and her eyes were open in death.

I went over and looked as closely as I dared. I've seen dead people and all that, but I still pause being near someone so obviously dead. "Don't see any blood. Was she the one shot?"

"Don't think so," he said, moving his hand lightly over her back and pushing her fine hair away from her neck. "No blood. Maybe she was poisoned or had a heart attack."

"Ray," I said in a quiet voice.

He looked at what I was pointing to. Against the wall was a body. Khaki-clad legs with topsiders protruded from under a bloody white tablecloth.

"Shit, Ray, who do you suppose it is?" I feared for Skyler. A shiver of dread went up my spine.

He walked over, reached down and pulled back the cover. I almost blew lunch right there. Staring back at us wide eyed and very dead was a man we had never seen before with half his head blown off. Ray nudged him with his boot and the man's head lolled over in the other direction.

"That's where the bullet went in," he paused and looked at me, "and you can see where it came out."

"Cover him back up, Ray. I'm gonna lose my lunch. Good thing we didn't have any lunch," I managed to say.

"Dude played Russian Roulette."

"How'd you know that?"

Ray, still kneeling at the body looked up at me with a somber expression—like one who has seen too much in his life. "One bullet in the gun and this is a contact shot. See the powder burn? Dumb fucker put it to his own head and pulled the trigger. Seen this shit in Nam."

My mouth was open but I couldn't speak.

"If this is what your crazy ass uncle is up to, he deserves what he gets."

I nodded, still numb. "I agree, Ray, but we're here to find Chris. If we do find Skyler, he's going to wish he put that gun to his own damn head. It's his fault we're here and that Chris is missing."

There was a stainless steel cart lying on its side with a bunch aluminum cases open and empty.

"What the hell you make of that, man?

Ray shrugged and bent over plucking a shell casing off the carpet.

".357. This is what we heard." He sniffed the shell casing in his hand. "Still warm. I love that smell." Ray scanned the room once more and said, "I wonder what was in those cases."

"Who knows? They're empty now. Let's get out of here."

"Come on, Hemmingway, let's go find this Black fucker. I wanna see if he wants to play roulette with my Glock."

Something was nagging me as we turned to leave the room. "Wait," I said turning around and scanning the room. "Look over there at that wall."

I pointed to where the marble shelf protruded at an angle. "That looks odd."

We both ran to the spot and Ray gripped the frame which was askew. Whoever went through this had left it open—just enough to catch my eye. Ray pulled it open to reveal another dark passageway.

"It's another secret passage," I said in excitement.

Ray held up his hand, which by now I knew meant *quiet*. "Listen, someone is down there. Let's move slow. I know I heard something down there."

"Right behind you, Kemo Sabé," I said, as we went deep in the bowels of Black's castle.

# CHAPTER 54

Skyler admired Miranda Bell as much as he lusted for her. She was the kind of woman he had always dreamed of—strong, beautiful, confident, sexy, and most of all, able to handle things. Right now, he was happy to defer to her command. Skyler admitted to himself that as of now, he was scared shitless. He knew his lifestyle choices had brought him here. He just wasn't a normal man. He always needed that thrill, that heart pounding elation when he was playing for high stakes—where it was all on the line. As far as the women in his life, and there had been many, he needed the excitement a new love brings and he would always disappear when the fire died. But this woman, my God, he thought, I would never tire of her. I could spend the rest of my years with her but he knew she would never give him the time of day. Who could blame her? There was a dangerous side to her, he just felt it. He could revel in that, he thought with a wry smile.

He watched her creep slowly down the dark passage as he and Donna Lee followed close behind. They were walking blind. Black had shut off the lights after he escaped the game room and they were feeling their way along the rough stone walls of the passageway.

"There has to be a switch here somewhere," whispered Miranda into the darkness. "I'm going to backtrack a bit. The first level had some lights. There must've been a switch when we branched off. I'll be right back."

Skyler grabbed her arm. "Wait, Miranda, you can't leave us here. I think it's best we stick together. You know, safety in numbers."

"Damn right," Donna Lee said, "You ain't leaving me here, that's for sure. I go where y'all go."

"Okay, okay," said Miranda. "Just stay behind me and let's go back a bit,"

They felt their way along the stone cold wall as they made their way back. The passage way seemed to wind through the interior of the castle—no stairs it just wound on a gradual incline. They got into a rhythm feeling their way along the wall. Skyler's hand was on Miranda's shoulder and Donna Lee's was on his.

Miranda heard it first. "Get down and don't say a word."

Skyler and Donna Lee crouched behind Miranda as they listened.

"Someone's coming," Miranda whispered. "Shhh, hear that?"

They all heard the low voices that seemed to be coming from the game room opening. Miranda judged it to be about fifty feet away and around several bends. Then there was total quiet for one minute, then two …

"Maybe they're gone," Skyler whispered. "I really gotta pee."

Donna Lee gave him a shove. "Tie a knot in it, Gramps. "That's if you have enough rope."

"Quiet," Miranda snapped. "Just be quiet. They could be up there waiting for us to make a move.

Donna Lee was crouched down behind Skyler. She did not have a lot of clothes on—short shorts, a tank top and her flip flops so she was damn cold. She was lost in her morose thoughts. Hartigan was such a fool, she thought. *He could've had me and we could've taken on the world. Even though they had only known each other a couple of days they could've been a great team.* Then to have him blow his brains out all over her was just too fucking much for this North Carolina girl. She had her hand on Skyler's back and she shivered as she crouched. Then a strange sensation came over her. It started as a cold shiver down her spine. When she realized that something was beginning to slide over her foot and then the sheer bone-chilling terror followed. Her scream echoed throughout the chamber.

"Snake! A fucking snake. Oh my god, a fucking snake!" she screamed as she jumped up and blew past Miranda and Skyler. "I'm getting the fuck out of here, right now!"

Skyler, who was petrified of snakes, was right behind her. Miranda had no choice but to follow.

# CHAPTER 55

The scream made my heart stop. Was it Chris, I thought in a panic, God please don't let it be Chris.

"That wasn't Chris, Hemmingway, but let's find those people," Ray said, switching on his Maglite. "They close."

Ray motioned for me to flatten against the stone wall as he moved toward the bend in the passageway. That was when all broke loose. Ray started to round the bend and collided with a moving freight train in the body of a hysterical young girl. The girl crashed head on into a very startled Ray. He stumbled backward as the woman bounced off his massive chest and crumpled to a heap on the cavern floor, sobbing.

"Fuck it!" she cried. "I'm dead. I don't care. Go ahead, just get it over with."

Ray looked at me with raised eyebrows just as the second body flew around the corner, tripping over the young woman. The man landed hard and rolled to a disheveled heap at my feet. I looked down in amazement to see none other than Chris's lost Uncle Skyler.

"Nick? Nick? Christ, is it really you?" He squinted up at me.

"It's me, Skyler," I said reaching down and helping him up. "Where's Chris?"

"Chris? What are you talking about, Nick. Chris isn't here."

My stomach knotted up and I grabbed him by the lapels of his suit and pulled him close. "Skyler, please tell me you've seen Chris or I'm going to kill your worthless ass myself."

He squirmed and tried to pull away. "Hey Nick, easy. I haven't seen hide nor hair of Chris. Honest. They're trying to kill us here. Tell them Donna Lee, tell them!"

The girl scrambled to her feet ignoring Ray's outstretched hand. She was a cutie with short tousled brown hair and a defiant look, dressed in cutoffs, a tank top and she was barefoot.

She glared at Ray. "Who the hell are you?" And then over at Skyler, pointing at me. "You know this guy?"

Skyler straightened and smoothed out his jacket after I had released my death grip.

"Nick this is Donna Lee. Donna Lee this is Nick, and that big scary looking fella over there is Ray. They're the good guys." He looked around with a puzzled expression.

"What is it, Skyler?" I asked.

"Miranda. She's ..." He looked back in the direction they'd come from. "Miranda was with us."

"Who's Miranda?" I asked, looking around.

"I'm Miranda," said a voice as an attractive woman stepped from the shadows holding a very large handgun in front of her. Ray's hand twitched toward his Glock.

"Don't even think about it." She thumbed back the hammer. I saw that her hands were steady as she moved into the light.

"Whoa, lady, hold on," Ray smiled broadly, raising

his hands in front of him. "Easy now, Darlin'. We're the good guys."

"Keep your hands where I can see them," she said in an even voice.

Skyler rushed over to her. "Miranda, I know these guys. They're here to help us."

She eyed me, the gun not wavering.

"Honest, lady," I said trying my award winning Nick smile. "We came up here to find him. It's a long story. I'm Nick and this here is Ray. We'll get you out of here."

She relaxed and dropped the gun to her side and actually smiled. "Thank God, we need all the help we can get."

Ray took over. "Okay, listen. How many in the house?"

Skyler and Donna Lee looked at Miranda who seemed to be in charge.

Miranda tucked the large pistol in the waistband of her suit.

"Where did you get that?" asked Skyler.

"Picked it up in the room."

"Was that the one Hartigan …"

"Yes," she said.

"Where did you get the bullets?" Donna Lee asked. "Chance … he … I mean there was only one bullet."

Miranda smiled. "Only one." She patted the butt of the magnum and looked at Ray. "But, he didn't know that."

Ray smiled and winked at her. "Knew it all the time. Jus don like shooting pretty ladies. That's all."

"Right," I said, shaking my head. "Come on, we need to move out."

"Where?" Donna Lee and Skyler asked in unison.

I turned back to Miranda. "Have you seen a young pretty woman about thirty or so?" I nodded at Donna Lee. "She's sort of an older version of this young lady here."

Miranda shook her head. "No. There were six of us at the start. I'm pretty sure that three are dead now, but I don't think any of us saw someone like that."

"Not me," said Donna Lee.

I looked at Ray who just shrugged and shook his head. "Don't mean she wasn't or isn't here, mon. First, let's figure out who is who." He squatted on his haunches and looked at Miranda. "We need to know who we're fighting here. How many men? Are they all armed? Where's Black?"

Miranda's eyes closed for a second as she was thinking. "Okay, I've seen two men—one a big German, his name's Dieter. I think he's like the head security guy and then there's a mean looking Cuban named Sanchez. Oh, and Marco. A big thug. So that's three by my count and I guarantee they are all packing." She closed her eyes again as if trying to squeeze more detail from her mind. "That's all. We didn't see anyone else except the cook, Helene, and her daughter. I think her name is Kristin."

I nodded at Ray. "We met the ladies when we came in and they are … umm let's say, they are occupied."

"You kill them, Nick?" Skyler asked with a flushed look on his face.

"Calm down, Skyler. We locked them in a storeroom. We haven't hurt anybody."

"Yet," Ray said and looked at me. "That must've been Sanchez on the ATV. He should be back by now. Teddy's diversion wouldn't have them fooled for long."

"Who's Teddy?" Miranda asked. "You guys got more troops?"

I nodded. "A sheriff's deputy who's after Black for his own reasons."

"Good, then call them in. The quicker the better," Miranda said. "We're sitting ducks in this cave."

Ray shook his head. "Can't, there's no signal. I think the man has a jamming device somewhere in this tomb. It's a sure bet that some of the cops are on Black's payroll. We don't know who the bad guys are. Y'all are stuck with us."

I spoke up, "I suggest the first order of business is to get out of this tunnel. Let's go back through the game room and into the main house and try to find a way out."

Ray shook his head. "No, I think there's a way out somewhere in this tunnel. This might lead down to the kitchen where we came in. Think about it, mon. That's why he built this—to escape. I say we go down as far as this will take us." He turned to Miranda. "What did you see the way you just came?"

"Nothing but dark. That's why we came back to find some lights."

Donna Lee stomped over, still barefoot. "Don't forget that fucking snake. There was a big snake that slithered over my foot back there and I ain't going anywhere in that direction. You understand me. I'll sit here first."

"No, you won't," Ray said in a firm voice. "Just stay behind me and I'll kill any damn snake we see. I promise." Ray said, pulling his K-Bar from its sheath. "I won't let anything happen to you. Now follow me, single file, and be quiet. We don't know where these guys will be. Nick, you have your gun so you bring up the six. Keep your eyes and ears open everybody."

I nodded and fell in behind Skyler. Miranda was next and Donna Lee was scrambling after Ray.

"If anybody sees my flipflops …" she called back to us.

This was scary. "Lead on, brave soldiers," I said as we proceeded down the cold stone passage behind the sweeping beam of Ray's Maglite. I could hear Donna Lee. "If I see that fucking snake … Hey, Ray, you married?"

# CHAPTER 56

We all heard the sound. We had only moved down the passageway about twenty five yards or so when a loud whir, followed by a metallic *thunk thunk,* echoed down the chamber. Almost like the sound power car locks make but much heavier and much louder.

I froze and slowly turned around. "What the hell was that?"

Ray came back and sidled up to me. "My guess would be locks. I bet we couldn't go back that way now if we wanted to."

"So we go on," I said, with more bravado than I felt. This did not feel good.

"We do," he said and then turned and played the beam of the light down the passageway's wall. "There gotta be lights in here."

Several long minutes later we came to a split in the tunnel. Ray stopped and shined the beam of his Maglite from one opening to the other.

"See anything?" I asked him.

"Looks like the one on the left heads down to the kitchen area. At least I think it does. The other inclines up after a few yards."

Donna Lee bumped in. "Come on guys. I gotta pee real bad."

Ray smiled. "Go back a little and do it, pretty lady. We won't watch."

I held up two fingers. "Promise."

"If you think I'm going back there where there might be snakes, you're crazy. No fucking way." Donna Lee stood there with her hands on her hips. Ray shrugged. "I don't know what to tell you. You want to run ahead faster, be my guest."

"That'll happen," she said with a pout. "Just hurry, okay? I can hold it a few more minutes. But I'm not going anywhere without you." She linked both her arms around one of Rays.

Ray grinned and wouldn't dare look my way. "Let's get a move on. We're going to the left and down. Be quiet and stay single file behind me."

We all grunted in assent. I was happy to have him in charge. All I wanted to do was find Chris.

The passageway that had been decent sized, narrowed considerably as we crept deeper in to the bowels of Black's castle. I knew there was no doubt that this would be in my next book. If I wasn't so scared about Chris, and the fact that there were people— exact numbers unknown—who would rather we didn't leave this place alive I'd have taken better notes.

It was more of a tunnel now and I was beginning to feel a little claustrophobic. I kept looking back over my shoulder, my trusty Beretta at the ready. Hey, what was that Miranda's story, I wondered? She had the look of someone who was used to this stuff—like Ray. Hell, he loves it. You can see it in their eyes. When this was done Ray would go back to the Cape and the restaurant to his lovely bride Jazz, and play the gracious island host ... and be bored to death. Miranda seemed to be cut from the same cloth.

It was easier to see as we descended down toward the kitchen. Ray crept forward swinging his light back and forth on the floor. He turned and put up his hand.

"Door's about twenty feet." He looked at me and shook his head. "Don't like the feel of this."

I nodded, "Too easy, man. They had us canned up in here and somebody with a MP-5 or something could have taken us out easily."

He nodded. "So ... I'm thinking either they all hightailed it the hell out of here or they're waiting for us in that big-assed kitchen. Too many places to hide and we'd be sitting ducks going through that door." He thought for a second and then smiled.

"What?" I asked.

He pulled out one of the flash bang canisters that Teddy gave us and bounced it in his huge paw.

Donna Lee stared at it. "You gonna blow us up? You can't be serious."

Miranda pushed her way past and stood in front of us.

"Look you guys, I'm an ex-fed, and so you can trust me to help. I'm here looking for a missing client, same as you. Can't say anything more than that."

I looked at her. She had a confidence about her. Plus, she was not bad on the eyes for an older woman.

Ray looked at her, nodded, and then turned to the rest of our little band of insurgents. "Okay, y'all stay back. Keep down and for god's sake please keep quiet. First one talks, I'll shoot you myself."

Miranda looked at us. "We *will* get out of here. We

all just need to stay calm and focused." To Ray she asked, "What do you plan on doing?"

Ray looked down at the flash bang in his hand. "I'm gonna see if that door is unlocked. If it is, I'm gonna toss this little baby in. If they waiting for us they gonna wish they were somewhere else." He motioned for us to gather around.

"Now listen. You all stay back here."

"What if it's locked?" asked Skyler. "What then?"

Ray just smiled and headed down to the door.

# CHAPTER 57

Black looked at his man Sanchez with a scowl. "What do you mean you don't know where Marco is? I sent him to look for Dieter hours ago. Call him."

Sanchez shrugged. "He don't answer, Mr. Black. I tried …"

"Try again. Now."

"Yes Sir, but it keeps rolling into voice mail. I tried both of them, Dieter and Marco. Same thing."

"Where are our guests at this moment?"

"I …I don't know Mr. Black. You sent me to the rear gate to check that fire."

Black, who was standing in the upstairs library, continued staring out the tall window, his fists at his side, clenched tight, trying to control his anger. He turned back to Sanchez, his was a face a mask of rage.

"Find those people, Sanchez, and see to it they are no longer a nuisance to me. Do you understand?"

Sanchez nodded. "Of course, Mr. Black, they must be in the inner passage. That's the only place they can be."

"Do it! And then find Dieter and Marco!"

Sanchez scurried from the room without another word.

Sebastian Black sighed and went to the bar and poured a generous portion of brandy into a crystal snifter. Without ceremony he downed it. He felt the fine brandy burn on the way down and immediately warm his gut. That was good.

Was it all over? he thought. Would this band of misfits be his undoing? Three generations of Blacks had lived here in splendor and had never been bothered—never had a problem, never had a scandal that couldn't be explained away or fixed. Speaking of which, where was Cobb? He was paid very well to ensure this type of thing never happened. He picked up the receiver on his desk and dialed.

"Sheriff's Office," a nasal female voice answered. "How may I help you?"

Black tried to control his voice. "Sheriff Cob, please. It's urgent."

"Sheriff's not in right now. How can I help yo—"

Black cut her off with a scream. "I don't care if he's dying. Get him on the goddamn phone right now! This is an emergency!"

Unruffled the woman deputy said, "Sir, please calm down and tell me the nature of your emergency."

"Get Sheriff Cobb on the radio and tell him to get his ass out to the Black estate right now!" he demanded, his voice barely in control. "Do you understand me? This is Sebastian Black. I need Sheriff Cobb!"

"Sir, Sheriff Cobb cannot …"

"I need Cobb!" Black screamed again.

"Mr. Black, Sheriff Cobb is with some men from the FBI right now and they specifically said that no way were they to be disturbed short of a nuclear attack."

"The what? The FBI? What are they doing there?" His throat tightened and the room began to spin.

"Sir, I am not privy to that. All I know is that he's been in there a long time with two men who said they were with the FBI and there are a bunch more waiting outside in two big black Tahoes. I don't know what's going on but it's big, so Sheriff Cobb can't be disturbed and if you want help you need to tell me what your emergency is, or get off the line." She said, having lost all patience with him.

Black stared at the phone in his hand and slammed it back into its cradle. What the hell was going on? The FBI? This was not good. Where the hell was Dieter? He would know how to handle this. Black opened the top drawer of his antique oak desk and pulled out a small automatic that he slid into the pocket of his blazer. He eyed the brandy, shook his head, deciding that he would need a clear head and went back to the huge window. What to do, he asked himself, as he looked out over his once magnificent kingdom that now seemed tarnished and alien. He saw a thin haze of smoke coming from the area of the rear gate where the disturbance had been. He'd sent Sanchez to check it out who said he'd looked around but hadn't seen anybody. He had raced back to the main house to find Marco and Dieter.

Black had the feeling that all was not well and that his time was growing short.

He heard several pops in the distance followed by more and then he realized that he was hearing gunfire. There it was again, but quicker like automatic weapons— rapid bursts, then silence for several seconds before more bursts followed, which were met by single reports from what could have been a handgun.

What the hell was going on? Were they being attacked? Who were they shooting at? Sanchez? Had to be, he was the only one left. Maybe Marco found Dieter and they were back. Nevertheless, he knew it was time to go.

He ran across the floor to the bookcase and pulled on a leather bound volume of Edgar Allan Poe that was on the fourth shelf up, at eye level, third from the right. There was an audible click and a section of the bookcase opened out. Black looked around his study one last time. Was this it? Was it all coming down around him? He shook his head sadly and disappeared behind the wall of books, pulling it closed after him.

# CHAPTER 58

"What was that?" Donna Lee asked in a scared voice.

"Gunfire," I said. "It's coming from outside, I think."

Ray padded back to us. "Hear that?"

I nodded and raised an eyebrow. "Calvary?"

"Could be," he said. "Maybe Teddy brought in the troops. 'Bout damn time. Was beginning to wonder where he got to."

Donna Lee scurried over to Ray and clung to him. They were close as two people could be with clothes on. He didn't seem to notice and looked at the rest of us.

"Okay, the door's not locked to the kitchen and my guess is that they're busy shooting back at whoever is shooting at them. So now's the time to decide. Do we stay here and wait it out or do we keep going?"

I looked at the others and said, "I say we move."

"I vote we go on as well," agreed Miranda. "I don't like being holed up here. We'd be sitting ducks from either direction."

Skyler straightened his shoulders and smiled bravely at her. "I'm with Miranda." Of course he was, I thought.

"Miss Lee?" Ray asked his adoring second skin.

"I go where you go," she said in a shaky voice, still clutching his arm. "Just don't leave me."

Ray looked at us again, made up his mind and turned to me. "Nick, I'm going in toward the right, you go left. Keep low with your back to the wall and make sure nobody is behind you. Try not to shoot the old lady or the girl, okay?"

"You going to toss the flash bang in first?"

"You bet your ass. They'll get over it. Now, the rest of you stay here and wait for the all clear from me." He paused and then added, "If we don't come back and you hear trouble, crawl your asses back up the tunnel as far as you can go and wait."

Donna Lee shook her head furiously. "I … I'm not going near those snakes. No fucking way!"

Ray put his massive hands on her shoulders and said in a calming voice, "Now listen to me pretty lady, I'm not going to let anything bad happen to you. I promise."

Her doe eyes searched his and then gave him a weak smile. "I think I love you."

In spite of the circumstances, I couldn't help but laugh. Ray shot me a murderous look and I stopped in mid-guffaw. I knew he was trying to calm her down so she wouldn't panic. Miranda came up, put her arm around Donna Lee and clasped her hand. "Come on, honey. Let's let them do what they have to do. You and I'll stick together. I won't let anything happen to you." Skyler moved to her other side and stood close in a reassuring gesture.

Donna Lee squeezed Miranda's hand and gave her a grateful smile. "Okay, Miranda. Thanks." She looked at Skyler and said, "You too, Skyler. Thank you. I'm not usually a wimp but this is way outta my league."

Skyler smiled. "Mine too, young lady. Believe me, this is not what I had in mind when I was invited to the back woods of Vermont."

Ray interrupted. "Now I suggest you all get back a bit and sit with your backs against the wall. Stay close together, and remember, be quiet."

The three of them sat huddled together as Ray and I readied to breech the door. Just another average day in the life of a mystery writer, I thought wryly.

# CHAPTER 59

Deputy Ted Adams had stopped his patrol car outside Black's rear gate, which now hung askew on its hinges. He made a small show of inspecting the damage caused the night before when Nick and Ray had crashed the jeep through it. He walked around, went through the motions for the sake of the camera mounted on the stone gate post and then got back in his car and drove away. He parked down the road out of sight, retrieved a long duffel bag and a gas can from the trunk and then doubled back toward the gate. He hugged close to the fence while he poured the contents of the five-gallon can along its base. When he was close to the entrance, he placed the can behind a thick laurel bush, soaked the rag he'd brought, and stuck it into the can. He waited several seconds to make sure all was clear, then lit the fashioned wick with a disposable lighter, and ran like hell.

They wanted a diversion. They got a diversion. The can exploded in a fireball as the flames spread along the base of the fence where he had poured the gasoline. The inferno licked high up and formed a wall of flame catching the thick ivy and laurels and anything else that would burn. Now, that's a diversion, he thought with a wry grin as he ran through the smoke, and disappeared into the woods on the inside of the gate with the duffel bag slung across his back.

Sanchez, on the ATV, rounded the corner with the dogs on his heels just as the road ahead of him exploded in a blast of sound and smoke. Sanchez hit the front brake out of reflex and went head first over the handlebars. The dogs turned and fled back in the direction of the castle in a flurry of yelps. The ATV had flipped and crashed to a stop on its side—the motor still whining while Deputy Ted Adams, smiling, headed back into the forest.

Sanchez had rolled to a stop, bruised and battered, and stared through the smoke at the fire burning at the base of the perimeter fence. The bastard had tossed a flash bang in front of me, he thought, not a grenade, or else I'd be dead. The dogs came back to him and circled nervously, still barking. He lay still where he had landed and waited for several long seconds, but saw and felt no one's presence. A chill was forming in his gut and he knew that was never good. He rose slowly, checking for wounds and found none serious enough to worry about. He looked around and found his rifle in the gravel near the ATV and slowly panned the woods on both sides of the narrow road. He fired several short bursts into the trees but no fire was returned.

Whoever was there was gone now, he thought. But where to?

He waited another minute and then ran over to where the ATV lay on its side and tried to push it over, to no avail. It was too heavy. The motor had flooded and stalled out. Sanchez could smell the gasoline leaking from the carburetor and decided it probably wouldn't start even if he could right it. He noticed that the handlebars were twisted and bent under from the impact. Screw this, he thought and ran back toward the castle—the now not-so-brave dogs way ahead of him.

Minutes later, Sanchez leaned against the wide column under the portico of the castle entrance and tried to catch his breath. The dogs were nowhere to be seen. He was not sure what to do first. Black had said to make the problem go away. Did Black know there was somebody out there coming after them? Easy for him to say *to get rid of them,* he wasn't the one to pull the trigger and Sanchez had some problems with killing innocent people. That's not what his Special Forces training had taught him. Of course he wasn't a "Green Beenie" anymore and that really wasn't his fault, but nonetheless he was out here in the god-forsaken woods making a hell of a lot more money doing very little except pampering this rich guy's ass. Where the fuck was Dieter, he wondered, and Marco? Maybe they got smart and hit the road. No, Dieter was loyal to Black for some reason and Marco, a soldier like him, would never turn tail and run.

Sanchez looked around and got another chill. This one traveling up his spine. He listened but heard nothing but quiet. Still ...

The silence was then shattered. "FBI. Put your hands in the air," the distinct voice from a megaphone commanded. "You are surrounded." Sanchez's blood ran cold.

Sanchez darted behind one of the columns and raised his MP-5. He popped the magazine and checked it—about half full and he had a spare in the pocket of his tactical pants. Fuck them, he thought. Jesus, what the hell was happening? The FBI? *You gotta be shitting me.*

"Come out where we can see you with your hands in the air," the voice in the woods repeated.

"Fuck you!" Sanchez screamed and fired off a short burst of three rounds in the direction of the voice then ducked back behind the column. He had about ten exposed feet to the door and knew he probably wouldn't make it. He didn't come through those damn wars to give up like this. No sir, he would die first!

The distinct staccato from an assault rifle erupted and bullets tore into the stone column that Sanchez had wisely stayed behind. The column was 4'x4' of solid stone and mortar that rose up and curved into an arch and then down into the next column. Another burst peppered the wall of the castle behind him— showering him with stinging shards of stone.

"Throw your weapon out where we can see it and come out with your hands high," the tinny voice commanded. "It's no use, you are surrounded."

"Fuck you!" Sanchez screamed again and squeezed off two more bursts at the voice in the woods. He was promptly answered by another blaze of bullets. The rounds ricocheted all around him and he felt a stabbing pain in his left leg. Shit, I'm hit, he thought, and felt his thigh. His hand came back with warm sticky blood. *Not good.* Now what, he thought. Do I die or give up. He knew there were only two choices. He had the horrible feeling in his gut that he wasn't going to get away this time.

Another hail of bullets smacked into the column in front of him and then in the insanity of the moment, he heard a blaring car horn and the sound of a vehicle approaching fast down the gravel drive. *What the hell?* He remained behind the column.

The shooting stopped for a moment and Sanchez peered around the other side of the column to see the Black Chrysler 300 barreling into the courtyard in a cloud of dust with Marco driving and Dieter, whose face was a bloody mask, was leaning out of the passenger window spraying the woods with his own MP-5. The car careened around the circle and then headed back toward the garages. The man or men in the woods began firing at the car so Sanchez knew this was probably his best chance to get the hell out of there. He stood, took a deep breath and counted. He'd go on three, he resolved. *One ... two ...*

Marco skidded the Chrysler to a stop at the side of the garage and he and Dieter leapt out and took cover around the corner of the stone building. It seemed as if an all-out war had begun. Automatic weapons fire persisted from the woods. The smell of cordite permeated the air as Marco and Dieter returned the fire sparingly. They didn't have much ammo and they needed to get back in that house—to the armory in the basement.

It was at that moment Sanchez made his move ... *three!* He waited a beat and then ran for the door in a low crouch, one arm shielding his head and face.

Sanchez didn't feel much pain when the next burst from the woods hit him high in the shoulder and the back of the head. The impact and momentum propelled him flat and hard into the heavy oak door where he stayed suspended for one long second, his hands stretched wide, and then his body crumpled to the porch in a heap, his hands leaving a bloody plea down the door.

Marco saw it happen. "Shit, Dieter, they got Sanchez. Now what?"

Crouched low next to Dieter, Marco released the magazine on his MP-5. He shook his head and slapped the magazine back into the weapon. "Fuck."

Dieter's trained eyes scanned the woods behind them. "How many you think there are?"

"Hard to tell, man. I'm thinking one, maybe two. One keeps us busy while the other circles around. I only got about ten rounds left. What about you?"

"A couple rounds, that's all. We got to get into the house. We can re-arm and maybe …"

Marco shook his head. "No way, man. We don't have a fucking chance and you know it."

Dieter gave him a withering look. "I'm not giving myself up. We'd be in prison for the rest of our miserable lives. Not me, man. I've been through a lot of shit and it's not going to end for me here, in this fucking forest. I'm going out with a fight."

"Dieter, I can't man. I got no real dog in this fight and besides I gotta …"

Just then another burst from the woods tore into the side of the building where they were crouched. They both ducked and scrambled toward the back of the building.

They huddled behind a small low wooden box that housed the garage's air conditioning unit. It was about four feet high and six-foot long. Marco had the bizarre thought that it looked like a big casket—maybe it was to be his.

"I wonder where our brave employer is right now, eh Dieter?" panted Marco, not caring what Dieter thought anymore. "The little fuck is probably hiding in a fucking closet pissing his pants and you and I are either gonna wind up in prison or dead."

Dieter gave him a hard look. "You want to give up, Marco? Go Ahead. Walk out there with your hands in the air, you idiot. They'll cut you down like a dog."

Marco got close to the German. "No, you hear me, Dieter. You got a wife and daughter in there. What do you think is going to happen to them with you dead, huh?"

Dieter eyed the man next to him with contempt.

"What?" prodded Marco, leaning closer into the big German's space, his voice rising. "You think I'm wrong? Let's throw these fucking weapons down and walk out of here before it gets worse. If you don't give a shit about your daughter, I do. I love her, you know."

Dieter said nothing.

Marco raised his head, peered over the top of the air conditioning unit and listened.

"Hear that? Nothing." The shooting had stopped. "Come on, Dieter, save yourself."

They looked at each other for a long minute and finally Marco said, "Fuck it, man. You wanna die? Go ahead, but do it without me."

Marco stood, raised the assault weapon in the air, and yelled. "I'm coming out, you bastards. Don't shoot." He walked toward the side of the garage with his hands in the air. "Hey, don't shoot, man, I'm coming out …"

The single 9mm Parabellum entered the base of Marco's head and he toppled dead, face first, to the gravel drive. He lay, still clutching the MP-5 with its ten remaining rounds in his outstretched hand, in a widening pool of his own blood. Dieter watched him fall—his vintage Luger still aimed where Marco's head had been.

Traitors and cowards were shot in wartime, Dieter thought. And this was certainly war. Now, he needed to find his wife and daughter. It was time to get the hell out of there.

# CHAPTER 60

We all tensed as Ray knelt before the door leading to the kitchen and a way out of this god-forsaken tomb. I didn't even care at this point where Black was, but I did care very much where Chris was. Don't ask me why, but I had a feeling she was okay. Her voicemail left me with the feeling that she had managed to escape and that she was safe.

Ray looked at me with a raised eyebrow.

I held up one finger, motioning for him to wait one, then turned and coaxed the others back. "Keep going. You all wait around the bend in the passage."

Donna Lee grabbed onto my arm. She was not holding it together well.

"Come on," I said to her as reassuringly as I could. "We're going to be fine. Now get back and let Ray do his thing." I had this sudden feeling that something wasn't right. *Wait a minute ...* I looked at Skyler

"Skyler, where's Miranda?" I asked.

Skyler whirled around, his panicked eyes searching the darkened passage behind us. "What the ... Miranda, Miranda, where are you? She was just right here."

Nothing.

"Miranda?" I called. There was still no answer. She had disappeared.

"You guys be quiet," Ray hissed from his position at the door. "Want to tell everybody we here?"

"Ray, Miranda is gone," I hissed. "She must have gone back through the tunnel. Want me to go back and look for her? Give me the flashlight."

He shook his head. "No, mon, it's too late to worry about her now. She can take care of herself. Let's get through this door. Remember you go in left and stay low."

I nodded and gripped the Beretta.

Just then we heard several muffled bursts from automatic weapons.

"Things heating up outside," Ray said.

"Must be Teddy," I said.

"Or the cops."

"Good cops or bad cops?"

"Hard to tell in this place. Let's do this," he said. He turned and went to the door. He looked back at me, smiled and gave me the thumbs up. He was ready.

"Down," I said to Skyler and Donna Lee, "cover your ears and close your eyes. I did the same.

Ray cracked the wooden door and tossed in the flashbang. A second later, the corridor was rocked by a loud explosion. He waited a beat and then went in with me right on his heels.

The huge kitchen was filled with smoke as we entered but I could see Ray on the other side of the door. He was crouched with his back to the wall. We both scanned the room, fully expecting gunfire. There was none. We waited several minutes as the smoke settled. There was no movement, no sign of life.

"Ray," I said in a low voice, "there's no one here."

"Stay down. Let me see if the ladies are still in the storeroom."

He scrambled over to the door and beat on it with his fist. "Hey. Hey, ladies, you okay in there?"

"What do you think? You ... you, pigs!" came the muffled response from inside. "Let us out of here. My husband will cut your throats for this."

Ray gave me a quick smile. "They good." He looked around again and said to me, "Get the others. Let's move."

"What about Miranda?"

"Her problem. Let's see what's outside."

I ran back and poked my head into the passage. "Skyler, Donna Lee, let's go. Now!"

Skyler looked back and then at me. "What about Miranda? We can't just leave her here."

"Her choice, Skyler. All I care about is finding Chris."

"But—"

"No buts, Skyler. Move your ass!" I grabbed his arm and shoved him toward the door.

Donna Lee had already brushed by me looking for Ray.

The gunfire outside had stopped for the moment. We were all huddled by the service entrance we'd come in through.

"What now, Ray?" I asked.

Ray put up his hand. His raven eyes scanned the large kitchen, looking for any sign of movement. He saw and heard nothing. "Okay, Nick, I'm going to check outside. You three stay put in here. Got it?"

"Why don't we just stay here and wait for the cops?" Donna Lee asked.

Ray gave her an indulgent look. "'Cause, pretty girl, we don't know who the good guys are and the bad guys wants us dead."

Skyler looked confused. "What do you mean? The police ..."

Ray silenced him with a withering look. "How about you just shut up and do as I say. You the reason we're in this damn mess." Skyler wisely obeyed.

"Nick, get them behind those storage racks and wait for me to get back."

I nodded, gathered my two charges and moved them to cover. Ray moved quickly to the hall and then disappeared.

One gunshot from outside pierced the silence and then all was silent, again.

# CHAPTER 61

Sebastian Black knew this day would come and he had prepared for it. He had no idea where his men were but he was not waiting for them now. The gunfire from outside meant trouble and he knew things had gone terribly wrong.

Black closed the panel of the bookcase behind him and entered the passageway. He paused, and listened for a long moment. Hearing nothing, he turned and pushed a spot on the stone wall a few feet down the corridor. The wall pivoted inward opening into a plush, dimly lit chamber. Black stepped through and closed the heavy door behind him. He was standing in his inner office, his command center. The room was furnished much the same as the rest of the castle: rich leather chairs facing a massive solid teak desk, a glowing gas fire, rich 18th century art, and bookshelves lining the walls behind his desk. This had been his father's sanctuary and his grandfather's before that—a place they could go and not be disturbed. He spent many nights here by the fire, reading a leather-bound classic, sipping fine brandy, and indulging in the occasional cigar.

Black gave his favorite room a wistful look, knowing that he would probably never see it again. He sighed, opened a closet, pulled out a large aluminum briefcase, and laid it open on top of his desk. In a hurry now, he went to a painting hanging near the fireplace and pulled on one corner. It swung out, hinged to one side, revealing a large wall safe. Black entered a code into the keypad, opened the safe and pulled out two velvet bags wrapped with a gold cord that he placed in the top compartment of the case. Then he began stacking banded hundred dollar bills in neat rows in the bottom. He had close to five million in cut diamonds in the pouches, several hundred thousand in cash, along with two forged passports, I.D.s with credit cards in each name. That would ensure him a nice, safe getaway. The cash would be used to grease any rough spots he might encounter on the way.

He closed the safe's steel door and swung the painting back in place. *Now for the hard part.* He had to get out of the castle unseen. He wondered if Marco had found Dieter.

He didn't register the blow to the head before everything went black.

Miranda Bell stood over Black's crumpled form, holding the .357 she had clubbed him with by the barrel end.

"There, you little bastard. That's for playing with my life."

Black lay in a fetal position, his hands close to his head as blood oozed from a nasty gash behind his right ear—his neat blue blazer rumpled, bloody and dirty.

"You monster, I should cut your balls off. You're lucky I don't have a knife."

Miranda wanted to kick him in the head for the shit he'd put all of them through and for what? The thrill? Fuck him, she thought, and stepped over his body to the large desk where the aluminum briefcase lay open.

Her heart quickened when she saw all the green faces smiling up at her. Christ, there must be ...

She stared into the open case. Looking back at her were stacks of crisp Benjamin Franklins. She pulled a few stacks out and fanned the bills. They were in ten thousand dollar bands, two rows of five, two deep—two hundred thousand dollars. Then she saw the velvet pouches in the top compartment and pulled them out.

What do we have here? she said to herself, as she untied one. She almost fainted when she saw what was inside. Miranda knew diamonds and knew exactly what she was looking at. She had worked a high-dollar case that involved diamond smuggling before she left the bureau. Diamonds were a very soluble form of money, and they were easy to hide. She quickly opened the other pouch and saw that it too was full of cut diamonds. She ran her fingers through the brilliant stones—they varied in size and weight but she knew she was looking at a fortune.

There must be ... God, she thought, there are millions here and this was why she was here. It was true that she had originally traced the eccentric millionaire, Malcolm Burke, up here. She was good at what she did, and that was to find people. But this time, when she figured out what was at stake, she'd decided that it was her turn. Then she found a sympathetic ear in town to help her. She had answered the ad with the right pedigrees and Sebastian Black had taken the bait. Funny what a little leg shown at the right moment—the dangle of a high heel, sexy polished toes brushing up against a leg and the rest was easy. That's all it took and she smelled the money. She had beat Black at his own game and now she would skip with the bounty. She deserved it.

Now she had to get out of here. She almost jumped out of her skin when Black moaned on the floor beside her.

She went back over to his body prepared to whack him again. She knelt down and felt his pulse. His breathing was shallow but he was still alive. She raised his eyelid and saw white. He would be out for a long time. Good she thought, let someone else find his sorry ass and put him in jail. She felt his jacket pockets and relieved him of the small Walther automatic and the spare magazine. It was a PK .380—not the most powerful gun in the world but it would do the trick. She would have loved to find more .357 cartridges but didn't have the time to look.

She turned and went back to the desk, thought a second, stuffed one of the pouches in her waistband under her black turtleneck and then snapped the case shut. She decided to go back through the castle. She didn't want to join back up with the others now. She had the prize and had no intention of surrendering it—or mentioning it to any of them. She had planned long for this moment. Pretty soon all this would be over with and she'd be gone. She thought for a moment. She needed a phone. She looked back down at Black, set down the case and felt his pants pockets. Nothing.

I know he had one, she thought. I saw the bastard using it. She went back to him and rolled him onto his back, his head lolled to one side. Miranda reached into his blazer, checking the inside breast pocket and to her delight, her fingers closed around a slim Blackberry.

"Good," she smiled, "I need to call my ride."

She looked at Black once more, fought the urge to kick him in the head. Then she slipped out of the chamber carrying the case.

She pushed the wall where she'd seen him come out but it didn't budge. I know this is where he came out, she thought. She felt around the edges, pushing and probing. When she was almost ready to give up and go back the way she had come, she found a small depression in the wall and she pressed it. There was an audible click followed by the door springing back several inches. She sighed in relief and pushed it open a crack. She waited a few seconds and then poked her head around the door.

The room was an office or library and it was empty. She saw that dusk was settling—perfect, she thought. She listened again and noticed that the gunfire outside had stopped. Satisfied that she was alone, she pulled out the cell and saw there was no signal. She looked over at the desk and saw the land phone, picked it up and dialed the number of the cell she had committed to memory.

It rang several times before a panting voice answered, "Hello?"

"It's me," she breathed. "I got what we came for. Where are you?"

"Outside. I got a couple of them, and now whoever is left is out there waiting me out. They think I'm with the FBI. Shit, Miranda, it worked! Did you get the money?"

"Yes, I got the money. Don't get too excited, we're not out of here yet. Where's your car?"

"I'm heading there now. I can be out in front in three minutes. Be ready. I'm not sure who's out there with what. Where's Black?"

"Taking a nap," she snapped. "Just hurry."

"Where's Thomas and the black guy?"

"Somewhere in the house, but they're moving down to the kitchen and planning to go out that way."

"I'll pull up to the front. Nobody's going to question me, I'm a cop."

"Right," she said, her voice dripping with skepticism. "Just hurry."

"Miranda?"

"What?" she answered with impatience in her voice.

"I … I love you. Be careful."

She took a deep breath. This had gone way too far. He was a love sick idiot. "Christ … just get the fucking car, will you?" She would have to deal with him later, but now, she needed him to get away from this place.

She cut the connection and moved toward the window. The long afternoon shadows gave way to dusk and it was getting dark. Perfect, she thought. Just five more minutes and they were home free. Nothing moved in the courtyard and she felt certain the others were going out the back to safety and wouldn't see her leave from the front.

She glanced back at the bookcase where the secret door was and satisfied that it hadn't moved. She headed out of the library and into the hallway. The castle was eerily quiet as she crept toward the sweeping main staircase and freedom.

# CHAPTER 62

Dieter had survived this world because he was smart and he knew when to keep his head down. The automatic fire from the woods had stopped. He thought they might be circling around him from the back but he heard nothing and it was getting harder to see as darkness was falling. His eyes traveled to Marco's body, lying face down fifteen feet in front of him. Dieter had a brief moment of regret. Marco was a good man and he had loved his daughter, Kristen, but war was war and Marco had been about to surrender. Dieter would never surrender. But getting away was another thing.

Helene and Kristen would be fine. They couldn't be charged with anything and he'd find them once the hubbub died down. But right now he needed a way out of there. He figured he had six rounds left in the Luger and knew that would not be enough in a firefight with an automatic rifle. There were plenty of guns in the basement armory but getting to them would be risky. He looked at the house again and decided the distance was too far with no cover. He remembered the way Sanchez had been cut to pieces at the door. The other Chrysler was around front but he was sure the tires had been shot out so that would be a fool's errand. The ATVs in the garage were the best bet and he thought he could reach one of them without being seen.

His mind went to his employer and he decided that his time with Sebastian Black had come to an end. The man was crazy. It was his fault that all this was happening, so Dieter made up his mind to escape and let Black fend for himself. He knew he had plenty of money hidden away.

Dieter scanned the yard around him and made his move in a low run toward the open bay door around the front of the garage. The crippled Chrysler sat on rims, partially blocking him from view as he scurried into the darkened bay.

Dieter ran to the ATV in the bay, jumped on, took a deep breath and turned the key. This was it, he thought. If this damn thing didn't start, he was sunk.

Ray heard the engine start as soon as he cleared the kitchen entrance.

# CHAPTER 63

I huddled in the kitchen under the cover of the storage shelves with Skyler and Donna Lee. Ray was outside checking things out.

"Where do you think Miranda went?" asked Skyler. "She wouldn't just leave us."

Donna Lee looked at him with disgust. "Well she did, Gramps. Apparently she thought she would do better on her own."

"She wouldn't," persisted Skyler. "I know her. She wouldn't leave us like this. Something must've happened."

Donna Lee scoffed. "Yeah right, how long we all known each other? Huh? Three days. Don't be a fool. You're thinking with your little head, like most men."

I had had enough and put up my hand. "Stop, okay? That's enough. It doesn't matter where she is now. We'll send somebody back. Important thing is for us to get out of here alive and to find Chris."

"But …"

"But nothing, Skyler. Just do what you're told and you might get out of here with your ass in one piece. And God help you if something has happened to Chris."

"Nick, I swear, I didn't know …"

"No you didn't, but the fact is we came up here looking for you. Your niece was worried that something might've happened to you and now we're here in this freaking mess. Now do me a favor and shut up." He saw the look in my eyes and decided it would be wise to do as I suggested.

Donna Lee clutched my arm. "Where's Ray? I'm scared."

I smiled at her. "He'll be back. Don't worry Donna Lee we'll get you out of here. Just hold tight. He's checking outside."

We waited. The only sounds we heard were from the two women locked in the storeroom. They were both pounding on the door and yelling. I was glad I didn't speak German because I knew what they were shouting wasn't nice. Every other sentence was punctuated with "You pigs, my husband will cut your throats," in harsh accented English.

I heard the ATV start. Ray was outside under the portico and facing the garage. I stood and ran to the door with Skyler and Donna Lee glued to my ass. I turned and told them to stay to one side of the doorway and to keep behind me.

I peered out and saw that Ray was getting ready to do something. He was crouched and I guessed he was about to time a flying tackle on the bad guy on the ATV. I heard the machine's engine rev and then accelerate around the bullet ridden Chrysler and onto the gravel drive. He could either go straight, past the Castle proper, or go around to the service entrance, which was where we were.

Ray had one chance to nail the driver before he got

out of the parking lot and disappeared into the night. Ray streaked across the lawn at a dead run to the point where he could intersect the ATV. The man on the ATV had his head down, was gunning the screaming machine and spitting a trail gravel and dust behind him. I could see he was a big bastard, powerfully built, with short gray hair and that he was gritting his teeth.

I watched everything unfold as if in slow motion. Ray raced toward the madman on an ATV, the man released the throttle and reached for his gun with his eyes on the fast approaching Ray. He did not see low brick curbing until it was too late. He screamed as he lost control of the ATV and flew over the handlebars when it hit the curb. Ray collided in mid-air with the man and the ATV as it was all happening. Ray had his arms around the man as they fell in a tangle of arms and legs. The ATV flipped and tumbled end-over-end, landing forty feet away in a tangled mass of handlebars, tires, and smoke as the strong engine still tried to run.

The man recovered and was on his feet before Ray could regroup and sent a vicious kick to Ray's chest as Ray tried to get up. Ray flew backward, landing hard on the gravel. He rolled to one side just as a heavy boot whizzed by his head. Ray managed to grab the man's foot and twist. The man went crashing down. Ray rolled away quickly and their eyes locked for a brief instant—each knowing one of them was not leaving alive. Ray leapt to his feet holding his K-bar. The man smiled and reached under his jacket. His face went white when he realized his gun wasn't there and that it must've fallen out during the crash. He patted his side again and then shook his head in confusion.

"What's the matter, lose your gun, mon?" Ray asked,

edging closer to the man. The man moved around with easy confidence as Ray circled him.

"You want me, you come get me," the man said with a heavily accented voice. "Come on boy." He was low, arms ready, eyes locked on Ray's and then he charged.

He came in hard. A powerful right aimed at Ray's head missed and caught Ray in the shoulder. Ray had moved aside just in time and the man stumbled, losing his balance and giving Ray the opening he needed. Ray spun and delivered a side kick to the man's knee.

I heard the sickening crunch of bone and cartilage as I ran toward them. The man screamed in pain and collapsed, gripping his already damaged knee with both hands. Ray spun and sent another kick that caught the man under the jaw. We all heard the loud snap and then the man was still. Ray doubled over, panting, with the K-bar still gripped in his right hand.

"Holy shit, Kemo Sabé. You dusted that freak. "

Between pants, he managed to say, "Didn't even break a sweat, mon."

"Riiiight. You okay?"

"Yeah, mon. Give me a second. Where are the others?"

On cue, Skyler and Donna Lee rushed out. Donna Lee flew into Ray and wrapped her arms around him. "Oh my God. Did you see that? Oh my God. I never … I mean you were awesome."

Ray blushed as much as his mahogany face would allow and gently untangled her arms. It was like pulling a mosquito off fly paper.

"We good, sweet thing, but now let's get out of here."

He looked at me. "You seen Teddy?"

"No man, I forgot about him. Where the hell is he?

He said he'd be here. Think that was him in the woods?"
I asked, looking around.

"Supposed to be. He said he'd lay down fire until we
could get out and then he would ride in and pick up
our asses. Well we gotta go before the real cops get here.
That Sheriff would shoot us for the fun of it."

I shook my head. "I can't leave here without Chris,
Ray."

"We don't know that she's here. Remember she
called you."

"Ray, that was hours ago and here we are and no
Chris. If she got out she'd bring help."

"Not if the wrong people picked her up."

"Ray don't say shit like that."

We both jumped when we saw the wash of headlights
bounce off the trees. There was a car coming fast from
the rear access road.

"Get down everybody," Ray yelled. "Now!"

I flattened against the disabled Chrysler with Skyler
and Donna Lee crouching along its side. Ray knelt next
to me as the car sped past, showering us with gravel. It
was a Cold River Police car.

I breathed relief. Teddy.

But the car didn't stop. It flew around the corner of
the castle toward the front and the long drive leading
away from the castle.

"That Teddy?" Ray asked, squinting into the darkness
after the car.

"I think so, but I didn't see him clearly. A man
driving."

"Has to be Teddy. Where the fuck he going?"

I shrugged and pulled Skyler up. "Around front.
Come on, let's go."

The four of us broke into a run heading around to the front of the castle. Ray was in the lead, I was a close second and Donna Lee had actually let go of Ray long enough to help Skyler along.

"Teddy!" I yelled as I ran. "Hey Teddy, it's us, man! Teddy, slow up!"

We skidded around the corner just in time to see the police sedan at the front door. Brake lights beacons in the blackness as a dark-clad figure, carrying a large case, raced down the front steps, opened the rear door of the cruiser and hefted the case inside. The figure then slammed the door, and jumped into the passenger side of the cruiser as it accelerated away. The whole thing didn't take ten seconds. The taillights of the car got smaller as it raced down the long tree-lined drive.

"What the ... if that was Teddy ... I don't get it," I said, looking at Ray for an answer.

Ray looked into the distance at the vanishing taillights for a long second and then shook his head. "Looks like Teddy made hisself a better deal."

# CHAPTER 64

Miranda looked over at Deputy Sheriff Ted Adams, as the car hurtled toward the front gate. His hands were white on the wheel and his jaw was set in a grim expression. She loosened the tie that held her thick blonde hair back and shook it out.

He glanced over at her. God she was beautiful, he thought. "I was scared for you."

She gave him a tired smile. "I'm a big girl, Ted. And I got what we came for." She stretched her longs legs out and slipped off her shoes.

"How much?" he asked in an anxious voice.

"Not sure, I think about two hundred thousand. I didn't have time to count it. I grabbed what Black had in his safe and got the hell out of there."

Ted looked at her, not believing his ears. "Only two-hundred thousand? Where are the millions you said he had stashed there? Two hundred is hardly worth it. Shit, Miranda, do you mean to tell me I killed people over two hundred thousand? That my career is over for a lousy two hundred thousand?" He shook his head and pounded the wheel with a fist. "Damn, that's hardly enough for us to get away."

Miranda ran a hand along the inside of his thigh and found the bulge. "Don't worry, Ted, things will be okay. Trust me, baby. Just trust me." She felt him getting hard under her touch and smiled to herself.

Ted slowed as he approached the gate to give the electronic eye a chance to open it. He put his hand over hers and said in a husky voice, "God Miranda, I've missed you."

She smiled at him and caressed him some more. "I can see that. I'll have to take care of that as soon as we get where we're going."

Ted slipped the sedan through the now open gate and sped away into the night, leaving Black and all his nightmares behind—or so he thought.

She turned to face him. "Everything set at the cabin?"

"All set and nobody knows about the place. We can disappear for a few days while things cool off and mmm … resume our relationship."

Miranda managed a smile. "Sure, baby whatever you want."

She was nervous now. What if dear Ted, the poor slob, figured out that she didn't need him anymore? He was a country boy but she didn't figure him for a fool. She had to be careful to keep him happy until it was safe to slip away with the diamonds and the money. She had trusted him to secure the place they were going to— private, secluded, where even the locals got lost trying to find it. He'd assured her that he had found the ideal place to hide out.

They drove on in silence. Miranda powered back her seat and stretched her long legs. "God, I feel like I've been through a freakin'war."

Ted turned serious. "We have, Miranda. We crossed

a lot of lines and they're going to be looking for us in no time flat. I don't know how you ever talked me into this, and now you're telling me that we're only talking one hundred thousand each?" He looked over at her. "You telling me the truth?"

Ah … the first sign of suspicion. She'd have to be very careful now or he would figure things out and maybe try to turn the tables on her. He didn't have a thing to lose now. He might even kill her. Who would know way out here in the woods? They'd never find her body. He did sacrifice everything for her—his job, his life and all for the promise of love.

Miranda nuzzled his neck and gave him a warm kiss on the throat.

He shivered and then shrugged her off. "Miranda, baby, come on, that's nice, but I gotta drive. Really. But you better look out when we get to the cabin. I'll light us a nice fire, open a bottle of wine and we can make love right there in front of the fire—all night."

She winced inwardly at the thought. "Sure, baby, that sounds good. I want to get slightly drunk in a warm bath first if that's okay with you. It's been a long few days and I need to soak. Please tell me there's a bathtub."

He nodded. "There's a bathtub and the hot water is on." She saw him smile in anticipation as he drove. They had the windows up, the heat on and the stereo playing so they didn't hear the State Police chopper as it streaked by overhead.

# CHAPTER 65

Chris sat strapped in the back of the State Police Bell Ranger helicopter as it raced toward Black's compound. All four doors were off the chopper for rapid deployment. Beside her was a nice but serious man in a black jump suit whose name patch said his name was Alverez. Another member of the team sat next to the pilot in the left-hand seat holding a rifle with a scope. They were alert and ready for business.

Chris spoke into the microphone of her headset. "Sergeant Alverez, are we getting close? I'm so worried about Nick, my boyfriend."

He nodded and said, "We should be down in five minutes. The ground units are already enroute. We'll get them out, Miss."

She continued to stare out into the darkness, watching the bottom-mounted searchlight sweep the forest ahead of them.

"Two minutes to target," the pilot said into the headset and Chris felt the chopper slow and begin its descent. "Get ready!"

Alverez put his hand on Chris's arm and said, "Now Miss Todd, you have to stay in the chopper until the scene is clear. Understand? I don't want you getting shot out there."

Chris nodded. "I'll stay put. You just find Nick. Okay? Please?"

He smiled. "This is what we do. If he's down there, we'll find him."

It seemed like days ago when she had collapsed into the trooper's arms on that dirt road, but it'd only been that morning—a mere ten hours ago. The trooper had radioed in and she'd been taken to the State Police Headquarters in Burlington and within the hour she was telling her story to a room full of astonished cops. It turned out that Mr. Sebastian Black and Sheriff Cobb had been on their radar for some time, and they were looking for an excuse to go in. She wasn't a lot of help with the logistics but they kept her in the loop while they planned their rescue. A take-charge female sergeant had whisked her away and found her a shower, some fresh clothes and coaxed someone to go out and get her lunch. The burgers, fries and milk shake never tasted so good. She only needed to find Nick and Skyler to make the day good again.

"There it is," the pilot said, pointing to an aura of light coming from the black ground. About a half mile away, Chris could see the hulking form of Black's castle looming in a pool of security lights. She had not seen the castle during the day and really couldn't be sure she was even there, but something told her she was right and that Nick was close. The Ranger moved in closer, hovering to land in the front courtyard. Chris saw flashing lights and a flurry of activity on the ground and prayed that Nick was down there and safe.

Alverez tugged at her harness to make sure it was secure. "Remember, Miss. Todd, stay put."

Chris managed a smile and gave him the *thumbs up* gesture. He grinned back and got ready to jump once the chopper hit the ground.

The Bell Ranger hit the ground with a bump and the two S.W.A.T. men leapt from the skids and hit the ground running. The confusion was deafening—sirens, radios squawking, men running and shouting orders. Chris scanned the men for a sign of Nick but could not see him in the confusion. There were no gunshots, so she thought it all might be over. Ignoring Alverez's warning, she unbuckled the safety harness and jumped out, ducking under the whooshing rotor blades.

The pilot yelled something to her but she couldn't hear it and didn't want to anyway. Nick was out there somewhere and she had to find him.

Chris looked frantically around and spotted a crowd of people near the back by a big garage structure so she ran toward them.

"Nick!" she screamed over the din as she ran as fast as her tired legs would take her. "Nick, oh my God, Nick? Where are you?" Her eyes burned with tears and her vision blurred. Then she spotted something that put her heart in her throat. Lying on the ground were several people but the one closest was a huge black man with a shaved head.

"Ray!" she cried out. "Ray … is that you?"

The cops that were standing over the people on the ground turned when they heard her.

"Ray!" she cried again.

Then she heard the only voice she wanted to hear. "Chris? Chris? Is that you?"

# CHAPTER 66

Once Ray had disposed of the big German all had gone quiet. We stood there expecting more chaos and when none came we heard the cavalry. It came in a wave of black SUVs with antennas all over them. Not usually what one would want to see coming in your direction. Even though we were the good guys, the victims, I wondered if the authorities would see it that way. Well, I'm guessing they thought they had a reason, and that would be enough, because they came at us hard. We were told to lay face down where we stood and put our hands behind our backs. We did as we were told. That was when Sky King, the police chopper, dropped in from the heavens whooshing and howling, displacing dirt and rocks as it landed.

Okay, I know I have done some crazy shit in my life but it still boiled down to one thing. I wasn't James Bond or any other type of superhero I dream up in my books. I was a freaking writer. I wrote mysteries and here I was lying face down in a gravel parking lot about to be handcuffed and charged for who knows what. I'm not optimistic enough to trust our legal system. Especially not after the past few days.

So in came the chopper with all the wind and the screaming pitch of its rotors and then I heard the voice of an angel—Chris, oh my God, it was Chris!

"Chris!" I cried and my heart was pumping out of my chest as I went to sit up.

"Chris, I'm here!"

That had been a bad idea. I felt a boot in the middle of my back and the cocking of a weapon. I knew they did that for effect. Who would go into a situation like this with no round in the chamber?

"Down," the nice FBI man screamed in my ear over the thunderous noise of the chopper. "Next time I'm gonna Taser your ass."

'Nuff said there. I laid back down as they had so politely asked. Chris was alive and apparently not under arrest. Hopefully she'd sort this mess out and we would get rewards or something—maybe even the keys to the town. I get silly when I'm scared.

"Nick? Nick? Where are you?" Chris called and the cops that were standing, parted and the love of my life stood there with her hands on her hips.

"You were supposed to rescue me, not the other way around."

"I wanted you to feel validated. Now please explain to these nice people who we are and that the bad guys are in there, not out here."

An official suit walked up and all I could see were his shoes and the cuffs of his nice pants. My neck hurt from craning it to look at Chris as the wise-assed FBI guy still had his foot in the middle of my back.

"Special Agent Smith, am I glad to see you." She pointed to me on the ground. "This is Nick, his friend Ray, and oh yes, the one who started it all, my Uncle

Skyler. I don't know this young lady." Chris looked down at Donna Lee who identified herself.

"Nick, this is Special Agent Smith, he helped me after I got away and believed my wild story. He's been very nice to me."

"Thanks," I mumbled. Sure, now Chris has a new hero. "Nice to meet you."

The suit spoke to the men who had us detained. "Okay guys, why don't you go have a look-see inside and I'll sort this out." He looked down at us "Okay, you can all get up now."

Ray straightened up and said to him. "Special Agent Smith, there is a maze of passageways inside there and that's where I think our infamous Mr. Black is hiding."

The FBI man looked at Ray. "Ex-Army?"

Ray shook his head. "SEALS."

The fed looked at him appraisingly and nodded. "Come on then, show my men where these passages are and where the weasel might be hiding."

I ran to Chris and we kissed and hugged and cried and all that stuff. I was happy again. I could watch the sun come up now that Chris was safe and back with me.

"Oh, baby, I missed you so. I was crazy with worry and they said that I killed you and hid the body."

"I would haunt you," she laughed between tears and hugged me tighter. "Oh, Nick, I love you so much my big hero man. You came to rescue me."

"I did. And I'm never letting you out of my sight again."

Chris pulled back from our embrace, and ran her hand lightly over my cheek. "I love you, Nick. I was so damn scared."

"Me too." I managed to get the words through the lump in my throat.

Skyler walked up with his head down, afraid to look at Chris. "Chrissy, I … uh … I'm sorry, Honey, for what I put you through. I truly am."

Chris disengaged herself from me and hugged her wayward uncle. "Uncle Skyler, if you ever put us through something like this again, I'll kill you myself. Do you understand? You're lucky to be alive!"

He traced something in the gravel with his shoe. "I know, Chrissy, I know. How can I ever make it up to you?"

I jumped in with that. "You can live the rest of your life like a normal person and quit running off like a dog in heat."

Skyler thought a long second and said with a dead-pan expression. "Can I think about that?"

We all laughed. I looked around and saw Donna Lee feeling one of the S.W.A.T. guy's muscles. "She don't miss a beat, does she?"

Skyler laughed. "She's a cute kid, so why the hell not? She's young, rich and single. Me? I'm old, poor and single. Doesn't have the same ring does it, Nicky?"

"Uncle Skyler, we mean it. No more of your tricks or you can do it alone," Chris said in a serious tone. "I mean it this time. *We will not* come after you again."

He held up his hands. "Okay, okay. I'll be good. Maybe ol' Abby will have me back."

"Not if she's smart," Chris and I said in unison.

There was a commotion from the front of the house and we moved toward the sound just in time to see the paramedics roll Sebastian Black out on a gurney—his head was bandaged and an IV bottle hanging above his head.

I jogged over to the stretcher and stared down at the man. "So you're the son-of-a-bitch who caused all this."

Black stared through me with a blank expression and then closed his eyes. I looked at one of the paramedics and raised an eyebrow.

"He'll live. Got a pretty good concussion, though," the female paramedic said as she wheeled him down the walk.

"Too bad," I said and watched them lift him in and close the rear door of the ambulance.

# CHAPTER 67

The cabin and barn were tucked into a small clearing that was partially hidden in the trees. The overgrown driveway was a twisted gash of dirt cut through the trees that led back one hundred yards from the road. Ted knew the nearest neighbor was a few miles south but he had never seen anybody there.

Ted pulled the Cold River Police cruiser behind the cabin and into the small barn. On his last trip out he'd left the doors open anticipating a triumphant return. There was a battered white Toyota Land Cruiser with Massachusetts plates on one side that Jack kept for his buddies when they came up to hunt and raise hell.

"This is it, honey," he said. They had driven miles into a tangle of dense woods and dirt roads.

Miranda had dozed a bit in the car, her head resting on Ted's shoulder. She straightened up and looked around. "Where in God's name are we, Ted?"

"We're only about twenty miles from Cold River but we're bordering a national forest. An old friend of mine owns this. He's in Boston and doesn't come up here much. He told me that if I take care of it for him, I can use it anytime I want. He comes up with his buddies two or three times a year to hunt and get drunk."

"What if he shows up now," she asked, annoyed that there was any possibility of an intrusion.

"I called him. Jack and his wife are in San Diego for three weeks and he doesn't think he'll make it up here at all this year. Maybe in the fall, he'd said."

Miranda smiled and patted his leg. "Good boy, you covered the bases. Now, find me some wine and that hot bath."

They entered the rustic cabin, Miranda headed to wash the day from her body and Ted went to gather some firewood. He'd have a roaring fire going before she finished her bath. Once the fire was started, he uncorked the wine and brought her a glass. Miranda sat in an old claw-foot tub working the hot and cold levers with her toes, and she had found something herbal in the cabinet that produced some bubbles.

Ted took in her long lean body through the soapy water while handing her the wine goblet that was actually a mason jar. Miranda smiled, took a long swallow, then leaned back with her eyes closed. "Nothing but the best, I see."

He knelt beside the tub. "We'll have it all someday, you'll see," Ted said, toasting her with his own jar. "You and me, baby."

Miranda still had her eyes closed. "Yeah, Ted, just you and me. Ted ... would you please do me a favor, sweetie?" She lifted one leg from the soapy water and ran her toes down his cheek. The soap and water dripped on him as she caressed his chin. She knew this drove him crazy.

"Anything," he answered in a hoarse voice as he

kissed her foot and ran his tongue along her perfect arch and down to her toes. He was so hard he couldn't see straight. "You name it, Miranda. You know I could never say no to you."

She smiled and leaned toward him. The water sloshed out a little onto the wooden floor. "Come here, baby." She kissed him long and deep, her wet hand found his hardness and rubbed it through his pants. Ted couldn't stand it. "Miranda, I'm getting in that tub. I want you so bad, baby."

She laughed, "That's just the pre-game, Ted. Now be a good boy and go out and get me a little more wine then get those clothes off. I'll be right out." She gave him another squeeze and said in a hoarse whisper, "Baby, I'm going to fuck you like you've never been fucked before and when we're done you will be completely mine."

Ted swallowed hard. "Yes baby, yes, whatever you want. Anything."

"Leave now and go get naked for me," she commanded. "I'm going to take you to a place you've never been before. Now, go!"

Ted's head swam with desire and he stumbled from the small bathroom.

He waited for her by the roaring fire on the old leather couch. He had chugged a jar of wine and was beginning to feel its glow in his gut. He was naked, just as she had asked. He was so hard it felt like he was going to burst. Five long minutes later, Miranda appeared with a towel wrapped around her body and smiled down in appreciation at him.

"Looks like you did miss me."

He handed her a fresh jar of wine and she drank.

Her eyes danced over the rim. "Now baby, I want you to lie down on the rug over there."

He bolted up and laid down where she had indicated, a few feet from the hearth. He felt the heat from the blazing fire competing with the burning in his loins. She went to him, dropping the towel as she walked. Her body was still damp and glistening as she knelt between his legs and took him in both hands, rubbing slowly. He groaned.

"You like this, baby?" she asked in a husky voice.

He groaned again and arched his back in rhythm as she played with his cock.

"Miranda, I'm going to …"

"Oh no you're not. Not yet baby." She squeezed the head hard as it bobbed back and forth. She smiled up at him and then lowered her head and took his shaft into her mouth. He cried out in pleasure. Then she stopped and sat upright. His was throbbing with pain, needing release.

"Oh baby, please …" he pleaded.

"My turn, baby." She turned her body, put a leg on each side of his face and lowered herself down to his waiting tongue. She arched her back and began grinding on his hungry mouth with a rising tempo, moaning in pleasure. His hands cupped her ass and pulled her deeper as his tongue found the sweet spot. She moved faster and caressed his shaft as she rode him. Then it became too much so she slipped off, hovered and guided him into her. They were both lost in the passion. She felt him go deep. He was so hard she felt the rising tide within her. He was moaning and thrusting into her with violent movements and then they both screamed as they came together. She held him tight as she felt his penis spasm inside her while she came in torrents and then collapsed on top of him, sweaty and spent.

They lay like that for several minutes and then Miranda rolled off and got up. Ted looked up at her. "Where you going, baby? I want to hold you." She smiled down at him, at his sweat soaked body, his limp spent penis. He looked so love sick, so pathetic. "You just stay there, baby. I'm going to get a cool wash cloth and wipe your body. You just lie there." He was too far gone to argue. He nodded. "Hurry back, my love. I want you to be with me."

Miranda went back into the bathroom and slipped on the fresh jeans and tee shirt Ted had brought for her, and under the tangle of dirty clothes she pulled the Beretta out, checked the mag and slipped it into the small of her back. She smoothed out her hair in the faded mirror and walked out into the living room still barefoot.

Ted was leaning on one elbow, sipping wine from the jar, the fire warming his back. He looked at her as she entered the room and his eyes showed confusion, then apprehension.

"Why are you dressed? Miranda, what's going on?"

"Oh, Ted, my dear Ted," she said, standing over him now.

"Miranda?" Then he saw the coldness in her eyes. "Oh no, Miranda, no ... no ..."

She smiled sadly down at him and shot him in the forehead.

# EPILOGUE

## PROVINCETOWN, CAPE COD

The low, open-aired, gray clapboard building was set back on the left at the end of Commercial Street, right on the water by the Town Pier. The club was marked by a bright orange neon sign that said: *MONTEGO RAY'S ISLAND RETREAT.* The catchy sign was flanked "tastefully" on both sides by fluorescent art deco palm trees crowned by a red and green neon parrot that was perched on top of the "M." The canopied entrance had several hefty potted palm trees on either side that gave the place what Ray proudly called "Island Flavor." Many a drunk had been found tangled up in those palm trees. And yes, I speak from firsthand experience.

*Montego Ray's* was a great little place located where the town ended and the pier began in Provincetown. Ray and his wife, Jazz, had built a place on the water that had a righteous mix of Key West, Montego Bay, and Cape Cod. They had brought the club to life with great Caribbean cooking, a lot of hot Island Reggae and a bunch of good people. I loved Ray and Jazz. They were my family, along with Chris, of course.

Inside, the huge paddle fans turned in lazy circles under the thatched straw ceiling that was adorned with fishing nets, seashells and old license plates, while Bob Marley sang about Buffalo Soldiers in the sun.

There were two live parrots and a couple of white cockatoos in big brass cages behind the bar that talked to you if you were drunk enough to listen. The pleasant clatter of plates, glasses and laughter filled the place while the smells of wonderful food drifted through the air.

It was good to be home, I thought. Chris sat next to me on one side and Ray was on the other. Skyler sat across from us in a tan Panama suit and white linen shirt, looking down into his Tom Collins, with extra fruit. He'd been quiet since our return. I think the brief glimpse into hell had dampened his spirit. One could only hope.

Ray's colorful mountain of a wife, Jazz, appeared with a tray laden with food. "You gots to eat," she said plunking it down on the table. On it were heaping piles of calamari, steamed clams, oysters, bread, and four fat red lobsters. Ray laughed. "Women think food cures everything."

"Men think it's sex," said Chris, digging her elbow into me.

I nodded. "Great combination. I won't turn down either."

We all laughed. I put my arm around Chris and closed my eyes. "God, I love you. I was so afraid that I'd lost you."

She smiled and nuzzled into me. "I know, my big hero man. You saved me."

Ray thumped his Corona on the table. "What about me? Hemmingway here couldn't find his ass with both hands without me."

"You be quiet now," Jazz said, punching him hard in the arm. "They's in love and if she wants Mr. Nick to think he saved her, jus leave that be."

"Jus saying …"

"Hush," said Jazz and raised her glass of tropical poison. "Now I wants to propose a toast to all you crazy people. Y'all had me worried 'bout to death."

She glared at her husband who tried to look small. "And you … you don' go runnin' off acting all brave and stupid again. What if somebody shot your big black ass? Huh? Who'd run this place? Who'd look after me?"

They all knew that Jazz ran Montego's without any help from Ray and he was very content in his role of the genial host while Jazz screamed and threatened the help into submission.

I laughed. "Jazz?"

"What?"

"Your toast …"

"Oh yeah." She pushed her bulk off the chair and stood with her glass held high. Her electric blue Mumu had scores of brown natives paddling like hell toward a large yellow sun while others roasted their freshly caught fish over small campfires. She maintained that each Mumu she wore told an important story and none of us would dare argue.

We all held our glasses high and waited for her words.

"To Chris, may God watch over you and this good man next to you and may the sun shine on you both."

"Saluté," I said, reaching toward the platter of food. The lobsters were calling my name.

Jazz shot me a look. "Not yet, you. Don' be in such a hurry." She shifted like a mighty ocean liner turning in a harbor, to face Skyler. I saw more natives on the back of her dress and—they were the unlucky ones. Her expression darkened and she said, "Now you, Mr. Skyler, you old fool, are damn lucky to be sittin' here eating my calamari."

Skyler looked back down into his Collins with a rueful look on his handsome face.

"Don' you be lookin' away from me. It was your gold digging ass that got you all into that mess. Foolishness, is all that was. Nobody wins money like dat."

I cleared my throat.

"What now, Mr. Nick?" she snapped at me.

"Jazz, the toast? The food's getting cold."

"Oh yea. I be done. God bless and I'm glad you're all back in one piece." She shot Ray a look and pointed a meaty finger at him. "We will talk 'bout you later. I heard all about you and that little southern girl with a crush on your big ass," she said and rumbled off toward the kitchen, screaming at some young waiter who had the bad luck of being in her way. The remaining help scattered in all directions like the parting of the sea.

Ray smiled and shook his head. "I love that woman."

"Hard not to," I said.

"Nick?" Chris asked. "Do you think Black will get what he deserves?"

I thought a second while swallowing a mouthful of calamari. "They found six bodies buried on the estate. He's going away for a long time. They think that one of them was his own mother. Remember the story Ted told us about the strange old woman his mother saw in the window?"

Ray nodded. "Looking back, I'm not sure how much ol' Teddy tol' us is true."

I shrugged. "Actually, he told us a lot of true things. First, that Black was a bad guy, next, that Sheriff Cobb was working for Black, and all that about Ted's mother and father appears to be true. I think Miranda, or whatever her name was, seduced poor lonely Teddy."

Skyler pounded his fist on the table. "I still don't believe she was bad. They never found her, or Ted for that matter. Hell, he could've forced her into it."

I shook my head. "I doubt that. The woman was slick. She had you all going. Looks like she went up there looking for that rich guy for a client and found out how much money Black had stashed in that castle and decided that she would get the whole prize for herself." I looked at Skyler. "She played you, too, man. Admit it."

Skyler, to his credit, didn't respond but just shook his head.

Chris broke in. "What I do know is that it was that German guy, Dieter, who snatched me from the hotel with Cobb's help. I'd like to be alone with that creepy shit Sheriff for five minutes."

"Ex-sheriff. He'll get his," Ray said. "They don' like cops in jail. They gonna call him Sally or Betty or something. He be pinup of the month."

We laughed, but I was troubled. "What do you think happened to Teddy and Miranda?"

"They off on a Caribbean island, sipping fancy drinks," said Ray.

"We don't know how much they got away with," said Chris.

I thought for a moment. "Well he baited the trap with the promise of five million. We could go on the premise that he had that much."

"They didn't find a dime in the castle. The FBI tore it apart," said Chris.

"Black insists he was robbed, but won't say how much was taken," I said around a mouthful of lobster. "It looks like Teddy found true love and a shitload of money at the same time. I guess we'll never know unless they find them. I will tell you this. I'm going to write this story. It's just too good to pass up."

"Use me in the movie, Hemmingway, and don't lie. You know I did all the heavy stuff."

I raised an eyebrow. "Would I lie?"

Ray laughed. "You gonna have your sorry ass climbing walls with a machine gun in your teeth and rescuing that damsel in the dress."

"It's damsel in distress," I said keeping a straight face.

"That what I said."

Chris linked her arm through mine. "I think I'm going to take my man here on a nice vacation, somewhere where we can lay on the beach, wear skimpy clothes and eat stuff that's bad for us."

I held my wrists out. "Take me, I'm yours."

When Chris finally dropped Skyler off in Hyannis, Abby Pierce was the perfect mix of crying concern, anger and calculated indifference. She did love the old goat. We would never understand the kind of man he was. He would always be drawn to the bright lights, the action and sexy women. It was his way.

Skyler went through his mail and found a slip from the post office stating that he had a package to pick up at the main post office between the hours of 8am and 5pm. He looked at the slip that bore no clue as to its origin and tucked it into his pocket and then promptly forgot about it.

Three days later, he found the crumpled slip, walked the six blocks downtown, and presented the slip to a woman too old to have orange hair. After a long minute, she returned carrying a large package wrapped in brown paper. There was no return address. Still puzzled, Skyler accepted the parcel and left the post office.

He hefted the package which was about eighteen inches wide, twenty-four inches long and four inches high. It was heavy, but not so much that he couldn't carry it. He walked over to the small park across the street and sat on one of the green benches, under the shade of a stately oak, and tore open the package. It was a briefcase, aluminum, with a recessed handle and a combination lock. He crumpled the paper up, then put it aside and tried the catches—they didn't budge. He looked at the combination lock in frustration. It was a small tumbler with four dials of numbers. Four digits. What the hell, he thought. Why would someone send me a case I couldn't open? He spun the dials in frustration and kept trying the catches to no avail. Then he noticed the card that was taped to the top right hand corner of the case. It had a palm tree in the corner and it read: *Your Birthday.* He sat and stared at the card for a moment. What the hell, he mused. It's not my damn birthday! And then a wide smile crossed his face. He looked at the combination lock and spun the dials to 1111, his birthday. November 11th—Veteran's Day.

The locks popped and he opened the case to see the stoic faced Benjamin Franklin—many times in many piles staring up at him. He counted two rows of five, two deep—two hundred thousand. He almost fell off the bench. He found another palm tree card tucked into the top pouch. It read: *Dear Skyler, you are a sweet man and I just couldn't bear the thought that you risked all for nothing. I know what you must think of me, but a girl does what she has to do to survive. Have a good life ... Miranda*

THE END

www.ingramcontent.com/pod-product-compliance
Lightning Source LLC
Chambersburg PA
CBHW050905250626
47155CB00001B/110